THE TRAITOR'S KISS

ERIN BEATY

[Imprint]
MAKE YOUR MARK

NEW YORK

REYAN

SEY LAMAN

Border Road

CRESCERA

Northern Road

Broadmoor

Garland Hill   Galarick

Western
Strong

*Sagitta
Crossing*

Tiegann Road

Sunset Road

Nai River

Span Road

TASMET

Fort
Jov

*Arrowhead
Crossroad*

BEY LISSANDRA

Western Sea

KIMISARA

2016

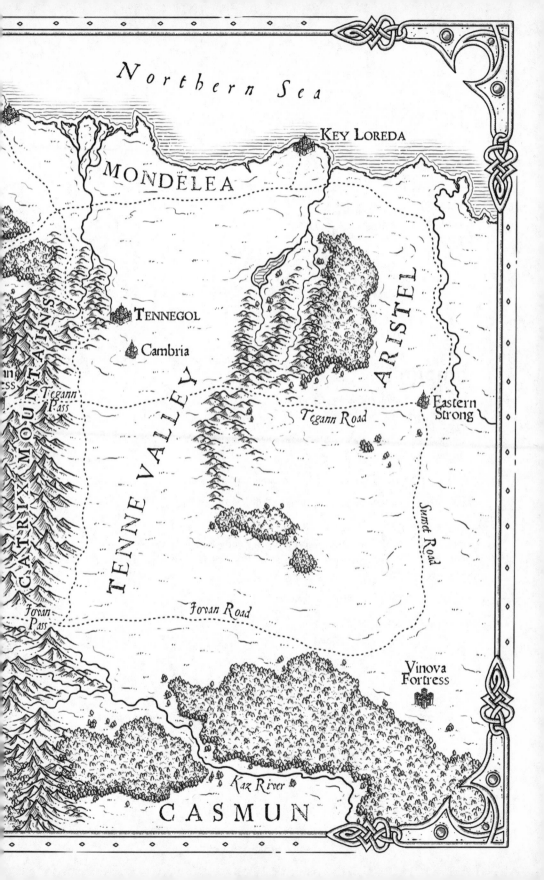

A part of Macmillan Publishing Group, LLC.
175 Fifth Avenue, New York, NY 10010

THE TRAITOR'S KISS. Copyright © 2017 by Erin Beaty. All rights reserved. Printed in the United States of America.

Library of Congress Cataloging-in-Publication Data is available.

ISBN 978-1-250-11794-6 (hardcover) / ISBN 978-1-250-11793-9 (ebook)

Our books may be purchased in bulk for promotional, educational, or business use. Please contact your local bookseller or the Macmillan Corporate and Premium Sales Department at (800) 221-7945 ext. 5442 or by e-mail at MacmillanSpecialMarkets@macmillan.com.

Imprint logo designed by Amanda Spielman

First Edition—2017

10 9 8 7 6 5 4 3 2 1

fiercereads.com

TREASURE   BLESSED   LOVE

MAY THOSE WHO   THIS BOOK BE   BY AN ALL-CONSUMING

ABUSE   EATEN   SWARM
                                                 OF FIRE
                                                 ANTS

For Michael, first and last.
And for Him: Fiat voluntas tua in omnibus.

1

UNCLE WILLIAM HAD returned over an hour ago, yet he hadn't summoned her.

Sage sat at her desk in the schoolroom, trying not to fidget. Jonathan always fidgeted through her lessons, whether from boredom or resentment that she—a girl only a few years older—was his teacher. She didn't care, but she wouldn't give him a reason to sneer at her. Right now his head was bent over a map of Demora he was labeling. He only put in effort when his siblings had similar work that could be compared to his. Sage had discovered that early on and leveraged it against his contempt.

She clenched her fist to keep from tapping her fingers, while her eyes darted to the window. Servants and laborers hustled about the courtyard, beating dust from rugs and building up the hay stores for the coming winter. Their movements coupled with the steady creak of wagons loaded with grain echoing from the road, creating a rhythm that normally soothed her, but not today. Lord Broadmoor had set out that morning for Garland Hill on errands unknown. When his horse trotted through the manor house gate in the early afternoon, her uncle tossed the reins to the hostler while casting a smug look at the schoolroom window.

That was when she knew the trip had been about her.

He'd been gone long enough to have spent only an hour in town, which was somewhat flattering. Someone had agreed to take her as an apprentice—the herb shop or the candle maker or weaver maybe. She'd sweep floors for the blacksmith if she had to. And she could keep her earnings. Most girls who worked had to support a convent orphanage or family, but the Broadmoors didn't need the money, and Sage more than earned her keep as a tutor.

She glanced to the wide oak table where Aster focused on her own map, eyes narrowed in concentration as her plump fingers awkwardly gripped the coloring stick. Yellow for Crescera, the breadbasket of Demora, where Sage had lived her whole life within a fifty-mile radius. As the five-year-old exchanged her yellow stick for a green one, Sage tried to calculate how much she would need to save before she could consider leaving, but where would she go?

She smiled as her gaze drifted to the map hanging on the opposite wall. Mountains that touched the clouds. Oceans that never ended. Cities that buzzed like beehives.

Anywhere.

Uncle William wanted her off his hands as much as Sage wanted to leave.

So why hadn't he called her yet?

She was done waiting. Sage sat forward in her chair and sifted through the papers stacked before her. So much paper, it was a waste, but it was a status symbol with which Uncle William could afford to supply his children. Sage could rarely bring herself to throw any away, even after four years of living here. From a stack of books, she pulled out a dry volume of history she hadn't looked at in over a week. She stood, tucking the book under her arm. "I'll be back in a few minutes."

The three older children glanced up and went back to their work without comment, but Aster's dark-blue eyes followed her every movement. Sage tried to ignore the knot of guilt forming in her stomach. Taking an apprenticeship meant leaving her favorite cousin behind, but Aster didn't need Sage's mothering anymore. Aunt Braelaura loved the girl as if she were her own now.

Sage hurried out of the room, closing the door behind her. At the library she paused to wipe her hands over the hairs that had escaped her coiled braid and willed them to stay flat for the next fifteen minutes. Then she squared her shoulders and took a deep breath. In her eagerness she knocked harder than she intended, and the sharp noise made her cringe.

"Enter."

She pushed the heavy door open and took two steps inside before sinking into a curtsy. "Pardon the disturbance, Uncle, but I needed to return this"—she held up the book, and suddenly her reason seemed inadequate—"and fetch another for, um, lessons."

Uncle William looked up from behind a half-dozen parchments scattered on his desk. A gleaming sword hung from the leather belt looped on the back of his chair. Ridiculous, that. He wore it like he was some protector of the realm; all it really meant was he'd made the two-month round trip to the capital city of Tennegol and sworn fealty before the king's court. She doubted he'd ever encountered anything more threatening than an aggressive beggar, though his expanding girth certainly threatened the belt. Sage ground her teeth and stayed locked in her low position until he acknowledged her. He liked to take his time, as if she needed to be reminded who ruled her life.

"Yes, come in," he said, sounding pleased. His hair was still windblown from his ride, and he'd not changed from his dusty riding jacket, meaning whatever was happening was happening fast. She straightened and tried not to look at him expectantly.

He set the quill down and gestured to her. "Come here, please, Sage."

This was it. She nearly ran across the room. Sage halted at his desk as he folded one of the papers. A glance told her they were personal letters, which struck her as odd. Was he that glad to see her leave that he was telling his friends? And why would he tell everyone else before her? "Yes, Uncle?"

"You were sixteen last spring. It's time we settled your future."

Sage clutched her book and contained her response to an enthusiastic nod.

He stroked his blackened mustache and cleared his throat. "Therefore, I have arranged your evaluation with Darnessa Rodelle—"

"*What?*" Matchmaking was the only profession she hadn't considered, the only one she absolutely hated. "I don't want to be—"

3

She broke off, abruptly realizing what he meant. The book tumbled from her hands and landed open on the floor.

"I'm to be *matched*?"

Uncle William nodded, obviously pleased. "Yes, Mistress Rodelle is focusing on the Concordium next summer, but I explained we fully expect it to take years to find someone willing to marry you."

Even in the fog of denial, the insult hit her like a physical blow, stealing her breath.

He waved an ink-stained hand at the letters before him. "I'm already writing to young men of my acquaintance, inviting them for visits. With any luck, some will admire you enough to inquire with Mistress Rodelle. It's her decision, but there's no harm in helping her along."

She fumbled for words. The region's high matchmaker took only noble candidates, or rich ones, or extraordinary ones. Sage was none of those. "But why would she accept *me*?"

"Because you are under *my* care." Uncle William folded his hands on the desk with a smile. "So we're able to make something good come of your situation after all."

Spirit above, he expected her to be *grateful*. Grateful to be married off to a man she would barely know. Grateful her self-matched parents were not alive to object.

"Mistress Rodelle has a far enough reach she can find someone with no objections to your . . . previous upbringing."

Sage's head snapped up. What, exactly, was wrong with her life before? It was certainly happier.

"It's quite an honor," he continued, "especially considering how busy she is now, but I convinced her your scholarly qualities elevate you above your birth."

Her birth. He said it like it was shameful to be born a commoner. Like he hadn't married a commoner himself. Like it was wrong to have parents who chose each other.

Like he hadn't made a public mockery of his own marriage vows.

She sneered down at him. "Yes, it will be an honor to have a husband as faithful as you."

His posture went rigid. The patronizing expression twisted away, leaving behind something much uglier. She was glad—it gave her the strength to fight back. His voice shook with barely contained fury. "You dare . . ."

"Or is faithfulness only expected of a nobleman's wife?" she said. Oh, his rage was good. It fed hers like wind on a wildfire.

"I will not be lectured by a child—"

"No, you prefer to lecture others with your example." She jabbed a finger at the folded letters between them. "I'm sure your friends know where to come for lessons."

That brought him to his feet, bellowing, "You will remember your place, Sage Fowler!"

"I know my place!" she shouted back. "It is impossible to forget in this house!" Months of holding back drove her forward. He'd dangled the possibility of letting her leave, allowing her a life outside his guardianship, only to drop her straight into an arranged marriage. She balled her fists and leaned toward him over the desk. He'd never struck her, not once in the years she'd challenged him, but she'd also never pushed him so far, so fast.

When Uncle William finally spoke, it was through clenched teeth. "You dishonor me, Niece. You dishonor the duty you owe me. Your parents would be ashamed."

She doubted that. Not when they had endured so much to make their own choice. Sage dug her fingernails into her palms. "I. Will. Not. Go."

His voice was cold to counter her heat. "You will. And you will make a good impression." He eased back down with that regal, condescending air she hated and picked up the quill. Only his white knuckles belied his calm exterior. He flicked his other hand in casual dismissal. "You may go. Your aunt will see to the preparations."

He always did that. Always brushed her aside. Sage wanted to make him pay attention, wanted to leap across the desk, swinging at him with closed fists like he was a sandbag out in the barn. But that behavior Father *would* have been ashamed of.

Without curtsying, Sage turned away and stomped out the door. As soon as she reached the passage, she began running, shoving through a throng of people carrying trunks and baskets, not caring who they were or why they'd suddenly appeared in the manor house.

The only question in her mind was how far away she could get by sunset.

2

SAGE SLAMMED THE bedroom door with a satisfying *bang* and walked across to the tall wardrobe in the corner. She flung the cabinet open and dug around for the satchel in the back. Her fingers found the rough canvas in the dark, recognizing it instantly despite not having used it in years, and she pulled it out and inspected it. The straps were still strong; no mice had chewed any holes she could find.

It still smelled like him. Like the tallow and pine pitch salve Father made for cuts and scrapes. He used it both on her and the birds he trained. She squeezed her eyes shut. Father would've stopped this. No, he never would have let it start. But Father was dead.

Father was dead, trapping her in her fate he'd always promised to shield her from.

The door opened, startling her, but it was only Aunt Braelaura, come to smooth things over as she always did. Well, it wouldn't work this time. Sage stuffed clothes into the bag, starting with the breeches she wore on rambles in the woods. "I'm leaving," she snapped over her shoulder.

"So I gathered," her aunt replied. "I told William you wouldn't take it well."

Sage turned on her. "You *knew*? Why didn't you say anything?"

Braelaura's eyes crinkled a little in amusement. "Honestly, I didn't think he'd succeed. I saw no reason to upset you over something so unlikely."

Even her aunt didn't think she was marriage material. Sage didn't want to be matched, but it was still insulting. She went back to her packing.

"Where will you go?"

"Doesn't matter."

"Do you expect it to go better than last time?"

Of course she'd bring that up. Sage furiously jammed extra socks into the bag. The nights were getting cold; she'd need them. "That was years ago. I can take care of myself now."

"I'm sure you can." So calm. So reasonable. "What do you intend to do for food?"

In response, Sage picked up the sling draped over a stack of books, wrapped it up dramatically, and stuffed it in the pocket of her skirt. Ugh. She'd have to change before she left.

Braelaura raised her eyebrows. "Squirrels. Delicious." She paused. "Available all winter."

"I'll find work."

"And if you don't?"

"Then I'll travel until I do."

She must have sounded serious enough, because her aunt's tone shifted. "It's dangerous out there for a girl on her own."

Sage snorted to hide her growing unease. She'd wandered the countryside for years with her father, and she knew very well what dangers—human and animal—she could face. "At least I won't be forced to marry someone I don't even know."

"You say that as if matchmakers don't know what they're doing."

"Mistress Rodelle certainly made the best match for you," Sage said sarcastically.

"Yes, she did," Braelaura said, unruffled.

Sage gaped at her. "You can't be serious." Everyone knew what Aster was. Her name—that of a plant—declared illegitimacy to the world. It wasn't the girl's fault where she came from, but Sage couldn't fathom why Braelaura forgave her husband.

"Marriage is not simple or easy," Braelaura said. "Even your parents knew that in the short time they had."

Perhaps not, but their love had been simple; getting married should've been easy. It shouldn't have meant being disowned by her mother's parents and shunned by half the village. But to them it had been worth it to be together.

"What exactly are you afraid of?" Braelaura asked.

"I'm not *afraid* of anything," Sage snapped.

"Do you really think William will give you to someone who will treat you poorly?"

No, she didn't, but Sage turned back to her packing to avoid answering. Uncle William had ridden day and night to fetch her as soon as he heard about Father's death. Then, when she ran away a few months later, he tracked her for days until he found her at the bottom of a ravine, too broken and frozen to climb out. He'd never said a word in rebuke, just lifted her up and carried her home.

A voice inside whispered that this matching was an honor, a gift. It declared she was part of the family, not just a poor relative he was forced to support. It was the best he had to offer.

It would be so much easier if she could hate him.

Sage felt her aunt's hand on her shoulder, and she stiffened. "He must have put down quite a sum to get her to take me."

"I'll not deny it." Braelaura's smile leaked into her tone. "But Mistress Rodelle wouldn't have agreed if she didn't see some potential." She brushed a dozen stray hairs away from Sage's face. "Do you think you're not ready? It's not as difficult as you think."

"The interview or being someone's wife?" Sage refused to relax.

"Both," Braelaura said. "The interview is a matter of presenting yourself. As for being a wife—"

"Father told me how babies are made." Sage flushed.

Braelaura continued as though Sage hadn't interrupted. "I've been teaching you how to run a household for years, if you haven't noticed. You did just fine last spring when I was ill. William was very pleased." Her hand lowered to rub Sage's back. "You could have a comfortable home and some little ones. Would that be so bad?"

Sage felt herself leaning into the soothing pressure. A home of her own. Away from this place. Though to be honest, it wasn't this place she hated so much as the memories.

"Mistress Rodelle will find a husband who needs someone like you," Braelaura said. "She's the best at what she does."

"Uncle William said it could take years."

"So it may," her aunt agreed. "All the more reason not to let emotions drive your actions now."

Sage set the bag down in the wardrobe, feeling defeated.

Braelaura stood on her tiptoes to kiss Sage's cheek. "I'll be there for you, every step, in place of your mother."

Since her aunt rarely mentioned Sage's mother, Sage wanted to ask questions before the subject changed, but twelve-year-old Hannah burst into the room, blond curls bouncing. Sage scowled. "Don't you ever knock?"

Hannah ignored her. "Is it true, Mother? Is Sage going to the match-maker? The *high* matchmaker?"

Aunt Braelaura hooked an arm around Sage's waist as though to keep her from running away. "Yes, she is."

Sage continued glaring at her cousin. "Do you actually have any-thing important to say?"

Hannah gestured behind her. "The dressmaker's here."

A cold sweat broke out over Sage. Already?

Hannah turned wide blue eyes to Sage. "Will she pick you for the Concordium, do you think?"

"Ha!" came thirteen-year-old Jonathan's barking laugh from the passageway behind Hannah. He was carrying a trunk. "I'd like to see *that*."

Sage felt sick. When was the interview? She'd interrupted Uncle William before he'd said. Braelaura began guiding her to the door, where Hannah bounced on the balls of her feet. "She's setting up in the schoolroom."

"When am I going?" Sage managed to ask.

"Tomorrow, love," said Braelaura. "In the afternoon."

"*Tomorrow?* But how can I possibly have a new dress made by then?"

"Mistress Tailor will adjust something she has on hand. She'll go over with us in the morning."

Sage let herself be led across the hall and stood numbly as Braelaura pulled the laces of her bodice loose enough for Sage to slip out. The room darkened suddenly, and Sage thought for a second she was fainting, but it was only Hannah and Aster pulling the curtains across the window. When they were done, Aster perched on a chair in the corner, obviously hoping, if no one noticed her, she could stay. Hannah danced around, chattering about how she couldn't wait for her own interview, and did Mother think Father would let her be evaluated at fifteen even though she couldn't be matched until the year after?

Her cousin also still imagined Sage had a chance at getting into the Concordium. Sage had no such delusions. The high matchmaker's primary job was to select the best from her region for the conference held every five years, but Sage wouldn't have wanted to go even if she was pretty or rich enough to be considered. She had no desire to be herded across the country to Tennegol and practically auctioned off like a prize head of cattle. Hannah, however, fantasized about it, as did girls all across Demora.

Braelaura pulled the dress off Sage's shoulders. The outfit was one of several she had and hated. How bizarrely unfair to have so many things she didn't want. Most girls would kill just to be evaluated by a high matchmaker.

Mistress Tailor was sorting through a basket on the table, but she paused long enough to point to the stool she'd set out. "Up," she commanded. "We've no time to waste."

Braelaura helped Sage step up and steadied her when the stool wobbled under her feet. She fought a wave of dizziness that had nothing to do with keeping her balance.

"Shift off," said the dressmaker over her shoulder. Sage cringed and lifted her under-dress over her head and handed it to her aunt. Normally a fitting didn't require full stripping—just a knotted cord measuring over her shift. She crossed her arms over her breastband and shivered, glad the window was covered against breezes as well as eyes.

Mistress Tailor turned around and frowned at Sage's undergarments. The boyish linen shorts were the only thing Braelaura had let Sage

11

continue wearing when they forced her into dresses. The shorts were far more comfortable than what women wore, and nobody could see them anyway.

The dressmaker pursed her lips and squinted at Sage from several angles. "Thinness is her main weakness," she muttered. "We'll have to fill her out, especially on top."

Sage rolled her eyes as she imagined all the padding and ruffles it would take to disguise her flat chest. Braelaura had given up putting lace and bows on her dresses long ago. They always had catastrophic encounters with scissors when no one was looking.

Cold fingers pinched her waist. "Good curve here, and solid birthing hips. We can emphasize that."

Sage felt like the horse her uncle had bought last month. *Solid hamstrings make a good breeder*, the horse trader had said, smacking the mare's flank. *This one can be mounted for ten more years.*

The dressmaker lifted Sage's arm to scrutinize it in better light. "Naturally fair skin, but too many freckles."

Braelaura nodded. "Cook's already brewing lemon lotion for that."

"Use it liberally. Are these *scars* all over your arms, child?"

Sage sighed. Most were so old and minor they could only be seen if looked for.

"Her father was a woodsman," Braelaura reminded the dressmaker. "She spent a lot of time outdoors before she came to us."

Mistress Tailor drew a bony finger down a long red scratch. "Some of these are recent. What have you been doing, climbing trees?" Sage shrugged, and the woman dropped her arm. "I shouldn't complain," she said dryly. "All your wardrobe repairs over the years have kept me afloat."

"Glad to be of service," Sage retorted, spirit rising a bit. Anger was more comfortable than fear.

The dressmaker ignored her and rubbed the stray end of Sage's braid between her fingers. "Neither brown nor blond," she grumbled. "I don't know what color to put with this." She glanced at Sage's aunt. "What do you plan to do with it for the evaluation?"

"Haven't decided," said Braelaura. "When we pull it back, it always escapes. It takes curling well, despite the fine texture."

"Hmmm." The dressmaker jerked Sage's chin around to look in her eyes, and Sage resisted the urge to bite the woman's fingers. "Gray . . . Maybe blue will bring some color to her eyes." She released her hold. "Gah! Those freckles."

Aster tilted her head in bewilderment. She'd always been envious of those freckles. When she was three, Sage caught her trying to make her own with ink.

"Blue, then," Mistress Tailor said, calling Sage's attention back to her, though once again, she addressed Aunt Braelaura. She turned to dig through the enormous trunk set off to the side. "I've got something that will suit, but I'll be up all night taking it in to fit her."

The seamstress lifted a mass of fabric and shook the folds out, revealing a blue-violet monstrosity Sage couldn't even imagine walking in. Gold-threaded designs—undoubtedly itchy—wound around the long sleeves and in similar patterns over the bodice. The low neckline had a draped collar, which would probably be embellished further to create fullness.

"It's off the shoulders," Mistress Tailor said as Braelaura and Hannah oohed and aahed. "Hers are rather nice; we should show them. But that means no breastband."

Sage snorted. It wasn't like she really needed one anyway.

3

THE TWO-STORY, WHITEWASHED building loomed out of the October mist. Sage hopped down from the wagon as soon as it stopped, so focused on the matchmaker's house, she didn't notice the mud puddle until she found herself sitting in it. Her aunt sighed as she heaved Sage up by her elbow and hustled her into the bathing room around the back. "Don't worry," Braelaura soothed. "This is why everyone prepares here."

Mistress Tailor was already waiting inside to help with last-minute adjustments. Sage wasted no time shedding her muddy clothes and climbing into the warm bath. "Rinse your hands, then keep them out of the water," Braelaura instructed. "Or your nail paint will peel off."

"How am I supposed to get clean?" In response, her aunt picked up a washcloth and began scrubbing Sage's back. Sage cringed but endured it. She just wanted this day to be over.

Once Braelaura was satisfied, Sage clambered out and toweled herself dry, then stood shivering as smoothing creams were spread over her shoulders, neck, and arms. Her body was dabbed with powder. "It itches," she complained.

Braelaura swatted her. "Don't scratch; you'll ruin your nails. The powder will keep you dry from sweat."

"It smells like chamomile. I hate chamomile."

"Don't be ridiculous. Nobody hates chamomile; it's soothing."

I guess I'm nobody. Sage held her arms up as her aunt wrapped the corset around her waist. Spirit above, it was the most uncomfortable thing she'd ever worn. The boning dug into her hips as Braelaura tightened the laces, trying to get it snug enough to hold in place. When Sage stepped into the first of three petticoats, the corset shifted and jabbed her in new places.

Mistress Tailor and Aunt Braelaura lifted the dress over Sage's head, and she shoved her freezing arms into the long sleeves. The pair then fussed around her, pulling the dress straight and adjusting it for the most cleavage before lacing the bodice in front. Sage swept her fingers over the velvet and lace flowing off her shoulders. After the interview, the dress would hang in her wardrobe until the day—months or years from now— she was presented to the man Mistress Rodelle had chosen for her.

While a man could approach a matchmaker about a girl he admired, it was ultimately the matchmaker's decision as to whether they should be paired. Often couples knew very little of each other before they wed. A fresh start was considered advantageous. Sage shared her father's disgust at that idea, but supposedly, matches were based on temperament— even the highly political ones, like those at the Concordium.

Marriages made outside the system were rarely stable or happy, though Sage suspected that had a great deal to do with how self-matched couples were ostracized. Perhaps Sage could convince her uncle to at least let her get to know this potential husband first. After all, he'd known Aunt Braelaura for years before they were matched. The thought gave her a glimmer of hope she'd not had before.

Aunt Braelaura moved her to a stool and draped a linen sheet over the outfit so they could paint her face. The twisting rags from last night were removed and Sage's hair cascaded in ringlets down her back. The two women pulled the curls away from Sage's face with pearl-studded pins, exposing her shoulders. Mistress Tailor made a noise of approval and handed Aunt Braelaura the first of many cosmetic jars.

"Do you think Uncle William will let me meet my match before he gives his consent?" Sage asked as her aunt spread cream across her cheeks.

Braelaura looked surprised. "Of course he will."

"And what if I don't like him?"

Her aunt avoided her eyes as she dipped her fingers in the jar again. "We don't always like what's good for us," she said. "Especially at first."

Sage couldn't help wondering if Braelaura was referring to her own match, but she was more concerned with hers at the moment. "So if Uncle William thinks this man is good for me, it won't matter what I say?"

"Honestly, Sage," her aunt sighed. "I think it's more likely you won't give the man a fair chance to win you over. You're so set against him, and he doesn't even exist yet."

Sage lapsed into a sullen silence, and Braelaura tapped her cheek. "Don't pout. I can't do this properly if you make such a face."

She tried to relax her brow, but her thoughts made it impossible. Her uncle's desire to have her settled and out of his hair would weigh heavily against his wanting to do right by her. He'd likely consent to the first man he thought wouldn't mistreat her, but that wasn't a recipe for happiness. Sage brooded as her aunt continued to apply creams and color to her face for what felt like an hour. At last she held up a hand mirror so Sage could see the result.

"There," Braelaura said. "You look lovely."

Sage stared at her reflection with morbid fascination. Not a freckle showed through the smooth ivory paint. Her lips were bloodred in striking contrast to her pallor, and her high cheekbones had an unnatural hint of pink. Violet powder on her eyelids made her gray eyes appear almost blue, which was probably the intention, but they were barely visible between her curled and blackened lashes.

"Is this what ladies at court look like every day?" she asked.

Her aunt rolled her eyes. "No, this is what a nobleman's bride looks like. What do you think?"

Sage twisted her scarlet lips in distaste. "I think I know why Mother ran away."

❦

Sage struggled to balance in the ridiculously heeled shoes as they made their way from the washroom to the front of the house. At the porch steps, Sage positioned herself behind her aunt, eyes downcast and hands folded to display her painted nails. Villagers loitered in nearby doorways and gathered at windows to catch a glimpse of the newest bridal candidate, and Sage flushed under her makeup. Did they stare because they didn't recognize her, or because they did?

Braelaura pulled the bell by the door, and a clang echoed through the streets, drawing even more attention. The matchmaker took almost a full minute to answer the door, and a trickle of nervous sweat ran down Sage's back.

The door opened, and the matchmaker stood imperiously in the door frame. Darnessa Rodelle was a tall woman, nearly six feet, and her graying hair was bound in a tight knot on the back of her head. At fifty, she had the shape of a potato dumpling and the fleshy, flabby arms that bespoke a life of comfort and good food, but her mouth twisted like she smelled something offensive.

"Madam Rodelle, Mistress of the Human Heart," said Braelaura, in what Sage assumed was some traditional greeting. "May I present my niece, in the hope your wisdom can find a husband to match her grace, wit, and beauty?"

Sage pulled her skirt away from her trembling knees and curtsied as low as she dared in the wretched shoes.

"You may, Lady Broadmoor," the matchmaker replied with a grand sweep of her hand. "Bring the maiden forth so she may honor her family name."

Sage rose and took a few steps forward. It felt like a play, with lines, positions, costumes—even an audience. A sick feeling began building in her stomach. None of this was real.

"Is marriage your wish, Sage Broadmoor?"

Sage flinched at the name change. "It is, mistress."

"Then enter my home so I may learn your qualities." The matchmaker stood aside to let Sage pass.

❧

Sage caught one last glimpse of Aunt Braelaura before the door closed, cutting off shadows and blending them into the gloom of the parlor. A thick, braided rug dominated the floor, with a low tea table centered on it and an upholstered sofa to one side. Though little light passed through the heavy linen drapes, Sage was relieved they were drawn against prying eyes.

The matchmaker circled her slowly, looking up and down. Sage kept her focus on the floor. The silence became maddening. Had she forgotten something she was supposed to say? The skin under her corset itched as sweat soaked the fabric. *Stupid, useless, nasty chamomile powder.*

Finally the woman directed her to an uncomfortable wooden chair. Sage lowered herself onto its edge and spread her skirts in a fan around her. She tried rotating her bodice to provide some relief from the itchy sensations. It didn't help.

Mistress Rodelle sat across from Sage on the wide couch and fixed her with a critical eye. "The duties of a nobleman's wife are simple but all-consuming. She places herself first in his affections with her looks and pleasing manners . . ."

The phrasing annoyed Sage. As long as she was pretty and in a good mood, her husband would love her? People needed love most when they weren't at their best. Sage blinked and refocused on the matchmaker, but the thought stuck in her mind like a thorn.

On and on the woman droned: she must be submissive; she must be obedient; she must be gracious; she must always agree with her husband. More about how she had to be what *he* wanted. The matchmaker leaned forward, tilting her head to look down her nose.

Abruptly she realized Mistress Rodelle had stopped speaking. Had she ended with a question? Sage answered with what she hoped the woman expected, question or no. "I am ready to be all this and more for my future husband."

"The greatest desires of your lord . . . ?"

"Become my own." Sage's responses had been drilled late into the night. It felt absurd, though, to make such a promise when she had no idea what this husband would want. Given the exaggerated claims this dress made about her figure, he was bound to be disappointed in at least one regard. The series of questions continued, and Sage's memory easily supplied the answers. So little effort was required, in fact, that it began to feel silly. None of the answers were her own—they were just what the matchmaker wanted to hear. The same answers every girl gave. What was the point?

"Now, moving on," the woman said, interrupting Sage's thoughts. Her lips curled back in a smile that did not reach her eyes. "Let us talk about your more . . . intimate duties."

Sage drew a deep breath. "I've been instructed in what to expect and how to . . . to respond." She hoped that would be enough to satisfy her.

"And should your firstborn be only a daughter, what will you say when you place the child in his arms?"

Next time I will have the strength for a son was the answer, but Sage had seen women suffer difficult pregnancies. Even the best of them were sick in the beginning and massively uncomfortable at the end, and that was before the laboring began. The idea of doing all the work of bearing a baby only to apologize stirred a smoldering furnace within. The heat of her anger felt delicious, and she embraced it.

Sage raised her eyes. "I will say, 'Isn't she beautiful?'"

Mistress Rodelle pinched off what initially looked like a smile before settling into annoyed expectation. "And then?"

"I will wait for my husband to say she is almost as beautiful as me."

Again the smothered smile. "Girls are useless to a lord. You must be prepared to apologize."

Sage's fingers curled around a fold in her dress. She'd once asked Father if he was disappointed his only child was a daughter, and he had looked her in the eye and said, *Never.* "Without girls, there would be no more boys."

"There's no denying that," the matchmaker snapped. "But in giving your husband no heir, you fail."

The last two words felt like they were meant for the present moment: *you fail.* What had possessed her to abandon the proper responses? Her mind scrambled to repair the damage, but nothing that wasn't both honest and insulting would come to her lips.

"Should you produce no heir after a time, will you stand aside for one who can?"

What would Father say to that? Sage looked at the floor and inhaled slowly to calm the tremor in her voice. "I . . ."

The matchmaker continued, "When you have a husband, Sage Broadmoor, you must endeavor to create more honor than you bring to the marriage."

Something inside Sage snapped when she heard that again—they were changing her name, like she should be ashamed of who she was. "Fowler," she said. "My father's name was Fowler, and so is mine."

A look of disdain crossed Mistress Rodelle's face. "You cannot expect to be accepted with such a name. 'Sage Broadmoor' sounds like a bastard, but 'Sage Fowler' sounds like a commoner's bastard."

"It is the name my parents gave me." Sage quivered with resentment. "They valued it, and so shall I."

The matchmaker's words lashed out like a whip. "No man of breeding would value such a name above the filth of a common whore."

Sage leapt to her feet, lightning flashing through her veins. Mistress Rodelle's thoughts were laid bare. And Sage had submitted to this, betraying everything her parents had suffered at the hands of people like her. "I would rather be a whore than the wife of a man of such *breeding*." Her voice pitched higher with every word. "*Your* name speaks of the same breeding, and *I want no part of it!*"

A palpable silence hung in the air.

"I think we are finished." The matchmaker's voice was so calm, Sage wanted to rake her painted nails across the woman's face. Instead she tripped across the rug and flung the door open. Aunt Braelaura froze in her pacing next to the wagon. When her eyes met Sage's, they widened in horror.

Sage hiked her skirt up to her knees and ran down the steps and across the street, stomping so hard her shoes were sucked off her feet into the mud. As she passed her aunt, collecting stones and muck on her stockings, she heard the matchmaker call out from the door in a voice everyone in the village could surely hear.

"Lady Broadmoor. You may tell your husband I will return the deposit on your niece. There is nothing I can do for her."

As the driver scrambled to help Braelaura climb up and then turned the wagon to the road, Sage marched out of the village without looking back.

4

SAGE CREPT INTO Garland Hill in the early morning light two days later, wearing breeches and her father's faded leather jacket. Uncle William had been so stunned by her disastrous interview that he hadn't raged or yelled as she had expected, just dismissed her from his presence. Until he felt ready to deal with her, Sage had a narrow timeframe to decide her own fate by finding work. Yesterday's inquiries in Broadmoor Village had yielded nothing, and asking around Garland Hill would probably be just as fruitless, but it was the only other place within a day's walk. She'd also come to a very difficult realization.

Her tantrum could very well affect the matching prospects of her younger cousins, and Aster already started at a disadvantage. After tossing and turning all last night, Sage knew what she had to do.

She had to apologize.

So now she stared at the bell outside the matchmaker's home as the village stirred around her. There were noises coming from behind the house, and she slipped down the alley and saw movement in the kitchen window. Taking a deep breath, she knocked on the back door just loud enough to be heard.

Mistress Rodelle peered with one eye through the crack before fully unlatching the door. She wore no face paint at this hour, and her gray-streaked hair was pulled back in a loose braid that draped over the shoulder of her plain wool dress. "You've come back, eh?" she grunted. "Thought of some better insults?"

Sage had been ready to identify herself, but it now appeared unnecessary. "Y-you know it's me?" she stammered.

"Of course it's you." The matchmaker scowled. "I know what you look like without your face caked and your figure padded. Do you think my evaluation begins when you ring my bell? What is it you want?"

Sage lifted her chin. "I would speak with you, please, woman to woman."

Mistress Rodelle snorted. "Where is the other woman, then? I see only a proud, spoiled girl-child on my step."

The insult rolled off Sage's back. Nothing said today could make things any worse, which was an odd kind of comfort. She held herself still until the matchmaker opened the door wider to let her in.

"Very well," Mistress Rodelle said. "Come in and say your piece."

Sage stepped past her into the surprisingly bright kitchen. The walls were a soft yellow color, and the wooden floor and table shone with polish. A cheerful fire crackled in the iron stove in the corner, on which a pot of tea steeped, pouring its minty steam into the air. Two teacups sat nearby, making Sage think the woman was expecting company, so she ought to hurry this conversation along. The matchmaker directed her to a wooden chair against the table in the center of the room and took the seat opposite. Sage studied the grain of the smooth oak planks for several seconds before clearing her throat.

"I've come to apologize, mistress. My words and actions were rude and disrespectful, and I wholeheartedly regret them and any pain they have caused you."

The matchmaker folded her fat arms over her chest. "Do you expect that heartfelt apology to change anything?"

"No." Sage worked her jaw a few times. "I don't expect it will."

"Then why bother making it?"

The embers in Sage's soul flared. "You see, the way this works is, I say I'm sorry for the horrible things I said, and then you say you're sorry for the horrible things you said. Then we smile and pretend we believe each other."

Mistress Rodelle's eyes sparkled with amusement, though her expression remained grim. "You presume to come into my house and lecture me on manners, girl?"

"I presume nothing. But I've made my effort, and I wait patiently for yours."

"You are on the wrong path." Again the woman's eyes didn't match her harsh tone.

Sage shrugged. "I have every right to ruin my own life." She twisted her mouth in a crooked smile. "Some might even say I have the inclination. But my actions are my own, not a reflection of the Broadmoor family. I'd like to trust my cousins will not suffer for my mistakes."

"Nicely put. It's a shame your words weren't so refined the other day."

Sage was growing weary of this exercise in humility. One could serenade a stone wall for hours, but it would never weep in response. "My father once told me there are some animals that can't be controlled," she said, picking at her painted fingernails. "It doesn't make them bad, just wild beyond taming."

To her surprise, the matchmaker smiled. "I think, girl, you're seeing yourself clearly for the first time." Sage raised her eyes to find a piercing, but much less hostile, gaze. "For a teacher, you're incredibly obstinate about learning your own lessons."

"I study every day," Sage objected.

"I'm not talking about history and geography." Mistress Rodelle waved her hand in irritation. "Look at me. I can barely read and write, yet I hold your future and the future of girls all across Demora in the palm of my hand. Not all wisdom comes from books. In fact, hardly any does."

Sage wrestled with the matchmaker's words. She wanted to reject them, but they sounded like something her father would have said.

The matchmaker stood and turned to the stove. She poured tea into the pair of cups as she spoke. "Now, I *am* sorry for what I said the other day. I aimed only to make you realize how much you didn't want to be matched." Sage's eyes widened, and Mistress Rodelle glanced over her shoulder with a shrewd smile. "Yes, I understand you well enough, and no, I never had any intention of foisting you on anyone."

"But—"

"And now your uncle realizes it, too, and he'll be more open to what I *do* want." She turned around and looked Sage straight in the eye. "I want you as an apprentice."

Sage shoved away from the table and stood. "No. Matchmaking is backward and demeaning. I hate it."

Mistress Rodelle set the cups and saucers on the table placidly, acting as though Sage wasn't halfway to the door. "Would it surprise you to learn I once felt the same way?" She eased back down into her chair. "You won't necessarily have to take my place someday. I just need an assistant."

Sage turned back, astonished. "Why me?"

The matchmaker folded her arms and leaned back in her chair, drawing a long groan from the wood. "You are intelligent and driven, if not yet wise. Your looks are pleasing, but you're not a beauty men will be dazzled by. I have the Concordium next year, and I could use some help picking the best candidates. Finally, you have no wish to marry, so you won't stab me in the back."

"How could I possibly do that?" Sage asked. "Stab you in the back, I mean."

"One of the simplest ways to get the result you want is to create a false choice." She flicked her fingers at Sage. "I can offer a man the choice between the girl I want him to marry and you, acting as a pleasant but less appealing option, and I don't have to worry about you bucking the process and stealing him for yourself." The matchmaker calmly raised her cup to her lips and blew the steam away.

"So you want me to be rejected over and over," Sage said, sinking back into the chair. "That's what I'm good for?"

Mistress Rodelle leaned her elbows on the table and eyed Sage over the tea. "That and other things. Matchmaking is primarily a task of reading people, collecting information, and piecing it together, which you have talents for. It's also not really rejection if you were aiming for it. Think of it as a game where the lowest score is the winner."

Sage wrinkled her nose. "Sounds manipulative."

"So it is. While blacksmiths bend iron to their will, matchmakers bend people to theirs." She took a sip and shrugged. "We aren't alone in our vocation. Actors and storytellers manipulate their audiences as well."

Sage eyed the teacup before her. The high-quality porcelain was sturdy and functional, just what she would expect in the home of a well-off but practical person. One who valued quality over looks. The matchmaker had known exactly when and how she would come to her. Sage raised the cup and took in the sweet whisper of spearmint—her favorite— rather than the more popular peppermint or chamomile. "How long have you been watching me?" she asked.

"Most of your life, but don't be flattered—I watch everyone. I knew your parents. They may have thought they matched themselves, but some of my work is subtle."

Sage's head rocked back like she'd been shoved. The cup in her hand dropped a few inches. "That doesn't sound profitable," she retorted. "How'd you collect your fee for that one?"

Mistress Rodelle arched her eyebrows with an amused look, and Sage plunked the cup back onto the saucer, sloshing tea over the side. She knew the answer already. "Your large fee for my aunt's match came from Mother's forfeited dowry."

The matchmaker nodded. "It was quite a tidy profit, actually. I have no regrets. Your parents belonged together."

Sage's only response was an openmouthed stare.

After several seconds of silence, the matchmaker rose from her chair. "You may think about my offer for a few days, but I doubt anyone else in the village will offer you a place," she said. "I'm not taking anything from your future. We both know you cannot be matched, wild Sage."

Sage stood and let herself be guided to the door. Before the matchmaker closed it, Sage heard her name called. She looked back over her shoulder.

"Your family expects a visitor today, yes?"

Sage nodded. A young lord was to go hunting with Uncle William, though his secondary purpose of being introduced to her was now pointless.

"Consider him an exercise in observation," said Mistress Rodelle. "When you come back to see me, be ready to tell me all about him."

5

CAPTAIN ALEXANDER QUINN peered over the jagged edge of a rock jutting from the hillside and squinted through the trees. The bright glade spread out below him, making it impossible for him to be seen in the shadows above, but he still crouched to stay hidden. His black leather jacket creaked a little, and he flinched at the sound, though it wasn't loud enough to give him away.

He'd pinned his gold bars inside his collar; they were too shiny—flawless—which declared how recently he'd been promoted and how little action he'd seen since. Once the awe of making captain a month before turning twenty-one wore off, the glare bothered him to no end, but at the moment he was more concerned with the enemy seeing the bars flash in the darkness.

To his right, twenty yards away, sat two of his lieutenants, both hooded—his oldest friend and second-in-command, Casseck, covering his blond head, and Luke Gramwell, hiding the ruddy tints in his brown hair. Quinn's mother was from the far eastern region of Aristel, and he'd inherited her dusky complexion and black hair, so he had no need for such precautions. Nor did Robert Devlin, positioned beside him. Rob had begged Quinn to pick him last fall. A new cavalry captain was granted his choice of officers so his first successes or failures were his own, but it had taken some smooth talking to convince the general to let the crown prince join a regular company.

At the moment Rob's hazel eyes were wide and his face pale, his gloved hands clasped to steady their trembling. Other than in height and eye color—the prince was slightly taller and Quinn's eyes were so dark they were nearly black—they looked so much alike, people often confused them. Quinn eyed his cousin, wondering if he'd worn the same terrified look just before his first battle. Probably. There was only one way to lose it, though, just like the shine on his gold bars, and that was experience.

Heavy snow and ice storms through March had confined the army to their winter camp in Tasmet, near the border with Kimisara. Patrols had started up again only a few weeks ago, and Quinn had been eager to prove his new company's worth. As the most junior commander, he had to wait his turn.

And wait.

His opportunity came last week, and his riders picked up the trail of ten men almost immediately. While he wasn't positive this group had come across the border, as far as Quinn knew they were the first potential Kimisar raiders anyone had seen this year. After two days of watching, he'd reached the point of needing to know more than just tracking could provide.

When the group of men came into view, walking—almost marching—down the road, every muscle in Quinn's body tightened. They carried themselves like fighters, and he didn't like the look of those staffs they carried. What if they smelled a rat? Beside him, Rob craned his neck to watch, going even paler, though Quinn hadn't thought it possible.

At that moment, another figure came ambling from the opposite direction. He slowed his pace briefly, as was prudent for a solitary man suddenly faced with ten. The group of ten also looked at the stranger with caution, but they obviously didn't feel threatened. Quinn's mouse could take care of himself, but five crossbows were backing him up from other angles in the shadows, just in case.

Quinn's tension increased as the men came together, and Ash Carter held up his hand in friendly greeting. The strangers offered few words from the looks of it, but seemed cautious. He turned and pointed back where he'd come from, probably describing the distance to some point ahead, or telling part of his story. Ash always said the trick to coming across as real was to change as few details as possible. Maybe that was why he was so good at this kind of scouting. Quinn would've had to change a lot more, starting with his name.

The talk concluded and both parties continued on their ways. A few glances were thrown back at Ash, but he never looked around. He didn't need to—over a dozen pairs of eyes were already watching their every move. Quinn relaxed and sat back. He'd never get used to putting his friends in danger. With a series of hand signals, he gave the pair on his right some instructions, and the lieutenants eased back up over the ridge behind them and disappeared.

A few minutes later, Ash scrambled down the hill to join him and the prince, having looped around behind them once he was out of sight. "They gone enough?" he asked quietly.

Quinn nodded. "Cass and Gram went ahead to watch. What did you learn?"

"Definitely not from around here," said Ash. "Most didn't speak, but the two accents I heard were Kimisar. Not that uncommon in these parts, though."

The province of Tasmet had belonged to Kimisara less than fifty years ago, and Demora had annexed it after the Great War, using it as a buffer against invasion more than anything else. For many this far south, Kimisar was still the primary language. It made identifying raiders more difficult.

The prince, who'd been uncharacteristically silent for the last three hours, stared at nothing. Ash leaned over and punched him lightly on the shoulder. "Wake up, Lieutenant."

Rob jerked out of his thoughts and scowled at his half brother. "Watch it, *Sergeant*."

Ash grinned. "Yes, sir." Ash had trained as a page and squire like the rest of the officers, but refused a commission last summer, never wanting to risk outranking his brother. Most soldiers treated him like an officer, though. He often joked that his position in the army reflected his life as the king's bastard son: all the perks of rank, but none of the responsibility.

"Any distinctive metalwork?" asked Quinn, drawing the talk back to the matter at hand. Kimisar soldiers usually carried symbols to invoke their gods' protection.

Ash shook his dark head. "Nothing visible."

"Did you find out where they're headed?"

"They asked how much farther the crossroad is. I told them they'd reach it by sunset," Ash said. "They looked happy to hear that."

"Weapons?"

"A few carried short swords—not long enough to draw attention, but bigger than knives. Couple bows, but that's to be expected if you're living off the land and traveling as light as they are." He paused. "Those staffs didn't look right, though. They looked hinged on the top."

Quinn nodded grimly. "Folded pikes. We've seen those before." It also pretty much proved the group had entered Demora with hostile intent, but in twelve years with the army, he'd never met or heard of any Kimisar who hadn't. Raids had been especially numerous in the last two years as Kimisara had suffered some sort of blight that destroyed half their harvest. There wasn't much in Tasmet to steal—the population was sparse, and the granaries were all the way north, in Crescera. "The bad news is that means they're ready to repel horses. The good news is they're not as strong as solid pikes."

Ash smiled. "Also that we're just as good on foot as on horseback."

"I guess that settles it, then," said Quinn, pushing to his feet. "It's time."

"Time for what?" said Ash.

Quinn wore a wicked grin as he brushed dirt off his black jacket. "Time to welcome your new friends to Demora."

6

THE ATTACK STARTED from ahead of the travelers, Quinn and his men taking advantage of the rocky landscape and a bend in the road to make noise that echoed around, confusing their prey. The strangers unfolded their pikes and dropped into a military formation to repel the riders coming at them, but ricocheting sound masked the second group, which was closing in from behind. By the time the strangers realized what was happening, the low sun obscured their view of the rear attackers. Half the group attempted to turn and face the new threat.

It was their first mistake.

Two of the foreigners went down with crossbow shots, but the other two archers held their aim, better as a constant threat than a couple more wounds. The riders passed on both sides and swept around, dismounting while the group struggled to reorient themselves. Before they'd fully recovered, the riders closed in on foot.

Quinn created the widest hole in the defense by grabbing the end of one pike with his left hand and sweeping up with his sword, shattering another right at the hinge. With his arm high in the air, he was exposed, but Casseck came into the opening and took out the only man who could have struck a blow, not that he'd had time to realize his momentary advantage. The captain grinned over the success of the move and focused on the next threat.

Prince Robert to his right drove his sword into the gut of one of the Kimisar, and Quinn moved to his side, ready for what he knew was coming. Rob staggered back, eyes wide. Without looking away from his cousin, Quinn slashed and blocked the weapons coming at both of them.

"Rob!" he yelled. "On your right!"

The prince recovered and pulled his sword from the body in front of him, but he was too slow for the weapon coming at him. Quinn had already switched his sword to his left hand to grab the dagger on his waist. In one move, he drew the knife and sent it into the neck of Rob's attacker. With the sword in his left, he deflected a swinging pike, but not fast enough, and while he didn't feel the wound, he couldn't ignore the blood pouring into his left eye. He swung around to cover his weak side and switch sword hands again, but the man who'd wounded him collapsed with a spear in his back.

Ash Carter stepped up on the man at Quinn's feet to wrench the spear free. The man groaned, but he wouldn't be getting up anytime soon.

Quinn looked around with one eye. The fight was over.

Ash raised an eyebrow at Quinn. "You're bleeding."

Quinn wiped his left eye and looked at his friend. "So are you."

The sergeant swept bloody black hair away from his forehead. "I'll live." He looked to his brother. "Are you all right, Rob?"

Robert's complexion had gone a pasty green. "No."

Quinn stepped closer and put a hand on his shoulder. "You hurt?"

"No," Rob gasped. "I'm just . . . going to be sick."

Ash appeared under Rob's other arm, propping him up. "Let's go for a walk." He led his brother away. Though Ash was significantly shorter, Rob leaned on him heavily.

Quinn watched them go before turning back to the pile of bodies. Rob's first taste of combat wasn't quite as glorious as the prince expected, but it never was. Quinn felt no amusement, only sympathy. Lieutenant Casseck offered him a pungent-smelling rag, and he wiped his face and forehead.

"That'll have to be sewn up," Cass said, squinting at the cut.

"Later," said Quinn. "I want to talk to the survivors."

"I don't think there are any." Casseck shook his head. "It's like they didn't even try once they saw our numbers."

Quinn frowned. "Explains why it was over so quick." He walked over to the man Ash had speared. "What about this one?" Quinn pushed his sword under the man's chin to make him lift his face. "Why are you here?" he asked him in Kimisar.

The man raised up on his arms to look at Quinn and grinned as he whispered something Quinn couldn't hear.

Quinn squatted beside him, looking for hidden weapons before leaning closer, keeping his sword a few inches under the man's throat, and now angled upward. "What was that?" he asked.

"Go to hell," the man said, throwing his arms wide. His weight came down on the point of Quinn's sword, impaling him through the neck. Blood gushed over Quinn's hand, and he swore and released the weapon, but it was too late.

Quinn rolled the shuddering body over with his foot and pulled his sword free. He searched the dying man's face for a clue as to why he'd done such a thing, but the dark eyes only stared blankly as an expanding pool of red formed on the gravel road beneath him. Quinn had seen death before, had dealt it plenty of times, but there was something horrifying about a man who took his own life. He shivered and drew his left thumb diagonally across his chest, whispering, "Spirit, shield me," as several men around him did the same.

He was more careful as he prodded the rest of the bodies for signs of life, but none still breathed, meaning he had no prisoners for questioning.

Damn.

7

THE ROCKY LANDSCAPE made burying the Kimisar bodies time-consuming, but Quinn insisted on doing that rather than burning them or leaving them to rot. His company returned to the main army camp five days later, where word of their confrontation had already been carried by courier. Quinn tried not to smile too much as heads turned and faces gathered to greet them. No one could doubt he'd deserved his promotion now.

Quinn led his company down the wide path between rows of wooden shelters set up for storage and smithing through the winter. Within a few weeks, they'd all be dismantled and the army itself would begin to move like a bear awakening from hibernation. The stables were already half down with cavalry patrols active. He drew his brown mare to a halt outside the structure and signaled for everyone to dismount.

A small body crashed into him as his feet touched the ground. "Alex!"

Quinn gave his younger brother a squeeze, glad he was surrounded enough that only his friends could see him. "Hey there, Charlie."

The page stepped back, looking embarrassed. "Sorry, sir. I forgot." He brought his hand to his forehead in a proper salute, which the captain solemnly returned.

When Quinn lowered his hand, he brought it down on Charlie's dark hair. "You're getting shaggy, kid."

Charlie grinned, revealing he'd lost another tooth in the last two weeks. He'd turned nine last month, but to Quinn he'd always be the wide-eyed toddler who followed him around when he visited their home in Cambria. As he'd joined the army before Charlie was born, Quinn had been almost a mythical figure for the majority of Charlie's life. "I heard you were in a battle," said Charlie. "Were you hurt?"

"Just a scratch." Quinn lifted his own over-long hair and tipped his head so Charlie could see the stitches over his eye. Cass had done a good job and the swelling was down, but it still itched like hell. "You should see Ash's. Much more impressive."

Charlie looked around for the other faces he knew before seeming to remember he had a purpose. "I'm here to take Surry for you, sir. You're requested in the general's tent for debriefing."

Quinn nodded, trying to ignore the flutter in his stomach. Reporting after a patrol was standard for a commander, whether or not he'd seen action, but this would be his first. He handed the reins over to his brother and patted the mare on the neck before pulling a small bundle from his saddle. "Take my bags to my tent when you're done brushing her down."

"Yes, sir."

Quinn straightened his uniform as he turned away, brushing road dust off his black leather jacket. He caught Casseck's eye, and his second-in-command nodded in acknowledgment that he would take over until Quinn returned from his meeting. As he headed for the general's tent, rising over the others several rows away, Quinn tried to strike a balance in his pace. He didn't want to look too eager, but he didn't want to keep his superiors waiting, either.

The sentry outside the tent saluted, and Quinn returned it as he ducked inside. He kept his hand up, rendering the gesture to the officers gathered around the wide table. His immediate superior, Major Edgecomb, was there as expected, and the regimental commander stood beside him. The general looked up from his seat, his close-clipped gray beard and hair looking as though they were made of iron themselves. Behind him stood his staff officer, Major Murray, and another man Quinn didn't know.

"Captain Alexander Quinn reporting as ordered, sir," Quinn said.

"At ease, Captain," the general said. "We'd like to hear your account now."

No pleasantries or congratulations on a successful engagement with the enemy. Quinn didn't know that he expected much, but the five stern faces were a little unnerving. He cleared his throat and approached the table, which had a map laid out on it. Without flourish, he described his company's arrival on station and how they discovered the trail of men headed north and then east.

"We tracked them for two days. They set sentries in the evening and appeared to have a hierarchy. Before attacking, I sent Sergeant Carter to intercept them and make close contact." Quinn unrolled the bundle he had with him and laid several silver medallions and a roll of parchment on the table. "We recovered these from the bodies, and this map, which is too vague to determine anything from."

The general looked up sharply. "You make it sound as though you made your decision to attack before making contact."

"Well, yes, sir," Quinn said. "But I obviously would have called it off–"

"Describe the attack, please."

Quinn swallowed. "We ambushed them here." He pointed to the spot on the map. "I used a scissor sweep, taking advantage of the angle of the sun–"

"What time was it?" Major Edgecomb interrupted.

"About an hour before sunset, sir."

All eyes went back to the map, and Quinn felt he'd made a mistake, though he couldn't see how . . . unless this was about Robert. The general must be upset Quinn had put the crown prince in danger, but he'd conceded months ago when Quinn had requested his cousin as one of his lieutenants, saying that keeping Robert away from action made him look weak. With winter weather cutting off communication with the capital, it was doubtful King Raymond knew of his son's new duties, and it was the general who would have to answer to the king and council if something happened to the prince.

Quinn cleared his throat. "There were only three injuries. All minor. Prince Robert wasn't among them—"

"Yes, we know," Edgecomb snapped. His eyes drifted to the general, who frowned back.

The unknown officer picked up a medallion and traced the raised design of Kimisara's four-pointed star with his thumb. "You have no prisoners for questioning."

It was a statement, not a question. Quinn knew better than to make excuses. "The survivor killed himself. It's not something I'd ever seen before, but yes, sir, I failed in that respect."

Every man shifted uncomfortably.

The general seemed to make a decision. "I would speak to the captain alone."

Sweet Spirit, this was bad.

The four other officers saluted and disappeared. After several seconds of silence, the general sat back in his chair and looked up at him. "This was our first potential raid in months. You can understand my disappointment."

Quinn silently cursed the dead Kimisar. "Sir, a man who wants to die will find a way."

"The suicide is secondary. Your primary mistake was timing."

"Timing, sir?" Heat rushed to his face. "The ambush was perfect."

The general shook his head in exasperation. "I'm not talking about your tactics—those are fine. You attacked too soon."

"Sir, we tracked them for days. We knew who they were, and their weapons proved they were hostile. There was nothing left to learn."

"*Think*, Captain." The general leaned forward and tapped his forefinger on a junction on the map. "A few more hours and they would've been at Arrowhead Crossroad. We'd have a better idea of whether they were headed north or east. We'd know if they were splitting up or meeting someone. As it is we know *nothing*. Because *you* couldn't wait to take them down."

Quinn reddened and said nothing in his defense.

The general sat back again. "You're in a command position now. These aren't mistakes you can afford to make." His voice gradually became less harsh. "You must see the bigger picture. Acting quickly has its merits, but so does patience. It's a delicate balance, and not everyone who walks it makes the best decision every time."

Quinn looked down at his feet, trying not to sink into himself.

"Son," General Quinn said, "you must learn *patience*."

8

SAGE SQUINTED THROUGH the peephole that looked into the bathing room. In the last five months, she'd learned to judge quite a bit through that hole, once she got over the sense of voyeurism.

"Well, what do you think?" asked the matchmaker.

Sage leaned back and made a face. "I don't like her. She's spoiled, rude, and overbearing."

Darnessa rolled her eyes. "I can count the number of girls you've liked on one hand. She's a Concordium candidate—of course she's a spoiled brat. Have you learned nothing?"

Sage sighed and began listing her observations. "Graceful and poised when she knows she's being watched. Thinks every man will fall in love with her if she flashes those big blue eyes. Servants detest and fear her. She's cruel when displeased, which is often."

Darnessa nodded. "Good. I see the same things. What about her looks?"

"Pleasing figure. Tightens her bodice too much, though; she looks like she'd spill out of it if she bent over too far." Sage suppressed a smile. "Her face still has some youthful roundness to it. She'll thin out in the next few years. Complexion is pretty good, except she styles her hair to cover some pockmarks on the forehead. She's not naturally that blond, but she looks better than the false red of that girl last month."

"Anything else?"

"Clubfoot."

That surprised the matchmaker. "Really?"

Sage nodded. "Hides it with a special shoe. I imagine dancing is somewhat painful." She chewed her lip thoughtfully. "Maybe that's the reason for the showy cleavage. When she can't keep up, she can use the hill scenery to keep suitors hypnotized."

Darnessa snorted in laughter and gestured for Sage to pull the heavy blanket over the peephole.

Sage tugged the weaving down and turned back. "Perhaps that's why she's so short-tempered. She's afraid someone'll find out and ruin her chance at getting in." She frowned. The girl had probably been told her entire life that a high marriage was all she was good for. And since the Concordium was held only every five years, at nineteen she had only one chance at getting in.

Darnessa rolled her eyes. "You're better at this than you realize."

Sage shrugged. "It's just figuring out motivations. Sometimes it's interesting." She tipped a thumb at the wall behind her. "They're almost done in there. How do I look?" She lifted her arms over her simple but pretty dress.

"You look very sweet." Darnessa reached out to tuck away a strand of Sage's hair. Sage stiffened a little, but didn't lean away as she had in the first few months of the job. "Now get back there and be ready."

Sage lingered in the kitchen until the front bell rang. Then she waited a few more minutes before slipping out the back door into the warm April sunshine. The younger brother of the girl in Darnessa's parlor leaned against the family's carriage, tossing his cap in the air. Sage cleared her mind and began making a mental list.

A sword was belted at his waist. Right-handed.

As she walked closer, the polished gleam of the metal hilt caught the sun and nearly blinded her. The scabbard was equally flawless. Rarely used. The boy was only seventeen, though, and under his very rich family's thumb, so he could be forgiven for not having found himself quite yet.

His embroidered tunic and white linen shirt were neat to the point of fussiness, and he looked a bit uncomfortable in them. The polished but worn boots and tanned face told her he enjoyed being outdoors. Her heart lightened considerably. He had some potential, at least in conversation.

He looked up as she approached, straightening and settling his feathered cap on his sun-kissed blond hair. Sage put on her best smile.

❧

Darnessa walked into the kitchen, toweling her wet hair. "You can write Lady Jacqueline down as coming with us to the capital," she said. "We'll find her a rich count who hates dancing."

Sage didn't look up from her seat at the table, where she wrote notes in a large, leather-bound book. "They certainly waited until the last minute to have her evaluated."

Her employer shrugged. "With her pedigree, she was pretty much a given, and it's a long way to travel twice. Her family will stay with relatives nearby until we leave next month. They're looking over the contract now."

"Why don't any of the families come with the brides?" asked Sage, searching for a page she wanted. "That's a lot of trust they put in you to make a match without them."

Darnessa lowered herself into a chair and propped her feet up. "We banned them from the Concordium generations ago. The crowding and backdoor attempts to arrange matches defeated the entire purpose." She pointed and flexed her feet as she spoke, working the soreness out from the fancy shoes she wore for interviews. "Have you finished the letter to General Quinn about our escort?"

"Not yet," Sage said. "We only got that last confirmation this morning, so I wasn't able to write out all our planned stops until today. I was waiting for your decision on Jacqueline, too. I thought I'd include all the names. Better too much information than too little." She tossed the draft of her letter across the table for Darnessa's approval. "Sister Fernham is expecting me in an hour, so I'll finish it tonight."

"I don't know what the convent will do while you're gone," Darnessa muttered as she squinted at the page, but Sage knew she didn't mind the

41

lessons she taught to the orphans in her spare time. "How did it go with Jacqueline's brother?"

"Fairly well," Sage answered. "We went for a walk, and I got him talking about himself pretty quickly. Considerate and attentive, though a bit vacant. I made a joke and it went right over his head." He was a bit of a flirt, too, but she wasn't foolish enough to think he was attracted to her. Young men were eager to impress any girl who flattered them, and she'd grown used to turning that to her advantage. "Overall a nice young man. If she wasn't already coming with us to the capital, I'd say he might be a good match for Lady Tamara."

"No, but when we get back from Tennegol, I'll be ready when he comes knocking for his match," Darnessa said.

"Something he said makes me think maybe his parents have a match planned for him down in Tasmet."

Darnessa frowned. "Are you sure? Something that big should have gone through me."

"It sounded like an agreement between families." Sage had a special section in her book for those matches. Tasmet, like Crescera, was a province of Demora, though it was still adjusting to being part of the country. Matchmakers had been established there for less than forty years—not quite two full generations, but as Tasmet nobility were mostly transplanted from other regions of Demora after it was ceded by Kimisara in the Great War, the practice had taken hold quickly. Every year a higher percentage of the general population used matchmakers. In another forty years, Tasmet would be like the rest of the country in that only the poorest—and most scandalous—marriages were self-arranged.

"*Another one?* This is getting out of hand." Darnessa swung her feet down to the floor and sat up straight, shaking her head and grumbling. "It's not just the loss in my planning. If it doesn't work out well, people might think *I* put them together."

Father had always said those in power feared losing it, but Darnessa's anger didn't feel like vanity to Sage. If she'd learned anything over the winter, it was that the matchmaking guild had high standards and tight control. Even a whisper of matching for personal gain was dealt with swiftly, and as the head of Crescera's guild, Darnessa took her leadership role very seriously.

"I don't know what's going on lately," continued the matchmaker. "But I'm glad it's a Concordium year. We'll be able to compare notes and see if it's part of a bigger trend."

"He didn't seem too enthused about the girl." That was truth, but Sage had offered it to make Darnessa feel better.

The matchmaker relaxed a little. "Hopefully that's a sign he'd rather have me find him a wife. We'll pair him up after we return. I'll get Jacqueline what they want, and the family will come back to me."

Sage bent over her work again, marveling at the power her employer wielded so casually. Yet in all her travels, in all the people she'd met, the matchmaker hadn't found anyone for herself. In five months, Sage had never detected any bitterness on the subject, though, which gave her the courage to finally ask, "Why did you never marry, Darnessa?"

"Same as you," Darnessa answered with a conspiratorial wink. "My standards are too high."

9

ON CHAPEL DAYS, camp routines were reduced to a minimum, giving the soldiers a chance to rest or catch up on duties. Captain Quinn usually set aside an hour or two to spend with Charlie, but since he hadn't seen his brother in almost three weeks, this time he promised him the whole afternoon. He used it as an excuse to avoid people, too. Every hearty slap on the back or congratulations Quinn received over last week's ambush felt like a punch to the gut—he didn't deserve to be celebrated.

Charlie, as usual, wanted to practice some sort of skill for at least part of their time. The page was still in the early stages of swordsmanship, which was to say, he was helping the blacksmiths make, repair, and maintain blades for a year. As a firm believer in the process, Quinn wouldn't interfere by giving actual fighting lessons no matter how much his brother begged. An informal archery competition was developing on one side of the camp, so Quinn talked Charlie into knife throwing as far away from everyone else as possible.

For his age and size, Charlie was already adept at hitting the target, so Quinn wanted him to work on greater distances. Charlie balked at first. "But I want to draw faster and smoother. *You* can do it like lightning."

Quinn raised an eyebrow at his brother, wincing a little as his forehead wrinkled. The sutures had come out yesterday, and the warm April sun made the scab itch and burn. "Which do you think is more useful in battle, hitting your target from farther away or looking pretty while you miss?"

Charlie gave a resigned sigh and took three more steps back. Quinn smothered a smile. It hadn't been that long ago that he'd been in Charlie's shoes.

After several rounds of throwing and another range increase, they were pulling their daggers from the target wall when Charlie turned to him. "Is something wrong?" he asked.

"No, why?"

Charlie shrugged as he worked to free a blade stuck between two planks of the wall. "You seem distracted. And you missed four times. You never miss."

"Most people wouldn't call this *missing*," Quinn said, tapping the hilt of a dagger stuck three inches from the center of the painted target.

"You would."

Quinn tried to act like nothing was wrong. "Everyone has off days."

They'd walked back to the range line before Charlie spoke again. "When we passed Captain Hargrove earlier he said something, and you made a face."

Charlie was too observant for his own good sometimes. "What kind of face did I make?"

The boy didn't look at him as he set the practice daggers on top of a barrel. "You looked embarrassed."

"I don't like people making such a fuss over me just doing my job; you know that."

Charlie picked a knife, then set his feet and focused on the target. "It's not that. You've been unhappy since you came back."

Charlie knew how to keep a secret, but it wasn't the fear his brother would tell all the other pages about his failure that kept Quinn from explaining. Nor was it because he didn't want to lose Charlie's admiration—his brother thought too highly of him already, and he should know Quinn wasn't perfect. No, it was because Quinn hadn't figured out how to make this right. Until he did, he would carry it himself.

At that moment Charlie yelped as he was lifted off his feet by Ash

45

Carter, who'd snuck up behind them. Quinn was glad Ash had chosen to grab the page, as he'd been so distracted himself he'd not seen the sergeant approach. His friend could just have easily taken him by surprise.

"Dereliction of duty, soldier!" shouted Ash, throwing Charlie over his shoulder and spinning in a circle. "You must be on guard at all times!" He set a laughing Charlie on his feet and held his shoulders so the page wouldn't fall over. "Sweet Spirit, you're getting big. How've you been, kid?"

"Good. Squire Palomar said he would put me on the duty roll soon," said Charlie with a proud grin.

"So I heard," said Ash. "Show me what you've got here." The sergeant gestured to the knives and the target. When Charlie's attention was focused away, Ash's dark eyes sought Quinn's own with a meaningful look. Something was up.

They waited for Charlie to throw the six practice blades plus the one he carried on his belt. Then Ash and Quinn offered their own daggers for him to throw. With nine knives to remove from the target, the pair would have a few minutes to talk privately while Charlie retrieved them.

"You and I have been called to the general's tent tomorrow morning," said Ash quietly as soon as Charlie was out of earshot.

Quinn folded his arms to cover the sick feeling in his stomach. He'd managed to avoid his father for the last few days and hadn't pushed for another assignment. "What about?"

"Don't know," said Ash, focusing downrange.

"Maybe he wants you to put on lieutenant."

"Perhaps, but I doubt it. He knows why I don't want it."

That didn't mean the reason would always be accepted. Quinn wondered if the general felt Ash having greater authority in their rider company would strengthen it. Maybe his father wanted the calming presence Ash brought to everything. Ash's rank didn't matter to Quinn, though, as long as his friend worked for him.

Ash glanced up at him. "You look worried."

"After last week's fiasco, don't you think I should be?"

The sergeant shook his head and looked back to Charlie. "Everyone makes mistakes, Alex," he said. They had been friends as boys, but Ash so rarely used Quinn's first name anymore that the captain knew it was to reassure him how deep his trust still went. "You're still new to being captain. It's expected."

Except not everyone was the general's son, and now his blunders also had bigger consequences. The stakes would only ever get higher. Quinn watched his brother turn back to them, struggling to hold all the knives in his small hands. How much longer before Charlie's life was in his hands? He exhaled heavily. "When is this meeting?"

"An hour after morning muster." Quinn nodded in acknowledgment. Ash retrieved his dagger from the jumble Charlie carried back to them, then rumpled the boy's hair before looking back to Quinn. "Don't be late."

◆

The next morning, Quinn reassembled and brushed off his already spotless uniform, cinching his sword belt over his jacket with growing apprehension. Was he being demoted? He'd never heard of such a thing, but his mind had run wild with possibilities long after half carrying Charlie to the pages' tent, having allowed the boy stay with him and his officers by the campfire late into the night.

Ash Carter waited patiently for him outside the tent Quinn shared with Casseck. When Quinn could delay no longer, he joined the sergeant and the two walked side by side through the camp, taking several shortcuts between the rows of tents. In the past week, more of the permanent structures had come down, meaning the army would start moving very soon. Quinn wasn't likely to get away from it on his own for a while, though.

At the general's tent, Quinn paused to watch several other officers stream in. This was a much bigger meeting than he'd realized. Inside, a dozen senior officers gathered around the table laid with maps and reports, and he understood what it was: an intelligence briefing. Relief washed over him as he understood this was actually a good thing.

Quinn and Ash took places in the back, standing with the lower officers. He caught a glimpse of his father at the far end of the tent, writing at a desk. The general's personal section had the comforts of rank—a wide bed, a wooden cabinet, and a washbasin, but no privacy curtains. An officer was never truly off duty. Quinn had only ever seen the area divided from the rest on the occasions Mother visited.

Major Murray called the meeting to attention, and the general stood and walked over to the table. Once everyone was at ease again, the senior officers took turns reporting on their action in the past week. A Kimisar squad was tracked crossing the border to the east and had been lost in the foothills of the Catrix Mountains. Local villages reported seeing groups of men like the one Quinn intercepted, but no raids, and the men had vanished like smoke. Quinn's own skirmish was detailed by his battalion commander with no comment on his lack of patience.

The meeting continued with attempts to find a pattern in all the events reported. Quinn wasn't asked for any insights, nor did he offer any. He cringed inwardly as the consequences of his mistake piled up. Were it not for him, they might be able to do more than speculate.

The only thing to do now was learn from it.

When the discussion was spent, Major Murray picked up a sheaf of papers and began reading orders out loud. Quinn straightened when he heard his name.

"Captain Quinn: you, three officers, and thirty men will leave for Galarick in two days. From there you will escort the brides from Crescera to the capital for this summer's Concordium. Submit the names of your men by sundown."

What?

"A ceremonial guard?" he blurted out.

Eyes around the table shifted to him, and the captain on his right smirked, but Quinn focused on his father, who returned his gaze calmly. The parchments describing their orders were passed over, and Ash took them. When the meeting closed and everyone was dismissed, Quinn lingered, waiting for a chance speak to his father alone.

"Too bad my father's not a general," Captain Larsen said from beside him. "I'd've liked to *squire* around a bunch of ladies for a few weeks." He made a show of folding up his orders and tucking them into his jacket. "Well, I've got to have fifty men ready to ride by sundown. Pick one out for me, will you, Quinn? I like blondes." Larsen sauntered out while Quinn glared at his back.

From his side, Ash held up their orders for him to take, but Quinn ignored them. After a few seconds, the sergeant folded the papers—there were several—and cleared his throat. "I guess I'll tell everyone where we're going."

He left Quinn standing alone, clenching and unclenching his fists. The last colonel finished talking with the general and departed, leaving only the two of them in the tent. His father watched him from the table with a map still laid across it. "I know you're not happy with your mission."

"Why wouldn't I be?" Quinn crossed his arms. "Matchmakers and preening noble girls as far away from danger as possible. It's a cavalry officer's dream."

His father pinned him with a look as sharp as his sword. "You're not in a position to look down on any assignment right now."

After several seconds of silence, Quinn dropped his gaze. "And this is how I will learn patience. This is my punishment."

The general sighed. "Yes and no."

Quinn looked up. The *no* interested him.

"In truth, I'm to blame for your mistake. You weren't included in these meetings before, and you should've been. I didn't want to be seen as favoring you." His father cleared his throat. "What I'm going to tell you now wasn't brought up earlier, and I don't want it spreading through the camp."

His father had his full attention now.

The general gestured to the map. "My gut says that squad you caught was headed east. I think the D'Amirans are communicating with Kimisara."

That was quite an accusation, though not outlandish. The D'Amiran family had unified Crescera, Mondelea, Aristel, and the Tenne Valley into the country they called Demora over five hundred years ago, but decades of corrupt and decadent rule led Robert Devlin's ancestors to overthrow them three hundred years later. While the family wasn't destroyed, they existed only on the fringes until the Great War forty years ago. With the annexation of Tasmet, a new dukedom was created and awarded to General Falco D'Amiran for his role in wrestling it away from Kimisara. It was only a fraction of their former power, and given their history, many suspected the D'Amirans wouldn't be satisfied with scraps from the Devlin table.

"Does Uncle Raymond know of your suspicions?" Quinn asked.

His father shook his head. "Not yet. The winter was so bad I wasn't able to send sensitive dispatches across the mountains—even the south pass at Jovan was blocked until last week. The king is almost completely unaware."

"So I'm to be the courier of your concerns." That at least felt important.

"That and more." The general leaned over to point to the map again. "The bridal caravan will travel through Tegann."

Duke Morrow D'Amiran's stronghold. Quinn suddenly knew why Ash had been included in the meeting. "You want us to spy on the duke."

"Discreetly, yes."

Quinn wasn't quite won over. "I don't have much experience with that kind of spying, just land reconnaissance."

"Then consider this your chance to learn something new," his father said.

Quinn grimaced. Acquiring new skills had always been a top priority. Casseck called it his obsession. Father had framed it that way to trap him.

On the other hand, all the general had to do was issue an order. His father wanted him to embrace the mission, not just obey.

When Quinn didn't object, the general smiled a little. "Whom do you want to take?"

Quinn folded his arms. "Can't I just take my officers?"

"I've been going back and forth on that," the general said. "On one hand, I don't like Robert Devlin out of my sight. On the other, the prince is probably safer away from the border."

"I won't tell him you said that."

The general continued, "Thirty men should be adequate to protect him, especially so deep in Demora, but I don't want the fuss he'll create, either." He paused. "I leave it up to you."

It may have been a bone thrown to make Quinn feel better, but he took it. "I don't want to break up what we have, so I'll take Rob, but give him a false name."

"Very well, and keep him away from the ladies," said his father, glancing out the open tent flap. "By the way, you're taking Charlie, too."

Quinn threw up his arms. "That just proves you're sending me away from anything important."

"Nonsense." The general eased down into a chair. "You need a page along, and he asked to be assigned to you for his birthday gift. He's good at his job."

Yes, Charlie was competent, but Quinn wouldn't be able to treat his brother like just any other page. It was hard enough giving commands to his closest friends, even orders they didn't mind. He squeezed his eyes shut and rubbed his forehead, forgetting the wound and flinching back when pain shot through his temple. "Father, please reconsider. Carting these women around is bad enough. I feel like a nursemaid."

"I'll leave the decision to you, but he already knows, so you'll have to be the one to break the news to him."

Trapped. Again.

His father pulled a parchment closer to read and raised a hand in dismissal. "You have a lot of preparations to make, so I suggest you get started."

Quinn retreated before things could get any worse.

10

CASSECK AND GRAMWELL had already spread out a map and were marking it with the places the bridal caravan would stop overnight. Robert and Ash wrote out lists of supplies and personnel. They all jumped to attention when Quinn walked in the tent, but he motioned for them to relax. "I guess everyone's heard."

Rob grinned. "As far as punishments go, it's not too bad."

Quinn shook his head. "Don't get any ideas—you're going under a false name. This is bigger than just an escort."

Casseck raised a blond eyebrow. "Bigger how?"

"It's an unofficial reconnaissance mission." Quinn leaned over the map and traced his finger along the Tegann Road and tapped the fortress at the pass. "The general is particularly interested in what's going on here."

Rob's eyes widened. "Is Duke D'Amiran up to something?"

"Possibly." They had to approach this mission with a neutral mindset, otherwise everything they observed would look like treason.

Ash offered Quinn the papers he'd ignored earlier. "Am I the lead scout in all this?"

"Yes," said Quinn, taking the pages. Among them was a letter to his father from Crescera's high matchmaker, Mistress Rodelle, detailing the arrangements she'd made for the journey. He scanned the precise handwriting, appreciating the logical way the information was presented. "We'll be at Baron Underwood's three nights, which is good. He's a friend of the D'Amirans."

Robert peered over his shoulder. "So is Lord Fashell near the end. All Tegann's supplies come through his estate."

Quinn chewed the inside of his cheek before looking up at Ash. "What do you think about making a contact in the ladies' group, with a maid or something? She could feed you information we can't observe."

Ash made a face. "Can't I do actual scouting this time? It's damn stressful to be undercover that long."

Quinn's experience was limited to terrain scouting; Ash had always been the one to do the closer work of questioning people, using a carefully constructed story to gain their confidence. "Seems pretty easy to me."

Ash shrugged. "Sometimes people get hurt."

"Hurt? Picket duty is far more dangerous."

"Not physically," Ash said. "If the contacts find out you're using them, it destroys everything you've built. And lying is lying. It never feels good."

"What would you have me do?" Quinn asked. "Send someone with less experience?"

"I didn't say I wouldn't do it, just that I'm getting tired of it. Besides"— Ash brightened—"the scenery will be nicer than I'm used to."

The women. As a sergeant, Ash didn't have to wait until he was twenty-four to marry like the officers. Though he was illegitimate—the result of the king's liaison with a maid after the death of the first queen— few families would shun a chance to merge with the royals.

Quinn pulled his friend aside. "Are you interested in being matched?" he asked quietly.

"Maybe." Ash avoided his eyes. "I don't think a girl would look at me twice if she didn't know who I was." That no one looked at him twice was his biggest advantage in spying. He glanced at his brother. "Rob says he'll wait for the next Concordium, unless Father says otherwise. What about you?"

Quinn's own parents were a highly political match, and it had worked out well, but he'd always resisted the idea. He hated feeling like a sum of what he owned rather than a person. "I plan on avoiding it completely."

"There's more to life than the army, you know."

Quinn didn't want to talk about marriage. The letters from Mother on the subject lately were bad enough. "You're my lead, then. Get your story ready, and make sure everyone knows it."

Ash nodded and walked back to Robert. "Put me down as a wagon driver. Lower me to private, too. It'll give me flexibility."

❧

Several days later, Quinn stared down at the remnants of a campfire. Anyone could see a group of men had stayed here two days ago. To the captain's trained eye, however, there was much to cause concern. First, the number of travelers was ten—which was typical for a Kimisar squad. Second, they posted roving patrols as far as four hundred yards out. And third, they traveled quickly. Unburdened with wagons and the need to stick to roads, they covered twice the distance in one day as the escort unit, and he didn't have the time or resources to track them down.

Ash Carter came up behind him. "I'm glad we brought the dogs. We might never have found this otherwise."

Quinn nodded. "They're headed north, into Crescera. Do you think they intended to meet with that group we dispatched a few weeks ago?"

Ash shrugged. "Don't know. But that courier said there's activity all over the border since we left."

Quinn had a packet of dispatches for the king and his council in Tennegol, but messengers from his father would find them along the way with updated reports. The first had caught up with them last night, bringing news that the army had mobilized and stretched out to meet a number of incursions.

He was missing out on everything.

"I've never seen a raid this small so far north," said Quinn. "They were only a couple days from Crescera." This group could already be there.

"Must be after food. All the granaries are up here."

"On foot? How could they carry enough grain back to justify the trip?"

Ash frowned. "Maybe they'll steal horses here. Last I heard, Kimisara had eaten half of theirs."

54

"That makes sense," Quinn said. "Makes it easier to sneak in, too. I wonder if what our army's reacting to down south is a diversion from a bunch of little raids up here." He was already writing the report in his mind for the courier to take back, glad he'd made the man wait.

The pair remounted their horses and headed back to the road, where the caravan waited. Quinn frowned as Robert's dark head came into view. If there were Kimisar in the area and they realized Rob was with the escort, Quinn had no doubt they would come after him. Kimisara had a long history of hostage taking in addition to raiding, and the crown prince would be a target too tempting to pass up. Quinn felt he could protect Rob against superior numbers, but when they met with the women in a few days, it would be more complicated.

He hadn't thought to post picket scouts around the group as it traveled, but it now seemed necessary, especially if there were more squads out there. An idea formed in his head as he balanced the need to protect Robert with his plans for spying. He turned to Ash. "I have a new job for you, my friend."

11

SAGE HEAVED HER trunk onto the wagon, then arched her back and stretched. The matchmaker rolled her eyes. "I hired men for that."

Sage hopped down from the cart. "Seemed silly to let it sit in the dirt till they got around to it."

"You're making this trip as a lady," Darnessa admonished. "Every stop along the way is a chance to observe people we need to know about, and if you ruin that image, you won't be able to get close to them."

"Yes, yes." Sage straightened her skirt. "I just wanted to wait as long as possible before putting on the yoke." The monthlong journey to Tennegol would be exhausting, but Darnessa had promised she could wear breeches on the way back.

She dutifully played the part of a shy noble girl as the women arrived, most meeting for the first time. Many obviously saw one another as rivals. Sage pictured a burlap sack full of cats and wondered which would come out with the most scratches.

The matchmaker introduced her. "This is my assistant, Sage, but you will call her Lady Sagerra Broadmoor. She'll be traveling as one of you, and you'll follow her instructions as if they were my own."

"She looks like that girl with the fowler who trained my father's hawks when I was young," said a blonde, leaning in to squint at Sage.

"She very likely is," said Darnessa. The matchmaker probably meant to sound kind, but Sage felt patronized.

Lady Jacqueline crossed her arms. "*Sage* is a peasant's name. Or a bastard's. Which is she?"

They talked like she wasn't there. "I can speak for myself," Sage snapped.

The young woman turned her head, peering down as if Sage were an insect she could crush with her high-heeled satin shoe. "Then which is it?"

"Neither, but you can bet your pretty ass you'll be kissing mine before we get to the capital." Sage smiled and curtsied. "My lady."

Jacqueline looked ready to bite back, but Darnessa slashed her hand through the air between them. "Enough. Her name is Lady Sagerra Broadmoor as far as anyone else is concerned, and if one of you leaks otherwise, you'll regret it for the rest of your life." Jacqueline turned and stalked away, several others following her lead. The matchmaker scrunched her mouth to one side. "That probably could've gone better," she said.

A hand slipped into Sage's, and she looked down in surprise—Lady Clare. She remembered the sweet face—and that *hair*. Dark, glossy curls the color of maple syrup cascaded over one shoulder, not a strand out of place. Clare smiled shyly. "I'm glad to meet you, Sagerra," she said. Clare squeezed her fingers and left to say good-bye to her family.

Sage watched her walk away, feeling unmoved by the gesture. Over the winter, girls who'd never deigned to speak with Sage for years had suddenly wanted to be her friend, which was flattering until she realized their kindness was only designed to get them better matches. No one was ever nice to her unless they wanted something.

❧

It was only ten miles to Galarick, and the bridal group arrived shortly after noon. Sage located the library almost immediately and intended to spend the rest of the day there but found herself wandering restlessly on the walls. Galarick's layout resembled a fortress with an inner and outer ward and barracks for soldiers, but it was only a glorified manor house—all the grandeur of a castle but little of its strength. Fortifications were unnecessary this deep in Demora, especially since the border with Kimisara had been pushed so far south.

When horns announced the arrival of their military escort, Sage's curiosity was enough that she found a spot on the inner wall to watch them parade in. There were about thirty soldiers total, and horses outnumbered men nearly two to one. Several hunting dogs walked among them, deftly avoiding hooves. The riders, all dressed in black jackets, breeches, and boots, dismounted as one and began unloading carts and leading horses to the stables. There was talk and some laughter, but not as much as she expected.

Darnessa also watched from nearby, wearing the sharp look Sage associated with sizing people up. Sage drifted over to stand beside her.

"Are those the wagons?" Sage pointed to the plain carts pulled alongside one another. "I thought they'd be fancier." The ten or so wagon drivers and attendants wore simple clothing—brown breeches and vests over white linen shirts.

"They'll dress them up tomorrow," said Darnessa. "Have you ever seen soldiers before?"

"Not to remember." Soldiers posted west of the mountains stayed mostly in Tasmet and had frequent clashes with Kimisara. While Uncle William may have sworn fealty and carried a sword, these men *lived* that vow in a way her uncle never had to. Sage shivered with the thought of what their blades may have already experienced.

"That's the captain there, with the gold on his collar." Darnessa gestured to a rider with dark hair. His features were handsome, at least from this distance, his bearing proud. The matchmaker eyed her sideways. "General Quinn's son. Quite a catch."

No doubt.

General Quinn had married the sister of the previous queen. Those weddings and several others at the time had pulled the richest families in Aristel into a tight alliance, which proved critical in defeating Kimisara's last major attempt to invade a few years later. The more she learned about matching, the more Sage suspected the nation was held together by it.

She frowned as the young man directed some of the handling. "Do you think his father sent him to the Corcordium to be matched? He can't be old enough."

"I'm not sure. He won't be eligible for three years."

"Bit long for an engagement," said Sage. "Should I bother putting him in the book?"

Darnessa nodded. "It's rare for soldiers to come close enough for us to size them up. Go ahead and make pages for each officer."

Just then a bell tolled, announcing the noon meal. The Baron of Galarick had provided the ladies their own room for dining and entertaining themselves, but Sage was loath to join them. "I'm not that hungry. I think I'll just grab a bit in the kitchens and eat in the library, if you don't mind."

"As long as you actually eat. You're too thin." Darnessa squeezed Sage's arm.

Sage twisted away. She was so used to the matchmaker judging people, it was hard to tell whether she was being critical or motherly, and neither made her comfortable. "I will."

Darnessa left her alone, and Sage watched the soldiers for a few more minutes, feeling a strange envy. The men below all moved and acted with a sense of purpose, whereas she always felt lost. True, the matchmaker kept her busy, and true, Sage sometimes enjoyed her work even though she would never admit it, yet Darnessa wasn't much different from Uncle William in the way Sage was bound to her. The soldiers were also bound to the commands of others, but it was by their choice, and they all played an important role in every mission, if not the fate of the nation.

Sage tapped a rhythm on the wooden rail in front of her. She was good at teaching; perhaps Darnessa could recommend her to a wealthy family—not this year, but maybe at the next Concordium. The matchmaker would probably retire then, and Sage would be old enough for people to take her seriously. Depending on who hired her, she might be able to have her own home.

She'd taken this job out of desperation and questioned it often despite Darnessa's assurance that she was suited for it. Now she saw it was the best decision she'd made in a long time. It was a step toward freedom.

Sage smiled and set off to find her ledger. She had work to do.

12

DUKE MORROW D'AMIRAN watched the sunset from the northwest tower of the massive stone fortress, his back to the hazy, narrow Tegann Pass. Spring had struggled to take hold of the landscape this year. Only the scattered evergreens produced any color on the slopes, which rose sharply behind him like a granite curtain.

His pale-blue eyes followed the man striding boldly across the drawbridge, pausing as the portcullis was raised to let him in. The Kimisar's clothing was as colorless as the land, the edges of him indistinct against the background. D'Amiran stroked his blackened beard as he searched the shadowy woods for signs of the other Kimisar he knew were out there. Only one was visible, and after a few seconds the duke realized he was looking at a fallen tree rather than a soldier in wait. It disturbed him to see the Kimisar were so efficient at hiding, though as they were his allies now, he should be pleased.

This alliance was distasteful, but Kimisara's desperation made for more agreeable terms. At the moment the southern nation wanted only food, though once it was back on its feet, he had little doubt Kimisara would return to nibbling away at the Tasmet province, if not mounting another full campaign to take it back. They could have it as far as he was concerned; only the rich deposits of copper to the south were worth keeping. The dukedom belonged to his family as a reward for his father's service in the Great War forty years ago, but it was almost an insult. While it seemed grand on paper, the land was drab, rocky, and barren.

As a child raised in Mondelea, he'd taken one look at the fortress and land that was to be his new home and wept.

He'd expected his father to be angry over those tears, but he'd only taken him aside and explained it was nothing compared to the centuries of humiliation his family had already survived after being ousted from the throne by the Devlin family. This place was only a stepping-stone to taking back what was rightfully theirs. *I may not see the day,* he said. *But you will.*

His father had been right about the first part. The Spirit had claimed him eleven years later, and Morrow suffered several setbacks as both he and his younger brother were prevented from advancing through military ranks—Rewel had failed to even make lieutenant. Blocked by the rising star of General Pendleton Quinn, the king's new pet, on the battlefield and in marriage. But if the duke had learned anything in his forty-three years, it was that not all battles were won in direct ways. Sometimes they were achieved, as with the steady rise and fall of the ocean tide he watched in his youth, benign and reliable—useful, even—until one day it tore away the side of a cliff.

The tide was coming in. He only needed to be patient a little longer.

Footsteps behind him called D'Amiran's attention to his guest's arrival on the tower platform. Two guards flanked the foreigner as he met their nobleman for the first time. Neither the mistrust of his host nor the grandeur of his surroundings appeared to unsettle him. He stood with his arms crossed and his feet planted, the rough weave of his cloak hanging off his broad shoulders to his knees.

When the young man didn't look inclined to speak, the duke decided to begin. "You are Captain Huzar, correct?"

The man nodded once from inside his hood but said nothing. Kimisar were darker than Demorans from Aristel, and even this close he almost faded into the shadows. Swirling tattoos on his exposed forearms added to the shapeless effect.

"Are your men in place?"

Huzar responded in a thick accent that hardened every consonant. "Yes. By your calendar, they have arrived."

62

D'Amiran allowed a tiny smile. "Excellent."

Huzar was unmoved by the praise. The lack of deference irritated the duke, but he ignored it for the moment. Things were going too well to quibble over a few phrases of respect from someone who had probably never addressed anyone as important as himself. D'Amiran clasped his hands behind him. "And they all understand their parts?"

"As instructed, only their parts. If some are captured, which is doubtful, they will not be able to inform on the others. Or you."

"Your men must not frighten the group." The duke lowered his chin to give Huzar a piercing look. "It only needs to be isolated from communication. As long as they believe nothing is wrong, they'll continue on their way here."

Huzar's lips tightened at the implication his soldiers did not understand their task. "They will not act unless necessary." He paused. "When shall we expect our hostage?" He couldn't manage the soft g, and it came out as a hissing *sch*.

D'Amiran waved his hand. "My brother is seeking him. Prince Robert is a cavalry officer, so it's only a matter of time until he patrols away from the main force. When your men carry him through the pass at Jovan, much of the army will follow, and we will act. As long as your men in the south can bring the prince back through the pass here, he is yours."

13

A LINE OF servants carried trays to the ladies' dining room at sunset. The women ignored them as they set places and filled wine goblets. When the head server announced the evening meal was ready, the guests made their way to the long table.

One server's mouth twisted in disgust as the higher ladies forced the lower ones to defer to them in small ways. His ears perked up when the conversation began, but after a few minutes he suspected it would bore him to death—luxuries they owned, marriage proposals they'd turned down, and other, even less interesting topics. Only their impression of the soldiers held any interest; they'd be amused to know the girls compared notes. None had recognized Prince Robert, which was a relief.

The matchmaker's letter had given only surnames, but the ladies addressed one another by first name, leaving him at a bit of a loss until he realized they'd arranged themselves in the same social rank as the list. He studied each girl in turn, attaching names to faces. The unnatural enhancements were distracting—how could they stand the paint on their eyelids? Some of the hair designs looked positively painful; they made his own scalp itch and reminded him he hadn't had a trim himself in two months, when it occurred to him one lady was missing. He counted again. Only fifteen.

Bowing deferentially, he approached the head of the table. "Mistress Rodelle, may I inquire if all your ladies are present? I see an extra plate."

The matchmaker scanned the table and sighed. "Yes. She's probably in the library and didn't hear dinner called." The blonde on her left snorted.

He decided there was little more to learn tonight and felt glad for a chance to escape. "Should I fetch her, mistress?"

The blonde—Lady Jacqueline—interjected, "We've already finished the first two courses. It would be rude for her to show up now."

Mistress Rodelle gave the girl a warning look, then turned back to him. "If you'd take a small meal to her, I'd appreciate it. Thank you."

He bowed and stepped back and around the table to assemble a tray of food. The bread was all taken, and he'd just decided this girl would have to do without when the lady at the matchmaker's right waved him over. With an inward grimace, he went to her, but to his surprise she handed him her loaf.

"You can take this to her; I have plenty." Lady Clare smiled and met his eyes—the only lady to have done so. They weren't all snobs, apparently.

He slipped out of the room and down the dark passageways he'd already memorized in the few hours since arriving. At the library door he balanced the tray on his knee long enough to lift the latch and nudge it open with his elbow. *Deliver the food, get a look at her, and get back to the barracks.* Based on placement of the empty seat and Lady Jacqueline's disdain, it was safe to assume this was the last on the list, Lady Broadmoor. He doubted he could find a way to get her first name tonight, though.

She didn't look up from her seat at the table by the fire, so he cleared his throat as he approached. "Forgive the intrusion, my lady, but I've brought you some supper. The other ladies said you wouldn't be joining them."

The girl lifted her head from between stacks of books. "Oh, thank you." She stood and shuffled papers and books aside. "I've made a bit of a mess, but you can tell the steward I'll clean up before I leave."

She'd been writing in a large ledger. Trying not to be obvious, he maneuvered closer to see. About half the pages looked to have been used, but the book was divided into sections with dog-eared corners, so it wasn't a diary. His eyes flitted over the scattered scraps of paper around her. Each appeared to have the name of a man on it. The open page had the information of a nearby paper copied on it. Transcribing notes. Interesting.

Her precise handwriting also closely resembled that of the letter from the matchmaker. A strange coincidence to be sure, especially considering what she was writing. He tried to get a better angle, but she gathered a few pages and shoved them into the ledger before closing it. Then she piled a few more books on top and moved them aside. The remaining loose scraps she collected in a stack before turning to toss them in the fire behind her. As the flames blazed higher, he was better able to observe her features.

She looked young, maybe just sixteen, and on the tall side, though perhaps due to her shoes. Her face lacked the doll-like beauty of the other women, but she smiled like she meant it. He couldn't tell the color of her eyes with her back to the fire, and a halo of fine hairs had escaped her simple braid, giving her a windblown appearance. The color was also difficult to nail down as the dancing light gave it red and golden hues. And either the shadows were playing tricks on him, or her nose was slightly crooked, like it had been broken at some point in the past.

Her eyes met his boldly, and she let him study her without embarrassment or indignation. As her own gaze swept over him, he curled his fingers under the tray, suddenly conscious of his dirty fingernails. She gestured at the table. "Just put it anywhere there's room. I'll serve myself."

He realized how long he'd stared and hastily set the tray down, sloshing the soup and clattering the tableware. She dropped back into the chair and reached out to help him. "I don't think I've seen you before," she said.

"No, my lady," he replied, mopping up soup with a cloth. "I came with the escort. The kitchen was short staffed, and I was told to make myself useful."

"You're a soldier?" Her eyes brightened, and he nodded. "It's good of you to help. And who wouldn't want a glimpse of our lovely ladies? Are you spying for your captain?"

Her tone was light, but he flinched and immediately cursed himself for it. She continued as though she hadn't noticed his reaction. "I suppose it's natural for people to be curious about them."

She spoke of the group as though she wasn't a part of it. Or—strangely—like she owned it. "What's your name?" she asked.

"Ash," he answered without thinking. Then, remembering how he should act, he straightened and bowed. "Ash Carter, my lady. I mostly drive wagons."

Her half smile took on a wistfulness. "Ash is a nice name. It reminds me of the woods where I grew up. How long have you been with the cavalry?"

"All my life, my lady. I've been serving with Captain Quinn since he was given command, but I've known him since I was a boy." He halted, realizing he gave more information than he should have.

She tilted her head to the side like a bird as she looked up at him, and he instinctively felt he'd made a mistake, though he could not decide how.

"Well, Master Ash," she said. "My name is Sagerra, and it's a pleasure to meet you. What have you brought me to eat?"

"Cold chicken with apricot sauce and vegetables, my lady, as well as bread and cheese and butter. This is Cook's specialty." He lifted the cover on the bowl. "Onion soup."

Lady Sagerra had leaned forward to sniff the steam rising from the dish but jerked back in revulsion. "Ick. They put onions in everything here. I can't imagine an entire soup based on them."

He paused, lid still in midair. "Truly, my lady? It's my favorite."

She gestured for him to close the steaming vessel. "You eat it, then."

"My lady, I couldn't!"

"Why not?" she replied. "If I send it back uneaten, what happens to it?"

He blinked. "They'll throw it to the pigs, I suppose."

"And you'll get none."

He shook his head. "I'll get some in the kitchens later, my lady."

Sagerra made an unladylike retching sound. "Suit yourself, but you'll be lucky to get cold dregs. Meanwhile, next week's pork roast will taste like onions."

He suppressed a smile. Maybe he could develop this into the connection the soldiers wanted within the brides' group. And that ledger she had was interesting. He didn't want to seem too eager, though. "My lady, it really is improper."

"Please?" she asked simply. "Just sit and relax for a few minutes. I haven't talked to anyone all day. I've never talked to a soldier ever."

He pulled a chair from the side of the table so he could sit across from her. Sagerra tossed him the spoon, and he caught it, grinning shyly. "I don't know if I'm worth much for conversation, my lady."

"Then eat." She pulled the bread loaf apart and leaned across the table to offer him one of the pieces, and he eyed it nervously. It was much larger than the one she kept for herself. "I'm not that hungry," she said.

He took the bread, careful not to touch her fingers. "Thank you, my lady."

She sat back and dug into her own food. He followed her example and didn't speak, though his eyes kept drifting to the ledger on the edge of the table. What was its purpose?

"So, Ash," Lady Sagerra said after she'd eaten half her plate, "where do you come from? Near the Tenne Valley?"

His mouth was too full to answer right away. "Yes, my lady. How did you know?" *And why do you care?* he asked silently.

"Your speech is quick, something I've noticed in people from that side of the mountains."

He relaxed a little. One of the first things he'd noticed was her own Cresceran accent—she made the slightest separation in words he combined into one, such as *anyone* and *everything.* "I left home for the army when I was nine, but I guess home never left me."

"Do you miss it? Your home?"

His answer required a careful dose of truth, but not too much. "I did at first, but they kept us busy, and that helped. The army is my family now."

It suddenly occurred to him that she, too, had left her family behind for a new one, but unlike him, she'd never be returning home. Did she feel as he had years ago, traveling into the unknown, feeling excitement and a sense of duty, but also a terrible loneliness and fear of the future? As his eyes drifted back to the ledger under the stack of books, he wondered if she buried herself in work as he had.

Sagerra's hand appeared in his line of sight and picked up the book on top. "Were you looking at this?"

"No, my lady," he said quickly, before realizing she wasn't talking about the ledger.

"Oh." She sounded disappointed. "Well, it's a rather interesting account of King Pascal the Third's reign. Are you familiar with him?"

He knew quite a lot about the kings of Demora, but she didn't need to know that. "Not really, my lady."

Sagerra sighed a little. "Soldiers don't need to know history, I guess." She placed the book back on the stack and returned to her food. "I suppose it was a little much to hope for."

She thought soldiers uneducated. Ignorant. Not worth talking to. He ducked his head to his soup to hide the blood rushing to his face.

"Were you schooled at all in your training?" she asked.

No, he wanted to say. *We just learned to stab things and march.* Instead he cleared his throat. "Not as much as your ladyship was, I'm sure."

He needed to moderate his tone or he would get in trouble. Or worse, he'd lose his cover and look like a fool in front of the whole company.

"I guess education doesn't count for much in your work," she said.

He clenched his jaw and focused on a chunk of bread dissolving in the now-cold soup as she continued, "It probably makes life easier."

"Easier if I don't know any better?" he snapped before he could stop himself.

She frowned. "That's not what I meant."

"Easier to be as obedient as a child? To not question anything?" Perhaps there was an element of truth in such accusations, but he found it insulting nonetheless.

"Of course not," she said. "But . . . an army's success depends quite a bit on soldiers following orders, wouldn't you agree?"

"I wasn't aware my lady was such an expert in military affairs."

Sagerra exhaled heavily. "Do you or do you not follow orders you're given?"

He wouldn't be here right now if he didn't. "Yes, ma'am."

"Have you ever argued over your orders or tried to get out of them?"

"No, ma'am." He wiped his thumb against his nose and looked away.

"That was my only point, Master Carter," she said, sagging a little in her chair. "I can even relate to it. We have more common ground than you think—"

"I think it's obvious we have nothing in common, my lady." He shoved away from the table and stood. "I'll be excused if I may."

He didn't wait for her permission to leave. As he yanked the door closed behind him, he caught a glimpse of her face, flushed with anger.

To think he'd actually liked her at first. She'd seemed rather unpretentious, but she was just as bad as the girls around the table, knowledgeable only about fashion and book learning.

He stomped back to the barracks, ignoring everyone he passed. Halfway there he realized he should probably tell somebody he'd left those dishes in the library, but he decided Lady Sagerra could find someone to take care of them. Soldiers were too stupid to know what to do unless someone gave them directions, anyway.

A part of his mind whispered that it wasn't her fault. A woman, especially one raised in the sleepy farmlands of Crescera, wouldn't have needed to know anything about the army. She admitted she'd never met a soldier. If he hadn't been acting the part of a wagon driver, he could've shown her just how educated he was, could've explained that the best soldiers were thinkers.

But she hadn't been that far off on the importance of following orders.

He reached the captain's door before he realized it. A quick glance around told him the passage was empty, but he went ahead and knocked a code on the wood. After waiting a few seconds with no answer, he opened the door and went in to write his report.

14

DARNESSA LOOKED UP from her embroidery as her apprentice poked her head in the door. "Just wanted to say I'm turning in," Sage said.

"Did you get supper?"

"Yes, a servant brought me some in the library. I figured you sent him."

Darnessa nodded. "I did. You really shouldn't avoid the ladies so much."

"I had a lot of work to finish." Sage hesitated. "Did you know that servant was actually one of the soldiers from the escort?"

"Really?"

Sage opened the door wider, then stepped inside and leaned against it to close it. "He said he was just making himself useful, but I think he was really observing for Captain Quinn."

Darnessa chuckled. "You should have heard the girls at dinner mooning over the officers. They'd be all too pleased to learn the men are spying on them." She glanced up and saw Sage frowning pensively. "Does that surprise you?"

"I suppose it makes sense from a military standpoint." Sage shrugged. "We're under their care."

Trust Sage to completely ignore the romance of the idea.

"I thought at first he'd be a good source of information on the officers," she continued. "So I started the usual routine to get him talking."

The anger in Sage's voice made Darnessa look up. "Did it not go well?"

"No." She stood straight and threw her hands up. "He got all bent out of shape! All I did was ask him what kind of schooling he had."

"And of course you didn't come across as condescending." Darnessa shook her head and looked back down.

"It's not my fault he's ignorant!"

Darnessa sighed. "Not everyone enjoys book learning as much as you, Sage."

"A whole lot of good it does me in this job." Sage folded her arms across her chest and leaned on the door again.

Darnessa grimaced. "Then perhaps you should focus instead on the things that will help you do your job. Like getting to know those girls." The matchmaker pointed to the door behind Sage. "We'll need to find matches that will suit them."

"You already chose the girls," Sage protested. "What more is there to do until we get there?"

"How can you expect to be able to match them properly if you don't get to know them?"

"I know what they think of me."

"And whose fault is that? It took you less than two minutes to start flinging insults this morning."

Sage's face went scarlet, but she said nothing. Darnessa watched her until she started to twist her hands. "Did you get this soldier's name, in case I hear about it?"

"Ash Carter. He's a wagon driver." Sage was staring into the fireplace and didn't notice Darnessa jump.

Ash Carter!

Darnessa quickly looked back at her sewing. While most knew the king had a son named Ash—one of the most common names for a boy born out of wedlock—*very* few knew his mother's last name was Carter. His official surname was Devlinore. The illegitimate son served discreetly under General Quinn alongside the crown prince, and using his mother's name was logical. If this was him, it was a huge stroke of luck.

The more she thought about it, the more likely it seemed it *would* be him, taking advantage of the chance to visit his family and friends in Tennegol. And he wasn't an officer—there was no limit on when he could be matched. She tried to remember the young man from dinner. He was dark in complexion. Both his and the prince's mothers had been from Aristel, so that fit. Sage might be able to uncover the truth for her, assuming she hadn't done too much damage. "Did you talk about anything else with him?"

"We were actually having a nice chat. He seemed like someone I'd get along with if I didn't have to act like one of the brides."

There was a touch of regret in Sage's voice, which gratified Darnessa, but something else set off a fine-tuned sense in the matchmaker. "Let's just hope he doesn't tell the other soldiers about tonight. It will only make learning about them harder."

Sage flinched. Good. After she cooled off she'd see apologizing was necessary. Darnessa just had to let her think it was her own idea.

"Better get some rest, then," Darnessa said finally. "We start early tomorrow."

Sage nodded wearily. "Good night."

Darnessa waited until the door closed behind the girl before letting loose the smile she'd been holding back.

Oh, wild Sage, I will pair you up yet.

15

QUINN WAS STUDYING a parchment covered in notes when Charlie brought him dinner. A glance at the time candle told him the page should have been in bed long ago, but he couldn't bring himself to scold his brother for trying to take care of him. The plate lay untouched as the officers filed into the room and stood side by side later. He continued frowning at the page for several seconds before placing it on one of the stacks spread around him and looked up.

"Sorry, just thinking." The apology was unnecessary, but in the past, he'd been made to wait by officers emphasizing their rank. He considered it a disgusting habit. Grabbing a fresh sheet of parchment, he dipped his quill in the ink pot. "Report."

Each man detailed what their teams had learned that day about the grand house and its people, routines, and surrounding land. Quinn covered the page with information and started another before they finished. Finally he tossed the quill down, flexing his right hand. "Very good. Some gaps, but over time everyone will get better at knowing what's useful."

He leaned back in his chair and chewed his lip before continuing. "Servants are often the best sources of information, so have your teams act helpful and ask questions. They can flirt with the maids, but no trifling. Which reminds me . . ." He sat forward to search for a particular parchment. "Here's Mouse's notes on the ladies. Memorize the names and put them to faces tomorrow."

Casseck took the page and scanned it. He frowned at the bottom. "Is there a reason there's so much written on this last one, sir?"

"Mouse actually talked to her one on one. She was in the library, and he took food to her there."

Cass eyed him over the sheet before passing it to Gramwell. Quinn ignored the look.

Robert squinted over Gramwell's shoulder. "It says she was writing notes on people. What does that mean?"

"She was copying notes on various nobles—likes, dislikes, descriptions, properties, that sort of thing. Nothing to cause concern."

"Sounds a bit concerning to me, sir." Cass raised one eyebrow.

"I thought so, too, at first," said Quinn. "But then I considered that she's the lowest lady, so maybe she's trying to ingratiate herself with the matchmaker by doing some work for her. Mistress Rodelle's pushing fifty, so maybe it's getting hard to record everything herself."

Gramwell nodded without looking up. "Makes sense, sir."

"That's all I have." He looked down to signal their meeting was over, but he could tell Casseck had remaining questions. Still, his friend came to attention and saluted with the others. When Robert and Gramwell left, however, Cass stayed and closed the door behind them. He sat in the chair across from Quinn and waited as he pretended to sort a few parchments. They dropped formalities when they were alone, but Casseck always waited for Quinn to initiate it.

Finally he sat back. "What, Cass?"

Casseck shrugged. "I was just thinking Mouse hasn't made a solid contact in the group. I thought that was the goal."

"He hasn't met everyone yet. What's your point?"

"Why not Lady Broadmoor?"

Quinn shifted in his seat. "We planned on one of the maids."

"I think she'd be better. By your own assessment she's got the matchmaker's ear. Could be handy if there's trouble."

Cass was right. His eyes drifted to Ash's summary of the last couple days of extended patrols. There was evidence of another Kimisar group out there. He'd have to report it when the next courier came.

"Besides," Casseck continued, "it said *she* struck up a conversation with *him*. I'm surprised Mouse didn't jump on that opportunity."

"The conversation ended when she implied the army is full of simpletons."

"So I read." Cass leaned forward and put his arms on the table. "But, Alex, that doesn't make sense. It said she started out friendly and shared her dinner with him, so why the sudden disrespect? Sometimes Mouse is a little oversensitive. Wouldn't be the first time he jumped to conclusions."

Quinn grunted. "Maybe you're right." He ran a hand through his shaggy hair and scratched the back of his head. "He left in a huff, though. I don't imagine she's eager to speak to him again."

"I might be able to intercede, explain that Mouse is a little touchy about schooling because he never learned to read."

Quinn considered this for several seconds. "You know, that has potential. If he ever takes her dinner again, she'd feel safe leaving that ledger open around him. He could get a better look at it."

"I thought you weren't worried about it."

"Doesn't hurt to be cautious."

"Of course not," Cass agreed. "But then, maybe you doubt Mouse's ability to hold his own around her. Is she pretty?"

Quinn bristled. "My soldiers are not here for flirting, and certainly not with Concordium brides."

"Of course not," Cass said again, this time with a hint of a smile. "So should I talk to her tomorrow? Try to smooth things over on Mouse's behalf?"

Mouse had made a mess of things. Quinn sighed inwardly. "All right. Give it a try. If it works, we'll use her as our contact."

Casseck stood and stretched. "Just make sure Mouse is ready for his role." He turned to leave. "And get some sleep, Alex. The next few weeks will be tougher than you think." He paused with one hand on the door latch. "She'll need a code name of her own."

Quinn tapped his quill on the table as he read over Mouse's notes for the tenth time. They were like a flock of gabbling birds, these ladies, following the lead of the one in front. "Starling."

Cass nodded as he opened the door. "Starlings are smart birds."

"I know. Annoying as hell, too."

16

PORTERS CAME FOR the ladies' trunks early the next morning. Sage was up and ready, but many of the ladies took some prodding. With servants bustling around everywhere, she resisted the urge to get involved and followed her trunk to the outer ward where the line of wagons awaited. The morning was chilly, and she hugged her cloak tighter as she studied every face milling about for the one she'd met last night. After a few minutes, she found him tugging a broad cloth over one of the wagons.

The rose patterns sewn into the fabric indicated the special status of the travelers, as the design was normally reserved for royal use. There was always a princess named Rose, and many families used variations on the name to imply royal connections—they had a Rosalynn in their own group. Rather ironic that otherwise plants and flowers indicated illegitimate or very low birth, except in her case, but Father had taken pride in flouting convention.

Sage watched Ash Carter tie the canopy to the frame. His name declared he was either a bastard or a peasant—or both. Neither bothered her. He was taller than she'd realized, and broad across the shoulders, though not bulky. The subordinate posture he'd worn last night was gone; he moved about his work with confidence and efficiency. She edged around a pile of baggage, wanting to get close enough to speak to him without attracting too much attention. Surely he wouldn't be rude if she approached with so many others around.

A rider's black uniform appeared in front of her, and she looked up into friendly blue eyes on a face capped by straw-colored hair. A lieutenant, judging by the silver bar on his collar.

"Good morning, my lady," he said. "Can I help you? You look like you've lost something."

"Begging your pardon, sir," she said, "but I was hoping to speak to the wagon driver. I met him last night, and I think he misunderstood something I said, so I wanted to apologize."

The lieutenant glanced over his shoulder. "I heard about that."

Had it been that bad? Were all the soldiers now upset with her? The lieutenant didn't look angry. In fact, he was smiling.

This was a good opportunity to start learning about the officers for Darnessa, but she wasn't likely to get anywhere with any of the soldiers until she made things right with Ash Carter. Maybe she could do both.

The soldier offered his arm. "Let me intercede for you, my lady. I can see you won't be easy until this is smoothed over. I'm Lieutenant Casseck, by the way."

"Thank you." She took his elbow and let him lead her. "Pleased to make your acquaintance, sir. I'm Sagerra Broadmoor."

"You have to understand, my lady," the lieutenant said as they walked. "Carter's a little sensitive because he can't read."

She looked up in amazement. "Can't read?"

Casseck shrugged. "It's fairly common among soldiers. They learn mostly by reciting. If you don't learn to read before joining, you never will."

"That's a shame," she murmured.

They reached the wagon just as Carter hopped down from the seat. He saluted the lieutenant, his dark eyes drawn briefly to their linked arms.

"My wagon is almost ready, sir." He bowed awkwardly to her and looked up from under straight black brows. "Good morning, my lady. It's a . . . pleasure . . . to see you again."

"Lady Sagerra was just telling me about last night," said Casseck before she could speak. "I believe she's worried you parted on poor terms."

"Yes," Sage rushed to explain. "I didn't mean to offend you. Please forgive me, Master Carter."

79

"There's nothing to forgive, my lady." He hesitated, his words sounding as forced as her own. "I apologize for causing you concern."

And there it was again: his diction and speech were positively formal. They didn't match his education, but Casseck had said he learned by listening. He was obviously smart.

Carter bowed to her again and began to walk around the wagon. Sage remembered the way he'd looked at that stack of books, realizing how humiliated he must have felt when she rubbed his face in the fact that he knew nothing about them. She knew what Father would have done.

"I can teach you to read," she blurted out.

Carter turned back, his mouth dropping open, and the lieutenant pulled away to look down on her. "That's very generous of you, my lady," Casseck said.

It wasn't very proper, either, for a lady. Darnessa wouldn't be happy, but Sage could also use time spent with Carter to learn about the officers. "It's no trouble at all," she insisted. "I have little else to do on the journey. And—and perhaps it would help Master Carter's career prospects. Do you think your captain would approve?"

Casseck looked more amused than anything else. He covered his mouth with his hand as he looked at Carter. "I think Captain Quinn would thoroughly approve."

"Would he?" said Carter. His face was unreadable.

"I think I can speak for him," replied Casseck. A tension stretched out between the two. Carter must feel embarrassed that the lieutenant had told her.

"We can start right away," said Sage. "I have a slate in my trunk. I can ride on the seat as you drive and show you letters." She curtsied to Lieutenant Casseck and hurried away before either he or Carter could object. This would be much more fun than cramming in the wagon with a bunch of vipers. It felt like a challenge, too, to see if she could get him reading simple sentences by the time they arrived in Tennegol.

Sage found her trunk still waiting to be loaded on the cart and unlocked it. As she dug around for her slate, Darnessa appeared at her elbow. "What are you doing?"

The matchmaker must have been watching. "Apparently that soldier I told you about, Ash Carter, can't read, so I offered to teach him." Sage pulled the slate out, speaking rapidly. "If I ride up front with him, it'll leave more room for you ladies in the back. I can also get some information on the officers."

She paused to wait for Darnessa's objection, but her employer was staring at the two soldiers. Casseck was still talking to Carter, who wore a thoughtful expression. After a few seconds the matchmaker turned back to her.

"Make sure you wear a hat," was all she said.

17

MOUSE MENTALLY REVIEWED each name as he watched Casseck and Gramwell assist the ladies into the back of the wagons. Lady Broadmoor had vanished, but any minute she'd be needing his help to get up to the driver's bench, so he waited. Her apology had taken him by surprise, but he'd still thought once Casseck told her he couldn't read, she'd decide once and for all he wasn't worth her time. Instead she'd offered to teach him.

The riders mounted up and there were fewer people on the ground, yet he didn't see her. Had she changed her mind?

"Master Carter?" came her low voice, and he spun around, looking for her. It took him a few seconds to realize she was above him, sitting placidly on the bench. A straw hat was tied to her chin by a green ribbon.

He grabbed the reins from the hook and scrambled up. "How did you get up here?"

She tilted her head to the side and raised an eyebrow. "I climbed up."

Gray. Her eyes were gray. And he'd forgotten to say "my lady."

"Sorry about this hat," she said, touching the wide brim and leaning away so he could settle on the bench without bumping into it. "Mistress Rodelle insisted."

There were honey-colored freckles he'd not noticed last night scattered across her nose and cheeks. This close, he could also smell the lavender and sage scents in her dress, which he much preferred to the floral perfumes the other women were drenched in. He cleared his throat. "I won't be able to give your lesson proper attention until we're steady on the road for a few minutes, my lady."

She nodded. "I expected as much. We'll just do what we can." She tapped her fingers against the slate on her lap, then folded her hands over it awkwardly.

The seat was wide enough for both of them, but not cushioned, and he wondered how long it would be before the discomfort got the better of her. Hopefully more than a few hours. He found her slightly intriguing. Still annoying, though. Starling was the perfect name for her.

When the command came to move out, Ash slapped the reins on his team and the wagon lurched forward. For the next few minutes, the sounds of horses, creaking wheels, and jangling tack echoing off the stone walls around them were too loud for conversation. Once they exited the gate, the noise dropped, but neither spoke as the line of travelers turned onto the road east and spread out a little.

Starling fidgeted with the slate on her lap again, waiting for him to tell her he was ready to begin. His eyes were focused straight ahead when he finally spoke. "May I ask why you want to teach me, my lady? I can't repay your kindness."

She looked surprised by the question. "I enjoy teaching. I taught some of my cousins to read a few years ago." Her fingers drummed the slate as she paused. "I'm sure there's some things you could teach me."

"Like what? I can't even read."

"Well," she said, "as you pointed out last night, I don't know much about the army."

An alarm went off in the back of his mind. Why would she want to know about the army?

"I've met only Lieutenant Casseck so far," she continued. "Who are the other officers?"

There was no doubt in his mind anything he said would end up in that ledger. Their names weren't something he could really hide, however, so he pointed out Gramwell and said he was a good rider, neglecting to mention he was an ambassador's son.

"And your captain?" She squinted at the dark figure riding near the front of the column. "What's he like?"

He shrugged. "Keeps to himself mostly."

"I imagine command is lonely."

He turned to look at her in surprise. "What makes you say that, my lady?"

"Well, maybe not on this assignment, but I imagine he has to be ready to order any of his men into certain death." The right side of her mouth twisted up in a crooked smile. "Not exactly a position for making friends."

She was either very perceptive, or she knew much more about military matters than she let on. He wasn't sure which option was more disconcerting. "I'm ready to begin whenever you are, my lady."

"Wonderful," she said. "Do you know the alphabet song, the one children learn?"

"A little, my lady, but it's mostly nonsense to me."

"Not after today," she said firmly, drawing the first set of letters on the slate.

And so the lesson began. He sped things along by pretending to discover he knew more letters than he realized, such as the ones in his name or that designated certain units in the army. Starling pounced on the opportunity to ask about them, and more than once he feigned a distraction with the wagon to end her line of questioning.

"So we'll travel an average of just over twenty miles a day," she was saying. "How does that compare with how fast the army can travel?"

"That all depends." He cast his eyes around for something. "If there are roads or—look, my lady. I think I'd like to try some of what I've learned." He pointed to the sign posted at a crossroad they approached.

Sagerra frowned a little before looking where he indicated. "Go ahead."

He stumbled through sounding out the letters. With her patient correction, he managed to come up with "Maple Glen" and "Flaxfield." Acting pleased with himself, he pointed to an angled sign, which became visible as they passed. "That one starts with a—"

"Wintermead," Sagerra said, cutting him off. "It says Wintermead." She stared straight ahead without seeing.

He watched her from the corner of his eye. "You do not like Wintermead," he said cautiously.

Her lips tightened into a thin line, and she reached up with her left hand and grabbed her upper right arm, fingers digging into the muscle. He'd seen similar actions in soldiers. When getting sutures or a bone set, they'd pinch a tender area to draw their focus away from the surgeon's work.

"I'd forgotten we would pass through this area." Sagerra swallowed twice before forcing the words out. "My father died there."

She wrinkled her forehead and turned ghostly gray eyes to his face. The raw emotion she directed at him was so intense he couldn't look away. "I thought I'd finally begun to get over it, but at times it feels like it was yesterday, and it's like I've been gored by a wild animal."

Her right hand gripped the wooden bench between them, and he had the shocking urge to cover it with his own hand and offer her some comfort, but that would have been very inappropriate.

"We don't have to talk about him," he said, "but it might help."

"How so?"

He shrugged. "Maybe it would relieve some of the pressure that's built up, like draining a festering wound."

Sagerra pursed her lips, looking slightly amused. "An apt, if somewhat disgusting, analogy."

He ducked his head. "Sorry. I'm a soldier. It's what I know."

Her silence felt louder than the rhythmic clatter of the horses straining to pull the wagon. He could see something building up inside her.

"His name was Peter," she said abruptly. Her eyes glazed over, and he held his breath, waiting through a full turn of the wheel at his feet. "He had dark hair and blue eyes and would read to me by firelight while I mended his shirts. When I read now, sometimes the words in my head are in his voice." She turned away and gazed down the road, her voice dropping so low he could barely hear her. "I worry someday I'll forget how it sounded."

Now the urge to take her hand was so strong he lifted his cap and scratched his head to prevent it. "You and your mother must have been devastated."

Sagerra shrugged. "She died long before that. I don't even remember her."

He waited, but she made no mention of a stepmother. Had her father raised her alone? He'd never heard of such a thing. Motherless girls were always passed on to female relatives, at least until fathers remarried, but it was obvious she was close to him. "How old were you?"

"Twelve."

Again she said no more. "Do you have any brothers or sisters?" he asked casually.

"No."

Another curt answer. Something wasn't right. Was he prying too much? He'd dropped quite a few "my ladys," so maybe she was displeased over that. He was debating how to proceed when Casseck rode up alongside the wagon.

"Carter," the lieutenant said sharply, making him jump. "We'll stop for a rest and meal just ahead." Casseck gestured to a bend where the road passed near a wide stream and a grove of trees. It appeared to be a common resting place for travelers. Much of the grass was worn away, and the remnants of fires could be seen. "When you're finished tending the horses, Captain Quinn wants a word with you." He nodded to Sagerra. "My lady." She half smiled and nodded back.

Mouse guided the cart into position, thinking more about her silence than where the wagon was going. It didn't feel like anger he'd run up against. It felt like a wall. He knew because he had one, too.

⚭

The officers ate their midday meal in a tight circle out of view and earshot of the ladies while soldiers moved about, tending horses and passing out food. Charlie waited on the officers, holding a pitcher of water off to the side. A soldier nearby started telling a rude joke but caught the captain's sharp glance and lowered his voice. Quinn looked back to his lieutenants. "I saw smoke. Our left picket has something to tell us."

Casseck nodded. "Corporal Mason will be patrolling on that side. Is there anything he should tell him, sir?"

Quinn shook his head. "Not at the moment. Anyone see a signal on the right?" Three negative answers. "Keep an eye out, we should hear from him soon. Gram, how's the road ahead?"

"Clear, sir," Gramwell replied around his mouthful. "Manor House Darrow is ready to receive us. I told them we'd arrive in time for supper and left two men to scout around."

Quinn nodded curtly and held up his cup for Charlie to refill with water. "Good. Anything else that needs reporting?"

Casseck cleared his throat. "How's our mouse doing?"

"Fine, if a little uneasy. Starling asks a lot of questions."

Casseck glanced at a nearby group of soldiers. "He didn't look uneasy."

Quinn sighed. "He's just playing the part; let him do it." He sipped his water, trying to put what wasn't right into words. "There's something off, though. Has anyone learned more about her?"

Robert waved his hand for attention. "Overheard some ladies talking. Lots of spite. Jealousy over Cass speaking to her earlier." He gave Casseck a wink. "Once, they said 'her kind,' like she's not 'their kind.' Whatever the hell that means."

Quinn rubbed his lower lip with his thumb. "Apparently both her parents are dead. Maybe she came from a convent orphanage."

Gramwell cleared his throat. "There's a Broadmoor Manor and village northwest of Galarick; I passed by it coming from Reyan. Lord Broadmoor is well regarded, but I don't know anything more."

"Clear as mud," grumbled Quinn, ripping apart a piece of dried beef. "Nothing truly conflicts, but nothing quite matches, either. She could be someone's hidden bastard, a high noble girl who came down in the world when her parents died, or something else entirely."

Across the circle, Casseck leaned back and folded his arms. "Sounds like Mouse has his work cut out for him."

18

IN THE EVENING the group stopped at the home of Lord Darrow, the first of several estates the matchmaker had arranged to receive them. After dinner with the lord, Sage buried herself in their host's library, recording what she'd learned that day in her ledger and reading whatever caught her interest. To her surprise, Ash Carter appeared once his duties were complete and shyly asked if he could practice writing letters. By the time she went to bed, Clare, who'd volunteered to be her roommate, was asleep, so Sage was spared dealing with her.

The second day of travel went as the first, and after another reading lesson and late night, this time in Lord Ellison's library, Sage returned to her room to find Clare sitting in a dressing gown by the fire, her burnished curls framing her creamy face. "There you are," she said. "I made us some tea."

Sage eyed Clare as she dropped her ledger on the lid of her trunk. The other ladies had barely acknowledged her in two days, so the kindness must be designed to curry favor. Clare shouldn't have worried, though; she was the most valuable match they had.

Clare held up a cup and saucer. "I was wondering if you'd be back before it got cold."

The scent of spearmint with a hint of orange drew Sage to her side. The library had been chilly, and she couldn't resist the promise of warmth from both hearth and tea. She sat with her legs folded beneath her on the sheepskin rug and accepted with a thank-you.

"You stayed so late," said Clare.

No sense in being rude. "There was a book I've never seen before—and not likely to again." Few households had books written in Kimisar, even harmless geology tomes. "And Private Carter came by for a reading lesson."

He'd also frustrated her attempts to learn about the officers. Both yesterday and today, she'd tried to get him to open up by showing interest in his life, which wasn't hard—the army was fascinating. Usually it was easy to get a man talking, but whenever the conversation wandered, he brought her back to a reading lesson. It was nice to have such a willing student, though. He especially liked to watch her write, probably because his attempts were so clumsy.

Clare shifted her silky blue robe. "Mistress Rodelle told me you tutored your cousins and also orphans in the village." There was none of the disdain Sage expected. "She said you're never happy unless you're teaching or learning."

Sage pursed her lips, uncomfortable at how close to home that statement was. "I think . . ." She hesitated. "I think it goes back to my father. We didn't have a home, but we always had books he traded and borrowed. He schooled me himself."

The thought of Father usually brought a terrible, soul-ripping emptiness, but this time there was only a dull ache. To her surprise, she almost missed the pain.

Sage changed the subject before Clare could say anything. "It's also a side effect of being stuck in bed for over six months." Uncle William had pulled her from the ravine and packed her mangled ankle in snow until it could be set once they got home. Then pneumonia had set in, made harder to battle by her grief and depression. "My two youngest cousins would creep in with me, and I'd read to them. I taught them letters, and the next thing I knew, Uncle William sent their tutor packing."

Clare's brown eyes widened. "How old were you?"

"By then? Thirteen. The younger ones preferred me, but Jonathan resented it. I'm only a few years older than him, and a girl besides."

"I've never met anyone your age—boy or girl—who knows so much,"

Clare said shyly, her voice ringing with honest admiration. Sage looked down at the liquid in her cup, unsure how to respond. "I always enjoyed lessons more than my brothers," Clare continued. "I wish I could've learned more."

Was Clare asking her to teach *her*?

Sage cleared her throat. "How far did you go in your studies?"

"Mostly just what I needed to know: sums, reading, and poetry. Botany, too, but that was limited to mostly edible plants. History was my favorite, though. I used to steal my brothers' books to read at night." The last was said with a naughty grin.

Sage felt herself smiling. "You know, we'll be at Underwood in two days. I imagine there's a sizable library there."

"I wouldn't even know where to start."

"You will if I help you."

Clare's face lit up. "I'd love that." They fell into silence as they sipped their tea. After a while Clare said, "May I ask you a question?"

Sage grimaced. Now Clare would ask about matching. The conversation had been designed to make Sage to open up. Maybe she should let Clare try to get Ash Carter talking. Sage nodded warily and set her cup down by the hearth.

"Why don't you want to be friends with any of us?"

Sage's mouth dropped open, and she quickly snapped it shut. "Maybe you haven't noticed, but no one wants to be my friend."

"I do."

Sage pulled her knees up under her skirt and hugged them against her chest. "I've never had friends."

"Never?"

Sage shrugged. "Too low for noble friends, too high for common ones when I lived with the Broadmoors."

"What about when you lived with your father?"

"We traveled a lot. Most other girls thought I was a boy, since I always wore breeches. So not really, no."

Clare looked at her with pity. "I'm sorry."

"Don't be. I had Father. He was all I needed."

That was plainly a strange concept for Clare. "I rarely saw my father. He probably would've married me off years ago if it weren't for the law."

"You know how that law came about, right?" Clare shook her head, but she looked genuinely interested. Sage lowered her knees and reached for the kettle to pour a fresh cup, falling into her schoolmistress tone. "Young noble girls were dying by the score in childbirth, and King Pascal the Third commissioned a study that found pregnancy was much safer for a girl after the age of seventeen. He wanted to craft the law according to that, but his nobles revolted, and they compromised. Since then, anyone properly matched must be at least sixteen."

Clare shifted her eyes away and bit her lower lip. "My sister was married at sixteen, two years ago. And now it's my turn."

"How do you feel about that?"

Clare shrugged, her face blank. "Does it matter?"

Sage didn't know how to answer. Often she felt it better to accept what couldn't be changed, but she'd rejected what had seemed to be her fate. She snorted. Maybe it was fate that rejected her.

"What about you?" Clare asked. "Will Mistress Rodelle find you a good match while we're in the capital?"

Sage nearly spat out her tea. "What in the world gave you that idea?"

"That's what Jacqueline's been saying. Everyone thinks it's how Darnessa will pay you."

"Well, it's not." Sage tapped her finger on her teacup. "What else does she say?"

Clare tucked her feet under her nightdress. "She says I lower myself by associating with you."

Sage grinned. "How do you like it, down here in the dirt with us common folk?"

Her friend smiled back. "I like it very much."

19

QUINN FROWNED AT the messages they'd collected from the picket scouts in the three days since leaving Galarick with the ladies. Just before the group reached Lord Darrow's manor on the first day, one of the four scouts reported coming across a Kimisar squad. They'd stopped the next night at Lord Ellison's, where a message arrived from another scout, saying he, too, found a traveling group of Kimisar. Knowing he couldn't go after them and still guard the women he was supposed to be protecting, Quinn instructed the scouts to shadow the squads for now.

Then, this afternoon, two more squads were reported. They were all traveling east, same as the escort. With ten in each, Quinn's men were now officially outnumbered.

But it was the forward scout's report that disturbed him most. He'd pushed ahead and passed their fourth stop, Baron Underwood's castle, and entered the Tasmet province. Instead of Kimisar squads, he saw traveling groups of Cresceran men, supposedly headed to work in the mines south of Tegann. It wouldn't have caused concern except in questioning local taverns on the increase in business, the numbers didn't make sense, so the picket had left his assigned area and followed some of them. Disregarding his primary mission risked a hanging, but Quinn trusted this scout above all others.

Right before they arrived at their evening stop, the scout's coded message arrived:

Paid soldiers, not miners. 3,000 strong.
Camping 40 miles south of Tegann. Waiting.
Returning to post. —C

An entire regiment was gathering in Tasmet. Quinn kept expecting one of his father's couriers to catch up to them, though, so he hadn't reported it yet. If there wasn't a messenger waiting at Underwood tomorrow, Quinn would send one of his own.

And Starling—Lady Sagerra—kept asking questions every day and on evenings Mouse found her for extra lessons. Innocent questions that always led to deeper ones. Questions that, when added up, could be very valuable information to their enemies. How was the army organized? How could Ash Carter advance through the ranks? What weapons had he trained with, and who did he report to? What kind of food did soldiers eat? Were even the cooks and pages trained in combat?

Every night she wrote in that ledger.

Every day he saw more signs that the ladies did not consider her one of their own.

Every instinct he had screamed one thing.

Lady Sagerra was a spy.

20

THE FOURTH MORNING dawned gray and drizzly, but Sage intended to ride with Ash Carter again anyway, so she dressed warmly, and gladly put on her hat for once. The ladies bustled about excitedly; their next stop would last three full days at Baron Underwood's castle. A banquet was planned for the second evening, and they tittered over the prospect of dancing with the army officers and other noble guests. At one point Sage overheard Jacqueline whisper loudly that "Sagerra can dance with the kitchen staff," and her audience burst into giggles.

Sage was too absorbed in her own concerns to care. If Darnessa realized just how little information Sage had gained after so much time with Carter, there would be hell to pay. She'd stayed up all last night debating how to confront him about his strange silence.

He already sat on the driver's seat, staring at the low-hanging clouds with a frustrated expression. She had to call his name twice to get his attention.

He looked down and removed his cap. "Good morning, my lady. I'm afraid today it would be better for you to ride in the back of the wagon."

Sage opened her mouth to protest that she wouldn't melt, but then she noticed a crossbow on the bench beside him and a sword belted at his waist. She glanced around at the other soldiers. They were all armed with twice as many weapons as usual. Did they expect trouble?

Looking back at Carter, it struck her that the sword hung to be drawn by his right hand. He always wrote—rather poorly—with his left.

"Perhaps it would be best," she said. "Consider this an apology." She pulled an apple from her pocket and tossed it up to him, aiming slightly to his left in a small test.

He held reins in both hands, but he dropped them into his left and caught the apple with his right. "Thank you, my lady."

Odd, that.

Sage walked around the wagon and waited her turn to climb in. With the rain, none of the ladies wanted to be close to the open back, so she took a seat nearest the rear gate, across from Clare.

Once the caravan started moving, Sage felt her suspicions that the soldiers expected something were on target. They started at noises and constantly scanned the trees along the side of the road. After about an hour of travel, a dog bolted off into the forest, and the caravan drew to an abrupt halt. The hound vanished into the brush, and every man stopped and waited.

Sage leaned outside to look. Carter stood on his bench seat, crossbow in the crook of his right arm. It might mean nothing except he'd learned to use both it and the sword with his right because most everyone else did, but somehow she doubted it. Why pretend to be left-handed with her?

He stared into the woods like the rest of the soldiers, an intense look of concentration on his face. She surveyed the trees but saw nothing. When she glanced back at Carter, she found him watching her.

He wasn't smiling.

Sage ducked back under the wagon cover. Clare started from her doze and looked questioningly at her, and Sage shrugged back. The other ladies were oblivious, however, and complained at the delay. After several minutes the dog came trotting back like nothing was wrong, and the soldiers relaxed a little. Lieutenant Casseck rode down the line, telling all the men they'd responded well to the drill. Judging from the lingering anxiety on every face, it hadn't been a drill at all.

Captain Quinn rode up beside their wagon, and Sage peeked around again to observe him, as he rarely came this close. She'd never seen him do anything resembling actual work, either. He carried himself as proud as royalty; she expected he'd been just as coddled his whole life as the actual prince. After speaking quietly to Carter, Quinn handed him something—a rolled scrap of parchment. Carter opened the note and frowned at it.

Sage leaned back out of sight, mind racing, hardly noticing the wagons were moving again. Maybe it was a diagram. Or maybe he'd learned enough to read what was written. He'd advanced pretty quickly.

Or maybe he already knew how to read.

It was silly to assume he could read based on a few seconds' glance, but in combination with the signs he was right-handed, it left a bad taste in her mouth. Why lie about such things? What did it gain, other than time with her?

No threats materialized over the rest of the morning, and the light rain kept them from stopping to rest and stretch as usual. They arrived at Underwood an hour past noon, well ahead of schedule, and the riders' faces showed their relief. The high walls of the crossroad fortress offered security from whatever was out there. Underwood marked the border between Crescera and Tasmet, but Tasmet had been part of Demora for over a generation now. Surely they didn't feel threatened.

Sage wanted to ask Lieutenant Casseck about the soldiers' alertness and reaction—and perhaps slip in a sly remark about Ash Carter's reading progress—but before she could get his attention, he and the other officers disappeared. She pushed between a line of soldiers carrying trunks and weapons to the barracks. They all made way for her, but she couldn't see Casseck's blond head over theirs. Even Carter had vanished, leaving their page to tend to the horses from his wagon. The boy looked too small for such a job, but he handled it with competence.

She considered him for moment. A page's job was to attend to officers' needs, so he would know them well. She changed directions to bump into him as he led the horses away. "Hello, young fellow," she said. "Have you been with us all this time?"

He stopped walking and bowed. "Yes, my lady. Good afternoon, Lady Sagerra."

"You know my name, good sir," she teased, "but I don't know yours."

"Charlie Quinn, my lady."

It was almost too good to be true. "Are you related to Captain Quinn?"

The boy nodded enthusiastically. "He's my brother."

Sage put on an impressed face. "I've heard so much about him; you must be proud to be his page." The boy glowed, and guilt settled in her stomach like a stone. It didn't sit well with her to manipulate a child, but she was getting a little desperate.

"I haven't had lunch, have you?" she asked, and Charlie shook his head. "After you're done with the horses, would you like to have lunch with me in the garden? I plan on taking my meal out there, as the rain looks to be stopping."

"I'd be honored, my lady."

Her mouth twisted in what she hoped was a smile. "No, Master Quinn, the honor is mine."

21

THE RELIEF OF arriving at Underwood was short-lived.

"Two more." Quinn tossed a message on the table in the barracks meeting room. "Two more of those damn Kimisar squads." He closed his eyes as he pinched the bridge of his nose and tried to think.

"The forward picket hasn't reported anything new," Casseck pointed out as he scanned the scrap of paper and passed it on.

"The forward picket hasn't reported at all," snapped Quinn. Damn, he was testy. He took a deep breath and opened his eyes. "No couriers since Galarick, and no messages waiting for us here."

"So send a courier of our own," said Rob.

"We could hole up here and signal with red blaze," suggested Gramwell. Every army unit carried packets of powder that when burned made red smoke, calling all forces within sight to their aid. "The Kimisar could never take this place with seventy men."

"Unless there are more Kimisar squads out there," muttered Rob.

Gramwell disagreed. "They'd need hundreds to breach these walls. If there were that many, surely we'd know it."

"We can't stay here," said Quinn. "Underwood is loyal to the duke, and no one is near enough to see the signal. The Kimisar our scouts saw have all been heading east, so maybe they don't even care about us. If they find out Rob is with us, though, that could change. The general will realize he's not heard from us and investigate, if he hasn't already, so right now we should focus on getting word of the gathering army to

Tennegol. I think there's no question that the D'Amirans are planning something, but they're waiting."

The prince frowned. "For what?"

"What happens during the Concordium?" said Quinn. "Fat, rich noblemen from every corner of Demora leave their lands and go to the capital wearing as much gold as they can carry and escorted by their finest troops. They travel even slower than us, so most left over a month ago; any that had to cross the mountains went north and around through Mondelea."

Cass raised his eyebrows. "No one's home. By the time word reached them in Tennegol, it could all be over and the passes sealed."

Quinn nodded. Anything his father sent through the south pass to Tennegol would probably be stopped by Count D'Amiran at Jovan, but if the Cresceran brides didn't show up at the Concordium, the alarm would be raised early. While the nation was busy trading brides and dowries, the D'Amirans would make their move, flanking the Western Army from behind. Quinn tried not to think how all their friends—his father—could be wiped out. He could tell everyone else realized it, though. For the first time, Quinn was glad Charlie was with them. His brother was safer, if only barely.

"So what do we do?" asked Gramwell.

"We pretend nothing's wrong while gathering as much information as possible. Our scouts will also look for subtle ways to disrupt things. Maybe once the ladies are safely through the pass, we can send a team back to burn some of their supplies or something. Ash stays where he is for now, doing what he does best."

Rob cleared his throat. "What about Starling?"

Quinn pushed his dark hair out of his eyes. Its length was getting annoying. "What about her?"

"Have you realized who she spends her time with, other than Mouse?"

Quinn gritted his teeth. "Rob, if you know something, you'd better tell us right now." His cousin had a flair for the dramatic, but lives were at stake.

"Lady Clare." Rob looked to every face, but no one seemed to understand why that mattered. "Clare Holloway's sister is married to Count Rewel D'Amiran, the duke's brother. I stood in for my father at the wedding two years ago."

Quinn looked to Casseck, who raised his eyebrows. The evidence against Starling was circumstantial, but it increased every day. Now they had the possibility of two spies.

A knock on the door announced a servant with a tray of food. Quinn realized how hungry he was; he'd skipped breakfast with the urgent matters of the morning and had only an apple. The map was swept aside and the meeting paused. He'd inhaled half of his first plate and was pouring more water into his cup when he realized someone was missing from the scene.

"Where's Charlie?"

22

LIEUTENANT CASSECK CHECKED the kitchens after he walked through the stables but found no sign of Charlie other than the properly tended cart horses. The page reveled in attending the officers, so Casseck worried something had happened to him. He decided to head back to the barracks. If Charlie still hadn't returned, Quinn would raise hell. They all would.

A high wall of hedges bordered the garden, and Casseck glanced through a gap as he cut around it and stopped short. There was Charlie, sitting on a bench in the sun, chattering to Lady Sagerra, who listened intently. Charlie's legs swung back and forth as he animated his speech with several hand gestures, and she laughed when he came to some conclusion. Casseck ducked back behind the hedge, hoping he hadn't been seen.

He watched her hand Charlie a bread roll while she took her turn talking. The boy was mesmerized as Sagerra told a story that ended with her pretending to smash her face on something. Charlie cringed.

She certainly knew how to talk to children.

Sagerra leaned forward and appeared to ask a question, and Charlie responded eagerly, like he wanted to please her, which made Casseck nervous. But Charlie didn't know anything dangerous, and he was a smart kid. He wouldn't give anything away. Not willingly.

Casseck spun around at the crunch of footsteps on the gravel behind him. One of the brides was heading for the garden, though how she walked in those shoes he couldn't imagine. Her blond hair was elaborately pinned around her freshly painted porcelain face. And she was very well-endowed. Not that Casseck was much for ogling at cleavage, but it caught the eye, especially in the low-cut pink dress she wore. She met his eyes and smiled, and he bowed as she shifted her parasol to offer him her hand. He raised it to his lips. "Good afternoon, my lady."

"And you, too, sir," she said. "I don't believe we've been properly introduced yet."

He stood straight. "I'm Lieutenant Casseck, Lady Jacqueline."

Her sky-blue eyes widened. "So you know me already? I'm flattered."

Quinn had made them memorize the names. This one was easy—she always put herself first. She presented an opportunity to get closer to Sagerra and Charlie, though, so he offered his arm. "Would you care to walk in the garden, my lady?"

"That would be lovely!" There was a hard gleam in her eyes as she took his arm. Within a few steps she was leaning heavily on him, like she was tired or in pain. Casseck held her up, bending away to avoid the parasol she held over herself with her other hand.

Jacqueline laughed as they turned the corner, though she didn't sound amused. "Oh, *there* she is," she said, nodding at Sagerra, whose eyes darted toward them, then refocused on Charlie. It was not a friendly look. "We didn't see her at lunch, but it doesn't surprise me to find her out here. You'd think with all those freckles, she'd avoid the sun, but I think she'd *sleep* outside if she could."

Jacqueline directed their path away from Sagerra and Charlie, and Casseck reluctantly followed her lead. Though he knew the answer, he asked, "Are you friends with Lady Sagerra, then?"

"Certainly not. I don't associate with commoners." Casseck froze in his tracks, and Jacqueline glanced up. "You didn't know?" She looked distressed. "Oh dear! I thought surely the matchmaker told you, seeing as you men are protecting us. I can't believe she wouldn't have explained."

"Lady Jacqueline, are you saying Sagerra's not a lady?"

Her lacquered fingernails flashed as she waved her hands before clutching his arm. "You mustn't tell anyone I told you, sir. I just . . . thought you knew."

"So why is she with you?" The woman obviously wanted to tell him.

"That is Mistress Rodelle's business. They didn't want anyone to know. I'm not even sure what her real name is." Jacqueline turned pleading eyes up to his and breathed so hard Casseck worried about the strength of her bodice. "I shouldn't have said *anything*! Please promise me you won't tell anyone!"

"Of course not, my lady."

23

CHARLIE STOOD AT military attention, looking pleased with himself. "Sir, I had lunch with Lady Sagerra. I'd like to report our conversation."

Quinn was torn between yelling and laughing at the boy. Casseck struggled to keep a straight face as he leaned on the closed door behind Charlie. Quinn forced himself to focus sternly on his brother. "You didn't ask permission, though. Lieutenant Casseck had to go searching for you."

"You said we needed to know more about her. It was a target of opportunity," Charlie said gravely.

Cass started coughing. Quinn leaned back in his chair and covered his mouth with his hand. "Very well. Report."

"First, sir, I'd like to assure you we didn't talk about Mouse. She didn't even ask about him."

Quinn relaxed a little. "What did you learn?"

Charlie grinned triumphantly. "She was seventeen last month." Age mattered to him. He launched into a narrative of broken bones and climbing trees and how she tutored her four cousins while she lived with her aunt and uncle at Broadmoor Manor.

Not much was useful, but it was more than Mouse ever got from her. "What else did you talk about?"

"Me mostly, sir. She wanted to know about my home and family. We talked about how I came to be a page, my travels with the army, the places I had seen, and how I'm training to earn my commission, like you."

Information on me by proxy. Oh, Starling, you are clever. Over Charlie's head he could see Casseck come to the same conclusion. "Did she ask about any of us?"

"Just if I was well treated. I said yes, but nothing else so I wouldn't accidentally say something about Robert or Ash or you."

Quinn reviewed the conversation to find what was tickling his mind. "When you told her about your time with the army, what are some of the things you said?"

Charlie looked thoughtful. "We talked about how big the army is, how fast it can travel, the different kinds of soldiers, how they get supplies." He shrugged. "Girls don't know any of that stuff. She thought it was interesting."

Quinn's heart sank. "I'm sure she did."

Casseck closed the door behind Charlie after Quinn dismissed him. "He thought he was helping. I doubt he told her anything we wouldn't consider common knowledge."

"She has a way of making you trust her," said Quinn. He tapped his lip. "But Charlie is a pretty good judge of character. Back home he knew which servant was stealing that one time, and he always knows when someone's lying to him."

Casseck sat down across from him. "Lady Jacqueline's information actually makes sense now. Starling is Mistress Rodelle's secretary."

"But why does she travel as a bride?" Quinn threw up a hand. "And why does she ask so many questions about the army?"

"You think she's a spy?"

"She speaks Kimisar; did you know that?"

Casseck raised his eyebrows. "It was never in Mouse's reports."

"*I* speak Kimisar, and so do you. That doesn't make us traitors." Quinn ignored the look his friend gave him. "The other night she was reading a book on mining by a Kimisar geologist."

"Heavy reading."

"But not unusual from what Mouse has seen. Could mean nothing other than she likes rocks."

"Alex."

The seriousness in his friend's voice made Quinn finally meet his eyes.

"We need information beyond what Mouse can learn."

Quinn nodded reluctantly.

He needed to know what was in that ledger.

24

AFTER CHAPEL DAY services, Sage and Clare spent most of the second day in Lord Underwood's library. Her friend devoured the books Sage picked out for her, and Sage alternately read and went over her ledger, adding what she'd gleaned from Charlie. The boy had readily answered every question she'd asked about the army; at the age of nine he knew much more than her. It only emphasized just how much Ash had avoided saying. What was he hiding?

Since Charlie was the captain's brother, once she got the page talking, she focused on his background. He spilled more information about his home and family than even she could remember. The Quinns had a distinguished military history, and it seemed the sons were following in their father's footsteps, the captain achieving his most recent promotion well before his peers. So either Quinn was quite accomplished, or as the general's son everyone was motivated to make him seem so.

When she and Clare broke from their reading for the noon meal, Sage paid attention to the escort soldiers she saw. They were still anxious, posting their own guards on the walls and around the ladies' quarters, which chilled her. Deep in their own country, they acted like they were in hostile territory. Maybe she could maneuver to talk with Lieutenant Casseck tonight and ask him about it.

Hoping Ash would appear for another reading lesson, Sage lingered in the library after Clare left to rest before the banquet. She wasn't sure whether she was ready to confront him, but Sage found she missed his company. Or maybe she just missed how he always seemed glad to see her. She shook her head as she returned a book to the shelf. First Clare, and now Ash. Companionship was hard to accept at first, but having had a taste, she now craved it.

Clare was already dressed when Sage returned to their room. Sage offered to style her friend's hair and Clare accepted, though she seemed strangely subdued. Silence was comfortable to Sage, and she worked Clare's sleek brown curls into a fountain knot as she considered how to approach Lieutenant Casseck.

Sage suddenly realized Clare had asked a question. She pulled a hairpin from between her clenched lips. "What was that?"

"I said, do you already have a husband planned for me?"

"I don't know," Sage said. Clare's question didn't sound designed to gain a favor; it felt like fear. "I don't really do the deals. I mostly collect information that goes into them. What kind of husband do you want?"

Clare looked down at her hands as they played with the ribbons of her bodice. "Just someone kind, really, and not terribly older than me."

A memory clicked into place. Clare's sister Sophia had married Count D'Amiran two years ago, and Darnessa commented once that no respectable matchmaker would've matched any girl to that cruel man. Sage pinned the last of Clare's curls in place. "Does this have anything to do with your sister's husband?" she asked.

"I guess. She's not happy." Clare sniffed like she was holding back tears. "He's . . . not kind. And now she carries his child. The second actually." Her words began to tumble out faster. "He got angry and pushed her down the stairs last year, and she lost the first baby. Now he just hits her."

Sage sat on the bench and put her hand on Clare's shoulder, which had begun to shake with the effort it took to keep from crying. Clare looked up at her with the wild fear of a trapped animal. "I didn't want to come . . . Father lied . . . I'm only fifteen . . ." She sobbed, and without thinking Sage threw her arms around her friend and pulled her close.

A fierce protective feeling flowed through Sage as Clare cried out the fears she hadn't allowed herself to show before. Sage rocked and soothed her friend. Uncle William may have been a prat, but he never would've done such a thing to her. "No," she whispered over and over. "Never. I won't let that happen to you."

Eventually Clare's sobs tapered off. "But what can you do?" she hiccuped.

"I don't know, but I'll think of something. If you're only fifteen, it's against the law to match you."

"But I can't go home unmatched. Father would kill me."

Sage tipped Clare's face up to her own. "Clare, I swear to you: I will not let it happen."

Clare's brown eyes widened at Sage's absolute promise. "I believe you," she whispered.

"Good. Let's get your face cleaned up. We don't want to be late for dinner."

25

SAGE STAYED WITH Clare most of the evening and kept men away from her, though she still wanted to speak with Casseck. It was a proper banquet in a grand hall with many guests. Though he was already married, Baron Underwood set out to impress the bridal caravan and local nobles with how much he could provide as their host. It was a ripe opportunity, but Sage dropped her usual information collecting in favor of propping up Clare, who looked increasingly weary. When they sat down to dinner, Clare's rank forced them to separate by several seats, and Sage watched her for signs of another breakdown. With her eyes on her friend, she shoved a forkful of food in her mouth, only to realize the dish was made almost entirely of large, slimy onions. Sage gagged but forced herself to swallow, then rinsed her mouth with wine several times. The combination didn't sit well in her stomach, and she couldn't eat another bite of anything, even plain bread.

After dessert, Sage slid back to Clare's side and began planning an escape for both of them. Lieutenant Casseck was present, but between the alcohol and several sickening, onion-tasting burps, Sage had long abandoned solving any mysteries that night. A pair of young men approached as music started, and she turned her and Clare's backs to them, not caring if they came across as rude.

Darnessa stopped in front of them. "Is everything all right?"

Sage shook her head. "Clare isn't feeling well, and now I would rather leave, too. Can you make some excuse for us?" She gave her employer a look saying she would elaborate later, and the matchmaker nodded.

As they made their way to the wide double doors, Casseck intercepted them. "Lady Sagerra, you're not leaving already? I'd been hoping for a dance, my lady, or just a chance to talk."

"I'm afraid neither of us is very well tonight, sir. You must excuse us." Sage made to step around him, but he blocked her way. He wanted to talk to her. It was the opportunity she'd hoped for, but she wouldn't leave Clare. Casseck eyed her for a few seconds, then signaled another officer to approach.

To Sage he said, "If you aren't well, perhaps some fresh air in the garden will help." A soldier with ruddy hair and bronze eyes appeared at Clare's elbow. "This is Lieutenant Gramwell, my lady." The young officer bowed and offered Clare his arm.

Clare looked back, but Sage leaned closer and whispered, "He can hold you up better than I can. I won't let you out of my sight." Shaking slightly, Clare grasped his arm and let him lead her away. Casseck offered Sage his own, and she took it and followed them outside.

Casseck directed their path to the garden without speaking, letting the distance grow between them and Clare and Gramwell, but keeping them in view. She ought to get Clare back to their room. She looked exhausted.

"Is the lady all right?" Casseck asked.

Sage shook her head with a sigh. "I think this trip has overwhelmed her."

"And how are you, Lady Sagerra?"

"I . . ." She glanced around. "I have concerns."

"Anything I can help you with, my lady?"

Clare appeared to have relaxed a little. Three days of observation had also led Sage to believe Lieutenant Gramwell was a decent fellow. Maybe time with him would make Clare feel more hopeful about her future. "I haven't seen Private Carter since we arrived," said Sage. "I hope your captain isn't displeased with his progress."

"Not at all, my lady," he assured her. "Carter is just busy. The captain sent him on a patrol today."

"Oh?" she said, though she wasn't surprised. "I thought he only drove wagons."

Casseck winced. "The captain insists all under his command be competent riders."

"And fighters," she added. "Your page told me everyone had combat training, even the pages and cooks."

There was a pause. "It seems you've learned a great deal about the army."

"Not really." She shrugged, hoping Charlie wouldn't get in trouble for telling her so much. "I just knew nothing before this journey." She tilted her head to look up at him. "Which makes me wonder if I'm wrong when I observe that you soldiers have all been on edge since yesterday."

Another pause. Lieutenant Casseck was a thinker. "You are astute, my lady, but I can't say anything about it."

His sudden tension was contagious. A chill went up her spine as she recalled Ash staring into the woods, ready to fight whatever was out there. "Are we threatened somehow?"

"Possibly. But again, I can say nothing more."

"I . . ." She hesitated. "I wish I could help. Being a woman is frustrating sometimes. I feel helpless."

The shadow that was his face tilted to the side to look down at her. White teeth flashed in the dark as he smiled. "Perhaps if we need some trees climbed, we'll ask you."

Sage chuckled. "I suppose your page told you about that."

"He did." Before she could ask anything more, he said, "Do you know Captain Quinn has a sister your age? I believe she'll be matched at the Concordium, too."

Sage wasn't fooled by the change in subject. She also already knew that from Charlie. "Lucky her."

Casseck stopped walking. "My lady, have I offended you somehow? Your speech is cold."

"You're trying to distract me." He stiffened and dropped her arm, and she knew she was right. "I'm not a child, Lieutenant. If you won't be honest with me about this danger, you should know I have a knack for finding things out."

"I believe you, my lady," he said quietly. "But you must believe me when I say we don't fully understand this threat, and I have strict orders not to discuss it with anyone. The captain doesn't know who he can trust."

Sage crossed her arms. For someone who held himself apart, Quinn kept a tight rein on everyone. She'd watched him for days now and was always put off by his regal bearing and the way he seemed to rely on Casseck to do all his work. "I wonder about Captain Quinn. Is he really as wonderful as Charlie thinks?"

Casseck pressed his lip together like he didn't want to smile. "He's not perfect, no, but no man is."

"And he's your best friend."

That startled him. "How did you know?"

She shrugged and resumed walking. Casseck also admired the captain as much as Charlie did, so his opinion would never be objective. "Just the way you talk about him. Your posture when he's mentioned. He's like a brother to you."

Casseck offered his arm again. "More than my own four brothers."

Sage took his arm and allowed him to slow their pace. "So tell me about your family."

26

QUINN SLIPPED INTO the girls' empty room. There wasn't much time. Casseck could hold off Starling's return for only so long. The glow from the hearth cast enough light to locate a candle, and he lit it on the embers. With it he could more clearly see the two beds and trunks at their feet. He knew which trunk was hers by sight.

The lid was locked, so he set the candleholder aside and pulled out a small pick and went to work. A few seconds later it opened, and the captain took a moment to observe how everything was arranged before reaching into the contents to search. What he was seeking lay at the bottom. He leaned down to grasp the large, leather-bound book, catching a whiff of lavender and sage from the fabrics. The scent muddled his thoughts briefly, but he pulled the ledger free, closed the lid, and opened the book on top.

By the light of the flickering candle, he scanned every page of Starling's writing: names, descriptions, property, likes, dislikes, personalities, diagrams of lineage and marriage connections. Not a word about the army or its movements, and nothing that seemed coded. A tension he hadn't fully acknowledged began to ease.

Toward the end he came to a section on eligible men, which included his officers. Mouse had told her very little, but the insight and information she'd gained on each of them after only a few days amazed him. If Mouse could get closer to her, she would be incredibly useful around D'Amiran. His mind explored the possibilities of such a source as he flipped to the last written page.

Captain _____ Quinn, born ~488, eligible ~512
1st Army, 9th Cavalry
Parents: General Pendleton Quinn, Lady Castella Carey
  Quinn

At first he was tickled she hadn't managed to learn his first name, but his stomach twisted as he discovered how she saw him. *Arrogant. Distant. Proud. Secretive.* As well as Starling read his friends, Quinn was disturbed by his own portrait. Below was an accurate summary of his career and home. He shouldn't have been surprised when he saw his sisters listed.

Siblings: Serena ~490 M, Gabriella ~492 (509 C), Isabelle ~493, Brenna ~496, Jade ~497, Amelia ~499

They were all correct. She must have memorized them from her conversation with Charlie. Damn, she was smart. At the bottom was a last note.

Charlten (Charlie) Quinn, page, born ~500
Sweet, idealistic, smart, hardworking, idolizes brother.
  Training for commission as of 509, comm in ~518,
  eligible 524

Starling thought ahead.

But what about Starling herself? Quinn frowned and went back to a page he had glimpsed before.

Lord William Broadmoor, Lady Braelaura Fletcher
  Broadmoor
Jonathan 496, Hannah 498, Christopher 499, Aster 503 (B)

Four children, all young enough to be tutored by Starling. Charlie either had the truth or her story was a well-thought-out fiction. Quinn wouldn't discount that his brother believed her. Lord Broadmoor's wife had obviously been born a commoner, but Starling's last name implied she was related on the other side. She was older than the marriage, which created the possibility she was actually Lord Broadmoor's illegitimate daughter. Noblemen fathering children with servant girls was fairly common, especially before they settled down or after they had enough heirs—further evidenced by the listing of a bastard child among the Broadmoors. Starling could've been foisted off on a family she always assumed was hers and given a name that implied legitimacy. *If* Sagerra Broadmoor was her name—Lady Jacqueline seemed to think it was not. But Sagerra wasn't listed with her guardians or anywhere else he could find.

So who the hell is she?

His time was almost up. Frustrated, Quinn snapped the book shut. But the ledger wasn't dangerous in a military sense, and that had been his main concern. He replaced it in the bottom of the trunk and checked for other books, papers, or hidden compartments. Finding none, he straightened the contents to their original place. Quinn shut and re-locked the trunk, then snuffed and replaced the candle before slipping out the door.

He was almost too late. Casseck's voice echoed down the passage as Quinn ducked into the shadows. The pair of them passed his hiding place, followed by Gramwell and Lady Clare. Quinn smiled to himself. Starling may not be a spy, but he had a feeling the section in the ledger on Casseck was about to get a lot longer.

27

THE OFFICERS ESCORTED her and Clare back to their room, and Sage worried she'd talked too long with Casseck, until she saw the smile on Clare's face when Gramwell kissed her hand. She'd not misjudged the young man.

They helped each other undress in the light of the low fire, and Clare began making them some tea while Sage pulled out her ledger. It was best to write down what she'd learned while it was still fresh. Clare was bubbling over with details of her conversation with Lieutenant Gramwell, so Sage would take advantage of that, too. It wasn't until Clare referred to Gramwell by his first name, Luke, that Sage realized just what kind of impression he'd made on her friend.

Sage turned away to hide her smile and grabbed the candle to light it so she could start writing. The wax at the top was warm and soft.

Her smile died. Someone had been in the room.

28

QUINN TAPPED HIS fingers on the table as he waited in his workroom. He wanted her. She was better than Mouse.

But if Starling was in Mistress Rodelle's employ, he would need the matchmaker's permission to use her, especially given what—who—he had to hide. He also still didn't understand who she was, and he needed to.

The words she'd written drummed in his head. *Arrogant. Distant. Proud. Secretive.*

She wasn't wrong.

There was a knock on the door and Casseck entered, ushering the matchmaker inside. She was still dressed from the banquet, where the lieutenant had gone to fetch her. He helped her into the seat across from the captain and left them alone. Quinn folded his hands on the table and waited for her to recognize him.

"Thank you for coming, madam," he said before she could speak. "I apologize for not meeting with you before."

"I can understand why." She arched a painted eyebrow at him. "You're a busy man, Captain."

He shifted uncomfortably in his seat. "I need to ask you about Lady Sagerra."

"Indeed. I have some questions about Ash Carter."

He flinched. "I'll explain what I can."

Her blue eyes narrowed. "You can start with why you are toying with her."

Quinn shook his head. "I had no desire to toy with her."

"Really?" She leaned toward him over the table. "Should I bring your actions to the attention of Baron Underwood? Or perhaps your father?"

Ah, straight for the throat. Direct women were a rare breed. "You seem keen to protect her. Are you as protective of all the ladies?"

"Of course I am," she snapped. "Their parents entrusted them to me."

"But Sagerra is special."

"You singled her out, not me."

"Yes, I did." Quinn sat back in his chair and crossed his arms. "I need her. She has a unique position."

The matchmaker emphasized every word as she said, "And what would that be?"

"She moves easily between the ranks of nobles and commoners."

"Which apparently is *not* unique in our party." Mistress Rodelle smirked a little when he winced.

"She's also very observant." He laced his fingers and rubbed his thumbs together, choosing his next words carefully. "I heard a rumor Sagerra is not a titled lady; is that truth?"

"It's . . . complicated," she said, avoiding his eyes.

"Illegitimate?"

"No, a noble's ward. Common by blood." The matchmaker paused to watch him, but he kept his face blank. "She works for me as an apprentice, but as you've noticed, she can gather quite a bit of information if she plays a lady. Most of the brides resent her inclusion, but they also know she has the power to make or break their matches, so they tread a fine line in how they treat her."

Everything about Starling finally made sense. It was a relief to know she'd never truly lied. He tapped his lip, his mind racing. "I think I can work with that. I need information she can acquire."

"You want her for a spy?"

His mouth tightened. "That's not my preferred term, but yes."

She sat up straight. "I'll not have her used in your soldiers' games."

"This is not a game." Quinn shook his head. "This is deadly serious."

He waited for that to sink in, watching her anger dissolve into fear as he sat unmoving. "I need to know if I can trust you."

Some of the anger returned to her face. "Trust is a two-way road, Captain."

"Point taken," he said. "I will be as honest as I can, but I must keep some secrets." He paused. "Do I have your silence? What I would tell you cannot go beyond this room."

The matchmaker scowled. "You have my word on silence, but my own trust I reserve."

"Fair enough," Quinn said. "Part of my mission during this escort was to look for signs the D'Amiran family was communicating with Kimisara."

Her eyes widened. "And you've found evidence of this?"

Quinn shook his head. He didn't understand what the squads his pickets had found meant, and there was no sense in bringing it up until he did. "Worse. The D'Amirans are gathering an army. One strong enough to move against the crown."

"While half the nation's nobility is in Tennegol," she whispered.

"Yes. And we're the only ones who know."

"But . . . your father, the general, the army to the south—"

"Is spread out chasing dozens of Kimisar squads crossing the border." At least that's what they were doing the last time he heard from them. "They don't expect an attack to come from behind. I'd warn them if I could, but I think we've been cut off."

"So we will head back to Crescera, where it's safe?" the matchmaker asked.

"No. We need to continue on, observing what we can and pretending we know nothing. We're the only ones who can warn the king."

She flushed with anger. "You endanger us all by playing hero."

"What do you think happens if we turn around?" he asked calmly.

The color drained from her face. "They'll realize we know."

"And?"

"We become casualties."

"The first of many. I'm glad you understand this," he said.

Mistress Rodelle closed her eyes for several seconds, breathing deeply; then she opened them and looked straight at him. "How can I help?"

"I want the ladies blissfully ignorant. Anyone who knows is at risk, and that includes you now. If the duke thinks we're onto him, everything will be lost." He took a deep breath. "But I need Sagerra. As a lady, she can observe things we can't. With your help, I can exploit that."

Realization dawned on the matchmaker's face. "You don't intend to tell her what's going on."

"I wish I could, but for her safety and that of others, she must be kept in the dark for now." Observant as Mistress Rodelle was, she might already suspect Robert was with them. She did not ask, however, and it was better if she didn't know for sure.

"The less she knows the safer she is," he insisted. "I can only promise she will know what she must. I've no wish to see her hurt."

She gave him a steady look. "If you continue lying to her, that is unavoidable."

He looked down at his hands. "Yes, I know. I've accepted that. My job isn't always easy or straightforward. Neither is yours."

When he raised his eyes again, he found sympathy in her gaze. She sighed. "How do you intend to use her? From where you are, I don't see that happening."

"I want to accelerate her friendship with Ash Carter. She needs to trust him and follow his lead."

Mistress Rodelle shook her head. "She's too far above him. It already borders on inappropriate and will look suspicious."

"Exactly," Quinn agreed. "Every alternative I have draws too much attention to her. No one notices Ash's movements, which is why he's so useful to me. They're already familiar, so if I elevate his status, it will be easier for them to become friends. Effective tomorrow, he'll be a sergeant, and he'll no longer drive wagons."

The matchmaker crossed her arms. "Isn't Ash Carter the name of the king's illegitimate son?"

He focused back on her. "So it is. You're well-informed."

"Because I know the name of an eligible young man with royal blood? You insult me," she said.

The woman had been onto him from the start. "I assume that's why you allowed her to associate with him at all. Does Sagerra know?"

She shook her head. "Her name is just Sage, by the way, and no, she doesn't. I actually hoped to see if he was a suitable match for her. Had she known, she would've ruined the possibility with her own stubbornness."

Quinn rubbed his face to hide the heat spreading across his cheeks. He had a feeling the woman still wanted to make the match. "I think the sooner she stumbles onto that information, the better. Except for the matching part, of course." He leaned forward. "But now I need you to tell me as much as you can about her so we can handle her better."

Mistress Rodelle raised her eyebrows. "How much time do you have?"

29

SAGE WOKE EARLY the next morning, still itching to hit something. She'd gone through her belongings after Clare went to bed, trying to determine if anything had been disturbed. Nothing was precisely out of place, but it felt wrong. She combed through her ledger for signs it had been tampered with, finding two dots of candle wax on pages and a smudge she knew hadn't been there before. The book was what the intruder had been after.

And it had been Ash Carter.

He'd always been fascinated by the ledger. Before, she assumed it had to do with his inability to read, but in retrospect every minute they'd spent together had been about getting closer to it. And he wasn't the only one. Lieutenant Casseck had kept her from going back to her room early. She also knew enough about the army to understand neither would have acted without the direction of their captain, whom Casseck had said approved Ash's charade back on the day they left Galarick.

Sage finished her breakfast quickly and left Clare with a mumbled excuse about going for a walk. She stormed to the garden, hoping to burn off some of her restless energy, but it only reminded her of Casseck walking with her last night. The soldiers were just like the people in Garland Hill—only nice because they wanted something. She'd been a fool not to see it.

Distracted by her thoughts, she turned around a hedge and nearly collided with a man.

"Lady Sagerra," Private Carter said with an eager smile. "I was hoping to find you for a reading lesson today."

"I almost didn't recognize you," she said, looking him up and down. He wore the all-black clothing of a rider rather than the brown vest and linen shirt she was used to. His hands were scrubbed clean and his black hair had been trimmed, too, making him look older.

Ash grinned and lifted his arms to better show her his uniform. The outfit wasn't new—the wear in places told Sage it was over a year old at least. Her anger surged. Just how much about him had been a lie?

"I've been promoted to sergeant. No more wagons for me." He dropped his arms. "And I have you to thank for it, my lady."

"How so?"

The coldness in her voice seemed to catch him off guard, and he took a step back. "Captain Quinn said my effort to better myself made me stand out."

"And you want to continue that?"

"If your ladyship wishes to continue." Ash eyed her warily.

"Then there's no time like the present." Sage turned on her heel and stalked away as he scrambled to follow. He didn't try to make conversation as she led him into the castle.

In the library, away from the eyes of passing servants, Ash closed the door behind them. "Is something wrong, my lady?" he asked.

"You tell me," Sage said, walking over to a writing table. "I'd like you to try something before we start." She pulled a scrap of paper from the stack on a desk and used a stick of charcoal to write two sentences. Then she turned and handed it to him. "Read this aloud, please."

His dark eyes widened as they fell on her script. There was a tremor in his voice as he obeyed. "I've been lying to you. I already know how to read."

Sage crossed her arms. She'd thought hearing him say it would make her feel better, but it didn't. "Feel free to explain yourself. Start at the beginning, with the night we met."

He lowered the paper and swallowed. "I was ordered to observe the ladies."

That didn't surprise her at all. "So you're a spy."

"Of sorts, my lady."

"I don't understand," she said. "Why spy on us, on me?"

Ash pressed his lips together. "I was to make a connection within the group for Captain Quinn so I could report anything unusual."

Sage's stomach twisted. "So that's what I was."

"No," he said quickly, then grimaced. "Well, yes. I didn't want to use you, but then you offered to teach me to read, and Lieutenant Casseck saw it as an opportunity." He paused and added, "So did Captain Quinn."

Her eyes burned. "Do you have any idea how humiliating it is to know I spent days looking like a fool?"

Ash ducked his head. "Is it any worse than pretending to be illiterate and ignorant? At least your intentions were honorable."

But they hadn't been. Sage had wanted to help him, yes, but she'd also wanted information for Darnessa. Another thought occurred to her. "You weren't just promoted, were you? You were always a sergeant and a rider."

He nodded. "It's just easier to move around as a private. No one pays any attention to you."

She should have suspected that. So many of his mannerisms hadn't matched such a low rank. But she had liked him too much, and so had never believed he would lie to her.

"I'm sorry, my lady," he whispered. "I was only following orders. I hated every minute of it. Well . . ." He looked up with a sheepish smile. "I did enjoy your company."

How different, really, was he from her? Just because she was good at pulling information from men didn't mean she enjoyed it. Spirit above, she'd even resorted to manipulating Charlie.

Sage cleared her throat. "That's not the only thing." She gave him a piercing look. "Last night someone broke into my room and read through my ledger."

All the color drained from his face. She'd been right. It *was* him.

"Why?" She tried to hold on to her anger but only heard hurt in her voice.

Ash held his palms up, pleading. "You asked so many questions. You were always writing observations. To a soldier it looks . . ."

"Like spying," she finished. "Especially if that's what *you're* doing."

He nodded miserably. "I'm sorry. I didn't want to."

That first night she'd talked about following orders, and he'd been so upset. She had thought he was overreacting, but now she realized she'd hit a nerve. What else had the captain made him do?

"I wanted to clear your name, though," he said. "And with what the captain discovered, we needed to know for sure."

Sage straightened. Casseck had dodged her questions last night, but here was an opportunity to force some answers. Then she winced. Who was the real manipulator here? "I already know there's some kind of danger. What's going on?"

He shook his head. "I can't tell you. I don't even know everything. My job was just to find someone to trust."

"How can I trust *you*, Ash Carter? You lied to me for days."

His shoulders sagged. "I suppose you can't."

Sage felt a sudden pity. He'd failed in his mission, though he'd only followed orders. "Why was the captain looking for someone to trust?" she asked quietly.

"He wanted a contact we could come to if there was trouble or who could find me if they heard something strange." He looked down at the crumpled paper in his hand. "But you're right. I ruined that. I'm sorry." Ash took a step backward. "If your ladyship will excuse me, I'll leave now."

"Wait," she said, guilt welling up inside at the awareness of her own lies. This would be so much easier if she could tell him she was just as common as him. But would they still want her if they knew she wasn't a lady? "I don't want you to get in trouble."

Ash shrugged. "I still have time to make friends with one of the maids. It will just be harder now that I'm riding again."

"Don't be ridiculous," she said, fearing how Quinn might react if Ash failed. "I'll be your contact."

He brightened, dark eyes rising to meet hers. "You're not angry, my lady?"

She scowled, though her anger had pretty much dissolved. "I didn't say that. You know your captain could've just asked me what I was writing himself or explained what he needed."

"He never meant to hurt you," Ash said, taking a few steps closer. He stood straighter, taller. "I was to pass on his apology for my deception."

"Hmph," she said. Sage furrowed her brow as she looked up at him. "So you were going to tell me the truth at some point?"

He nodded. "I was going to tell you tomorrow."

"How? Weren't you going to be riding rather than driving?"

A handsome smile spread across his face. "I was given permission to ride with you, if you were agreeable."

She felt herself smile back, though she knew Quinn wouldn't have allowed such a thing unless it gave him what he wanted from her. "I'm not used to being called agreeable, but if it gets me off the wagon, you can call me anything you want."

30

AFTER LUNCH AND a much-needed nap to make up for such a restless night, Sage went looking for Darnessa and found her embroidering in the sitting room of her suite.

"How is Clare?" she asked before Sage could start.

"Oh," said Sage, scrambling to remember what Darnessa meant. "Better. This trip is a little much for her, I'm afraid. I have to do some thinking yet, but we need to discuss her future before we get to Tennegol."

Darnessa shrugged. "Very well, you can get back to me. Have you talked to Ash Carter lately? I haven't seen him much since we arrived."

Sage chewed her lip. "He's been promoted, so he has new duties." The matchmaker didn't need to know he was a sergeant all along.

"Indeed? Anything to do with you and your lessons?"

It was too casual. Darnessa was up to something.

"He seems to think so," Sage said. "He won't drive a wagon anymore, and he's offered to teach me to ride as a thank-you."

"I suppose that sounds fair."

Sage already knew how to ride quite well—Uncle William had been surprisingly open-minded and had even taken her hunting a few times—and she'd framed it that way to make Darnessa think Ash owed her something. Still, she'd expected some resistance. "I didn't think you would approve."

"Why not?" said Darnessa. "Ladies ride horses all the time, and I rather like the extra room to stretch out in the wagon."

"Yes, but riding with a peasant?"

Darnessa peered at Sage over the wooden hoop. "Is that what he told you about himself?" She looked back down and shook her head disapprovingly. "A handsome boy speaks to you in half-truths, and you believe him? You must be losing your touch, apprentice."

The matchmaker's willingness to let her ride with Ash left a bad taste in her mouth, but Sage left without saying anything more. Darnessa was manipulating her. She *wanted* Sage to spend time with Ash. And there could be only one logical explanation: the woman was trying to match her. She wanted it bad enough to let Sage back off from acting like a lady. That might not have bothered Sage—she wanted to spend time with Ash, too—except there was something else about him. Something Darnessa wanted her to discover.

So Sage went in search of the one person she thought might tell her. She found Charlie near the kitchens, ferrying food and supplies to the wagons, and she dropped in beside him and offered to help. It took some sideways questioning, but the page let enough information drop by the time they returned to the kitchen. After another round-trip, this time carrying a bag of apples, she made her way back to her room, feeling dizzy.

Spirit above, it explained *everything*—Ash's refined speech, the way he dropped formalities, his frustration with being ordered around . . . and Darnessa's attitude.

She stared at the hearth fire, letting the low, oscillating flames soothe her chaotic thoughts. The matchmaker couldn't help it, she supposed. Ash was the only man Sage had ever shown any interest in, so naturally the woman assumed it meant they should be paired. But Darnessa didn't know Ash spent time with her only because Quinn ordered him to.

A coldness swept over Sage. If Ash *did* have any interest in her, it would vanish as soon as he found out she wasn't a Concordium bride—she wasn't even a lady. He could have anyone he wanted. Even Lady Jacqueline wouldn't turn him down.

No, Darnessa was a fool. Sage had nothing to offer him.

Except whatever help the soldiers needed. And friendship.

Yes, she could do that.

Meanwhile, she was obligated to do her job. Sage pulled her ledger from the deepest layers of her trunk and flipped to the entry on Captain Quinn. With fingers that trembled, she gripped the quill and wrote on the blank page opposite.

> *Ash Devlinore "Carter" (B) born ~489*
> *Sergeant, 1ˢᵗ Army, 9ᵗʰ Cavalry*
> *Father: King Raymond Devlin*

Sage sat back as the dinner bell's summons echoed off the stone walls and into the window. She didn't think she could bear writing anything more that night, so she tucked the book back in her trunk under the breeches at the bottom. Suddenly she remembered the matchmaker's knowing smile when they parted earlier, and a sly smirk of her own twisted her mouth.

You want me to ride, Darnessa? Fine. You asked for it.

31

DUKE D'AMIRAN LOOKED up from his late dinner in the Great Hall of Tegann as the bound man was brought before him. The captive's black-and-gold livery was torn and muddy, and he reeked of sweat and excrement. D'Amiran covered his nose with a lemon-scented handkerchief and motioned for the gag to be loosened.

"Traitor!" the courier sputtered. He tried to spit, but his mouth was too dry.

The duke remained composed. The man would plead for death soon enough, but D'Amiran doubted he knew much worth the effort. He had a few questions, though, mostly about why his brother was having so much trouble finding the prince. It was making his allies restless.

"How did we acquire this man?" he asked.

Captain Geddes habitually tugged his left ear, which was missing a large chunk. "Our Kimisar friends caught him. He carried a dispatch from General Quinn intended to meet the escort commander when he stopped at Underwood." He pulled a bundle of papers from his jacket and laid it on the table. "The letters are in code."

The duke glanced through them as he addressed the prisoner. "Am I correct in assuming you don't know how to translate these?"

"Yes." The courier looked back steadily.

"I can find out for you, Your Grace," the captain offered.

D'Amiran shook his head. "I doubt General Quinn would go through the trouble of coding messages only to send the key with them." He pursed his lips. "It does bother me he'd use such precautions, though. He must have suspicions." D'Amiran covered his nose again as he gestured for the man to be taken away. "Focus your efforts on those topics, Captain."

The guards began dragging the courier toward the back door of the hall. The man didn't struggle, but he didn't cooperate, either.

"Do me a favor, Captain," the duke called through his makeshift mask. The head guard turned back. "Wait until I'm done eating before you get too involved. It's difficult to properly digest to the sound of screaming."

32

SAGE ROSE EARLY and dressed in her breeches, boots, and linen shirt with a heavy felt vest, binding and covering her hair with a wool cap and the hood from her faded brown jacket, then packed her belongings and left the guest wing before anyone else stirred. She strolled to the kitchens, blending in with the servants and common soldiers and grabbing a quick breakfast before heading to the stables. After locating the lead hostler, she asked him which of the horses was designated for Lady Sagerra. He pointed it out, glad to delegate another task on the busy morning. She picked through the cavalry's spare gear until she found a saddle with stirrups already set to the right length and carried it to the stall.

They hadn't patronized her by giving her a pony or a packhorse, but rather a spare mount of one of the riders. She offered the dark gray mare an apple and began brushing her down with a curry comb, making friends quickly. After checking the animal over for signs of lameness or injury, Sage pulled the saddle down from the stall door and heaved it over the mare's high back.

As she bent over to cinch the girth, she heard a familiar voice. "Boy, that saddle needs an over-cantle for a lady—you'll have to put it on before you cinch it down." Sage grinned and didn't acknowledge him.

Ash pulled the stall door open and walked up behind her. "Did you hear me? You have to put the side cantle over that first." He grabbed her arm, and she stood straight to face him.

"If you don't mind, I'd just as soon go without it," she said.

He froze in shock, his hand grasping her forearm. She came up to his chin, but this close she had to crane her neck to meet his eyes. "If you'd ever tried to ride in a skirt, you'd know why."

Ash released her arm and stepped back, his mouth falling open. The way his eyes roved over her was no different from the way others stared when they saw her in breeches, but she had to resist the urge to turn her backside away from his lingering gaze. He shook his head. "Riding in the front of a wagon or sidesaddle is one thing, my lady, but I think Mistress Rodelle will draw the line at this."

Sage winked at him. "Then I suggest you help me stay out of sight until it's too late."

Outside she turned her face to the sun and soaked in the warm rays. She wouldn't miss that silly hat, though she'd end the day with far more freckles than she started with. It seemed a fair trade for the freedom she gained. Once on the road, Sage observed the landscape with fascination. Crop fields were less common as the terrain became rockier, and the wooded areas they passed through were broader. The group was beginning to cross Tasmet, which wasn't technically another country, but it felt exotic to her. In Crescera, only the richer houses were built out of stone, while peasants built with wood and thatched with grass. Here even the poorest homes were made from stone and had slate roofs.

At first she was embarrassed, thinking she came across as a wide-eyed country girl, especially now that she knew Ash's true identity. He'd also been in the province with the army for years, so nothing was new to him, but he seemed to take delight in her impressions, pointing out trace veins of colorful minerals threading the walls they passed. Her self-consciousness slowly melted away.

Ash was also much more open to her questions about the army. He talked about his fellow soldiers like they were his brothers, which she supposed they were. Sage wondered how he felt about that. "You know about my family," she said. "What's yours like?"

He shrugged. "Not much to tell. My father is . . . well-known. I grew up seeing him from a distance. Mother was devoted to me, but I've only seen her a few times in recent years. The army is my family now." He avoided her eyes. "I suppose my name makes it obvious what I am."

"Which makes no difference to me," she said, realizing he wasn't ready to reveal himself yet. "Tell me about page training. I can hardly believe some of the duties your captain trusts Charlie with."

Ash drew his brows together. He had the darker skin of an Aristelan as well as the nearly black hair. She'd never be able to match his color even if she stayed outdoors all summer, contrary to her aunt's endless lectures on ruining her complexion. "What I remember most was the hazing, the way the older boys tormented the younger ones. Quinn's father was a colonel back then, and the day after Quinn arrived, he marched right up to his father and said he wanted out of the army if he was going to have to serve with twats like them for the rest of his life."

Sage chuckled despite her dislike of the captain. "I guess his father made him stay."

Ash shook his head. "His father told him he could go home if he wanted—it wasn't like anyone was showing the brats how to act any better." He smiled tightly. "Quinn took it as a challenge and went back to the pages' tent and picked a fight."

Sage snorted. "I suppose he won all the boys' respect that day and made lieutenant the next week."

Ash ignored her sarcasm. "No. Got licked pretty badly, but he refused to name whoever had beat him. I guess it was only right, seeing as he started it." He stared at his mount's ears. "That was the beginning of a very rough year for him. I'll never know why he didn't quit."

"What happened?" She found it a bit intriguing. "He obviously made it through and succeeded."

"Don't really know," said Ash. "He just worked at being and doing what was right, slowly gaining friends—myself among them—until just about everyone looked up to him somehow. He took that responsibility very seriously. Still does. By the time we were squires, all the fighting and hazing had stopped and the pages were handling duties usually left to squires, who were then able to focus higher."

The dedication Quinn's friends had to him ran deep, back into childhood. She couldn't help but feel it drove them all to please him now, even when his orders weren't pleasant. Though now he was forcing only minor lies and deceptions, it likely wouldn't stop there unless someone stood up to him.

Ash turned his face to her. The sunlight hit his dark eyes at an angle, making them shine with a rich mahogany color. "So the short answer is: at Charlie's age, we *didn't* do those things. What a missed opportunity."

Sage caught that Ash had been a page and squire himself, yet he wasn't an officer. She was about to ask why when he said, "How about you, Lady Sagerra? Did you get in any fights as a child? Or did you just throw pinecones down on your enemies?"

He was teasing, but she answered truthfully. "Three fights, actually. I lost the first. Father said I was being honorable with a boy too cowardly to pick on someone his own size. So in our next matchup I used my left knee to great effect. I don't think he walked straight for weeks."

Ash cringed. "And the third?"

"It was more a contest of wits against an unarmed opponent."

"You cannot leave me hanging with that."

Sage shrugged. "He was an empty braggart, talking down girls, points of which I mostly agreed with, but when he said he could beat any girl at anything, short of weeping, I challenged him to Kimisar arm wrestling." Ash had never heard of it. "That's because I made it up," she explained. "I would try to pull his arm down while he resisted with his elbow levered on a table." She held her arm out with her fist facing her to show him.

"Sounds like you had the easier part."

She nodded. "That's what he said. So I asked what was he afraid of, being he was so much better."

"Who won?"

"Depends on your point of view. I only pulled his arm down about so far." She opened her arm to a wide angle and turned to Ash with a wicked grin. "But then I let go." She snapped her arm back, demonstrating how he punched himself in the face.

Ash burst into laughter, startling their horses and everyone around

136

them. After the initial blast, he worked to bring himself under control. Sage thought for a moment he might actually fall off his horse. The other soldiers stared, but he waved them off as he gasped for breath and tears rolled down his cheeks. He finally calmed down and wiped his eyes with his gloved hands. "Oh, I can't believe you did that. It's positively diabolical."

"I couldn't believe it worked as well as it did," Sage said, shaking her head. "It knocked him right out of his chair and cut his lips on his teeth. There was blood everywhere." Ash started snickering again. "The best part was his face." She put her fist to her mouth again and made a comical expression of horror. "Of course, Uncle William didn't think it was so funny. Nor did the boy's father."

Ash clutched his sides like he was holding himself together. When Sage heard her own peal of laughter, it struck her she hadn't truly laughed in a very long time.

∽✦∾

Their first stop to rest and stretch made Sage realize a problem her clothing presented. An outside observer would assume she was a common man, so she couldn't sit with the ladies. She would've taken her breaks with Ash, but he had important matters to discuss with the officers and firmly insisted she couldn't be anywhere near them. Sage decided eating alone was a small price to pay for the privilege of riding.

When they stopped for lunch, Ash excused himself, mentioning he would take a turn on patrol as soon as they were back on the road. Sage had already established she neither needed nor wanted any assistance dismounting, so Lieutenant Casseck waited until she was on the ground before approaching. He also looked to be over the shock of seeing her dressed and riding like a man. "My lady," he said. "I have a request from Captain Quinn concerning his brother, Charlie."

She glanced over at Quinn leading his horse to where another officer and Ash gathered near a makeshift table with a map spread over it. "Why can't he ask himself?"

Casseck shrugged. "It's my job to carry out his ideas."

137

Sage rolled her eyes. She'd faint of shock the day Quinn did something himself rather than give orders. Or perhaps he was too embarrassed to face her after making Ash lie, in which case he wasn't lazy, he was a coward. "Go ahead, then."

"You're aware our situation has developed a degree of danger. The captain feels if he puts Charlie under your supervision, he'll have less to worry about. Charlie will still have page duties, but he'd be assigned partly to you and the other ladies. Carter can't ride at your side all day, nor can he eat with you, but Charlie can."

She tilted her head up to meet Casseck's eyes. "Am I correct in assuming if we're attacked, Charlie is less likely to be harmed if he's part of the women's group?"

The lieutenant grimaced. "Yes, but that doesn't mean we expect such an attack."

He might be telling the truth. That morning the soldiers were alert but not as nervous as before, though all had been fully armed. She opened her mouth to ask what they did expect, but Casseck cut her off.

"My lady, you asked how you can help us, and it is truth when I say this will allow us to focus more on understanding the threat. This isn't a minor request. Captain Quinn doesn't give up control easily, especially over his brother."

Sage sighed and nodded. "I will for Charlie's sake." She felt a little patronized, but the fact that Quinn was concerned for Charlie's safety gave her chills. Who out there would harm a child?

33

SAGE WATCHED ASH ride ahead on his patrol after lunch. He seemed confident he'd be back by the time they stopped for the evening, but the way Casseck frowned as he watched him go concerned her. Why would Quinn send Ash out alone? The captain strutted around giving orders as they prepared to move on.

She settled into the saddle and turned to Charlie beside her. "Your brother looks like a man of action, always in a hurry."

Charlie nodded. "Father says he assigned him this job to learn patience."

Sage stifled a laugh. Perhaps his father knew he wasn't quite as wonderful as everyone thought.

"Want to see my knife?" Charlie asked. "Mother had it made special." He unhooked the dagger belted at his waist, proudly displaying the gold initials inlaid on the hilt. It looked huge in his small hand. "My brother has one, too."

"My father gave me my own knife when I was your age," Sage said. "But I lost it." She told him how she had run away and when her uncle had found her and carried her home, the knife was left behind in the ravine.

Charlie's brown eyes widened. "Why did you run away, my lady? Was your uncle cruel?"

"At the time, I thought so." She smiled sadly. "My father had just died, you see, and when someone you love is in trouble or dead, you don't always think clearly."

"Father says clear thinking is an officer's most valuable asset," said Charlie solemnly.

"I imagine he knows from experience," she replied with equal gravity.

⌘

Ash hadn't returned by the time they arrived at the next estate. Middleton Manor had high and thick walls in the style she'd noticed in places they'd passed since leaving Underwood. Tasmet had endured centuries of fighting and invasions. She imagined if they traveled south toward Kimisara, such homes would be even more fortified. Sage helped Charlie carry her trunk to the room she and Clare would share, sensing a growing uneasiness in the soldiers as they watched the eastern approaches for their missing companion. Dinner had passed and the sun was setting when the escort began organizing a search party.

Sage, now in a dress, watched the officers confer from atop the estate's outer wall. Charlie fidgeted beside her, and she tried to soothe him despite her own fears. She intended to force some straight answers from Casseck tonight, but at the moment he was giving instructions. Captain Quinn stood at his side, arms folded. How could he look so unconcerned? Didn't he feel any guilt for having sent Ash out on his own? She'd never seen him go out on a patrol himself, and while Sage didn't know much about the army, that struck her as wrong. A commander should never order others to do what he wasn't willing to do himself.

Five riders were armed and mounting up when four short horn blasts sounded in the distance. The soldiers instantly relaxed, and Charlie sagged against her in relief.

Several minutes later, a large dog bounded down the road in the dusk, followed by Ash on his brown horse, riding as though he was eager to get back to them, but not rushed. The gate opened, and he trotted through, making a series of hand signals to the riders in the courtyard. Casseck jerked his head at the assembled team, and they headed back to the stables with their mounts.

Casseck approached Ash as he dismounted. "Sorry to make you worry, Cass," Sage heard Ash say. "But it was well worth it."

The lieutenant tilted his head and pointed with his eyes to the wall where Sage stood with Charlie, and Ash turned to wave at them before walking away with Casseck. Charlie made to run down after them, but she grabbed him.

"Wait, Charlie. I'm sure they have important matters to discuss. We know he's safe now; you should go to bed."

"But I'm sure he's hungry. I'll get him something to eat."

She shook her head. "No, it's late. I'll take care of it." The page made to protest again, but she raised a finger. "Your brother put me in charge of you, soldier, and I say, go to bed." She pointed to the barracks. "Now."

Charlie obeyed with a sullen "Yes, ma'am," and Sage headed to the kitchens and asked for a tray of food. Her arms full, she crossed the yard and pried the stable door open with her foot, using her hip to angle it just wide enough to pass through. Other than horses, the stables were nearly deserted, and she slipped quietly along the stalls toward the voices at the far end. Lieutenant Casseck was lecturing Ash.

She crept closer to the stall door and paused behind a dividing wall, just out of sight. Through a space between the planks, she saw Casseck looking down and to the rear of the horse, but Ash was out of view. "You had everyone scared, you know," the lieutenant said.

Including me, Sage thought.

Ash stood from where he'd been crouching, probably checking the mare's hooves. "I can take care of myself." His voice rang with confidence and authority, so different from the way he spoke to her.

Casseck wasn't cowed. "Not against a hundred and thirty men."

Sage stifled a gasp.

Ash snorted. "They're not all in one place."

Sage's brow furrowed. Were they surrounded? No wonder Quinn didn't want anyone to know. Darnessa would panic.

"All right, then, ten," Casseck conceded. "You're good, but you're not that good." Ash clenched his jaw and swept a brush over the brown mare, making her shiver and stamp with enjoyment. Casseck patted her withers as he continued. "We can't afford to lose anyone, least of all you. From now on, all patrols should be at least two men; three would be better."

Ash shook his head. "We don't have the manpower to spread out that much. It makes us vulnerable."

"We're already vulnerable," Casseck said. Before Ash could protest again, Casseck stepped closer, putting a hand on the brush to make Ash pay attention. "I mean it. No one goes out alone anymore, especially you. Your father would kill me if I stood by and let you act this way."

Yes, listen to Casseck. Sage wished Casseck were in charge rather than Quinn. He obviously cared more about the safety of his men.

Ash turned his face to glare up at the lieutenant. "I think you're forgetting who is in command here," he said slowly.

Sage needed to step in before Ash got into trouble. She moved around the wall, making enough noise that they wouldn't think she was sneaking. Casseck's eyes flashed to the opening as soon as she was visible, and Ash stiffened with his back to her. After looking to Ash's face for a long moment, the lieutenant pulled his hand down and hooked his thumb in his belt. "I'll speak to the captain. He'll make you see reason."

Casseck stepped around Ash, heading for the stall door. Ash pivoted to watch him go, eyes settling on Sage as Casseck passed her with a polite nod and disappeared. She hovered at the opening as Ash studied her with an unreadable expression before turning back to the horse. "How long have you been there?" he growled.

She might as well admit it. "Long enough to hear some things of interest." He said nothing and continued brushing with swift, angry strokes. Her temper rose to match his. "I didn't come to spy on you, if that's what you mean. I came because I thought you'd be hungry. You're welcome."

"And now you know who I am," he snapped. "Congratulations."

Her anger evaporated. He hadn't wanted her to know. Quinn probably made him hide it—he could gather more information as a commoner. "You're the king's son," she said calmly. "I've known since yesterday. I won't tell anyone."

He stopped brushing and leaned his forehead on the mare's flank. "You know this habit of yours is really annoying."

The venom in his voice didn't match the relieved slump of his shoulders, but he was upset, so she kept her tone neutral. "And which habit would that be?"

"The one where you go around digging up everything you aren't meant to know, hearing what you're not supposed to hear, forcing everything to the surface that should be hidden." Ash twisted around to look at her accusingly. "All the while deceiving me about yourself and your purpose." He spun back and flung the brush into a basket with a clatter, startling the mare from her dinner.

He exhaled heavily. "It was bad enough thinking you were going to be wasted on some rich, pompous old man. But I've read your book." He crossed his arms and turned to glower at her. "You're not in there. Not as a bride. Not as a Broadmoor. *You don't exist.* Yet you stand in front of me now, playing the concerned lady. This morning you were dressed and riding like a man; last week you played at being a teacher. The question is, who will you be tomorrow?"

She lowered her eyes. "I'll be your friend."

"I have friends. None of them gives so little and takes so much as you do." He advanced a couple steps and took the tray from her hands. "You can leave now."

He'd known for days she was lying—maybe from the beginning. If Quinn had suspected her of spying or being connected to the 130 men around them, Ash must have put a great deal of effort into trying to prove him wrong, finally breaking into her room to clear her name. Yet he still didn't know who she was.

And she couldn't tell him.

"Good night, Sagerra Broadmoor," he said. There was a finality in his voice, an unspoken *Good-bye.*

He only wanted the truth, and as her friend he deserved it.

"Sage," she whispered.

"What?"

She squared her shoulders and forced her eyes up to meet his. "My name is Sage."

His dark eyes held hers for several seconds, waiting, but she couldn't find her voice.

"And what comes after Sage?" he prompted gently. "Not Broadmoor."

"Fowler," she whispered. "My father was a fowler. Lady Broadmoor is my mother's sister. They took me in when he died."

"And now?"

She dropped her gaze. "I apprentice with the matchmaker. I'm her assistant."

"How does she pay you? By getting you a rich husband?"

"No, of course not." A deep flush crept up her neck to her hairline. "I don't want to get married."

"Ever?"

"Ever," she replied firmly, peeking up again.

Ash's eyes shifted at a noise behind her, and he lifted the food to show Lieutenant Gramwell. "I'll be right along, sir," he said. "I was just thanking Lady Sagerra, as she was so kind to bring this." He bowed to her over the tray, seeking to meet her eyes one last time.

"I hope you'll ride with me tomorrow, Sage Fowler," he whispered.

34

DUKE D'AMIRAN READ the hasty dispatch from Baron Underwood with widening eyes: *Prince Robert was in the escort group.* The message also confirmed what they'd learned from the courier: General Quinn's own son was leading the unit. Inwardly the duke kicked himself for not questioning their prisoner about Robert, but he'd assumed the man would know nothing useful on that front. It didn't matter, however, D'Amiran knew now. Both the king's son and nephew would be under his roof in a matter of days. He couldn't have planned it better.

Originally the plan had been to let the Kimisar in the south kidnap Prince Robert and carry him through the Jovan Pass so General Quinn would send a significant part of his force in pursuit. Those Kimisar would've headed north and back through Tegann Pass, and then both passes would be sealed, trapping many Demorans on the wrong side of the Catrix Mountains. Divided thus, the western unit of the Demoran army would be easier to defeat with his own forces now gathering. Then the Kimisar were free to ransom the prince back to Tennegol. Or kill him—D'Amiran didn't care.

The duke called for Geddes and updated the captain on the situation as he wrote a letter to his brother at Jovan, instructing the count to send their Kimisar allies through the pass without the prince. D'Amiran had assumed it was Rewel's incompetence that made his brother unable to find Robert, but it was because the prince wasn't, in fact, with General Quinn in the south. For all the thrill of knowing the crown prince was coming straight to Tegann, it was a slight complication. If the Kimisar didn't have a kidnapped Robert with them as bait, the general would send fewer of his soldiers in pursuit, but D'Amiran was too excited to worry about that.

"The prince is traveling under a false name," he told Geddes. "So that may mean the escort perceives a threat, which is all the more reason for us not to frighten them. I won't have them panic—my prizes may be damaged. In any case, I want a look at young Quinn. They say he's just like his father, though I'd hardly consider that a compliment." It was morbid curiosity that drove him there.

D'Amiran folded the letter and held the stick of wax to the candle on his desk. "I also wonder why the general assigned his own son to this mission."

"Do you think it's to spy on you, Your Grace?" Geddes asked.

Those coded letters—still untranslated—told him General Quinn trusted no one. "Undoubtedly. But he could also be trying to get the prince back to the capital, which may mean they have informants we need to weasel out. At any rate, we can't tell Captain Huzar about Robert. When you patrol out to the pass next, say only that Robert is on his way. Once we have the prince, perhaps we can force the Kimisar to support us just a little more before we hand him over." He might need them now, when his army faced Quinn's.

"I'm not sure we can trust them, Your Grace," the captain said, running a thumb along the scarred edge of his ear.

D'Amiran chuckled as he sealed the parchment. "I know we can't. But this famine and blight is in its third year. Kimisara will trade anything for food, and so they will do what I want."

Geddes brushed his brown hair down over his ravaged ear and held out his hand for the dispatch. "I'm prepared to retrieve your prizes myself."

The duke shook his head as he handed the letter over. "Relax, Captain; in this position we cannot lose."

"What of the soldiers escorting the brides?" Geddes asked, tucking the letter into his jacket.

"They're of no concern. At the moment they keep me from having to bring the women here myself. If things go badly in the south before we can march, there will still be time to turn on the Kimisar here." He chuckled. "We'll be heroes for saving and returning Robert. Maybe we'll even let the escort soldiers help, though perhaps young Quinn will meet with a fatal accident. If nothing else we can stretch them for information. Leave them unmolested for now."

35

MOUSE LAY ON his cot in the barracks, too full of thoughts of Starling to sleep despite his weariness. What had possessed him to push her like that? He tried to tell himself it was only because she would never be comfortable until she could be herself. In truth, it was the strain of his own deception that made him take foolish chances. He'd almost ruined everything, hadn't realized how much he'd be losing until the moment he told her to leave.

But she hadn't left.

Sage Fowler. He'd known her name, but hearing her say it had been a gift. She trusted him. She wanted to tell him, just like he wanted to tell her.

Then she stood there, blushing her freckles out of existence as he pushed further, demanding what he'd needed to know. Her answers had sparked relief. And disappointment.

He groaned and rubbed his face. He'd been lucky so far, but he was afraid sooner or later those gray eyes would disarm him completely at the worst possible moment.

36

SAGE LAY AWAKE in the bed she shared with Clare, thinking of the relief on Ash's face when she'd told him her name. He knew she'd lied and she wasn't a lady. He knew she was nobody.

And he still wanted to be her friend.

"Sage?" murmured Clare in the darkness, startling her. She'd thought her friend was asleep. "Are you awake?"

"Yes."

"Everyone's talking about you."

"Who's everyone?" Sage asked.

"All the ladies. They watch you and say awful things. I don't know how to defend you."

Sage frowned. This could mean trouble. "Are they keeping it to themselves?"

"Yes, they're afraid of Darnessa. They don't talk around her, but she knows. She told them you do nothing without her permission."

Sage shrugged. Father always said gossip was for small minds. "Then you needn't defend me. If I cared what people thought about me, I'd—" Sage broke off. She'd been about to say she'd be married, but it seemed a little indelicate considering where Clare was headed. She cleared her throat. "Where were you when I came back this evening?"

"Oh." Clare shifted. "I went for a walk with Lieutenant Gramwell again."

"Again?"

"We've been walking every day after dinner, but tonight the soldiers were busy with something, so we went later than usual." There was a long pause. "Do you think that's improper?"

Sage smiled and reached across the bed to squeeze Clare's hand. "Not at all."

37

HE ALMOST SIGHED in relief when he saw her eating breakfast at dawn with the servants outside the kitchen, dressed for riding. He sidled up to her on the bench and presented her with a large, ripe strawberry. "Good morning, friend," he said in a low voice.

Sage took it and peeked up at him shyly.

"I want to apologize for my anger last night," he said. "I was tired and being rather unfair, but I'm glad to finally understand your place in all this."

"There's no need for apologies. We both act under orders." There were no biscuits left in the serving bowl, and she offered him half of hers. "From now on I'll make my own choices, though I know you're less free to do so."

He accepted the biscuit, brushing his fingers against hers. "I get the feeling you're used to making your own way."

"You can thank my father for that." Sage smiled sheepishly.

He'd give anything to have met the man. "I look forward to hearing more about him today."

Her eyes shone out of her pale face. "I look forward to telling you."

Casseck wouldn't let him ride after yesterday's patrol. The lieutenant had been sly enough to present his case at last night's meeting in front of the officers, and the captain was forced to agree all patrols would have at least two riders from now on. At least he had pleasant company. And true to form, they were barely on the road before she started asking questions.

"Can you tell me what happened yesterday?" she said. "I wanted to ask about it last night, but we were interrupted."

The worry in her eyes was gratifying, but it was misplaced. They hadn't heard from the forward picket, so he'd gone to find him. It turned out he was only sick from a place he'd passed through a few days ago. The illness wasn't fatal to anyone, but it was . . . inconvenient, and it had slowed him down.

"It wasn't dangerous or even that exciting," he said. "A town nearby is under quarantine. They had some sort of dead animal in their well and the sickness spread quickly, but as long as we avoid the water in the area, we should be fine. It was worth investigating, though."

"What kind of malady is it?"

He hesitated. Sage wasn't squeamish, but he didn't feel like describing two days of diarrhea and vomiting. "A passing affliction I'd rather not detail to you, proper lady or no."

She caught his meaning. "A *passing* affliction?"

He chuckled at his unintentional pun. "Yes."

"Wouldn't *that* be handy to inflict on your enemies?" she mused.

He abruptly reined in his horse to stare at her. Sweet Spirit, it was brilliant.

"Is something wrong?" she asked, pulling back on her gray mare and glancing around.

"No, just . . . that's a hell of an idea." They could cripple Tegann on their way out. Maybe even the army to the south.

"Really? I was only joking."

"I'm not," he said. "Wait here. I need to talk to Casseck." He wheeled his horse around and waved to his friend. After a few minutes' conference, he returned to Sage's side and gave her a pointed look. "You must say nothing about this."

Sage shook her head. "You have my word." They watched two riders and a dog run ahead. Cass was already putting the plan into motion. "You can take credit for the idea," she said.

"Nonsense. If it does what I think it might, I'll get you a commendation."

He bent his head and looked over at her. "It would make your father proud."

She ignored his deflection. "You avoid calling attention to yourself when you do well, but accept blame even when unnecessary."

He shrugged. "I give credit where it's due."

"I think you'd make a good officer. Have you ever thought about it?"

"You're not the first to bring it up." He shook his head. "But my brother's a lieutenant. I can't be the same."

"The prince," she murmured. "You don't want to compete for promotion with him."

"Exactly. He's got it hard enough. I'd rather support him."

"I understand the desire," she said. "I just wish you wouldn't sell yourself short."

"And maybe I don't want a commission. It chains him to nothing but duty for years." He pointed to Cass and Gramwell, riding a few yards ahead. "See them? How they have to act all the time? Compare that to me, here with you. This is freedom they don't have."

Sage eyed him sideways. "You don't fool me, Ash Carter. You've got ambition and a natural command presence. But I admire your sense of duty and honor."

His face burned as he looked for a way to change the subject. "Speaking of honor, if your parents were married, and your father was a fowler and not a peasant, why did they name you Sage?"

"They liked the name, I guess."

"Not buying it," he said, looking ahead with a hand over his eyes to block the late-morning sun.

"It was Mother's favorite herb. Father said she'd fry leaves and eat them straight, especially while she was . . . when she was expecting me." She smiled a little. "Then when I was born . . ." Her voice faded and she dropped her eyes.

"When you were born . . . ," he encouraged.

Her freckles faded as she flushed. "Father said I smelled sweet and had soft skin, like sage leaves. Once he said so out loud, no other name

153

would do. And sage is for wisdom and knowledge, which were important to him." She bit her lip before continuing. "It has healing qualities as well. More than once Father said I was the only medicine that could ease the pain of Mother's death." She picked at her fingernails. "I like it."

"I like it, too," he assured her. "It has meaning." She colored a deeper shade of pink, but he pretended not to notice, focusing down the road. "Sounds like your parents were well-matched. Is that what made you choose your apprenticeship?"

"No, I kind of fell into it. My parents matched themselves. She was a fletcher's daughter."

"Let me guess," he said. "As a fowler his father sold feathers to her father for arrow making."

"Close. Father was raised in an orphanage and never knew his parents. He sold the feathers as an apprentice." A dreamy smile lit her face. "He would ration what he had to sell, so he could visit almost every day."

He found it impossible to look away from her. "He must've had a rough childhood, with no parents."

Sage shook her head. "Actually, the convent inspired his love of learning. Had he been raised outside it, he might never have been so well-schooled. He also had more choice in his apprenticeship, as he wasn't born into one. When he was thirteen, he saw Mother for the first time, and since the fletcher already had an assistant, Father chose the next closest thing. Nine years later, they ran off together."

"*Nine years?*" he said. "That's a lot of dedication."

"Says the career soldier," she retorted cheerfully before growing serious again. "They might've married sooner if her parents had approved. They were so horrible, Father refused to send me to them after she died. So I stayed with him, always traveling."

"What happened to him?"

"There was a bad fever in late summer. He nursed me through it before taking ill, so for a long time I blamed myself. When he looked at me near the end, he called me Astelyn. He thought I was Mother." She stared at a point between her mount's ears. "In a way I'm glad, because it gave him comfort."

Everything she'd had in life, gone at twelve. "I'm sorry," he said.

"It wasn't your fault."

"True, but I'm sorry I made you relive it for my own curiosity."

"No, you were right before." She exhaled and closed her eyes. "I feel much better having drained the wound. Most of the bitterness is finally gone. Maybe now it can properly heal."

She shook herself a little and looked at him brightly. "So tell me about your scar."

Her shift threw him off. "My what?"

"Your scar." She pointed above his left eye. "How did you get it? Looks recent."

"Oh, this," he said, rubbing his forehead. "Kicked by a deer that wasn't as dead as I'd thought."

"Liar." Her cheerful tone contained a trace of warning.

He supposed there was no real harm in telling her. "A collision with a Kimisar pike last month. But I do have a scar over here from a deer, like I said." He pointed to a spot over his ear. "I was thirteen."

She refused to be diverted. "You've been in many battles, then?"

"Of course," he said. "I've been with the army since I was nine. They were more like skirmishes than battles, though. Things are tense with Kimisara, but it's not all-out war." *Yet*, he added to himself.

They rode in silence for a stretch, but he knew what she was thinking.

"Yes," he said abruptly.

She jumped. "What?"

"You want to know if I've killed anyone. The answer is yes. Quite a few actually."

"Oh."

"The first was the hardest." He couldn't understand his compulsion to tell her, but neither could he resist it. "Well, it wasn't hard at the time, considering he was trying to kill me, but the way I felt after was a bit of a shock. It takes something away from you that you can never get back." He swallowed. He remembered everything—the screaming, the smell of

155

blood and fear, the feel of the other man's flesh yielding, the light fading from his eyes. "I was fifteen. I used a spear."

Pity shadowed Sage's face. "So it's gotten easier?"

He nodded. "On good days I tell myself it's easier because I'm more skilled or they would've killed me if I'd let them, I'm avenging friends, or that it's justified some other way. On bad days . . ." He stared down the road, unable to recall the face of the last man he'd killed, though it was barely weeks ago. How many other faces had he forgotten?

"You think it's because you enjoy it," she finished. "That you're a monster."

He met her eyes, terrified she saw him that way. "Yes."

Her smile was soft, reassuring. "You're not."

"How do you know that?" That she'd read him so well gave him hope she was right.

"Because you still worry about it."

38

THE THIRD MORNING of riding followed the comfortable pattern of the past two. Sage learned more about page and squire training, and Charlie told her about his grandparents who lived in Aristel. Ash's mother also came from the far east, but he said nothing other than she'd recently married.

For her part, Sage talked about catching young birds and training them with her father. When Charlie wasn't with them, she entertained Ash with stories of spying on suitors and how she and Darnessa figured out what men wanted in a wife.

"I would've expected your uncle to send you to Mistress Rodelle to find a husband, not to work for her," he commented.

"He tried last fall," she said. "He set up the interview and told me about it after. I was furious."

He grinned. "So you sabotaged it?"

She didn't answer right away. "No, I tried for my aunt's sake, since she tried so hard for me."

"Tried?" Ash said, drawing his brows down. "You say that like it was futile."

"It was. I ruined everything in a matter of minutes. Darnessa provoked me, but I certainly didn't display any maturity."

"You sound like you wish it'd gone better."

Sage puffed out her cheeks and slowly released the air before replying. "Yes and no. I could never be happy pretending to be something I'm not. I just wish being myself didn't cause so much trouble. Uncle William and I never got along, but he took care of me when I was at my very worst, and I owed him my best effort. And my best effort was awful." She smiled ruefully. "It's one thing to not want to get married. It's quite another to find out no one would ever want to marry you."

Ash raised his eyebrows. "I don't know if that's true."

"Do you know Darnessa hired me because I would compare unfavorably to other women? That men would choose girls she wanted for them when given a choice between them and me?" She hadn't thought of it in those terms since the first time. Why did it bother her now?

"*That* I find hard to believe."

"It's not difficult if you know what a man likes. Too many are distracted by looks and don't see incompatibility of spirit." Ash didn't look convinced, so she tried to explain. "Say a man prefers quieter girls of delicate build and blond hair, but what he *needs* is a more outgoing girl who will counter his antisocial tendencies. The one Darnessa wants to match him with is taller than he'd like, not very thin, and has brownish hair. So I color my hair darker, put on high shoes, and wear a dress that . . . fills me out a lot. When we meet, I chatter a lot and the other girl holds her tongue. Compared to me, she's closer to what he likes, and he picks her."

Sage left out how Darnessa called her a natural at doing exactly what made people uncomfortable.

"So you trick men into choosing what you want?" Ash sounded disgusted.

"I thought it was like that at first, but a good matchmaker gives people what they need. Most people focus on what they want. And we don't do that all the time. Some men just need to feel they're in control." Sage screwed up her face. "It's challenging and satisfying to create a match that grows into love, but I don't think I can do this forever. Someday I'll find Darnessa a new apprentice and try to find a job teaching. I'm just too young right now."

His expression became unreadable. "If the process works so well, why won't you use it yourself now and have Darnessa match you?"

"Because I'd rather make a mistake than yield my destiny to

someone else." She smiled crookedly at him. "And believe me, I'm damn good at making mistakes."

Ash turned his face away, but she could see his own smile. "I can relate to that," he said. Suddenly he squinted at a line of smoke to the southeast. With a tug of the reins, he pulled his horse off the road. Without thinking, Sage followed him, letting the other riders pass them by.

"What is it?" she asked, stomach fluttering, but he looked excited rather than worried.

He twisted around in the saddle. Casseck was nowhere to be seen—he must be patrolling away from the road. Ash made a few hand signals at the captain several yards behind them. Quinn shrugged and made a motion. *Go ahead.*

Ash looked back to Sage. "Want to see the fruit of your idea?" He leaned toward her and whispered, "If you can keep up." He kicked his horse and cantered ahead of her.

Frowning, she urged Shadow, the mare she'd ridden for the past two days, forward. Ash gestured for Charlie to follow, which he did with an eager grin. As they passed the dogs at the head of the caravan, Ash whistled to one, and it dropped in beside them.

They rode in silence for nearly an hour. Ash was alert to their surroundings and kept his crossbow ready and sword handy. Even Charlie had grabbed a spear, which made Sage uneasy, thinking of the first man Ash had killed. She felt helpless, though she wouldn't have been able to handle a weapon if she had one, but Ash wouldn't have brought her or Charlie along if he expected trouble.

After a few miles, they turned right onto a wide trail for another quarter hour. When the dog went bounding ahead out of sight, Ash halted his horse. "What is it?" she whispered, drawing up beside him.

He beamed at her like a delighted child. "Wait."

They turned back to the trees and, after a few minutes, Sage began studying Ash from the corner of her eye. In profile his nose was straight but slightly hooked, and his mouth twisted up a bit, hinting at the sense of humor he often buried. He sat straight in the saddle, with a natural grace and confidence she hadn't seen when he drove the wagon, though now she understood why. Sage knew him well enough to tell he was relaxed, but his head tilted and turned minutely in reaction to the forest noises while his eyes remained unfocused. *Seeing with your ears*, Father used to call it.

The sword at his side was plain but elegant—and deadly, no doubt, if he used it with the same grace and efficiency he had in everything else he did. She wondered if the king knew what a fine son he had. It was a shame his birth excluded him from an official place in the royal household. Was that why he had joined the army?

Sage glanced up to his face again and realized he was watching her. They were spared the awkwardness of talking by the return of the dog. As it trotted closer, she saw two small animals hanging from its mouth. Ash jerked his head at Charlie, and the boy dismounted and went to meet the hound, which dropped the animals in front of him. Charlie knelt and patted the dog and gave it a treat from his pocket, then pulled a scrap of paper from a hidden slit on the collar. Giving the dog one more scratch behind its ears, he stood and picked up what she could now see were a pair of fat rabbits.

He brought both to Ash and grinned up at Sage. Now she understood. The dogs exchanged messages with scouts farther out. Like her father, they probably used whistles that animals could hear but humans could not.

Ash set the rabbits over the pommel of his saddle and read the message before addressing Charlie. "You can mount up; I don't need to send anything back. He's probably already another half mile away." Ash tucked the note in his jacket, and Sage tried not to feel hurt he didn't show her what it said.

She could see Ash sympathized, but he had his orders. He held up the rabbits by the twine connecting them. "Do you fancy rabbit stew tonight? No onions."

Something caught her eye, and she reached for one animal's hind leg. "Caught with a snare," she said, pointing to a spot of fur that had rubbed off. Sage bent the leg experimentally. "This morning."

"Very good, Fowler." He said her name like it was a compliment. "Notice anything else?"

Sage studied one of the rabbits, trying to discern what wasn't quite right. She leaned closer and squeezed its middle. "Gutted already." Frowning, she squeezed harder, then pulled it into her lap. Her fingers found a slit cut in its belly, and she reached inside.

Ash smiled as she pulled out a glass container filled with water and sealed with a wax plug. "Our scout went back to the sick town and got us a gift."

Sage looked up in awe. "A weapon in a bottle."

39

IT TOOK LESS than an hour for them to get back to the road and the caravan. Casseck had returned from his patrol and now glared at Ash, who met his gaze without blinking. They eyed each other from several yards apart while Sage watched from her seat on Shadow, feeling uncomfortable. Finally, Casseck rode forward and past Ash to address her.

"My lady," he said. "Please don't go off like that again. Carter is so cavalier about his own safety, he neglects that of others. Captain Quinn would never forgive himself if something happened to you."

Ash kicked his horse and trotted back to speak with Quinn.

"I'm sorry," Sage said. "I didn't realize it was dangerous." She looked up at Casseck with feigned innocence. "Maybe if you told me more about our situation, I could act with prudence. Sir."

Casseck closed his eyes briefly, like he was praying for patience. "Mistress Sage, riding in the woods isn't helpful to us. You should observe the places we can't patrol."

"What, like banquets and dances and wedding plans?" she said sarcastically.

He looked at her steadily. "Yes."

She wrinkled her brow. "How could that be helpful?"

"Not all battles are fought in the field, my lady. Duke D'Amiran is an ambitious man, and tongues are looser around wine and pretty ladies."

"You called me Sage. You already know I'm not a lady," she accused him. *Dammit, Ash, do you have to tell them everything?*

Casseck smiled a little. "Then we're lucky you can play both. Servants like to talk, too." He dipped his head and urged his horse forward and away.

Ash rejoined her after reporting to the captain, but she didn't feel like talking. He didn't force conversation, though she felt him watching her sideways. As they neared their next stop, they came over a rise, and he pointed out the mountain peaks now visible on the eastern horizon. He knew she'd looked forward to seeing them for days, but she barely acknowledged the sight. When they rode into the estate, he stayed near her as they dismounted and walked to the stables.

"I would never put you in danger, Sage," he said quietly as he helped her take down her saddle.

She glanced up. There was a worry crease between his dark brows. "I know."

"What did Casseck say to you? You've barely spoken since we came back." He settled the saddle on a rail and took his mare's lead to pull her around behind Sage.

She turned around from brushing Shadow. Her eyes swept over their surroundings, but no one paid them any mind as they went about tending their own mounts. "Lieutenant Casseck asked me to keep my eyes and ears open when we get to Tegann. He said the duke is ambitious."

Ash scowled. "For someone so angry about the nondanger I put you in today, Casseck is quick to put you in harm's way himself."

"But if we're already in danger," she whispered, "what difference does it make? Especially if I can help?"

He stepped closer, forcing her to tilt her head higher to see his now-anxious expression. "I just . . . I got you into this. He should butt out."

Ash looked down on her as he had the night she confessed her name, like she was the only thing in the world—except this time there was no tray between them. Sage found her eyes drawn to his mouth, to the three short whiskers near the corner he must have missed in shaving this morning. She pulled her lips in to wet them with her tongue, anticipating . . . something.

Without warning Shadow stepped sideways, roughly knocking her against him. Ash caught her in his arms and looked up behind her, annoyance on his face. The top of Captain Quinn's dark head appeared over the horse's back. "Sorry about that, Carter," he said. "My sword clipped her accidentally."

"No harm, sir." Ash set Sage back on her feet, withdrawing his support as soon as she was upright, touching her as little as possible.

Straightening her like a vase on a shelf.

Face burning, she grabbed Shadow's reins and fled.

40

CAPTAIN HUZAR REGARDED Duke D'Amiran with a stony expression, his back to the fireplace of the Great Hall. His forearms flexed, and the duke noticed how the inked designs flowed into one another when Huzar's arms were crossed as they were now. He considered tattoos vulgar, but these had a sort of scrolling poetry to them.

"My sources say our men are sent through the south pass with no prince," Huzar said. "Why is this?"

The duke smothered a grimace. He'd have to find these spies and eliminate them. Or employ them himself—they were incredibly swift. With a cheerful smile, he gestured for the Kimisar soldier to join him at the table, which was laid with enough food for ten men, though he dined alone. "You should eat something, my friend. I know you're hungry, waiting out there."

Huzar ignored the invitation. "I will eat when my people can eat."

D'Amiran sat back in his ornate wooden chair and wiped his fingers on a linen napkin. "The truth of the matter is, I've discovered Prince Robert is on his way here, with the escort."

"And you did not tell us."

"I'm telling you now. I didn't want you inspired to take him sooner than we'd planned." He sipped his wine without taking his eyes off Huzar.

"Why should we not take him? He is the goal. The earlier the better."

"Earlier is *not* better—it could ruin everything. Nothing has changed other than the time he's in our grasp, and it's an advantageous change."

He set the goblet on the table. "I instructed my brother to have your men create as much havoc as they like on the eastern side of the mountains. They may keep anything they manage to carry back across the pass here—it's of no concern to me."

Huzar's face relaxed slightly, but he said nothing.

"The prince and the others will be here in two days. If your men have done their job—"

"They have," Huzar interrupted.

"—then there's nothing to be troubled over." D'Amiran clenched his jaw. "We'll hold the prince and signal when we're ready to give him to you. In the meantime, you shouldn't come here again until we call for you."

A servant set a large, steaming dish of sliced beef on the table. Huzar's stomach growled audibly. "I do not like the calendar. Why do you wait so many days before acting?"

D'Amiran leaned forward and scooped a pile of the meat onto a serving fork, dripping bloody juice across the table as he brought it to his plate. "Patience, my friend. Moving against the crown is no small matter. I must prove to my allies I have the ability to win, and I must know where the Demoran army is before I march." He stabbed the serving fork into the meat and left it upright. "Consider this: we could've slaughtered this cow months earlier, but we would've had much less to eat. Waiting until the time was right allows us to feed many more."

Huzar stared at the food. "More meat is no good if many starve waiting for it."

"Consider also that starving in solidarity does not help you perform your tasks." The duke put a forkful in his mouth and chewed deliberately.

The Kimisar captain swallowed. "Your points are taken. We shall wait. For now."

"I'll have my cook prepare a gift for you to take back to your men." D'Amiran smiled benevolently. "For your strength and patience."

Huzar nodded once. "We will need both."

41

MEN WONDERED WHY women loved embroidering, but Quinn suspected it gave them an excuse to focus away from a conversation, to avoid direct looks, as the matchmaker did now. He clasped his hands behind his back and waited for her to begin.

"Things are going well for Ash Carter," she said from her seat by the fire. "Though I didn't appreciate it when he disappeared with her for over two hours, attending page or not."

Quinn shrugged in what he hoped was an indifferent manner. "She was never in any danger. We needed to cement her trust after keeping so much from her."

"And that's the real reason?" she asked, pursing her lips.

"I'm not sure what you're implying. I felt obligated to let her see something important. That she follows Ash's lead is critical."

Mistress Rodelle continued speaking to her work. "I need you to promise me something."

His shoulders tensed with the urge to cross his arms. "I can't make blind promises."

"This is a simple request for Sage's safety." The matchmaker's evasiveness dropped as she looked up. "If she's to be under your command, you must assure me that as with any other soldier, she's able to defend herself."

His eyebrows shot up. "You want me to arm her and teach her to fight?"

The wooden hoop lowered several inches. This was important to her. "I don't want her helpless. It's unfair to make her risk her life without some knowledge in how to defend it."

Quinn closed his eyes and pinched the bridge of his nose. "It's not a pleasant thought, teaching someone like her to kill."

"The alternative is worse, Captain," she reminded him.

"She'll have to trust Ash more than she currently does."

The matchmaker looked down at her work again. "I think you know exactly how to do that."

42

SAGE'S THOUGHTS SWIRLED and tumbled like the leaves whipped about by wind from the coming rain. Every time she thought they'd settled, she caught sight of Ash, and her stomach fluttered. Until last night, she hadn't realized how rarely Ash touched her. When the horse knocked her into his arms, she'd felt the briefest . . . something.

But he hadn't even looked at her. And that something had vanished like smoke.

Ash had greeted her with his usual "Good morning, friend," and shortly after setting out, he'd left her alone with Charlie. Sage didn't blame him for being too busy to ride with her, but even with Charlie by her side she felt an overwhelming sense of loneliness. She told herself it was because Darnessa had said she had to ride in the wagon tomorrow since they would be arriving at Tegann and she had work to do. Even if doing so would be helpful to Ash and the soldiers, she didn't look forward to it.

The train of wagons drew to a halt, and Sage looked around. Ahead she could see a haze sweeping toward them over the hills. The soldiers began lashing down the wagon covers and pulling out rain cloaks. Ash brought his brown mare up on her right. "The rain will start soon," he said. "Captain wants you and Charlie to ride in the cart for the rest of the day. There's no reason for either of you to get soaked." He dismounted and raised his hands to her.

"I can get down myself," she said, irritated. Nobody ever offered to help Charlie on and off his horse, and he was only nine.

"I know you can," Ash replied. "But you're in pain, I can see it. You're not used to riding this much." He continued holding his arms out.

Three days of riding had caught up to her. Sage tried not to flush at the idea of him noticing which of her parts were sore. With a resigned sigh, she gingerly swung her left leg over the pommel to dismount facing him. She reached for his hands, but they slipped past her arms to grab her waist. He lowered her to the ground between the two horses, making no move to release his hold. Sage became acutely aware no one could see them.

Ash looked down on her. "Better?" he asked softly. She nodded and reached for the bridle, but his hands tightened, and she looked back up, startled. He leaned closer. "You have to play the lady again tomorrow, don't you?" he whispered.

The searching look in his dark eyes terrified her, and she tried to cover with a flippant response. "I'm afraid so. With a dress and everything."

He ignored her tone. "I'll miss our talks."

Heat seeped into her cheeks. "Maybe when we leave Tegann, I can ride again."

"I was hoping we could spend some time together in Tennegol. I could introduce you to my father. Maybe find you a teaching position there."

"I don't—I didn't . . ." She took a deep breath to steady herself. He was so close, he filled all her senses. The scent of his leather jacket mingled with the evergreen shaving lather he used. "I don't want special favors from you."

"I know. You're one of the very few who doesn't. You have no idea how that feels."

Her eyes drifted to his mouth. He hadn't missed a spot this morning. She licked her lips nervously. "Actually, I do. No one pays attention to me unless they want something."

"Which is why you prefer the company of children."

Sage blinked. "Generally, yes."

"And my company?" The gentle pressure of his fingers pulled her closer.

Panic welled in her throat, and Sage gripped his sleeves to keep herself upright, realizing only then that her arms rested over his. She locked her knees in place and forced herself to toss her head and lift her hands away. "Has been pleasant."

"*Pleasant.*" Ash dropped his hands and stepped back, his mouth pulling into a thin line. He shook his head and made a quiet noise of disgust. "I suppose I shouldn't have expected anything more."

He snatched the reins of the two horses and stormed away without a backward glance.

❧

Sage rode in the equipment wagon, trying to make out the shapes of the riders behind them. The rain pelting the canvas cover was too loud for any conversation with Charlie, who stretched out beside her and dozed against his saddle, and she felt grateful to be alone with her thoughts.

Ash had been right when he said she preferred to be around children. Their motives were simple and pure. They trusted completely, loved and wept without restraint, hated without guilt—things she hadn't done in the years since Father died.

Darnessa used her. Uncle William used her. Aunt Braelaura tried to make her into something she could never be. Clare needed her strength and guidance.

But Ash wanted things *for* her.

He wanted to make her happy, tried to include her when he could, offered to arrange something he knew she'd like, but would never ask for. And when he'd learned she wasn't a bride, he wanted to know if she would still be getting married. Why? He could have anyone he wanted. Until an hour ago, she never would've considered he might want *her*.

But then she'd panicked and ruined it. Ash wasn't the type to give up easily, though. Would he try again?

Did she want to say the right things if he did? Sage closed her eyes and remembered the way he looked at her, the way it felt when he held her waist and leaned close.

Yes. She did.

❧

Sage dozed off next to Charlie and napped through the afternoon until the next stop. She woke to Ash unlatching the rear gate of the wagon, and she struggled to sit up and catch his eye. He focused on Charlie, pulling the sleeping boy to the edge by the crate he lay across while she rubbed her face and prepared to say what she'd rehearsed.

Ash, I should have thanked you for your offer; it just took me by surprise . . .

He never looked in her direction, though, just hefted the boy into his arms and strode away without speaking. She was left to climb out on her own and follow the ladies to their rooms. At the last second, she remembered how she was dressed and went back to the baggage cart and pulled her heavy trunk onto her back.

43

LORD FASHELL HAD them for only one night, but he went all out, treating his guests to a full banquet. He'd even produced a quartet of musicians, which meant there would be dancing afterward, too. Sage struggled through dinner. She was seated far from Clare and next to the younger sons of the household. Like most men she met, they spent the evening trying to impress her with their accomplishments and connections. Belatedly she remembered she had a job to do, and her mind automatically began tallying what she would write down later, but she still listened with only one ear.

"As the nearest estate to Tegann, we have a great responsibility to Duke D'Amiran," the one on her right said.

Sage's head whipped around at the mention of the duke. "Oh really?"

The young man—green eyes, left-handed, sunburned, one inch taller than her, callused hands, well-used dagger at his side . . . what was his name? . . . Bartholomew—continued, "Almost everyone going to or from the capital stays here. Right now the pass is still closed to wagons, so there will be a backup of travelers. You ladies have places reserved at Tegann, of course, so you'll wait there until it's clear, but soon the fortress will be crowded. Some may turn back to us if the rains take too long to arrive."

"Father received several letters today, begging his hospitality in advance," put in the brother on her left (blue eyes, right-handed, missing half his left pinky). "Fortunately, he can afford it."

She widened her eyes. "You have an advantage over me! I have no idea who'll be there."

The brothers rattled off names, many of which she recognized but made little sense. Few had enough property to be considered seriously for a Concordium match, and most had something in common she couldn't put her thumb on. As she'd never met any of them, however, she encouraged the young men to describe each one, laughing and commenting on how witty their impressions were.

When the last plates were cleared away, both brothers asked her to dance, and she forced them to flip a coin to see who would get the favor first. As Bartholomew led her away, she cast a disappointed pout to the other—what was his name?—to placate him. She was pleased to see Lieutenant Gramwell had taken Clare to a quiet corner, reminding Sage she still needed to speak with Darnessa, and she grimaced. The matchmaker would probably not be happy over what was developing. Sage was surprised she hadn't already noticed.

"Is something wrong, my lady?" her partner asked.

"Oh, no," Sage said with false brightness. "I just remembered I tore the hem of my blue dress getting down from that wretched wagon, and I forgot to tell the maid to fix it." She made a sulky face. "I don't think it will be repaired in time for the first banquet at Tegann, and it's my best color."

"Now I'm disappointed, Lady Sagerra, that I shan't see it, if it looks even lovelier than this one."

She blushed. "Don't tease me; you know I'll be married in just a few weeks." Sage tilted her chin down and looked up at him through her long lashes. "I just hope he dances as well as you," she said a little breathlessly, leaning into him. He beamed and held her tighter.

As her partner spun her around, Sage caught Lieutenant Casseck watching her with an amused smile. Her own expression faltered. What if he told Ash about her flirting? Would Ash think it was a message that his feelings didn't matter to her? Would he suspect her motives if she tried to reverse what happened this morning?

Why did this have to be so complicated?

∽✖✑

Sage flipped through her ledger, adding notes from that night's conversations. A name mentioned caught her eye, and she stopped to read about him. Apparently the lord sounded familiar because he'd proposed to one of the brides last winter. She paused again when she saw another had proposed to Lady Jacqueline. Both were refused, of course. The coincidence struck her, though, and she turned to the pages where she'd summarized the information on the Concordium brides.

She frowned as she studied matches they'd turned down, or rather, their parents had turned down on their behalf. Girls with a chance of making it into the Concordium usually declined or delayed suitors in the year before the conference. Interestingly, not a single proposal had been presented by a matchmaker, but as Darnessa had complained last month, there were quite a few marriages that *had* gone through, of late.

Sage tore a blank page from the back of the ledger and tallied the recent matches between families from Crescera and Tasmet, finding and writing down fourteen—all arranged by the D'Amirans. Why? And why so many? Such unions weren't unheard of—they usually brought some advantage the families wanted, but fourteen in two years was well outside normal. She went back through the pages and copied the dowries next to the pairings.

Eight involved troops and arms, ostensibly to help protect from Kimisar raids, totaling over 1,800 men. Two were large sums of gold. Three traded massive amounts of wheat and other grains. The remainder was a combination of weapons, gold, and food. In total, it was enough for a small army.

The D'Amirans were building an army.

Sage drew a line down the middle of her page and listed the women with them on the other side. Next to each name she detailed the assets she knew by heart: money, militias, property, connections. Every lady was a prize. It was why Darnessa had chosen them.

And tomorrow, like flies in a web, they'd be trapped at Tegann and surrounded by spiders.

She had to tell Captain Quinn.

⚜

Casseck and Gramwell passed Sage and entered a room at the end of the barracks passage, but she waited until Ash appeared, headed for the same room before reaching out of the shadows. He grabbed her hand and twisted it back sharply before releasing it with a scowl. "Don't ever sneak up on me like that. I could've broken your wrist."

"I'm sorry," she gasped. Spirit above, she'd forgotten about how upset he was with her over this morning. Would he even listen? "I need to talk to Captain Quinn."

His scowl grew darker. "Why?"

"It's not a simple matter," she insisted. "And we can't be overheard."

Ash pressed his lips together. "Fine." He took her arm and led her back down the passage to a room she assumed he shared with another soldier. He grabbed a candle and stepped back out to light it on the torch outside, then closed and bolted the door behind him. He put his hands on his hips. "It's risky for you to come down here."

"You think a fowler doesn't know how to move through the shadows?" She didn't wait for his response. "First, I want to know why you won't take me to Captain Quinn."

"His speaking to you is dangerous. If people see it, they might think you know what we're up to. Tomorrow I'll be driving a wagon again. You can order me around as needed to speak to us, or go through Charlie." He paused. "I've answered you as best I can; now please tell me what is so important it couldn't wait until tomorrow."

"I know what's going on." Sage pulled out the folded parchment. "Tonight I learned who's been traveling this area and will be at Tegann when we are." She rapidly described what she'd written down. "Look at all these marriages. *Look* at the dowries that went with them. It's enough to build a small army. And here"—she pointed to the other column—"is what we have with us now."

He looked at her rather than the paper she tried to show him. "And what is your conclusion?"

She took a deep breath. "I think the duke is planning to take the brides and force their families to support him. By binding all the wealth of Crescera to his allies, he has an army and the resources to arm and feed it. He can take everything west of the Catrix Mountains with what he already has and keep it with what our women provide. Those men surrounding us, the one hundred and thirty I heard you talking about, are meant to make sure we get to Tegann and trap us there. Every noble with enough power to stop the duke will be at the Concordium, and it will be all over before they realize we haven't shown up."

"And you pieced all of this together on your own?" he asked slowly.

"Yes." Sage suddenly doubted herself. She lowered the page, embarrassed. Ash took the paper and scanned it silently. When she dared to look up again, she found him staring at her with what she could only identify as fear.

"Tell me," he whispered hoarsely. "Tell me right now that you were always on our side, that this isn't switching of loyalties."

Her eyes burned with tears. "You *still* doubt me?"

"Say it, Sage."

"I swear it!" she nearly shouted. "And you can go to hell if you don't believe me!" She turned to leave, but he caught her arm.

"I'm sorry, Sage. Don't go, please." He pulled her closer by her elbows, but not as close as he had that morning—she'd ruined that. "It's just . . . Sweet Spirit, this changes everything."

"So I'm right?"

"We'll discuss it tonight, but, yes, I think you're right."

"What can you do?"

"I don't know, but this is worse than we ever imagined." The seriousness of his voice frightened her, and she began to tremble. His hands slid up to her shoulders. "Thanks to you, however, we may be able to even the odds a bit."

"Me?"

"Yes, you," he said. "We have your weapon, and if it works, there will be a lot fewer enemies able to fight. We'll need time, though. It takes about three days for the sickness to take effect."

"Please let me help," she begged. "I'll go mad if you don't give me something to do."

Ash sighed. "Sage, you aren't a lady. Don't you understand what that means? If the duke finds out, you're worthless to him, except for information. He's already planning treason; do you think he'd hesitate to torture you? We haven't kept you in the dark because we don't trust you or think you capable, but to protect you. In that respect, I wish to the Spirit you were a lady. It would be easier to keep you safe."

She dropped her eyes. "I feel foolish now."

"Don't. We'd be both blind and helpless without you. That is truth." He chucked her chin gently. "Your ability to figure things out on your own is unparalleled, but also aggravating. You know too much."

Sage took a deep breath and let it out, resigned. "I will accept you cannot tell me everything now, if you promise to tell me what you can, and everything else later."

"I swear it."

Her shoulders slumped in defeat. "Now what? Play the lady? Flirt and keep my ears open?"

Ash nodded. "Yes. Casseck already told me how good you are." His smile was a little shaky. "And I have a real job for you, if you're interested."

44

THE ROOM WAS silent as they stared at Starling's parchment.

"It's useless to question what we would've done if we'd known," Quinn said to himself as much as everyone else. "Focus on what we can do now."

"Our list of options is pretty short," Rob said bitterly. "We'll be outnumbered seven to one, and that doesn't count the Kimisar. I'm the only one worth keeping. You're all dead and you know it."

Quinn folded up the paper and tucked it into his jacket. Where the army came from wasn't as relevant as how to stop it. "Look here," he said, sweeping a finger over the map. "We've been tracking these squads, thinking they were scattered randomly as they traveled east, but as more have been added, it's started to look like a circle."

With a charcoal pencil he traced every day's summary of positions relative to their own progress along the Tegann Road.

"It's a wheel," said Cass, "with us at the center. It's to isolate us from communication and keep us from escaping."

Quinn nodded. "Right. But since we were headed to Tegann, there was no reason to act unless we deviated. We were already doing what they wanted."

Rob grunted. "I feel so much better."

"*But.*" Quinn raised a finger. "There's a hole." He pointed to a spot on the north side of the circle. "There was never anyone here."

Rob brightened. "That squad we eliminated last month was probably supposed to be there."

"That's my thought, too," said Quinn. "So we might have a way out." He stood up straight. "Who's getting the sketch from our forward picket in the morning?" Gramwell raised his hand. "Let him know we'll keep up patrols at the fortress as long as it's practical, but we can't count on being able to talk to our scouts after tomorrow."

"What should he tell the other scouts?" asked Gramwell, bending down to write notes.

Quinn considered. "Send the north and west pickets to watch that gap. Have them signal if it closes. South can join east at the pass." Gramwell nodded and made more notes.

"When do we use our bottled weapon?" asked Robert.

"I want it in Tegann's cistern by the second night. There's a banquet planned then, and that'll be a good diversion."

"So who'll scout it?" said Casseck. "The quartermaster? It's logical for him to be concerned with where the water comes from."

"We're sending Starling."

Cass exchanged glances with Rob. "Is that wise?"

"It makes perfect sense," said Quinn. "She can take a tour and ask lots of foolish and innocent questions, and if she bats her eyelashes, all of them will be answered."

Rob frowned. "I think you're overestimating her charms."

"You didn't see her tonight," said Cass. "She had two young men wrapped around her finger in a matter of minutes, and I don't even think she was trying."

Quinn bristled. "Is that supposed to be a comment on something else?"

"Not at all," said Casseck mildly. "Just supporting your decision."

Quinn almost wished Cass had tried to talk him out of it, but it was too late anyway; she'd already told Mouse she'd do it. "Let's move on to other ways to make a stand. Whether or not the sickness works, and whether or not it works in time, we have to find ways to take out as many of D'Amiran's people as possible."

"Poison?" suggested Gramwell.

"I doubt we can get anything before tomorrow," said Quinn. "We'll have to watch for it in our own food, however. Make sure everyone knows."

"How about a fire?" said Casseck. "Tegann Fortress is almost entirely granite, which will give us safe places to hide. At the very least it causes panic and burns supplies."

Quinn nodded. "I like it. How much oil do we have?"

Cass shook his head. "Unfortunately, not much. We can pinch some at Tegann."

"Alcohol," suggested Rob.

"All we have is wine and ale," said Gramwell. "They aren't strong enough to burn."

"No," replied Rob with a grin. "But we do have the Stiller brothers."

The prince ducked out of the meeting a few seconds later and returned shortly with Privates Gregory and Tim Stiller, who came from a large family of Brewers and Stillers in northern Crescera. They drove equipment wagons and were steady, reliable soldiers, despite having been disciplined several times for distilling their own liquor in camp. The captain's sudden interest in their skill startled them.

"How much pure alcohol can you get from, say, a barrel of wine?" he asked.

The brothers exchanged nervous glances before Tim answered. "Maybe a fourth of a barrel, sir, but much of that is useless."

"Useless?"

"Poisonous, sir," clarified Gregory. "Not good for drinking and highly flammable."

"More flammable than drinkin' spirits?"

"Yes, sir." Gregory nodded. "Burns real sneaky, too. The flames are damn near invisible. Drinkable spirits burn much brighter. It's how we test it."

"Funny you should mention that," Quinn said, tapping his fingers on the table. "Starting fires is exactly what I want it for. How long does it take to distill?"

"A barrel's worth, sir? Six hours, minimum."

"Excellent. What would you need to build a distiller tonight?"

The brothers looked at each other again, reluctant to speak. "We, ah, don't need anythin' we don't already have on hand, sir," Tim finally answered.

Quinn eyed them. "All right, then. Get on it."

45

SAGE TOOK CARE with her appearance the next morning, making a true effort to blend in with the ladies. Ash watched from his seat on the wagon as one of the young men from the night before, Bartholomew, came to see her off. Casseck walked past and punched Ash on the foot, and the sergeant scowled and kicked back at his friend. Remembering what Ash had said last night, Sage turned a dazzling smile on the young man holding her hand. He helped her into the wagon, and she gave her traveling companions a smug look. *Talk about* that, she thought.

Had it not been for the gray curtain of fog wrapping the landscape, Sage might have enjoyed the scenery. But the hours dragged on as the wagon bounced and sloshed through the mud. Her dress became spattered and damp from choosing the seat closest to the rear gate, but she could see Ash driving the wagon behind her. A few times he caught her eye and smiled.

The weapons were out again, and the tension in the soldiers was worse than the day they reached Underwood. Sage twisted her hands in her lap until the raw spots from holding reins began to bleed. If she'd realized what was happening sooner, would they have had time to make a plan to escape? She couldn't shake the feeling that it was her fault they were now walking—willingly—into the snare because there was no alternative. She looked back to Ash, feeling guilty, and he shook his head a little as though he knew what she was thinking.

Whether or not it was her fault, she would do anything now to help him—them.

The weather made for slow going, and they arrived at Tegann at sunset—over two hours later than they'd hoped. Sconces set around the fortress spread their light in wide, hazy orbs. Their host, Duke D'Amiran, approached the matchmaker in the rapidly fading light and offered to have supper trays and hot water brought to the ladies' rooms so they wouldn't have to dress up and wait to eat. Sage allowed Lieutenant Gramwell to help her down from the wagon and looked around, hoping to observe something, anything, that might be useful. But she could barely make out the shapes of the walls or buildings. Only the inner gate could be distinguished, looking like the mouth of a creature ready to devour them whole. She shuddered.

As befitted her rank among the women, Sage waited until all were ahead of her before following on to the guest wing off the main keep. Ash walked behind her, carrying her trunk. When he set it down in her room, she moved to help him scoot it against the foot of the bed. He leaned close to whisper, "The cistern is in the southwest quadrant if you want to get lost there tomorrow."

Sage glanced back to the open door behind them. "Can you do me a favor and wash my clothes?" He looked at her in confusion, and she clarified, "My breeches and such. They're all muddy from riding."

He nodded, and she quickly opened the trunk and pulled out a bundle from near the bottom. Ash took it and winked. "They won't smell nearly as nice, though."

"That's just as well," she said, relieved he seemed to have forgiven yesterday's slight.

Clare entered as he left, followed by a servant carrying a basin of hot water. Sage's friend wore a dreamy expression, and if she wasn't mistaken, the shape of a folded square of parchment could be seen tucked under her bodice. Sage turned away with a smile and set about fixing them a pot of tea.

Once they were alone, sharing another cup after dinner, Clare confessed to Sage how she felt about Lieutenant Gramwell, how he returned her affections, and showed Sage a letter he'd written. None of it surprised Sage, of course, but she counseled caution and discretion.

"I know I promised I'd stop your matching—and I fully intend to do so—but you need to be careful. You don't know him very well, and doing things to get to know him better isn't good for your reputation. Honestly, I think you suit each other well, but he can't marry for another three years."

"Why does the army have that rule?" asked Clare.

"Life as a young officer is difficult and dangerous, and marriage and children are distractions they can't afford. By twenty-four, they've advanced to captain or are flushed out of the army." Sage shrugged. "It's been the law for over a hundred years, and no one remembers why it started. Personally, I think it was designed to keep nobles, especially younger sons who would only join to increase their match appeal, out of the ranks. Genuine commitment to the army is critical."

Clare pondered for a few moments. "I'll be eighteen then, but that doesn't seem so bad."

"And it would be a man of your choice, rather than being sold off like a cow."

Her friend eyed her curiously. "You don't like matchmaking very much. Why are you Mistress Rodelle's apprentice?"

"It's a long story, but no one would ever want to marry me—so I must make my own way. Darnessa offered me a job, and I took it."

That surprised Clare. "Why would no one marry you? Did the matchmaker tell you that?"

"I spent my childhood climbing trees and catching birds and wearing breeches," said Sage. "If there's a time when ladylike behavior can be instilled in a girl, it must have passed me by long ago, because my aunt tried for almost four years and got nowhere."

"You never lack for dance partners or dinner conversation," Clare said.

"Yes, but that's an act," Sage insisted. "I'm really just collecting information for future matches."

Clare looked doubtful. "I've noticed how some of the soldiers look at you. Especially that darker one you spend time with."

Sage dismissed the idea with a wave of her hand. "For most I'm a curiosity, just as you would stare at a boy in a dress. I've been riding and talking with them because they asked for my assistance."

"In what?" asked Clare.

Sage searched for a vague but believable reason. "They like to know the layout of the places we stay, mostly. They can't go into the ladies' quarters, but if they're to protect us, they ought to know if there are back doors and windows, that sort of thing."

"Oh, I guess that makes sense."

"Speaking of," said Sage. "Would you like to take a tour of the fortress with me tomorrow?"

∽✣∾

The next morning, Sage and Clare dressed for weekly chapel services with an eye toward catching the attention of someone who could be helpful. The duke's steward's son presented the perfect opportunity when he poured their tea at breakfast and asked if there was anything he could do to make their stay more comfortable. Sage was caught with her mouth full of toast and missed her chance to get his immediate attention, but Clare quickly claimed it.

With her fingers lightly touching his arm, the girl turned the full force of her large brown eyes on the young man and asked if there was anyone who could show them around after breakfast. "My friend and I have never seen a place so . . . magnificent."

Her victim nodded as though hypnotized and offered his humble services. Clare drew her lips back in a smile that glowed across her creamy cheeks, and slowly blinked her long lashes. "I look forward to it, sir."

He bowed and stumbled the rest of the way around the table, filling teacups in a daze. Sage blinked in admiration of her friend, feeling like an amateur in the presence of a master. Lieutenant Gramwell never had a chance.

186

Fortunately for them, Thomas Stewart was particularly proud of the fortress's water supply and led them straight to it when asked. There was no simple access, though. The cistern was two levels below ground and was enclosed on top and drained from valves in the bottom.

"It's naturally replenished by rain, so Tegann is impervious to siege," he bragged. "It's a little low right now, but the spring rains will arrive very soon. They'll also clear the pass for your journey."

But how to get in? They couldn't just pour the bottled water down a drain on the bailey wall.

"How do you maintain it?" Sage asked.

"Every summer we drain and clean the cistern." He pointed to a grate in the floor. "Boys climb inside and scrub the walls, and Tegann uses the river for water during that time."

Clare made a horrified face. "There must be months' worth of dirt and leaves and perhaps animals inside!"

"Oh, but my lady, we have a way to prevent that." He led them to a servants' passageway and a wooden hatch over a raised stone rectangle. "Anything that goes down the drains passes through this shaft."

Thomas opened the lid and pulled up the rope leading down. After a few feet, a mesh basket appeared. A couple small stones and dead leaves lay in the bottom. "This sits at the bottom by a screen and catches anything that can't pass through. We clean the basket and screen regularly."

Clare gushed over the clever design while Sage mused. It would be difficult to get in, but maybe not impossible. "How far are we from the top of the cistern?" Sage asked.

He lowered the basket back down the void. "It's about twenty-five feet from here. There's also an overflow drain into the sewer."

Clare peered down the black hole. "This is wider than I would've thought. Is the drain this wide, too?"

"It has to be, my lady. When we clean the cistern, one unlucky boy climbs through and scrubs this last section."

Clare shuddered. "It sounds dark and slimy and cramped."

"So it is, but it must be done on occasion for the safety and comfort of ladies such as yourself."

46

SAGE SHOOED CLARE off to walk in the garden with Lieutenant Gramwell while she drew diagrams of the cistern and the ways to get to the maintenance shaft. Darnessa knocked on the door, and Sage hid her work from the matchmaker and prepared to make excuses, but Darnessa didn't ask what she was doing.

"We need to talk about Clare," the matchmaker said.

Sage winced and nodded.

"She's getting far too much attention from that officer. I think it's a good match personally, but she's a Concordium bride. She needs to break it off."

"We can't match her," Sage protested. "She's only fifteen. Her father lied to get her in."

"I know," said Darnessa. "But I wanted to get her off his hands. It's better to let her marry too young than wed her to such a man as he gave her sister to."

"She told me about it the night of the banquet at Underwood. She cried herself sick." Sage grimaced with guilt. "I let Gramwell walk her through the garden, which is when this all started, though honestly it wasn't my intention. He was just strong and kind right when she needed it."

Darnessa knew as well as she did that Gramwell had to wait three more years to marry. She made a thoughtful sound. "Maybe we can find something wrong with her that will make her less desirable, and she can 'settle' for Gramwell. Remind me: Where is his family from?"

"Up north." Sage pulled her ledger closer and flipped to the page on Gramwell. "His father was ambassador to Reyan, but just retired to Key Loreda, where he's from."

The matchmaker brightened. "An ambassador's son! That works in his favor, and Key Loreda has a tradition where a bride lives with her future in-laws for a year before marriage. The couple is bound as if they were wed, but it's considered a mother-in-law's duty to train her son's wife."

Sage made a face. "Sounds awful."

"Not if your mother-in-law likes you, and Clare's a sweet thing. I can't imagine her not meeting any reasonable woman's approval. We'll see what we can do for her." Darnessa scanned the other pages on the officers and paused. "You don't think very highly of young Captain Quinn. Did he snub you somehow?"

"I've never spoken to him," Sage admitted. "I've just seen what he demands of others."

"A commander's job is to be demanding."

"Yet I never see him get his hands dirty," Sage protested. "I have more respect for someone if they don't make everyone else do everything for them."

The matchmaker shrugged and tapped the opposite page for Ash Carter. "Ironic you have so little on a man you've spent so much time with."

"I know him, so I'm less likely to forget." Sage took the book back. "Meanwhile, there are others to detail."

"I see you also discovered who he is."

Sage glanced up with a scowl. "You could've saved me some embarrassment by telling me."

Darnessa chuckled a little. "Honestly, I wasn't sure. I didn't want to taint your investigation."

"Hmph." Sage went back to her book. She wanted to finish her diagram.

"We could try matching him at the Concordium."

"I'll ask him," Sage said, trying to sound indifferent. She had no such intention. "I don't think he's interested, though. Too busy soldiering."

"If you say so." Darnessa stood to leave.

"Oh, by the way," called Sage. The matchmaker paused to look back. "Don't ask me for details, but don't drink any of the water after tonight. It may not be safe unless it's boiled. Tell the maids and ladies as best you see fit."

Darnessa only nodded, making Sage suspect Quinn was sharing things with the matchmaker that he refused to let Ash tell her.

Once satisfied with her summary of the cistern and other relevant information, Sage folded the two pages, tucked them under her bodice, and went to lunch. Servants were preparing the Great Hall for that evening's banquet, so a casual noon meal was set up on long tables in the garden next to the hall, but no soldiers were present.

Her information was critical, and she expected someone to check on her soon. The garden seemed a logical spot to find her, so she filled a plate and picked a bench under a tree to eat and wait. But as time passed, she wondered if maybe the library would be better. Sage was just about to give up when she spotted Charlie collecting dishes from other ladies. She gave him a genuine smile as he approached. "Hello, Little Soldier."

The page's grin melted her. He was such a sweet, eager boy—nothing like his proud brother.

"My lady, I can take your dish for you." Catching his meaning, she nodded and slipped her papers from their hiding place and tucked them under her plate before handing it to him.

She watched Charlie head back to the kitchen, wondering if the boy knew he likely held the fate of the nation between two dirty plates.

47

"THOUGHTS?" QUINN ASKED.

Casseck studied the diagram of the cistern. "Her drawings are better than Ash's."

"I won't tell him you said that."

"Who's going to the banquet, you or me?" asked Robert.

"Me," said Quinn. "I'll make a brief appearance so D'Amiran sees me."

Rob brightened. "Does that mean I get to take Charlie to the cistern?"

Quinn shook his head. "No. He's my brother and my responsibility. You're lying low from here on out. And you're back to being Lieutenant Ryan Bathgate if anyone asks, but I'd rather no one ask. If we smuggle you out or hide you later, it'll be easier if you were a ghost in the first place."

Robert sighed dramatically. "It was nice while it lasted. Maybe I'll buck for promotion after all."

Quinn rolled his eyes. "You have a long way to go. Questions?" He glanced around again. "Very well. Go shine up for dinner."

❦

Charlie crept through the dark hallway with his brother beside him. At the first sign of anyone, he was prepared to act like a page leading his drunken master to bed, but the passage was deserted. All the servants must be at the feast.

They found a rectangular wooden hatch right where Lady Sagerra's notes had described. The captain lifted the lid and pulled the rope up, counting the distance. Five feet to the basket. He pulled it out, set it aside, and glanced down at him. "We'll try feetfirst. I think there should be enough room for you to move around."

Charlie peered into the blackness. He wasn't afraid of the dark, but this wasn't just night—there would be no moon and stars to see by. His brother had said boys climbed down to clean it, so it must be safe. And Alex—his captain—needed him. This was something only he could do.

Before his courage could fail him, Charlie settled himself on the edge of the hole and looked back up, patting the bottles tucked in his vest. He raised his hands and whispered, "Ready."

Alex gripped his arms and lowered him down. Then the cover was replaced, and the smell of damp and stone wrapped around Charlie like a blanket.

He shimmied down to where the shaft met the horizontal drain. Which direction led to the cistern? He groped around until his fingers brushed across a wire mesh, and he followed it to its framed edge. It must be on the cistern side. He felt along the frame, trying to determine what held the screen in place. Charlie almost laughed with relief when he realized it was held simply by hooks on the sides. He eased the screen up, leaving just enough room to squeeze through.

Bending and twisting, he maneuvered his legs and body into the other horizontal shaft until he was far enough in to slide down the right side headfirst. From the feel of them, the walls were normally slimy, but with no rain they'd dried up. He controlled his descent easily, occasionally scraping his knuckles on the stones. The total darkness was unnerving. He couldn't even see his hands right in front of him.

Charlie went slowly, worried the noises might echo up and attract attention, until he came to an edge. There was an overflow drain along here somewhere, so he waved his arms around, trying to tell whether it was that or the cistern. A bit of heavy grit fell over the edge and splashed below. This was the right place.

He pulled his elbows in and slipped the first bottle from his vest.

From his sleeve he produced a thin metal rod and pierced the wax seal. His hands shook as he poured the water out, spilling a bit on his fingers. When it was finally drained, he repeated the process with the second bottle. By the time he was done, he was dripping with sweat. He wiped his face with his damp sleeve before tucking the bottles away again.

His mission complete, Charlie inched backward until he was over the trench. He rotated his body in the small space and replaced the mesh screen. After he gave a soft whistle, his brother's anxious face appeared above. Alex's hands grasped him and pulled him up.

His brother set Charlie on his feet. After the darkness of the cistern, the hallway seemed bright. "Done?" the captain asked quietly.

Charlie was heady with a sense of accomplishment. "Done, sir." He licked the sweat around his mouth and saluted before wiping his forehead on his sleeve.

Alex exhaled heavily and pulled him into an embrace. The gesture surprised Charlie, but he hugged his brother back, grinning. He couldn't wait to tell the other boys back at camp he was a real spy.

48

SAGE HAD CURLED and colored her hair a bit red with one of the tonics in her trunk, feeling overdone but thinking it would help her blend in better with the ladies. She'd even stuffed the top of her dress and made an effort to cover her freckles with powder. While she and Clare gathered with the others outside the Great Hall, Lieutenant Casseck walked around the ladies, scanning faces.

Clare fidgeted beside her. "Would it be rude to ask His Grace about Sophia? I haven't heard from her in months."

"Perfectly appropriate," Sage assured her. "His brother is married to your sister. That makes you family." Silently she wondered what kind of influence Ash could wield to keep Sophia safe. Being married to a traitor wasn't her fault.

Casseck passed them for the third time and stopped in his tracks. "Lady Sagerra?" he asked.

Sage smiled and held out her hand. "Good evening, Lieutenant."

Casseck kissed her hand and then Clare's. Any of the other ladies would've thrown a fit at being acknowledged second to Sage, but Clare didn't mind. At that moment Darnessa appeared and whisked Clare to the front of the line to be presented to the duke, who stood just inside the main doors receiving guests, and Sage was left alone with Casseck.

"Is it too presumptuous to hope for a dance tonight, my lady?" Casseck asked.

Sage hesitated. Ash wouldn't be here tonight, but surely he would hear about it from the other soldiers. She had to dance with somebody, however, and she rather liked Casseck.

As if reading her mind, the lieutenant smiled. "I'm sure Sergeant Carter won't mind."

Heat rose in her cheeks. Was she a source of teasing among his friends? "I'd be pleased to accept, Lieutenant."

"I look forward to it." He bowed and left, and Sage returned to waiting in line. The two ladies ahead of her glanced back before putting their heads together and whispering, but Sage was engrossed in the idea that Casseck hadn't recognized her. A whole world of possibilities opened up if she could look different enough to fool people. She eyed the maids scurrying about on errands as the line inched forward. With so many retinues coming and going, an unknown servant wouldn't attract attention.

The Great Hall was decorated with garlands of spring flowers imported from somewhere much warmer than Tegann, and rushes on the floor released sweet scents as they were trod upon by the multitude of guests. Tables off to the sides overflowed with meats, fruit, and pastries, which was all the more impressive to Sage as she knew just how far those things had to travel to get there. The ladies in front of her seemed oblivious to the splendor around them. Perhaps they were just used to riches and never gave a thought to where they came from.

The hall itself awed her with its size—the family living quarters of Broadmoor Manor could've fit inside without being stacked. It was a fairly recent addition to the fortress, constructed when the D'Amiran family was granted Tasmet as a dukedom forty years ago. Apparently over a hundred and fifty years of living in near exile hadn't dampened their taste for opulence. The high stained-glass windows depicted scenes from the family's history of uniting Demora into a single nation, though they left out the fight they'd picked with Casmun three hundred years ago, ruining trade relations. Their loss of the throne a hundred years after that was also omitted.

Sage had plenty of time to observe the duke while she waited to be presented to him, last of the ladies as usual. Morrow D'Amiran was over forty and blackened his beard and hair to give the illusion of youth, but his hands and forehead had the wrinkles of advanced middle age. She couldn't deny he was handsome in a conventional sense. His facial features were well cut, and his teeth were straight and white. He hadn't allowed himself to grow portly like Uncle William, and his manners were pleasing, but his crystal-blue eyes were cold and calculating. Sage curtsied low and focused on the floor as Darnessa introduced her.

"I don't know of the Broadmoor family," said the duke, holding on to her hand. "Where are your estates?"

"About a day north and west of Garland Hill, Your Grace," Sage replied, unsure whether she wanted to be interesting to him, but deciding to err on the side of blandness. It took a great deal of control not to pull away from his soft but firm grip on her fingers.

"Her uncle is a minor lord, Your Grace," put in the matchmaker. "He holds in trust everything belonging to her mother as her dowry." It was a statement carefully designed to imply Sage had a greater rank and wealth than her guardian.

"Yes, that would explain why I hadn't heard of her." He paused and looked her over as she tried not to squirm. "You look like someone who enjoys being out of doors."

Her complexion. He was commenting on her freckles. Now Sage wished she'd worn that ridiculous hat. She ducked her head and tried to look embarrassed. "This past winter was so confining, I'm afraid I overindulged in sunshine once spring arrived, Your Grace."

Her host gave her a genuine smile. "My dear, that is a sentiment I truly understand. Even years since arriving here, the mountain winters make me long for the mild climate of Mondelea I knew as a child." What had started as a wistful statement ended with a note of bitterness. His hand tightened on hers.

He'd been very young when his family came to Tasmet, and they'd lived in near poverty before that, but he plainly remembered his childhood home with longing. Sage went with a combination of empathy and flattery. "Your Grace shows me there is no shame in missing what I left behind in my own home."

His hand relaxed. "No, my lady, there is none at all." He bent down to kiss her hand. "I hope you will enjoy your time here and find pleasure in your new home, wherever it shall be."

"I thank Your Grace from the bottom of my heart," Sage murmured, lowering her eyes again as she sank into a curtsy.

The matchmaker curtsied to the duke and led Sage away. "Nicely done," Darnessa said in her ear. "Now go enjoy yourself, but don't forget you have a job, too."

Her employer didn't realize how much more than matching information was at stake. Perhaps Quinn hadn't told her everything after all. Sage hated keeping her in the dark, but as protective as Darnessa could be, it wasn't a good idea to tell her anything yet. At any rate, this wasn't the place to do so.

Clare was already dancing with Lieutenant Gramwell, so Sage mingled in the crowds, seeking to put names to faces. Amusingly, she found the caricatured impressions by the young men from their last stop were accurate enough for her to identify several nobles present. Not all the intended grooms had arrived yet; many higher, married Tasmet nobles were here, Sage suspected, to seal their allegiance to Duke D'Amiran before he took action. Once they departed, the others would have places to stay in the fortress. She hoped the comings and goings would delay D'Amiran's plan to wed the women to his allies for a few critical days.

Judging from the steady stream of young men who approached her for dances, she was an unexpected bonus in terms of the brides and would probably be awarded to someone the duke found loyal. That was, if her image as a highborn lady held. Sage took in the vast hall full of loyal supporters, knowing their combined assets, and compared it to the size of their own honor guard. She began to wonder if she should find a man who might like her enough to protect her—should the worst come to pass.

Yet she could never turn her back on Ash and the other soldiers. Win or lose, she would be firmly on their side, even if the latter meant losing everything.

As if bidden by her thoughts, Lieutenant Casseck appeared at her elbow. "I'm here to collect on my lady's promise," he said with a smile.

Sage took his hand, and he led her to the far end of the hall, where fewer people gathered. The duke was like the center of an archery target—like arrows, the density of people increased the closer one was to him. She was happy to avoid him, and as no one was close enough to overhear, she could also speak more freely.

"How did you find my notes from this morning?" she asked. "Were they helpful?"

"Most impressive," Casseck said. "Captain Quinn was very pleased."

"I didn't do it for him," Sage said a little bitterly.

"He's grateful nonetheless." Casseck twirled her around, keeping her back to the duke and those who orbited around him. She found herself facing an ornate window depicting General Falco D'Amiran driving the Kimisar out of Tasmet.

"When will he act on it?" No one paid them any attention, but she kept her phrases carefully neutral.

"It's done."

Sage missed a step in the dance. "Already?"

"Charlie wasn't even late to bed."

Of course Quinn had used his little brother. Sage gritted her teeth. "I'm glad he found the boy useful."

Casseck raised an eyebrow. "I understand your concern, but I'm not sure who else you think could have done it."

Sage turned her head, unwilling to admit he was right. Casseck swung her a little to the left, and she found herself looking at the stained-glass window again. "When did things go sour between the royals and the D'Amirans?" she asked to change the subject. "The Great War brought the family back into favor, but things went sour quickly." She nodded at the window.

Casseck glanced over his shoulder. "I'm surprised you don't know. It had to do with the Concordium twenty years ago."

The more Sage learned about matchmakers and the power they wielded, the more she was convinced they secretly ran the country. "I haven't been Mistress Rodelle's apprentice that long. What happened?"

"Apparently the good duke came home empty-handed. He was offered several matches but refused all of them."

"Sounds like he wanted someone he couldn't have."

Casseck shrugged. "Some say he wanted Gabriella Carey, but she married King Raymond a year before that, so I think the theory is off."

Quinn's mother was a Carey—Queen Gabriella's younger sister. She'd married Captain Pendleton Quinn around the time of her sister's engagement, but it had been a quiet affair for a union of such powerful families. The fanfare over the king's nuptials had overshadowed it, she supposed.

The dance they were doing involved several turns, yet Sage always found herself facing the window. "Are you trying to keep my back to everybody?" she asked, slightly exasperated.

Guilt flashed across his face. "I, ah, just like being able to keep an eye on the whole room. Soldier's habit."

"You don't have to apologize for that," she said. "I'm just glad you aren't embarrassed to be seen with the lowest lady of them all."

"From what I've seen tonight, my lady, very few have such reservations." He angled her a little to the side for a change.

"Was it just my perception, or did you have trouble finding me in the crowd earlier?"

"I did. You look . . . different." He winced. "I hope that didn't come across as insulting."

Sage barely heard that last part. Her heart was hammering at the thought of someone who knew her as well as Casseck not recognizing her.

Tomorrow she would test just how far that lack of recognition could get her.

49

CASS HAD STARLING at the far end of the hall. Her hair looked reddish, so for a few seconds Quinn wasn't sure it *was* her, but then she tilted her head to the side as she did when she was thinking, and he knew it. He made his way through the throng that surrounded the duke.

"Your Grace," the captain said with a bow. "I'm sorry I didn't meet with you last night when we arrived. We were so behind schedule, I had to catch up on critical business."

D'Amiran acknowledged him with a regal nod. "It was no matter, Captain; your officers took care of everything." He paused and looked Quinn up and down. "So you are Pendleton Quinn's son."

"I am, Your Grace." It didn't escape Quinn's notice that the duke had omitted his father's rank. As young men, both the duke and his brother had entered military service but washed out before either achieved captain. According to his father, Morrow D'Amiran had potential, but had relied too much on his own father's reputation. It was a lesson Quinn had taken to heart at a young age.

Light-blue eyes continued to study him. "Armand, is it? You don't look much like him."

"Alexander, Your Grace. My father's middle name."

The duke sniffed.

Either D'Amiran was trying to get under his skin, or he didn't remember what the general looked like. Quinn was almost a copy of his father, but with his eastern mother's darker coloring. "I actually find that advantageous, Your Grace."

"Indeed." The duke selected a flaky biscuit from the tray a servant offered him. "Will you be taking advantage of this assignment to visit your uncle, the king?"

At first Quinn thought it was a hint that D'Amiran knew his father had sent him to spy on him, but on reflection it seemed innocent small talk. "Of course, Your Grace. May I give him your regards, or will you be traveling with us to the Concordium?"

Too many teeth were revealed by the duke's smile for it to be natural. "I would be pleased if you would carry my regards to both him and your father."

In the form of my head in a basket? Quinn knew the look of a man who hated another, and he was only third on this man's list, behind his father and the king. His eyes darted to Casseck and Sage. Her back was to them. He waved a hand around to indicate the room as he again addressed D'Amiran. "Your Grace puts on a magnificent display. I believe this rivals anything I've seen at the palace."

"Yes, and you would know, having spent so much time there."

People were always jealous of his position, but Quinn wearied of it. Only Robert and Ash had it worse. He suppressed a smile. Third place again.

The duke continued, "I trust the accommodations meet the standards you're used to?"

"More than acceptable, Your Grace," he answered. "I thank you for your hospitality."

D'Amiran looked annoyed that his small digs never yielded a response. "Yes, well, I'm sure you have duties to attend to."

Once again, rather than act insulted, Quinn simply smiled and bowed at the dismissal. With a last glance at Casseck and Sage, he slipped out the main doors and headed back to the barracks.

50

SAGE ROSE BEFORE dawn and put on a plain wool dress, lacing the bodice swiftly in the dark. Then she combed darkening syrup through her hair before braiding and coiling it behind her head and covering it with a hood. A glance in her hand mirror showed the reflection of a simple maid rather than the grand lady everyone had seen the night before. Grabbing a bundle of soiled clothing, she let herself out of the room.

No one gave her a second glance as she headed to the laundry. Few stirred as it was—everyone was recovering from last night. Sage dropped her bundle in the empty washroom with other clothing belonging to their group and began looking for more places to explore, thinking to start in the kitchens. The cistern had its own outlet into the laundry, which inspired her to fill an empty pitcher from a shelfful of them. There was no time like the present to start spreading the contamination.

In the kitchen she found several baskets of bread and cheese set out on a central table. A hungover cook barely glanced up before gesturing for her to take one. "It's about time you girls started showing up. Go out to the main gate first. The guards are hungry, so be quick."

He assumed she was an errand girl. Perfect. Sage grinned to herself and grabbed a basket and a metal cup in addition to her pitcher and set off for the north side of the fortress. Balancing her burdens carefully, Sage passed through the inner gate and the outer ward and climbed the stone steps nearest the gatehouse. Two sleepy guards perked up as she walked in the door.

"Hello, love," one called from where he lounged in a rickety wooden chair. "You're a sight. Come give us a little wake-up?"

In that moment, Sage realized she was woefully unprepared to deal with the advances these men might make on a common maid. She nervously set the basket down and poured water into the cup. When she offered it to the guard who'd spoken, he grabbed her wrist and yanked her onto his lap. Sage yelped as he squeezed her rear end and whispered in her ear, "You got me woke, love. How's about you stay awhile an' keep me company? Hix here ain't much fun, but you looks lots of fun." His week-old stubble pressed against her cheek, and he gave her a sloppy kiss that reeked of sour wine.

Sage shrieked and shoved herself off of him, and he laughed before drinking the water. A wet trail dribbled down his chin and onto his blue uniform, joining several dark stains that looked like wine—or blood. He held the cup out to her and winked. She stared at it, unwilling to get closer, though a part of her wanted to give him *more* of the contaminated water, until he pulled the cup back and wiggled it. "Com'n get it, love."

The other guard, Hix, stepped forward and smacked him lightly across the back of the head. "Knock it off, Barley. She's got rounds to do." He took the cup and held it out for his drink. She poured his water ration with shaking hands and waited for him to finish it. He handed back the cup and grabbed two rolls from the basket, tossing one to his leering friend.

"Gimme a cheese, will ya?" Barley said, and the guard flipped a chunk at him. He struggled to catch it, cursing as it bounced out of his hands. Tipping his chair back, he snatched it off the stone floor and took a bite as he watched Sage retreat. "I'll look for you later," he called as she closed the door behind her.

Sage set down the basket and pitcher so she could straighten her clothes and wipe her face on her sleeve, feeling foolish for thinking it would be easy to just wander around like a servant. Some spy she was.

In the morning twilight made longer by the eastern peaks, she saw several guards in blue and white posted at intervals along the wall, the nearest of which looked at her expectantly. Sage took a deep breath as she gathered her things and reminded herself she was safer out in the open.

The next encounters went smoothly, and she progressed along the north wall. None of the guards made further advances, though one on the northeast tower eyed her long enough to make her blush. She stared at the mountains to avoid his gaze, watching a hawk fly up from the south and circle over a spot near the pass.

On the eastern wall, midway between guards, she passed a man sitting against the curve of a small, unmanned tower. "Spare a bit of bread, miss?" he asked quietly.

She stopped in her tracks, sloshing the water in the pitcher. "What are you doing here?" she gasped.

Ash squinted up at her and scowled. His dark hair stood out at odd angles from where he'd leaned against the wall. "I could ask you the same thing." He stood and moved closer to take a roll. "Because I know this isn't something anyone told you to do."

"It's called taking the initiative."

"No, it's called putting yourself in danger needlessly."

"I can take care of myself," she said, trying to forget the man in the gatehouse.

"No, you can't. Go back to bed." His voice had the air of a command.

"Not until I finish taking the rest of this around." Sage switched the basket to her other arm and brushed him aside. "It'll look suspicious if I stop now," she said over her shoulder.

"Dammit, Sage, this is not a game!" he growled to her back.

Fuming, she continued down the east and south sides, making it around to the circular tower at the southwest corner before she ran out of cheese and bread. There was still some water in the pitcher, so she decided to climb up the tower to the last guards before returning to the kitchen. The encounter in the gatehouse rattled her more than she'd ever admit. Part of her wanted to quit and go back to bed, but she certainly wouldn't after Ash ordered her to. She was hitching her skirt to mount the steps to the open trapdoor when she heard the men above talking.

"I'm tellin' you, sir, it was 'im," one was saying. "I seen 'im before, last time we escorted 'is Grace to th' capital."

"He doesn't look like the king, though," another replied. Sage froze. They had to be talking about Ash.

"'Is mother was onna them easterners—they got black hair an' dark skin. I'm tellin' you it was 'im, an' 'is Grace would want to know, sir."

Sage backed away to where she wouldn't be seen if they looked down. An authoritative third voice asked, "Have you told anyone?"

The first soldier replied, "No, sir. I couldn't place 'is face till I thought on it, and yer th' first I told."

"Then keep your mouth shut," came the harsh response. "His Grace already knows, and if you ruin his plans by running your mouth, you'll wish your execution was quick."

Sage didn't wait to hear any more and fled, thankful she wore her soft leather boots, which were silent on the stone steps. They knew who Ash was, and they were planning to take him. She had to warn him—now.

She dashed down the stairs all the way to the bottom, afraid the guards would notice her if she went back out on the wall. Now on the ground level, she forced herself to walk around the outer ward to the base of the small tower where Ash sat on the wall above. She picked up a stone and threw it against the structure. She missed and tried again until she succeeded in getting one right where she wanted. Ash's dark head leaned over the edge to look down.

Trying to be discreet, she made motions saying he needed to come down to talk to her. He shook his head, and she stomped her foot. Why wouldn't he believe this was important? Finally, he jabbed a finger at the building behind her and disappeared. She dumped the remainder of her water on the ground and put the pitcher and cup inside the basket before heading to the double doors.

The scents of metal and oiled leather met her as she pulled the right door open and let herself into the main armory. A single torch lit the empty passage from a bracket on the wall. Ash stormed around the corner at the opposite end. She had no idea how he'd gotten there so fast. He walked right up to her, grabbed her arm, and gently shoved her into one of several pitch-black storerooms.

"You know, I have a reason to be up there, unlike you," he whispered furiously. Ash closed the door and bumped against her hard enough that she backed into an open box stacked in the corner. Something sharp poked her, and she reached behind her to feel what it was and push it fully inside the crate. She could barely see in the faint light from cracks in the door, so she clutched Ash's vest to make sure he was facing her.

"Ash, they know who you are. They're going to grab you."

She had his full attention now. "Who knows?"

"The guards on the tower; I heard them talking. One of them recognized you."

He put his hands on her upper arms. "Tell me exactly what they said. *Exactly.*"

Sage repeated it word for word and added, "You have to get out of here, Ash."

She heard him shake his head. "They're not talking about me."

"The king's son, Ash. That's *you.*"

"They're talking about Robert."

"Prince Robert?" she gasped. "How—"

"He's been with us the whole time under a false name."

"But . . . how can you be sure they mean him?" After all, Ash was valuable to the crown, too. And to her.

"Just trust me. But you're right, we need to get him out. Today." He squeezed her shoulder. "I'm sorry I was angry. You'd think by now I'd know to trust your judgment, though coming out here wasn't—"

He broke off at the sound of the armory door creaking open, and two guards entered the hall, laughing and talking. They walked past Sage and Ash's hiding place and opened a storage closet at the other end of the passage and began rummaging for equipment. Ash leaned on the door to listen for a few seconds, then stepped back to her, and whispered, "They're getting crossbows for their patrol. Once they find the bolts they'll be gone."

A wave of horror swept over Sage, and she seized his collar frantically. "Ash, the bolts are in here."

"What?"

"There's a box of crossbow bolts behind me."

51

SHE HEARD ASH'S breath catch in his throat. Before Sage could say anything more, he pulled her close. "You must forgive what I am about to do," he whispered, reaching down to hike up her skirt.

"What—" But he silenced her with his mouth on hers. It was so sudden, so urgent, Sage didn't even register it as kissing as he pushed against her, forcing her back. With one hand up her dress, Ash lifted her off her feet and set her on the crates while the other tugged her bodice laces. He pulled his face back with a murmured apology before nudging her knees apart with his hip and maneuvering to stand between them.

Her bodice loosened, and he leaned forward and put his mouth at her ear. "Whatever you do, don't let them see your face."

Let who see her face? She couldn't see anything, which only made his closeness overwhelming. Then Sage understood. They needed an excuse to be hiding, and it had to look like they'd been here for a while. This act couldn't be one-sided, though—she had to do something. It was just so hard to think with his hands working her bodice open more. She fumbled with the ties on his vest, but they weren't coming loose, so she reached around to his back and untucked his shirt. Ash pulled her sleeve off her shoulder and dragged his lips across her collarbone and up her neck, leaving a strange trail of icy fire on her skin. His hand slipped between her bodice and thin linen shift—under where his hand had been when he helped her off the horse, right where she tucked her note yesterday. . . .

Sage had one hand under his shirt and halfway up his back, unsettlingly aware of the solid muscles at her fingertips. Heat from his breath burned her skin as his right hand pulled her hood off. Ash buried his nose in the loose hair at the back of her neck, inhaling slowly and deliberately. It seemed an odd thing to do. She turned her face into his collar. He smelled infinitely better—like soap with essence of evergreen... clean linen... leather... and something indefinable that left her only wanting to breathe more deeply.

Ash froze and then leaned back a little, brushing his eyelashes across her cheek as he brought his mouth to hover over hers.

"Sage," he whispered.

She closed her eyes and parted her lips. *Yes.*

The door opened, throwing blinding light across her face. She shrieked, and Ash shielded her with his body. A guard with the torch in his hand stood motionless for a second before bursting into riotous laughter. His companion peered around the door frame and joined him. Sage pushed her skirt down and attempted to pull her bodice back together, aware Ash was blocking her face from their view as he hitched his sagging breeches higher.

"Get out of here, you two," said the man with the torch. He stepped back and threw the door wider. Ash advanced on them so Sage could slip out behind him, and she grabbed her basket, keeping her face down and away. "Be glad we're in a hurry, boy, or we might've taken a turn, too."

She saw Ash's fists clench at the guard's taunt, but rather than swing at him, to Sage's relief he reached down to snatch up the hair cover she'd dropped. Her outer dress shifted with her steps, and she grabbed at the bodice to keep it from opening farther as she stumbled to the door and leaned against it. Panic seized her throat as the soldier grabbed Ash's arm and leaned to his ear.

"You tell your captain if any of you boys is caught like this again, he'll hear about it from Captain Geddes." The man shoved Ash at her. "Now run, boy."

Ash's hand was on her back, propelling her out, as the sound of laughter echoed out the door. She tripped on a clump of dirt and barely managed to stay upright. "In here," Ash whispered, guiding her to the tiny chapel at the base of the tower he'd sat against earlier.

Sage collapsed on the bench inside as Ash closed the door and pressed an eye to a crack in the boards. She hardly dared to breathe as he watched the courtyard for several seconds. At last he leaned back. "I think we're good. No one's out there."

With shaking hands, Sage hiked her stockings back over her knees, then stood and smoothed her skirt. Ash was barely a foot away, retucking his shirt. Her heart pounded so loudly she felt he must be able to hear it. "We have to tell Captain Quinn right away," she said in a hushed and hurried voice.

"I'll go as soon as . . ." Ash fumbled with his belt in the light coming through the dirty stained-glass window. When he'd finally found the catch he was looking for, he straightened and smoothed his rumpled hair. Sage suddenly found herself wanting to feel it in her own fingers. Cheeks flaming, she ducked her head to focus on straightening and re-tying her bodice.

Ash tugged her left sleeve back over her shoulder, startling her enough that she looked up into his shadowed face. "I have to go," he said softly. "But you should take a few minutes to fix your hair; it's a real mess. And your face is all flushed."

"Maybe I'm just not practiced in these sorts of things." She jerked away from the hand that lingered on her shoulder. In the last two days, she'd allowed herself to wonder what it would be like to be kissed—and by him—but had it all been for show back there? Had she been too eager to play the part in what was only an act for him? Her eyes burned with what she was afraid would become tears.

For a long moment, Ash said nothing. Then he whispered, "Neither am I."

He took a half step forward. With the bench pressing her knees from behind, Sage couldn't back away without falling. His vest brushed against her now-motionless hands, and she stared at them in confusion. What were they supposed to be doing? Ash was so close she could feel him breathing. She wanted to see his face but couldn't force her eyes higher than his collarbone. Instead she concentrated on the faint pulse visible at the base of his throat. His neck muscles flexed as he swallowed.

His next words were forced out like a confession. "If I was any good at it, it was only because I've imagined it so often."

Sage suddenly had to remind herself to breathe.

With the determination of having made a difficult decision, Ash reached up and tilted her chin higher. In the same movement, he slipped his left arm around her waist, drawing her to him. Their eyes met for a split second; she barely had time to realize what was happening as his face bent down to her own.

At first Sage trembled so badly she couldn't react. His lips pressed against hers, and she tried to yield, tried to respond in a way that would tell him what she wanted, but she didn't know how. Ash's confidence wavered against her lukewarm response, and he drew back. Sage nearly panicked. It couldn't end like that. She leaned into him, sliding her hands up to grasp the open collar of his shirt. *Don't stop.*

Their lips met again, and this time he was startled, but only for a moment. Then he pulled her closer, raising her onto her tiptoes. She closed her eyes as his fingers drifted up her jawline to bury themselves in her hair.

A sound—more a squeak than a sigh—escaped her, and his lips tightened against hers in a half smile. What was awkward only seconds ago became natural, and she didn't even have to think about surrendering to the gentle pressure of his mouth. Her second sigh was softer and on purpose, and he echoed it. They both smiled a little before coming back for more.

Her third sigh was as unplanned as the first, but his reaction was everything she could've hoped for. Ash's kisses became deeper, more insistent. His strong arms tightened around her as he lifted her completely off her feet. Sage's fingers slackened their grip on his shirt, and every muscle in her body relaxed against him. Without his support at the small of her back, she would've slid into a puddle at his feet.

Nothing in her imagination had ever come close to this.

Ash pulled back, and her eyes fluttered open. He was still too close to see clearly, his breath mingling with hers. "I . . . I have to go."

Sage nodded, brushing her nose along his. She felt her body sliding down his as he lowered her back to her feet. From the unchanged light in the cramped room, barely two minutes had passed, though she could've sworn it had been an hour.

He bent down and pressed his forehead to hers, and for another minute they remained melted against each other. She rested her hands on his chest, matching her shaky breaths to his. "You need to go," she managed to say.

He nodded and pulled his hand around to her jawline to trace his thumb over her bottom lip before leaning lower again. "You are so beautiful," he whispered against her mouth, finishing with the softest of kisses.

He gradually loosened his embrace, dragging his fingers across her cheek and waist like he couldn't bear to let go, stepped back, and tugged his vest straight. Then he was gone.

52

THE OFFICERS WERE only just stirring, but within five minutes they were dressed and assembled in the meeting room. A patrol was already scheduled for that morning; now they'd leave as soon as possible without inviting D'Amiran's guards along, which would likely offend their host. The four men would now include Robert and ride hard for the north gap in the ring of Kimisar, which they prayed was still open. They'd return with one of the picket scouts there and leave the prince to escape on foot with the other. If luck was with them, by the time anyone realized he was missing, he'd be far away.

There was no time to waste. Supplies had to be gathered and horses readied. Quinn dismissed them, and Rob and Gramwell dashed out of the room, but Casseck remained. When the door was shut, he seated himself across from Quinn and leaned on the table. "Why didn't Mouse bring Starling into the circle after overhearing this? She knows almost everything."

Quinn focused on the map. "It was the right decision to wait. Once she's in, it can't be undone."

"Alex." Casseck stared hard at him. "What are you leaving out?"

Quinn closed his eyes and massaged his temples with the fingers and thumb of his right hand. "He kissed her."

"I see." When Quinn didn't respond for several seconds, Casseck cleared his throat to cover what sounded suspiciously like laughter. "Well, it's about time."

Quinn looked up sharply. "You think this is funny?"

"Not at all. It's a tough thing to be jealous."

"You think I'm *jealous*?" Quinn slammed his hand down on the table.

Casseck deftly caught the ink pot as it bounced over the edge and set it back on the table. "It's not you she's falling in love with," he said quietly. "She needs to be protected, yes, but that's not the real reason you haven't brought her into the circle."

Quinn exhaled slowly, choosing not to respond to that point. "It's too early. We still have to get Rob out, and if we fail, the last thing we want is her involved. If we succeed, everything changes, and Mouse needs to teach her something while she still trusts him. But very soon. I promise."

"As soon as possible after that. Tomorrow."

Quinn closed his eyes and nodded. "Tomorrow."

53

D'AMIRAN KNEW OVERCONFIDENCE could be deadly, but right now, things were going well. Better than well: he had Robert.

He smiled as another lord signed his name to the list of committed allies. They'd all readily pledged their resources to his cause once he had all of the women in his possession, though he hadn't informed any of them of his pact with Kimisara. It was a minor detail, and the fewer aware, the better, especially since most hated the Kimisar after years of fending off raiding parties.

Lord Fashell approached and bowed low. "Your Grace," he said. "I've brought the latest provisions, some news, and a humble request." D'Amiran nodded, and the man continued, "Everything you wanted is being carried into your storerooms. My estate has been accommodating travelers bound for Tegann, and we're proud to provide these services to your cause."

"I've been pleased to count on them," the duke said graciously. "Your loyalty is noted and appreciated."

Dashell bowed again in thanks. "As for news, Your Grace, there will be a delay in some arrivals. An illness has been affecting many travelers in the area, and several cannot continue their journey at present."

"An illness?" Concern was etched along D'Amiran's brow. "How long before they can be expected to recover?"

"Only a day or two, Your Grace," Fashell rushed to assure him. "You might not have even noticed with all the activity and arrivals, but I felt you'd like to be informed."

Somewhat relieved, D'Amiran smiled. "Yes, once more I appreciate your attention to my needs. If that's your only news, I would hear your request."

"A minor item, Your Grace, concerning one of the ladies who arrived here two days ago." Fashell cleared his throat. "My son Bartholomew was quite captivated by Lady Broadmoor, and it was my impression she wasn't promised to anyone yet."

The duke frowned thoughtfully. "Broadmoor . . ." He recalled her—a rather plain little thing, freckled and thin with eyes that avoided his but observed everything else. "Yes, of course. I'm not sure what property she brings. Probably not much, as I'd never heard of her before."

"Property is not a concern for us, Your Grace, thanks to your generosity. We shan't object if you find it advantageous to give her to another, but if you had no use for her, I felt there was no harm in asking."

"Absolutely no harm, Lord Fashell." D'Amiran folded his hands. "I will consider your request, factoring in the service you've done me." He would leave it at that; he couldn't promise her to anyone just yet. If she'd caught the attention of Bartholomew Fashell, he needed to see for himself why.

Fashell bowed one last time. "That's all I hoped for, Your Grace."

Captain Geddes squeezed past Fashell at the door. "Your Grace," he said with a breathless bow. "The escort's patrol hasn't returned, and we haven't been able to find"—he glanced around at the others present and scratched his half ear—"them," he finished, trying to convey meaning with his eyes. "Though I wouldn't consider them late just yet."

"How many departed?" asked D'Amiran.

"Four, sir. None appeared to be officers, but they left early without telling anyone."

"Are all three officers accounted for?"

"We've seen only three today," said the captain. "It's been confusing, Your Grace. But I'm sure there are four: Quinn, Casseck, Gramwell, and Bathgate. The last hasn't been seen since yesterday."

The duke's eyes narrowed. "Then I suggest you find him."

54

SAGE FAILED MISERABLY to keep her focus that day. While she blamed her overheated complexion on the warm spring sunshine, in her mind she relived the events of the morning several dozen times, Ash's words echoing in her head. No one had ever called her beautiful, but there was no doubt in her mind that he meant it.

Once, she even allowed herself to picture the episode in the armory without deception or fear of discovery. Or, she thought wryly, without a box of arrows poking her in the rear. That only made her envision softer alternatives and that inflamed her cheeks even more, until she remembered the danger they all faced. Guilt nagged her, too—what kind of a distraction must she be to Ash?

At dinner she chose a seat where she could watch the officers at their corner table. Robert must be one of them. Ash didn't want her talking to the officers, especially here at Tegann, implying she would've realized who he was. Casseck was so straightforward, he almost seemed incapable of lying, but Gramwell . . .

The lieutenant's gaze wandered to Clare every few minutes. He'd ignored a lot of protocol by courting Clare, but no one objected. Before, Sage assumed he was so besotted, he couldn't help himself, but it made even more sense that no one had stopped him if he was the prince. Yes, it was entirely possible he was actually the prince in disguise.

As if the two had read her mind, Clare excused herself and left through the main doors, toward the gardens. Her admirer quietly followed less than a minute later. He would be gone after tonight, and he probably wanted to say good-bye. She smiled. If any of these women deserved the attention of royalty, it was her friend.

Sage bumped into Charlie on the way back to her room. He held up a bundle of clothing. "My lady, I'm to deliver this to you," he said.

It must be her clean breeches and shirt. She was glad to have them back. Sage considered asking Charlie about Robert, but that wouldn't be fair to the boy, and she'd promised Ash to stop asking questions he would answer later. So she simply said, "Thank you. Good night, Little Soldier."

He bobbed his head and hurried off. Rather than put the bundle in her trunk, Sage pulled it apart, hoping to find a message from Ash. A lump in one of her socks turned out to be a stub of a candle wrapped in a scrap of parchment.

If you trust me with your life, light this candle. When it burns out, meet me in the lower passage in the west barracks.–A

With a trembling hand, Sage lit the wick and nestled it in a holder. It would take less than two hours to burn out, so she changed into her clean breeches and curled up on the bed to wait. She'd toss the note in the fire before she left, but until then she held the scrap in her hand, reading the words over and over. *If you trust me with your life . . .*

She did. And tonight she would prove it.

⚜

Sage slipped around the corner and found him, leaning against the wall opposite the low-burning torch, arms crossed, silent as a shadow. His gaze followed her until she stopped in front of him. "I almost hoped you wouldn't come," he said.

He didn't want her involved because it was dangerous, but Quinn needed her, and so she had an unlikely ally in the captain. She wasn't doing this for Quinn, though. Her eyes traced the contours of the face she'd come to know so well in the last weeks—from the almost-straight black brows over eyes so dark and deep she could fall into them to the stubble she now knew by feel. "I came because I trust you," she whispered.

He pressed his lips together as he took her right hand in both of his and inhaled deeply. "Everything changes tomorrow. If you leave now, I will think no less and ask no more of you, and I'll still do everything I can to protect you from what's coming." He turned her hand over and rubbed a thumb along her palm, sending lightning up her arm. "But if you stay, you commit yourself. You become a player we depend on and confide in. There is no middle path or going back. You must decide tonight."

"You're a fool if you think I'm leaving," she said firmly.

He winced. "People will die, Sage. At our hands and theirs. The surest way you can be safe is by not getting involved. That is truth."

She curled her fingers around his. "I know. I'm not afraid." But she trembled.

"Will you promise to follow orders, without question or hesitation?" He eyed her with silent meaning.

For him? "Yes," she whispered. "I promise."

He sagged slightly and nodded. "Then there's something I must do first."

Ash raised her hand to his lips and kissed it, then, clasping her fingers tightly, he led her down the dim corridor to the last door. Without knocking, he pushed it open and ushered her into a windowless barracks room used for storage. Candles set in the stone wall illuminated a jumble of wooden chairs, tables, and cots piled on one side, and a stack of straw mattresses lay in the corner. Several pallets had been pulled to the middle of the open space and stacked two high with a large blanket over them. The implication stunned her—it was so unexpected, so unlike what she believed about him—her mind only registered denial.

She heard Ash bolt the door and remove his leather jacket, felt his hands on her shoulders as he turned her around to face him. He stroked her cheek with one hand while the other reached for his belt. "My sweet, innocent Sage," he whispered, and still her thoughts could gain no traction.

There was the snap of a release from his belt, and though she continued to meet his eyes, she saw a sheathed dagger in the hand he raised between them.

"Tonight I must teach you how to kill a man."

55

SAGE REACHED FOR the knife, and he rotated the handle to make her grip it with her thumb at the end of the hilt. "Hold it like this."

She'd wielded a knife before; Father had taught her years ago, but this was different. The way she now held it, with the blade extending from the small side of her hand, was useless for anything but stabbing and slashing. She swallowed. "I'm ready."

"Are you?"

Sage knew his deepest fear was that he was a monster, that he enjoyed killing. Now he had to expose her to the thing he dreaded most. She nodded with the confidence he needed to see, and his expression became fierce, determined.

Before starting, he showed her the places a man in armor was vulnerable, pressed her hands where the arteries lay closest to the surface, and demonstrated the blade angles that would exploit both. After that, he stepped around to guide her into a defensive position, laying his arms over hers to place them and forcing her into a crouch with his own body. She shivered with sudden cold as he stepped away to stand in front of her again.

He made her come at him with the sheathed dagger from several angles, admonishing her not to hesitate whenever she was reluctant. His criticism rankled her, but he was so serious, she suppressed the urge to snap back.

The third time she faltered in advancing, he wrenched the weapon from her hand and had her down on the mat with the covered blade at her throat before she could blink. Sage had always thought of him as a soldier, knew he'd killed men, but for the first time she comprehended just how powerful and deadly he was.

"Did I frighten you?" he asked, leaning back. She nodded. "Good." He tossed the knife into her lap as she sat up. "Get up and try again."

A grim determination settled over her, and she began to progress as he wanted, drawing occasional unsmiling praise. After nearly three hours, he slapped the dagger from her hand, saying, "Your weapon is gone; now what?"

Without thinking she jumped at his middle, driving her shoulder into his stomach. She'd surprised him enough that he crumpled with the blow and fell back on the mat. There was a sickening thud as his head hit the straw pallet. Horrified, Sage pushed up to her knees as Ash groaned and reached for his head. She leaned over him only to realize her mistake when he grabbed her by the throat and yanked her close to whisper, "You're dead."

She pounded on his arm with her fist. "That's not fair!"

"Do you think this is a game?" he asked. "Is there fairness in fighting a man twice your size?"

Her protest died. "No."

He released his hold. "Good. Again."

Ash came at her from behind, from the front, from the side. He twisted her arms behind her and bent her fingers backward to force her grip open, making her push and pull against him with all her strength. Sage learned how to use her dangling feet to find leverage and reach vulnerable spots if she was lifted off of them. He showed her which of her bones were strongest, where she was weakest, how to allow injury to gain a critical advantage, and how to fall. She landed roughly on the pallet more times than she could count.

All but two of the candles had burned out, telling her it must be nearly dawn. Sage was more tired than she'd ever felt in her life, but she dared not complain. She couldn't help that her reactions slowed, however, and her strength waned. Finally, she lay panting on the mat as he stood over her and nudged her with his left foot. "Again."

"I'm too tired," she wheezed.

"I don't care. Again."

"I can't," she whimpered, rolling to her quaking hands and knees.

"You can." He prodded harder. "Get up."

Anger surged through her, and Sage used its fire to slam her elbow into the back of his right knee. Ash fell backward with a grunt, and she grabbed his hair and jerked him the rest of the way down. She pressed her forearm across his throat as he scrambled to reach for her, and she leaned close enough to gasp, "You're dead."

He smiled for the first time. "Very good."

Sage collapsed against him. "No more, please," she mumbled into his sweaty shoulder.

Strong arms encircled her, and he pulled her closer, laying his cheek on the top of her head. "No more," he soothed. "We're finished."

She nearly wept with relief as she clutched his shirt and buried her face in it. "Why were you so hard on me?"

Ash tipped her chin up and looked at her with a fierceness that took her breath away. "Because if you die, it will be my fault, and I can't live with that." He leaned down, bringing his lips so close they brushed against hers as he whispered, "Or without you."

She didn't know who kissed who that time, but it didn't matter. A warmth radiated through her from the places they touched, bringing an energy she didn't think possible. The hands and arms that had frustrated her all night with their quickness and power now moved slowly and caressed gently. Ash tentatively explored the curves of her back and hips, and she encouraged him with her sighs to grow bolder, until she felt his hands traveling down and around her thighs.

Ash rolled from his back onto his side to face her, and she grabbed his waist with a need to be closer still. Her fingers brushed skin where his shirt had come untucked, making him moan softly into her hair. Sage smiled and slipped her hand under the fabric. She traced her fingertips up the hard muscles of his back, enjoying the way he responded to her touch. Then his mouth was on hers again with a hunger she felt equally, and he was tugging her top out to make her react in the same way.

His calloused hands were so gentle as they traced her spine. When he spread his fingers, they seemed to cover her whole back. Her own fingers found the texture of a broad scar under his shoulder—evidence of his deadly past and future, of his strength. But here, now, he was vulnerable to the softest touch. He trembled at the slightest noise she made. She felt dizzy with a sense of power, despite the fact that *he* was so much stronger. But Ash would never hurt her. Sage only had to say no, and he would stop.

She didn't want to say no.

Sage turned her face into his hair as he trailed soft kisses down her neck. A shiver ran through him as her breath grazed his ear.

"Ash," she whispered.

The hands on her back curled into fists, and his body went completely rigid. He buried his face in her shoulder, groaning, "Sweet Spirit, *NO!*"

She'd done something wrong. "You don't have to stop—"

"Yes, I do." His eyes were desperate as he leaned back and pulled his hands out from her shirt. "There are things you don't know, Sage."

"Then tell me."

"Soon, sweet Sage. I promise." He wrapped his arms around her and kissed her softly as the last candle went out. "Just not tonight."

56

NOISE IN THE passage outside woke her. Ash was still stroking her back as he had been when she drifted off to sleep. He'd pulled the musty blanket up around them, but most of her warmth came from him. "We need to get up," he whispered.

She snuggled closer. "I don't want to," she mumbled into his shirt.

He kissed the top of her head. "Neither do I, but we must."

Sage groaned and pushed the blanket back, realizing she could see a little in the light coming from under the door. The shadow of two feet appeared, and a knock echoed through the room. Ash pushed himself to his feet and padded across the stone floor in his socks. She smiled as she heard him trip on the forgotten dagger and curse.

The door opened a crack, and Sage threw her arm over her eyes against the burst of light. "I see the lesson went well," a voice said dryly. Lieutenant Casseck. She didn't care what he thought, but that light was too bright.

"Shut your damn mouth," said Ash. "What's going on?"

"D'Amiran's realized Robert is gone. He wants to see Quinn right away, but he's moving slowly from last night's wine." Sage wondered whether Casseck meant the duke or the captain.

Ash glanced over his shoulder at her. "Can you get her back to her room discreetly?"

"Yes."

"We need five minutes."

"Make it three."

Ash shut the door in the lieutenant's face, then reopened it when Casseck knocked again. "Thank you," Ash said grudgingly, accepting the candle his friend offered. He bolted the door and turned to her. "Let's get you back together first. Your hair is a real mess."

Sage sat up stiffly and began struggling with her breastband. It was loose in the back, and she wasn't sure she could fix it without taking off her shirt. Ash set the candle on a table and dropped down beside her. "Let me help." She cringed as he lifted the back of her shirt. His hands tugged the ties but it only became looser. "Oh," he said sheepishly. "The laces ripped through the eyelets. I hope you have another one."

He'd been through her trunk; he should know. But she only said, "I do."

She focused on lacing her boots while he tried to pull her hair down, but succeeded only in making a further mess of it. Sage swatted his hands away and picked it apart expertly. Ash sighed and stood, lifting her up under her armpits as he rose, and set her on her feet. He moved around to her front and loosened her belt so he could push her shirt back into her breeches. Even with the distraction of his hands in her trousers, she managed to put her hair in a single braid and tuck it around enough to hide it under her hood. He tossed her jacket to her and gestured for her to step off the mat so he could stack the pallets back in the corner. Once she felt in order, she tried folding the blanket before giving up and rolling it. He took it from her and tossed it on top of the corner pile.

Three minutes had surely passed, but no knock came to urge them out. Ash saw her glance at the door and said, "He'll come back when it's safe to take you to your room."

"Why can't you take me?"

"Because I don't think I can walk next to you without making it obvious what happened last night."

She raised an eyebrow. "I thought nothing happened." He ignored her and jammed his shirt back into his breeches. Her stomach twisted. Why wouldn't he look her in the eye?

The captain. He wanted to use her, but Ash didn't. She'd seen Ash's reluctance when he made her promise to obey orders, when he taught her to fight. What other orders had Quinn forced on him?

After last night the answer was obvious: Ash wasn't allowed to be with her, no matter how much he wanted. Anger rose in her chest. Did the captain think she wasn't good enough for Ash? It was none of his damn business.

"Are you ready to go?" he asked.

Sage crossed her arms. "No, I'm not. I want to talk."

He froze with one hand half in his breeches. "About what?"

"About the things I don't know yet. You said not last night. Well, it's morning."

Ash swallowed. A tap on the door saved him, and he nearly ran to answer it. "Thirty seconds," whispered Casseck through the crack. Ash beckoned to her.

She stepped up beside him. "Talk to me, Ash."

He pulled her against him. "Tonight, I promise. Everything."

His mouth was on hers, and she melted into him, barely able to wonder what was so wrong about this, why anyone would try to stop what they had when it felt so right. Even Darnessa wanted it.

A single knock interrupted them. "I'll see you tonight," he murmured before opening the door and handing her to Casseck.

The lieutenant led her to the end of the passage and handed her a small pile of firewood. "This is for Lady Sagerra's room," he said as though nothing was amiss. They walked side by side through the empty courtyard. Most of the servants must be eating breakfast and all of the nobles still asleep.

Sage knew she should care about her reputation, but what Casseck thought of Ash concerned her more. If he reported what he saw to the captain . . . "We didn't—"

"I know. I know him well enough to see that." He looked down on her. "It's you and your honor I worry about. As far as those harpies traveling with you are concerned, you're already bedding half the soldiers." Sage rolled her eyes, but Casseck remained serious. "If they talk where

225

others can hear, you may find yourself cornered by a man who thinks he can do what he wants with you. We'd be forced to kill him, hopefully before he got very far."

Sage thought of the guard in the gatehouse. "Maybe we could use that to our advantage."

Casseck stopped to stare at her. "No. Absolutely not. That goes too far. We will *never* use you in that way."

She met his eyes accusingly. "Captain Quinn doesn't mind using anyone to his advantage—including Charlie."

Casseck shook his head. "If you truly believe that, my lady, you don't understand him at all."

Sage turned away and continued, making Casseck scramble to catch up. She was done with everyone defending Quinn, done with not knowing anything, done with watching Ash crumble under his captain's demands.

Most of all, she was done being Quinn's pawn.

57

QUINN CROSSED THE ward to meet Duke D'Amiran's summons and climbed the steps to the top of the outer bailey at an energetic pace.

"Your Grace," Quinn called as he approached. "I'm sorry it took so long to find you; there was a miscommunication as to where you were." He bowed low, then stood straight with an inquiring look, trying not to appear as tired as he felt.

"I want an explanation, Captain," the duke said. "Four of your men left on a patrol yesterday—without my permission and unaccompanied by my guards."

Quinn blinked. "I wasn't aware we needed permission or escort, as we fall under the king's authority. In the future I'll make sure you're informed, however. We meant no harm."

"No harm?" D'Amiran growled. "What say you to the report of armed men roaming my lands, frightening my workers? If my few fields cannot be planted in time due to the chaos, who will pay for the loss? You? Soldiers destroy out of habit, but men like me must provide for their people."

The incident was obviously made up or falsely linked to his patrol, but Quinn acted contrite. "If my men are truly at fault for such damages, I assure you the crown will more than cover your loss."

"You're very free with the royal purse, Captain," the duke sneered. "Is it Mother's or Father's influence that allows you such liberties? Your rank already makes it clear that being the general's son makes for a fruitful career."

Quinn ignored the insult. "That's not for me to judge, Your Grace. I simply do my best to follow orders."

D'Amiran's face darkened. "In that case, Captain, I will issue new orders to you, being you are under my roof. You and your men are forbidden to leave this fortress until further notice. You will not patrol outside my gates, and you'll submit to a muster three times daily, conducted by my captain to make sure no other faces go missing."

"Who is missing, Your Grace?"

D'Amiran met his eyes coldly. "You seem to have lost one of your officers."

"I think Your Grace must be misinformed." Quinn's tone was bland, respectful. "We haven't mustered for the day, but I laid eyes on both only a few minutes ago."

"Yes, but there were three yesterday. Four, including yourself. When your patrol returned, one of your men had been replaced by another. One shorter and filthy."

Quinn looked back in bewilderment. "They told me Sergeant Porter fell off his horse and dislocated his shoulder. I can only suggest the man in question was him, and he wasn't sitting up as straight as when he left. I can bring him to you, Your Grace, if you'd like to speak to him."

"No," his host spat. "I'm sure you covered your tracks there."

"Your Grace," Quinn said carefully, "I'm not sure why you think I would do such a thing—or how. If we've offended you, violated your hospitality, or shown ourselves to be untrustworthy, I sincerely apologize and beg the chance to make amends. Perhaps we should leave. There's enough time in the day to gather the women and take them back to Lord Fashell's estate. We can wait there for the pass to clear."

"Don't be ridiculous, Captain." The panic that flashed across D'Amiran's face told Quinn the duke wasn't quite ready to act. "Not only are the accommodations inferior, a sickness is present there. I only want you to respect my authority in my lands—a right granted by the crown."

Quinn lowered his head. "As Your Grace wishes. Are there any other restrictions? May we continue to move freely within your walls and guard the ladies we're assigned to protect? We have only their honor and safety in mind, and idle soldiers are a commander's bane."

The duke waved his hand irritably. "Yes, of course. But if any more of your party comes up missing, I will hold you personally responsible."

"As you should, Your Grace," Quinn said. "My men should be mustered now, if your captain is ready for his first inspection." He stepped back and politely gestured for the guard behind D'Amiran to lead the way.

❧

Casseck dropped into a chair opposite Quinn at the table. "What was that about?" he asked.

Quinn rubbed his face as he detailed his conversation with the duke.

"I think he's worried about what he's lost with Robert gone," Casseck said. "Maybe he promised him to Kimisara."

Quinn yawned. "You may be right. He would've been a valuable hostage. Ash said earlier their people were starving."

"Speaking of Ash," said Casseck. "How are he and the others doing out there?"

"Porter said they're getting tired of squirrel meat, and they could all use baths, but generally fine. No injuries. Ash got sick that one time, but if he hadn't, we might not have gotten our bottled weapon. How's Charlie?"

"Fine. Out in the stables this morning, tending Surry and Shadow. Three days, right?"

"At least." Quinn rubbed his neck and yawned again. "What do we need to do today, Cass?"

"Everything's in hand. Two more small barrels of both kinds of alcohol last night. Gramwell's team is done surveying the sewers. Our watch rotations cover all the areas you designated, and we have a running list of who's here. There'll be several parties leaving today, and several more arriving. The men are tired, though."

"Well, now that we won't be riding, there'll be less to do. Make sure they get rest, though—they'll need it."

"You need some sleep, Alex. Go take a nap." Casseck tilted his head at the side door.

Quinn scratched the back of his head. "I may just do that." He stood to walk to the attached room they shared.

"Starling is coming to the meeting tonight." Casseck made it a statement rather than a question.

"Yes."

"She still doesn't know, does she?"

"No." Quinn wouldn't look back as he pushed the door open.

"Mouse." Casseck waited for him to pause. "I suggest you wear body armor when you tell her."

58

SAGE SLEPT STRAIGHT through lunch and dinner, waking with a start as a tray of food settled on the table near her head. Clare sat on the edge of the bed and brushed hair from Sage's eyes. "How are you feeling?"

Sage sat up with a groan. She felt like she'd been run over by a wagon. "I've felt better."

"Where were you all night?" Clare asked. "I heard you leave, but you never came back. I went looking for Darnessa after a few hours."

The matchmaker had been waiting when Sage returned that morning, disheveled and smelling like sweat. Though Darnessa had stopped short of calling her a harlot, it was a lecture Sage didn't care to remember. She rubbed her face and tried to think. "Privy," she said. "The soldiers said we passed a village with a nasty illness. I must've caught it."

"Is that why Darnessa told us not to drink the water?"

"Probably. I guess she didn't tell me in time."

Clare smiled sympathetically. "I brought some dinner. Are you up to eating?"

Sage's stomach roared in response. "Yes, thank you. I think the worst is over." Clare handed her a cup of herbal tea and watched as Sage tried to drink it slowly. "Did anything interesting happen today?"

"Lots of departures and arrivals. Duke D'Amiran's angry about something. He spent most of the day stomping around the outer walls, staring at the forest."

Sage smiled to herself. "What has our escort been up to?"

Clare offered her a roll of soft bread. "Haven't seen most of them, other than the regulars who patrol around us on occasion. I think they're lying low. One of the maids said the duke was yelling at Captain Quinn this morning."

Feeling guilty, Sage said, "I'm sorry you didn't see Gramwell today."

"He told me last night he wouldn't be able to write or come near me for a while, but if the duke said anything interesting, I should tell you." Clare narrowed her eyes. "Why would it be dangerous for one of our escorts to speak to me?"

"Did he say 'dangerous'?" Sage asked.

"No, but I'm not a fool, and you're even less of one."

Ash must have felt this way when she asked questions. "Clare, there's trouble brewing, and I can't tell you the details, but not because I don't trust you. Anyone who knows is at risk."

"And when events come to a head, how am I to act in a way that's helpful if I don't know anything?"

"I'll tell you. Or one of the soldiers will. Or Darnessa." Sage added the last, suspecting the matchmaker knew much more than she revealed. They eyed each other stubbornly until they heard a knock on the door.

Clare stood and set the tray of food across Sage's lap. "I will try to be content with that for now." She walked around the bed to answer the door and came back with a note. Before Sage could stop her, Clare opened it herself and glanced at it, then handed it over.

Main chapel, 1 hour before midnight.–A

She looked up at Clare, who gazed back with raised eyebrows.

"You weren't sick last night, were you?" Clare asked. "You were with him." Sage pressed her lips together, and Clare rolled her eyes. "Just tell me when I should start worrying that you haven't come back."

❧

Sage waited nervously in the dark chapel, as eager to see Ash again as she was to confront the captain. The air behind her shifted, and she felt the heat of someone at her back. She yelped as an arm slipped around her waist. A gloved hand slammed over her mouth, and she was lifted off her feet. She bit down hard on the hand, bracing her arm to elbow her attacker with all her strength.

"For Spirit's sake!" Ash hissed in her ear. "It's only me."

He released her, and she spun around to shove him. "You scared the life out of me!"

Ash's teeth flashed in the dim light as he shook his left hand in the air. "Good reaction, though." He took off his glove and flexed his fingers. "Ow."

"You deserved it." Her heart was pounding so hard, she felt it in her fingertips.

"So I did." He pulled her to the side, glancing around. "We're going to a planning meeting, but I have to explain something first." Sage's heart had begun to slow, but it leapt again. Ash took a deep breath. "Robert's gone, so now it's safe to tell you who he was."

"Lieutenant Gramwell, right?" She wanted to show him she'd discovered it on her own.

"How did you figure that?"

"You didn't want me to talk to the officers, so it must be one of them. Gramwell wouldn't leave Clare alone, and who but a prince would be so bold with a Concordium bride? He also told her he wouldn't see her for a while." She heard Ash groan softly. "I'll do everything I can to make the match happen. She'd be a wonderful queen."

"For once, you're mistaken." His head snapped up at a noise near the altar. He tugged her arm. "This way."

Ash led her out a side door and pulled her toward the soldiers' quarters. Along the way she tried to figure where she went wrong in her logic. He ushered her into the barracks, pausing to close the door behind them.

"Quinn," she said as he turned to face her.

Ash jumped. "What?"

"Prince Robert was acting as Captain Quinn."

He swallowed. "Yes." He glanced anxiously at the captain's door.

She waited, but he didn't say anything more. After a few seconds, she prompted, "And Casseck is really the captain?"

"Will you stop it with the theories?" Ash reached up to her face with his right hand, his dark eyes locking onto hers. "There's something I need to tell you. Something important."

"Yes?" she whispered, the mystery forgotten. Now she understood why he was nervous. He wanted to say what he couldn't before. The words that would change everything.

Ash hesitated. "I've practiced telling you so many times, but I still don't know how."

She leaned closer and placed a trembling hand on his upper arm. *Please*, she thought but could not say. *I don't need fancy words, I just need—*

The captain's door opened, throwing a shaft of light across them. "Captain?"

Without lowering his hand, Ash slowly turned his head to acknowledge Lieutenant Gramwell, who now realized his intrusion.

"Sorry, sir. Begging your pardon, sir, but we're ready when you are."

Ash gave a short nod. "Thank you. I'll be just a couple minutes."

Gramwell shut the door after casting an apologetic look at Sage. Once again they were alone with the light from a single torch. Ash continued to stare at the door, clenching his jaw.

"*You,*" she whispered. "You're Captain Quinn?" His dark eyes turned back to her, filled with shame. Fury of comprehension raced through Sage like wildfire, burning every nerve ending in her skin.

It was all a lie.

Everything about him was a *lie*.

There was no Ash Carter.

Her vision clouded over, and she wrenched away, yanking her hand back from his arm, only to reverse and send her clenched fist flying at his face. With the hand that had rested against her cheek, he deflected the blow and seized her wrist, forcing her arm down in a swift arc. His left arm clamped around her, pinning her arms to her side and pulling her roughly against him.

"I may deserve it," he said, straining to hold her. "But a broken nose will slow us down in ways we can't afford."

His right arm was across her body, pressed between them, jamming her left hand under his elbow, and he'd wrapped one leg around hers to pin them together. She couldn't move an inch. "You two-faced son of a *BITCH*!" she hissed. "Is this how an honorable officer of the realm behaves?"

"In protection of the crown, yes." His coolness only infuriated her more, and she twisted and pushed against his iron hold, her left wrist screaming in protest. Her struggles made him fight for balance on one foot. "You weren't always honest about your identity and motives either, *my lady*."

It was a cruel thing to say. Every second the Ash she knew drifted farther away, but he'd never been real. "Mine were never intended to use or hurt people, *Captain Quinn*." She spat his name like a curse.

He looked down on her without blinking until she turned her face away. She'd fallen for his act like a lovesick schoolgirl—she who prided herself on her judgment, her ability to see through the fronts people presented. And why? Because she wanted a prince, a fairy tale. The tidal wave of anger receded, leaving behind a gaping chasm of hurt, which was worse, and she sagged against him with a muffled sob.

Quinn relaxed his leg and eased the pressure at her back enough to pull his right arm free. She might have escaped his grasp in those seconds, but she no longer cared enough to try. He wiped her tears away with his fingers as she stared into empty space. It was humiliating. She hadn't even cried when Father died.

"I never wanted to hurt you," he whispered.

She would not answer, would not look at him, would not even nod or shake her head.

"Sage, please, I'm so sorry it had to happen this way. Only truth from now on—I promise."

How could he think that promise meant anything? "I don't want your truth. I hate it." Her voice sounded dead to her own ears. "I hate you."

"I'll say it anyway: *I love you, Sage Fowler.* Of everything I've said and done, *that* is truth."

Of all the things he could have said, that was the worst. Her left hand no longer restrained, she drew back and slapped him across the face with all her might.

59

SAGE IGNORED CASSECK'S and Gramwell's apologetic smiles as she brushed past them into the room. She didn't hate them, though—all of the blame rested on the captain, who now pulled a chair around the table. He gestured for her to sit, which Sage did without looking at him. She'd refused to go back to her room. Maybe it was defiance; maybe it was loyalty to Darnessa and Clare. Maybe she just couldn't stand to be left out. But when he offered to release her from any part in their plans, she'd simply turned her back on him and walked to the meeting room door.

The lieutenants stood silently on the opposite side of the table as Quinn seated himself beside her. They acknowledged her as one of their own and not like some pet as she feared they would, though perhaps their deference was inspired by the fading red handprint on their captain's cheek.

What she learned was frightening. The 130 men she'd heard about were in fact 200 Kimisar soldiers, though at least ten had been killed. As Quinn showed her how the squads were arranged around them, her mind made a connection.

"Their commander is here." She pointed to a group near the pass. Everyone stared at her.

"What makes you say that?" asked Quinn.

"That morning I was on the wall, a trained hawk circled that spot before landing. It came in from the south."

"How do you know it wasn't just a regular hawk?" Quinn asked. In response, she raised an eyebrow, and he snorted humorlessly. "Right. A fowler would know."

Most of the meeting was devoted to refining the soldiers' response if the duke acted before the sickness hit. Her responsibility would be to gather and hide the ladies, and if they were taken, to be alert for a rescue attempt. So after everything she'd done for Quinn, he wanted her to sit on the side and watch. "I can do more," she argued. "As a woman I can provide . . . unique distractions."

Quinn waved her idea aside. "I leave it to you to have a fainting spell as necessary, but we're talking about battle, Sage."

Somehow her name on his lips was an insult; he had no right to address her so casually. Sage crossed her arms. "*I'm* talking about battle. D'Amiran's guards are as lecherous as they come. We can use that to our advantage."

Quinn's eyes widened. "Don't even think about it." Casseck and Gramwell shifted uncomfortably. "Besides," he continued with a meaningful look, "you promised to follow orders, as I recall."

"And *you* promised . . ." She faltered. An awkward silence fell as the lieutenants looked everywhere but at their captain. Sage pinched her upper arm to anchor herself. She would not cry. Not here. Her fingernails dug into her flesh through both jacket and shirt, but she maintained her composure.

"Mistress Sage," Lieutenant Casseck said, "this is what we need from you. It's truly important, and it leaves a man free to fight."

Sage squeezed harder as she turned to Casseck. His expression was open, honest. For the sake of that honesty, she backed down, but she remained silent for the rest of the meeting.

Gramwell left when dismissed, but Casseck stayed behind.

"I need to check on a few things before taking her back," Quinn said. "Can you wait with her?"

Casseck nodded.

Once Quinn was gone, Casseck pulled up a chair and sat facing her, but didn't speak. After a full minute, she asked, "How long have I been involved in this?"

"Since the night he met you," Casseck said. "The code name for the first agent to go into a situation is 'Mouse,' because he's supposed to be the crumb catcher no one notices. But you saw him, and that changed things."

Her hands clenched under the table. He'd used her from the first day. "Did I have a code name, too?"

"He called you Starling."

Starling. A useless, annoying bird that gabbled all its secrets.

Casseck watched her fight back tears. "It was never easy for him to lie," he said. "In fact, as time went on, the harder the act wore on him."

"What's done is done," Sage said dully. She just wanted to go to sleep and forget everything. "If he hadn't been playing the Mouse, you might never have realized what was going on." He nodded, and they were quiet again. Finally, she said, "I remember Mouse being mentioned during the meeting—you talked about him like he wasn't there."

"That's a spy tactic. It throws off anyone who might overhear and alleviates confusion about who is doing what, as who, and what everyone's relationships are." Casseck scooted his chair closer and put his elbows on the table, plainly relieved to address something professional. "The habit is also useful to those who change identities. It keeps the personas separate in their own mind, makes it easier to take one off and put the other on."

The implication made her feel sick. *I love you, Sage Fowler.* Which was the person who'd said that? Did it even matter? One person was a lie and the other she hated.

Casseck shook his head as if reading her thoughts. "No, Mistress Sage, I'm his oldest friend, and I can tell you—"

The door opened and Sage and Casseck nearly jumped out of their seats as Quinn walked in. He looked from face to face before striding to the door of the bunk room. "Whatever you were about to say, Lieutenant, keep it to yourself."

Casseck shrugged sheepishly at Sage.

Quinn returned a few seconds later, stuffing something into the breast of his jacket. "Things look clear enough to take you back." He stalked out the door without waiting for her. Sage glanced at Casseck before pushing back her chair and following.

"Sage," Casseck called, and she paused to look back. "Just . . . go easy on him." He grinned a little. "Or at least don't hit him again."

Captain Quinn waited for her in the passage. "Nice chat?" he asked, raising an eyebrow.

"Very informative," she answered coolly.

"Anything you want to say to me?"

"No, I think I've expressed myself enough for one night."

He rubbed his cheek. "I deserved that."

"At least we agree on something." She felt a little satisfaction, but she also knew he was fast enough to have ducked the blow. He'd let her hit him.

The walk back was silent. Only the guard posted at the entrance to the Great Hall was in sight, and he didn't seem interested in anything but scratching his ear. They made it to the guest wing without seeing anyone else. At her door she turned to leave him without a word, but he caught her elbow.

"You're in this now, for better or for worse," he said, "so you need to take extra precautions." She nodded reluctantly, and he continued, "From now on, don't go anywhere alone unless you absolutely must, and then always make sure someone knows where you are. Don't trust any notes we don't hand to you, and don't trust any you don't recognize as mine."

He reached into his jacket, pulled out a knife, and pressed it into her hand. "Carry this on you everywhere you go."

Sage looked down at the sheathed dagger. The handle was black and had inlaid gold letters: *AQ*.

"If you're in trouble, any of my men will recognize it, and if none of my men are around . . . you remember what I taught you."

She didn't want this knife—his personal one—but his logic was sound.

His hands were still on hers. "Are you going to be all right?"

She gripped the weapon and nodded.

"Good night, Sage." He pulled her hand up to his mouth and brushed a featherlight kiss across her knuckles. She pulled away at the touch of his lips, and he released her.

Sage backed into the room, refusing to look at him as she shut the door in his face. She shoved the bolt home, and the sound echoed through the silence.

How she would face tomorrow, she didn't know.

60

QUINN WENT ABOUT his duties and inspections the next morning, contemplating how his father wanted him to learn patience. Well, he was learning it now.

It was his habit to walk several daily turns on the inner and outer walls, and if he dallied where he could see the garden, so be it. From his current angle he could see Sage sitting on a stone bench. She'd tinted her hair and wore a dress that made her look like another of the painted peacocks he was protecting, but he recognized the way she walked, knew how she tilted her head when she smiled, saw her fold her hands as she did when she was stressed. A pair of young men hovered around her, vying for her attention. He leaned on the wooden rail and watched, silently willing her to look back at him, but she never did.

His attention was so focused, he didn't notice Casseck approaching until he was right next to him.

"So what did you say to her last night?" he asked.

Quinn looked at his hands. "The truth."

"I see. What was her response?"

"Nonverbal, but clear." He rubbed his still-sore cheek.

"I'm sorry."

"I expected the reaction, but I still had to tell her." The hurt and fury hadn't been a surprise, but the blank look that had taken over afterward had been worse. That she'd mustered enough emotion to hit him after that deadness had been a relief.

"She'll cool off, Alex, just give her time. You can make it up to her."

Quinn snorted. "If D'Amiran doesn't kill us all first."

"Always sanguine. Which reminds me, I came up here to report."

Quinn stood straight. "Go ahead."

"We've got so many arrivals that they're putting up tents now." Casseck nodded to the inner ward, where a large circular canvas was being laid out. "Only a few guards with them, though, so that means we don't have much more to worry about than D'Amiran's soldiers."

"And the Kimisar." Quinn gestured to the top of the granite keep. "The flags up there were moved around this morning. I'm guessing that's how the duke talks to them, though I've no idea what it means, and there's no way for the scouts to tell us." He tapped his lip as he watched the activity in the ward. "Good news on the arrivals, though they're all too late to catch the sickness. If it works."

"That's my other good news," said Casseck. "I just found Charlie in the privy. Not feeling too well."

It *was* good news, but Quinn couldn't manage a smile over the twisting guilt in his stomach.

61

THE MAID ENTERED the bedchamber to prepare it for the evening. She stacked more firewood by the hearth and swept the ashes away from the embers before coaxing them back to life. Then she swung a kettle over the low flames so the ladies would have hot water for tea and wiped her hands on her apron. This room was easier to tend than the others—the occupants were far less demanding. For that reason, she often found herself putting extra effort into it, simply because the ladies were so kind and appreciative. Tonight, though, she had a touch of stomach-ache, and she hurried through her duties so she could have time to rest before dinner.

She dusted and plumped the cushions on the chairs, replaced the lowest candles, and had just moved to turn down the beds when the door opened behind her and a castle guard stepped inside, leering at her. He was huge and dangerous-looking, with a large chunk missing from one of his ears. His intentions became obvious when he bolted the door behind him and made a kissing face. She cast a frantic look at the small window. Would anyone come to her aid if she called? He smirked while she tried to decide if she could make it to the opening before he got to her.

She dove over the bed, rolling across the satin coverlet and to her feet on the other side, and lunged for the open window. She took a deep breath to scream as loud as she could, but his hand clamped over her face and yanked her backward. Within seconds he had her pinned to the floor, and he released her mouth only to clench his meaty fingers around her throat.

"I suggest you stay quiet," he whispered maliciously in her ear. She began to cry.

He slid a large knife from his belt and tapped her on the shoulder with it. "I'm not actually in the mood just now, but that may change, depending on how you answer my questions. We can start with something simple." He leaned back and looked down at her. "What is your name?"

"Poppy," she whimpered. "Poppy Dyer."

"And where are you from, little Poppy Dyer?"

"Garland Hill."

"You were hired by the matchmaker as a ladies' attendant for the journey?"

She nodded, tears streaming back into her hair. "Please, don't hurt me."

"You're doing well, Poppy." He smiled, but it gave her no relief. "Let's try some harder questions. What are the names of the women who sleep in this room?"

Poppy choked against his hold. "Lady Clare Holloway and Lady Sagerra Broadmoor."

The man shook his head in disappointment. "Now, see, I know that ain't exactly accurate, little Poppy." He trailed the blade from her collarbone to her waist and sliced the laces of her bodice open, generating a brief, futile struggle. "Let's try again, shall we? What are the names of the women who sleep in this room?"

Mistress Rodelle didn't want anyone to know Sage was really her apprentice. But no silly matchmaker's secret was worth keeping in the face of this man.

"Clare Holloway," she sobbed. "And Sage Fowler."

"Much better," he said pleasantly, resting the tip of the knife on the neckline of her linen underdress. "Now let's find out how much you know about Sage Fowler."

62

SAGE MADE HER way back to her room in a fog. She couldn't remember half of what had happened that day. Like a horse wearing blinders, she'd focused only on what was directly in front of her. That way she never saw Quinn, never had to think about him.

She flopped down on the bed, wishing she could fall asleep right then, even in the ridiculous dress, corset and all; but there would be a meeting tonight, and she had news to contribute. Quinn would probably fetch her soon, unless he was too cowardly to come himself.

Someone knocked on the door, and Sage groaned and rolled off the bed, then slumped against it. The sky outside the window was still light, so it was too early for Quinn. Clare wouldn't knock, so it must be Darnessa. "Come in," she called.

As Darnessa opened the latch and stepped inside, Sage felt a rush of anger. So much of the emotional turmoil of the last few days reminded her of when Uncle William had told her she would go to the matchmaker, and all of it, past and present, had been orchestrated by this woman. She pushed herself upright and faced Darnessa.

"How long did you know?" Sage demanded. "From the beginning?"

Darnessa sighed as she closed the door. "Since Underwood. I agreed to let him use you. It wasn't supposed to happen this way."

Sage advanced a step, eyes narrowing. "How, exactly, was it *supposed* to happen?"

The matchmaker wrung her hands, looking small for once. "You were just supposed to be friends. You were supposed to trust him, help him. I hoped when this was all over, maybe you would let yourself see him as something more."

"Some. Thing. More." Sage's hands curled into fists. The fragile control she'd maintained all day began to crack.

"I just wanted you to be happy. You *were* happy," Darnessa insisted.

"He lied to me."

"You lied to him, too."

"On your orders!" Sage screamed.

Darnessa dropped her arms and drew herself up. "I did not do this for my own amusement, Sage. Nor did he."

Furious as she was, Sage knew the first part was true—the matchmaker never abused her influence and punished those who did. As for him . . . It was easier to hate him than to admit she'd fallen for the idea that a prince had loved her. She wasn't as blind to position and power as she'd thought. "He's not who I thought he was."

"And who am I, Sage? The high matchmaker—or Darnessa?"

"What is that supposed to mean?"

"We each play several roles in life—that doesn't make them all lies." Darnessa moved closer, raising her hands in appeal. "I am the high matchmaker of Crescera. I make calculated decisions that affect the lives of hundreds, if not thousands. That's who I am." She stopped when her skirt brushed against Sage's and reached across the gap. "I'm also just Darnessa. I'm your friend."

Sage stepped back before Darnessa could touch her. "You are *not* my friend," she spat. "You've been playing high matchmaker so long you've forgotten how *not* to manipulate people. Friends don't do that."

"You're not an authority on friendship." Darnessa dropped her hand. "But you're right. I'm sorry."

"Mend a broken plate with that apology, and I'll accept it." She pushed around Darnessa and stalked to the door, throwing it open only to find Clare standing outside with a guilty expression. Turning back, Sage addressed the matchmaker. "Good night."

Darnessa nodded, her face crumpling like a used napkin. Clare moved out of the matchmaker's way, then stepped inside and bolted the door behind her. For a handful of seconds she and Sage eyed each other from a few feet apart.

"Are you okay?" Clare whispered.

"No," said Sage. "It was all a lie." She burst into tears, and Clare put her arms around her and let her cry.

63

QUINN WIPED CHARLIE'S forehead with a cool cloth. "How are you feeling, kid?"

"Better now." Charlie clutched his stomach and shifted on the cot in the room Quinn shared with Cass. "I'll get up in a minute and finish my work."

Quinn shook his head. "No, stay here. All this will last a couple days more. Just rest."

"How do you know?"

The knot in Quinn's stomach tightened. "I've just seen this before."

Charlie nodded. "I'll get the bucket, though."

"No, I've got it." Quinn stood and picked up the foul-smelling bucket covered with a soiled, wet towel. "I have to take care of some things, but you stay here and call if you need anything. And drink this tea when you feel you can. Those are orders."

Charlie nodded, his feverish eyes closing as Quinn backed away.

Quinn carried the bucket to the privy and dumped and rinsed it out himself. Then he washed his face and hands in water that had been boiled and tossed his shirt in the steaming cauldron the soldiers had already started to wash contaminated clothes. He couldn't afford to have anyone get sick, least of all him.

But he'd let it happen to Charlie. The logic was indisputable—the page wasn't a fighter they would lose; they needed an early sign that the sickness would work; and Charlie was already exposed when he dumped it in the cistern. None of it eased the feeling of guilt.

Quinn slipped back into his room, placed the bucket where Charlie would be able to use it again, and changed into a fresh shirt before going to collect Sage for the meeting tonight. He arrived early, afraid she would head to the barracks unescorted.

She answered the door, dressed in breeches and ready to go, and he stepped inside before she could push past him into the corridor. A low fire in the hearth provided the only light, but his sight was already adjusted enough to see the puffy redness around her eyes. She'd been crying.

Because of him, what he'd done.

He didn't realize someone else was in the room until there was a movement by the fireplace, but it was only Lady Clare. She stood to acknowledge him, and he wondered what she knew. Not much, he decided. Sage wouldn't have wanted to endanger her friend, but from Clare's hostile look, he could tell she knew enough to blame him for Sage's tears.

"Captain Quinn," she said, offering her hand. "I don't believe we've been formally introduced."

Quinn touched his lips to her fingers. Sage watched impassively. "Lady Clare, it's a pleasure to meet you."

Clare pulled her hand back. "I was just leaving to speak with one of the maids. I imagine you'll be gone by the time I return." Her brown eyes were hard with a silent message: *If you hurt my friend again, you will answer to me.*

He bowed, and she left with a last glance at Sage. When they were alone, Quinn cleared his throat. "Say what you need to," he said simply.

Sage looked confused. "About what I learned today?"

"Well, that." He shuffled his feet. "Or anything you'd like to say to me. Anything you want to know—I'll answer it all now."

A ripple of surprise went over her face, a spark of life in an otherwise spiritless posture. "All right, then. Why did you keep lying after I told you who I was? And don't say to protect me."

"Mainly to protect Robert." He tried not to fidget. "I reassigned our original Mouse at the last minute, and since I'd never gone undercover myself, I took the opportunity to experience it. We still needed a captain, however, and Rob looks a lot like me. I thought after a few days I'd step back into the role and no one would notice as long as he stayed a bit distant.

"When you offered to teach me to read, I couldn't really say no, so I played along, especially because you and that ledger became more interesting. I also enjoyed the freedom of not being the captain." He tried to smile. "And your company."

She waited, saying nothing.

He took a deep breath. "Thing was, we realized we were surrounded, and keeping Rob hidden became a necessity. If I'd gone back to being myself . . ."

"You would've revealed him," she finished.

He nodded and looked down. "Every decision I made has put us in the best possible position to foil D'Amiran's plan—and Robert is safe now. I regret nothing except that you were hurt. But . . ." He hesitated. "I also could've told you earlier. I was a coward."

"You didn't have to kiss me," she said stiffly. "Not after the armory, at least."

"I didn't have to, no." He raised his eyes to meet hers. Kissing her had been like tasting sunshine. "But I wanted to."

Sage blushed and looked away, hugging her elbows across her stomach, but whether from anger or embarrassment he couldn't tell.

"You're a complication, Sage, one I never could have planned for. I wish I could make you understand." He shrugged helplessly. "But I don't really understand it myself. I just know how I feel."

Her gray eyes focused back on him, but she remained silent.

Quinn swallowed. He'd been a fool to think his lies had been forgivable. That he loved her only made them worse.

"I don't even know your first name," she said abruptly. "But I suppose I can just call you Captain like everyone else." She looked away again and flushed a deeper shade of pink.

Sweet Spirit, no wonder she treated him like a stranger. "It's Alexander," he whispered. "Alex."

"Alex," she whispered back. There was a softness to her voice.

It was enough. For now.

64

ALEX. HIS NAME echoed in her mind every time she looked at him. It was a strong name, one that suited the man who now held the attention of his officers with a natural confidence and command. But it had a softness and intimacy, too, when he'd whispered it in her room. Occasionally, she caught his dark eyes, and there was a trace of uncertainty in their depths. Darnessa's words returned to her.

We each play several roles in life—that doesn't make them all lies.

Gramwell was reporting on the test runs of what D'Amiran's people would and wouldn't notice. The soldiers had obtained several casks of oil and two kinds of very pure alcohol and planned to place them around the fortress to aid in creating panic and destroying weapons. Several of the duke's guards were observed to have skipped the evening meal or eaten lightly, and Sage noted the absence of three lords at dinner, which was taken as evidence the sickness was spreading.

"But those lords may have picked it up on the way here," she pointed out, worried they depended too much on her idea. Spirit above, how did Quinn make life-and-death decisions with so little information?

"Given Charlie fell ill this afternoon, I'm optimistic," he said.

He'd made his own brother sick to test the weapon. What a Quinn thing to do. She crossed her arms and looked away, though not before catching the guilt on his face.

Sage paid attention to where they would stage oil and alcohol so she could keep the women away from those areas. When the discussion turned to how to take out the long, single-room barracks in the outer ward, hopefully with a number of sick guards inside, Sage listened with one ear as she studied their map of the fortress. It was based mostly on her own sketch, with a few additions. She barely glanced up when Gramwell left and returned with two enlisted men who looked enough alike to be brothers. The officers began questioning the soldiers on how to start a big fire in a hurry.

"It's not hard, sir," the shorter man was saying. "You jest need t' spread it around. It vapors into th' air pretty quick, but then it thins out. If you catch it right at th' beginnin', it can be good and explosive, though."

That caught Quinn's attention. "Explosive?"

Both soldiers nodded, and the shorter one continued, "In a closed space it's deadly. Can I show you?"

"If you can do it without killing us," Quinn said with raised eyebrows.

"Sure, sir. I jest need a bottle and a bit o' the spirits."

The materials were procured and the shorter man poured a thimble-ful of clear liquid in an empty bottle. He held his thumb over the mouth and swirled the liquid around a bit, until most of it seemed to disappear. Then, keeping it plugged, he set it on the table and gestured for everyone to back up.

Quinn pulled Sage away, and she peered around him to watch. His arm stayed protectively in front of her, ready to sweep her behind him if necessary. This close, she couldn't help breathing in scents of leather, evergreen soap, and linen—a mix that was distinctly his. She felt herself leaning against him. To get a better view.

The taller soldier brought over a sliver of wood lit from the torch on the wall—a little nervously, Sage thought. Quinn's arm curled around her a bit, muscles taut as a bowstring.

In a swift move, the first soldier released the bottle and the second dropped the burning stick in the opening, then both jumped away. A loud *pop* echoed through the room as blue flashed through the bottle, spouting flame out of the mouth for a few seconds. Then it was over. The shorter man picked up the bottle and swirled it again, and a trace of the blue flame inside flickered and vanished.

Quinn released her and stepped forward. "Excellent. How do we make that happen in a large room?"

The pair looked doubtful. "You need t' get it in th' air, sir," the shorter man said. "You could throw in a couple bottles like this t' break and scatter it around."

"But it vapors quickly, right?" said Casseck.

The man shook his head "It would take a while still, sir, t' get that effect. But maybe that'd be enough—flames would spread like a flowing river, jest not like this." He waved the bottle in the air.

The discussion turned to that possibility, but Sage found herself stuck on the memory of a fire-breather she'd seen as a child. The man would spit a fine cloud of alcohol into the air and touch it off with a torch. One time he created a ring of mist, stepped back, and lit it as it hung in the air in front of him. She smiled.

"I have an idea," she said.

"You always do." Quinn was looking at her, and the room fell silent. "Tell us."

"Well," she said, conscious that everyone was watching her. The captain nodded encouragingly. "I was thinking of bellows."

"Bellows?" he echoed, forehead creasing. "Like to build up a fire?"

Sage twisted her hands. "Yes, well, a few summers ago, it was really hot, and my cousins and I took bellows and put water in them and sprayed one another. If—if there's only a little water inside, it comes out not as a stream, but a mist. . . ."

Quinn's eyes widened. "A flammable mist." She nodded, and grins spread on every face.

"That's brilliant," said the taller enlisted man. He gaped at her. "Who are you?"

"Private Stiller, this is Sage Fowler," said Quinn—*Alex*—with a smile that sent warmth through her veins. "Our secret weapon."

65

D'AMIRAN SHADED HIS eyes against the sun and took a few minutes to observe the girl before approaching. She looked so innocent, sitting on the bench under a budding tree in the garden, a heavy book open on her lap. Not overly pretty, though, and rather skinny. What was it Quinn saw in this commoner? He shrugged to himself. Perhaps she simply gave him what young men wanted; as a false bride, she didn't have to preserve her virtue.

Geddes was of the opinion that Quinn's attachment was not superficial, though. All the better that the boy-captain was gone for this conversation. D'Amiran had granted Quinn's request to take a team to the river to collect fresh water that morning—accompanied by his own guards, of course. The fool expressed concern about the low level of the cistern and whined about how his hunting dogs felt cooped up, but it served the duke to have him out of the way for a few hours.

When his shadow fell over her, she looked up and started to her feet, but he motioned for her to stay seated. "May I join you, my lady?" he asked.

"You honor me, Your Grace," she said, her pale eyes wide in awe.

"I was merely curious what you were reading," D'Amiran said, easing himself down onto the warm stone seat and leaning in. "It's not often I see a lady so absorbed in such a large volume."

"It's from your magnificent library, Your Grace," she said shyly. The girl shifted her knees toward him so he couldn't scoot closer. She probably had that dagger Geddes had seen Quinn give her tucked up her skirt. "I hope you're not upset I removed it. It's so much nicer out here for reading."

"Not for long, though." D'Amiran pointed to the gathering clouds over the eastern peaks. "We'll have our rains at last, and the pass will clear. In a few days you can continue your travels."

She gave a dreamy sigh. "I shall miss this place, I think. Coming from the open fields of Crescera, I always imagined mountains would be dark and forbidding, but they're not. Tegann nestles within their arms like a lover, and I've never felt so safe."

The little fowler was *good*. D'Amiran felt charmed in spite of himself. He turned his attention to a page approaching from the keep.

"Your Grace," the boy said with a bow. His face was pale and he didn't stand up quite straight, like his stomach hurt. "You wanted to be informed when Captain Quinn was returning from the river."

Next to D'Amiran, the girl's head went up. The duke smiled to himself as he addressed the boy. "Very good. Tell Captain Geddes to meet me on the south wall."

When the page was gone, D'Amiran turned back to the girl. "I've enjoyed our chat, however brief it was, but you must excuse me, my lady. I have matters to attend to."

She put out her hand to touch his arm. "May I ask why our escort went to the river?"

"It seems your captain doesn't trust I can provide enough water for everyone here," he said. "Or perhaps he just doesn't like the taste."

"From your cistern? Oh, I saw that wonderful system, Your Grace. The captain is no doubt overreacting. How silly."

Her expression was a mixture of fear and resentment, which puzzled him, but perhaps she was afraid someone would discover her connection to Quinn. D'Amiran bowed and kissed her hand before departing for the outer ward and the south wall. Captain Geddes waited in a spot where they could watch the approach to the rear gate.

Quinn hadn't objected to not being allowed to carry weapons, but it looked like a few of the hunting dogs they'd taken had caught some rabbits. None of the dogs looked eager to return to the confines of the fortress, as they danced around the escort soldiers, burning off energy. For a few minutes the duke and his captain watched the wagons make their way up the slope.

"Did Your Grace speak with the girl?" Geddes asked.

D'Amiran nodded. "Not to my taste, but I see some of the appeal. She's positively enchanting when she wants to be." The duke smiled. "I imagine the little slut plans to seduce him so he'll do the honorable thing and marry her, but I don't think she has yet. It would ruin his career and create a huge scandal, which would've been amusing to watch. My question is, would it be more soul crushing to take her from him before or after he gets a taste? Each has its own poetry, don't you think?"

Geddes tugged his ravaged ear. "I don't think you should wait any longer, Your Grace."

"Yes, I agree." D'Amiran sighed. "With this sickness, though, we'll have a hard time marching anytime soon." He brooded for a moment. "I thought it was a sign the Spirit blessed my cause when the rains were late. I felt sure of it when we learned the prince was coming right to us, but now I'm plagued with problems. Robert escaped, this wretched illness delays my allies, and my idiot brother keeps coming up with excuses not to march yet."

"All will be in place tomorrow, Your Grace," the captain soothed. "A few delays were inevitable."

"Eliminating the escort could be messy. Their vigilance is irksome, and we can't challenge them head-on without risking some of the lives I need." The duke inclined his head toward the party now entering the gate below. "We probably should've taken them just now, while so many were at the river, but that moment has passed. Can we take them during one of the musters?"

"Not without losing a number of our own men, Your Grace. They chose the location well," the captain admitted.

D'Amiran waved his hand. "It wouldn't have been much fun anyway. I don't know how Quinn managed to get the prince out, but that little shit has caused a great deal of complication. I want him to suffer, and I want to tell his father all about it. So that leaves the girl."

Geddes cleared his throat. "She visits him in the barracks in the evening, dressed as a man, but he accompanies her to and from those trysts. Perhaps we can separate them and then grab her. Being that she's not a lady, what else could we assume but that she's a spy?"

"And hang her?" D'Amiran smirked. "It would certainly provoke him, but it's a little too prosaic." He gazed wistfully into the distance. "I need poetry in my life to combat this drab place."

"Then use her as you wish, Your Grace; she's only a commoner. Nothing would bring Quinn to her aid faster. And raising arms against you would be treason, punishable by death."

"Yes." The duke dragged out the syllable. "That is positively a ballad."

The page from earlier came running up the nearest steps, crouching even more than before as he approached. "Your Grace!" he gasped, clutching his stomach.

D'Amiran backed a step away from the boy. He smelled like sewage. "What is it?"

"You have a visitor. From the forest."

Huzar. The duke grimaced and looked to Geddes. "Meet him and bring him to my chambers. I'll receive him there."

"He's already there by now, Your Grace!" the page blurted out.

D'Amiran narrowed his eyes, and Geddes stepped in. "How long ago did he arrive, boy?"

"Perhaps thirty minutes ago, sir."

"And we're just now learning this?" roared Geddes, cuffing the boy with an open hand.

"Begging Your Grace's pardon, but I had to use the privy before I could tell you! It was urgent."

Geddes raised his arm to strike the boy again, but D'Amiran lifted his hand to stop him. The captain froze. "Why was no other messenger sent in your place?" the duke asked.

The page cringed away from Geddes. "All the other boys are sick, Your Grace. Worse than me."

"All of them?" The boy nodded.

D'Amiran made a disgusted sound and turned away. Geddes trailed him as he headed down the steps and around the ward to the inner gate. As they passed the gardens, the duke caught sight of the Fowler girl and Lady Clare walking together. The former watched him as he walked up the steps to the keep, and he knew in that moment she wasn't Quinn's target of affection—she was his spy. He would enjoy making them both pay.

When he reached his chambers, pausing outside to catch his breath from the climb, he realized Captain Huzar had dispatched an underling this time. D'Amiran seated himself and studied the emotionless face before him.

"I have a message from my commander." The Kimisar soldier enunciated consonants and dragged the soft g as Huzar did. He'd given no greeting.

Annoyed, the duke gestured for him to continue. The Kimisar would be enlightened on how to properly address a nobleman once things were settled.

"The Kimisar are returning home."

"WHAT IS THIS?" roared D'Amiran, leaping to his feet.

The young man continued without flinching. "The agreement is broken. We keep our side, but you do not. Your army does not march. There is no prince. We wait no longer for other promises. We return home, taking payment along the way."

"I will hunt you down and hang every one of you by your entrails along the border—"

"You will not. We will be beyond your reach before your sick soldiers can mount their sick horses."

The truth of the statement enraged the duke, and he seized a knife from his nearest guard and advanced on the Kimisar, who up close he could see was little more than a boy. "You are wrong about one thing," D'Amiran said. "There is no 'we.'"

The youth reacted with only the slightest grimace as the blade cut deep into his neck. He held himself upright even as his blood sprayed across the hearth rug. D'Amiran stayed close until the soldier collapsed in a heap, relishing the small victory of a Kimisar groveling at his feet as was proper. D'Amiran smirked as he wiped his face and handed the knife back to the guard.

"Have this mess cleaned up and hang him over the side of the keep so they know not to wait up for him." He turned and headed for the bedchamber to change his ruined shirt and wash the blood out of his beard. "And bring me the girl. Tonight."

66

QUINN—ALEX, SAGE reminded herself—came to fetch Sage as soon as it was dark. She let him in the room, and he immediately started pacing. "Everything's changed twice today."

"I heard you went to the river," she said.

He nodded. "We got some clean water and managed to make contact with our scouts. They've found Robert and also a courier from the main army, which now occupies Jovan. It seems the general decided to set up his headquarters there, though I don't know why."

"Sounds like good news."

"Yes and no," he said. "Now that the rains have started, most of the army will be stuck on the wrong side of the Nai River as it floods. But there's a battalion just on the other side of the pass here. They could get here in five or six days, once they know to come. The pickets want to cross the pass and call for help, but without red blaze, it will take twice as long."

"Red blaze?" asked Sage.

"Special packets sealed with wax," he explained. "When burned they make red flames and lots of red smoke. They're only used for absolute emergency to call all forces within sight. I have five."

She remembered a detail from her tour with Clare. "They have some of that in the keep so Tegann can call for help. Theirs is green, though."

Alex nodded. "Green is for local militias. Red is for the royal army, though supposedly anyone loyal to the crown should show up. I'm debating using one ourselves tomorrow. If nothing else, it may frighten D'Amiran's allies if they think the army is headed this way."

"So how will you get some to the scouts?"

"I can't," he said, kicking the bedpost in frustration. "Even if we could get out of this rock, there's that ring of Kimisar around us, and according to the scouts, they're on the move again."

Sage recalled what she needed to tell him. "I saw a man escorted into the keep. He looked Kimisar to me."

He stopped pacing. "When?"

"About an hour ago."

"Is he still here?"

"I . . . I don't know."

Alex waved his hand. "I'll ask my patrols what they've seen. Are you ready to go?"

"Yes. Clare is telling everyone I'm ill."

He grinned. "They're dropping like flies around here, thanks to you." She blushed, and he took a few steps closer, looking serious. "We owe you so much, Sage."

Her pulse quickened at the look in his eyes. She'd been terrified when she heard he went to the river, thinking they might be ambushed. Then she remembered what else had happened that day. "The duke came to see me while you were gone."

Alex froze. "What did he want?"

"Idle talk." She repeated the conversation for him. "You don't think it means anything, do you?"

He frowned. "Maybe, maybe not."

"Normally he chats up Clare, but she'd gone to get some water. Maybe he was just looking for her."

"You were alone?"

She nodded.

"Dammit, Sage, I told you not to go off alone."

"I was in plain sight," she argued. "It was only a few minutes."

"We're counting the hours until all hell breaks loose." He reached for her arm. "A lot can happen in a few minutes."

He didn't trust her enough to decide what was too risky. She elbowed his hand away furiously. "Don't I know a few minutes can change everything!"

The blood drained from his face, leaving his normally dark skin pale. Alex reached for her again, brushing his fingers down her arm, leaving a trail of goose bumps. "Sage, please. I don't care what he does to me, but you . . ."

How did he keep doing that? How did he make her want to claw his face one minute and kiss and reassure him in the next?

"What's that?" The moment ended as his dark eyes snapped to the window. The sound of shouting came from the courtyard. He crossed the room to look out. "Something's wrong." He pivoted back to the door. "Stay here."

Sage ignored his command and made to follow him. "I thought I wasn't supposed to be alone."

She expected him to force the issue, but instead he grabbed her hand. "Then for Spirit's sake, stay close and do what I tell you."

She barely got the door closed behind them before Alex rushed her down the passage and outside. All around the inner ward, people were staring up at the keep.

In the pillared bowl atop the tower, a great pyre blazed, casting a golden glow over the granite walls. The bloody body of a man painted with the white four-pointed star of Kimisara hung by his neck below. A soldier in black sidled up to them and said everyone was describing the man as a captured spy.

"I think that Kimisar you saw is still here," Alex observed dryly.

67

SAGE WATCHED THE officers argue over what it meant.

"If you're going to make a point with a body, you hang it where everyone can see it," Casseck insisted. "It's hanging over the west side, not from a pole over the top. The Kimisar are all to the west. They've abandoned D'Amiran."

"That must have been the unlucky bastard who delivered that news," said Gramwell. "But why would they leave? Is someone coming from that direction?"

Alex held up a hand. "Doesn't matter. Now this morning's report makes more sense. Their absence leaves an opening to get red blaze to the scouts, but it may not be open for long. Now is the time." Casseck and Gramwell nodded. "Once the scouts have it, a pair of men can get to where the signal can be seen in two days. It'll be a minimum of five days more for reinforcements to arrive, but let's assume ten total. We'll lose the man who goes out, so that leaves us with twenty-nine to take control here."

"Doable," said Casseck. "Especially if the remaining scouts can make their way in."

"Which would bring us up to thirty-three." Alex crossed his arms. "So now we need to get out. What about the sewer, Gram? You found a drain by the river on the south side." He indicated the spot on their sketch.

Gramwell shook his head. "The end's covered with a grate of iron rods—old, but solid. I got one vertical bar loose, but the rest are stuck fast. No way any of us can fit through. Charlie could, but he'd never make it that far in the dark alone, especially if the forest is crawling with D'Amiran's guards."

Alex nodded in agreement, and Sage felt relieved Charlie's illness made it an easy decision.

"How about a dog?" asked Casseck. "It's far, but not impossible."

"They're all sick now," Gramwell said. "Apparently the illness affects them, too. We're lucky they contacted the scouts early today."

"How large is the gap in the grate?" Sage asked.

Gramwell rolled up his sleeve to show the marks he'd made on his arm. Casseck dug out a knotted cord to measure. "Looks like about seven inches high and a bit less than a foot wide."

Sage laid the cord on the corner of the table to visualize the size. After a few seconds she looked up. "I can get through."

Alex sighed. "I knew you were going to say that."

Casseck and Gramwell exchanged glances but didn't dare say anything.

"Maybe I should check on Charlie while you three discuss it," she said. It would go better if she wasn't there.

Without a word, Alex pointed to the side door and she ducked into the attached room. She knelt by Charlie's cot and brushed sweaty hair from his forehead. His breathing was deep and regular, a sign he would be much better by morning. Alex's sword lay on the bed next to Charlies's, and she suddenly knew he'd been the one tending to his brother. There was only one other person he ever entrusted Charlie to, and that was her.

Alex pushed through the door and came to stand at Charlie's feet, arms crossed. "I don't like it."

She didn't look up. "Do you have a better idea?"

"Not yet. I just need time to think."

"We're out of time." She pushed herself to her feet to face him. "I know how to move through the forest quietly and how to find my way at night. I can climb trees and rocks. No one will notice I'm gone until it's too late—maybe even not at all. You can send me off before the evening count."

"And when you run into one of D'Amiran's sentries?"

"With the sickness there are fewer out there." She raised her chin. "And you've taught me to fight. I can make it."

His eyes narrowed. "One lesson doesn't make you a warrior, just less helpless."

"*You* brought me into this." She crossed her arms to mirror his.

"I never should have." He closed his eyes and put a hand to his forehead. "You don't need to punish me. I do that well enough myself."

"This isn't about you and me," she said. "This is about what needs to be done and the only person who has a chance of doing it."

"I know you hate me." He dropped his hand and focused on her. For the first time she realized how tired he looked. Did he ever sleep? "But I can't lose you, Sage. It would kill me."

"Alex," she said, and he flinched. That she'd never heard his name before last night made Sage wonder if anyone ever used it, and what that did to him. If everyone only ever called him "sir" or "Captain," it would be easy to forget he was anything else. Had he taken the role of Mouse to escape that?

"I'm probably safer out there than in here tomorrow," she whispered. "Let me go."

His shoulders slumped, and she knew she'd won.

68

SAGE WATCHED ALEX brace his feet and bend down to grasp the carved stone lattice over the sewer drain. The thick grime around it came up with the cover, but she could see it had been removed recently, and clumps of dirt and moss pressed back in to hide the fact. It was very heavy, and he lifted and rotated it out of the way only as much as she needed to get through. Together they stared at the blackness below.

"You're sure you want to do this?" Alex asked.

"I'm the only one who has a chance of making it."

He nodded without looking up from the hole. "You know the way through?"

"As well as I can."

"And you know where to meet my scouts?"

"One point south of the pass."

"And you have the knife I gave you?"

"Right where I can reach it."

Alex turned her to him and grasped her by her elbows, leaning down to touch his forehead to hers. She wasn't sure who was shaking more. It was so easy to imagine he was Ash again, and she let herself think it, feel it. Sage closed her eyes and matched her breathing to his.

He raised one hand to sweep a few stray hairs to the back of her neck. "Let me say it one last time, Sage. Please."

"No." She pulled away, shaking her head. He wasn't Ash, and she didn't want to hear it.

He released her, hands dropping to his side. "Then let me say I'm s—"

"No," she said again. It didn't give her as much satisfaction as she thought it would to watch her words hit him like blows.

He opened his mouth again to say something, but then pressed his lips together and nodded.

"I'm ready," she said, though she wasn't.

Alex nodded and clasped her arms again, then lifted her up and lowered her slowly into the damp hole. "Got my feet," she said when her boots touched the bottom of the tunnel, and he let go. The way his eyes searched told her he couldn't see her in the shadows.

"If you're in trouble, I swear I will never stop until I get to you," he called softly.

Sage could've pretended she was already gone, but she couldn't leave without answering.

"I know."

69

SAGE CREPT THROUGH total darkness, feeling her way through the twists and turns Gramwell had described. She had to walk hunched over, sliding her feet through the frigid, slimy water. Occasionally she stumbled on stones or—worse—softer, unidentifiable objects. Fortunately, her toes were numb with cold after the first few minutes.

She tried not to think of him—*Alex*. Of his pleading eyes and his soft touch, of the way his hands shook as they released hers. Of his promise to abandon everything for her if she was in trouble. If the soldiers failed, she might never see him again. Or she might see him hanging from the top of the keep.

No matter how much she hated him, he didn't deserve that.

She tripped on a protruding stone and clutched at what she hoped was a tree root growing through the wall to stay upright. The numbness in her fingers and toes seeped into her limbs. Was this what it was like to be dead—seeing and hearing and feeling nothing, wandering in the dark forever?

A glimmer of light shone on the walls ahead, and she stumbled toward it with a grateful sob. Another turn and the grate glowed at the end of the tunnel. A dozen steps more and she was gripping the bars, listening for insects and nocturnal creatures, concentrating to sort them from the echoes behind her. Nothing sounded disturbed.

Relieved, she felt along the vertical bars until she found the weak one. She yanked it free, letting loose a shower of dirt and rust. Her eyes caught her pale hands glowing in the moonlight, which inspired her to rub the grime onto her face, neck, and hands. It was like the day she met the matchmaker, only this time she was trying for the opposite effect. The thought made her smile a little, and she used it to focus on her task, like Alex needed her to.

Once satisfied with her camouflage, she crouched down and began to work her body through the largest gap in the metal grate, arms and head first, facedown. Being skinny and flat chested was finally an advantage. The sash she'd sewn together to hold the red blaze rested snugly against her waist and caused no problems. Her hips, however, were a different story.

Sage grunted and strained to squeeze them through, mentally grumbling that she should have brought a pound of butter to grease the way. She eased her breeches down a little and wriggled back and forth, painfully gaining another inch. The corroded metal bars scraped her exposed flesh, and she bit her lower lip to keep from crying out as she pushed with her toes and pulled with her arms. With a flash of agony, she surged out another foot, smacking her face on the rock she'd grabbed hold of and bashing her knees on the grate. Even with pain coming from so many places at once, she gasped and groaned in relief.

But now she was wet all over, and muddy and bleeding to boot. Sage eased her legs the rest of the way out and pulled her breeches back to her waist. She sat up and looked at the tunnel, debating whether to bother replacing the bar. Instead she reached through the grate and pulled the rod out, hefting it in her hand. It wouldn't hurt to have another weapon. Pausing once more to listen for signs of disturbance, she descended carefully down the embankment and headed southeast.

The rocky terrain and late spring made for less undergrowth, so Sage had little to slow her progress. Before long, she'd put about three miles between herself and the fortress and turned east along a steep rise when she sensed something was wrong—the forest was too quiet. Sage pressed her back against a tree and held her breath to listen. To her right, maybe forty yards away, a twig snapped in sharp protest of being stepped on.

She wasn't alone.

She couldn't hold her air in forever. As quietly as she could manage, Sage exhaled and inhaled several quick, shaky breaths, trying not to create large puffs of steam in the frigid air, though he surely knew where she was already. She gripped the rusty iron bar in her sweaty hands. Over her thudding heart, she heard the crushing of dry leaves. Closer.

Sage took a deep lungful of air and launched into a sprint along the ridge. A large shape crashed through the brush after her. Wind whipped past her ears as she ran faster than she ever had in her life, but she knew her wind wouldn't last.

He was gaining on her.

She dodged between trees, gasping for breath and changing direction as often as she could spring off rocks. The moonlight made her able to see where she was going, but it also made it easier for him to follow. His panting was right behind her. A swerve to the left gave her a glimpse of a hand reaching for the hood of her jacket. Seconds later, fingers brushed against it.

Sage swung around and smashed the metal rod against his outstretched forearm. He yelled, and she heard bone snap, but her split second of triumph ended as she lost her footing and tipped backward, tumbling down the steep slope. Her makeshift weapon went flying as she tucked and rolled, covering her head and neck rather than trying to stop her fall. The man grunted in pain as he fell after her.

Sage bounced over bracken and rocks until she crash-landed against a log at the bottom of the ravine, knocking the wind completely from her body. She couldn't breathe. For a panicked moment, she thought she'd never breathe again, but then blessed air surged into her lungs, shocking her with its cold burn. She gasped and coughed uncontrollably.

"You little bastard!" A large hand grabbed her hair from behind. Sage was yanked off her feet and hurled against a tree. Stars swam in her vision, and she felt her bound hair come loose. He let her fall to the ground on her hands and knees in front of him. She saw his foot come up just before it kicked her hard in the ribs, and she flipped onto her back on the sharp rocks. A moan of pain escaped her.

"Well, well, what have we here?" he taunted. "A little girl lost in the woods."

Alex's dagger pressed against the small of her back. By some miracle it hadn't been lost. It wasn't much of an act to whimper and reach for her bruised back. She just had her fingers on the hilt when the hulking shadow reached down to pick her up by her throat.

His breath stank and spittle landed on her face as he brought her up close. "Don't worry, sweetheart. His Grace will make everything better."

The stars—real and imagined—faded, replaced by expanding blackness as Sage pulled the dagger free of its sheath. She rammed it up and into the soldier's exposed armpit with every ounce of force she could muster. The pressure on her neck eased just long enough for her to catch half a breath, and she wrenched the hilt to sweep the blade within. Hot blood spilled over her hand, and then a second gush told her she'd found the artery. The edges of her vision were going white as the hand finally released her, but it was too late, and Sage was falling—though she never knew if she hit the ground.

70

QUINN WATCHED THE time candle slowly burn away the night hours. Cass had gone to bed long ago, urging him to do the same, though his friend must have known it would be impossible for him to sleep. Silence was his companion, and Quinn embraced it, let it soak into him.

Silence meant Sage hadn't been caught. Silence meant she was safe.

She hated him.

He'd made up his mind not to tell her again he loved her until she was ready, but he could be dead by this time tomorrow; and so he'd tried, but she would have none of it. That had hurt worse than the night he'd said it the first time, and that had nearly killed him.

He glanced at the candle. Three a.m.

Casseck said she would cool down, she'd forgive him in time, but Cass didn't know her inner fierceness like he did, didn't understand the pain and loss she'd suffered when her father died. She'd had no one for so long. He knew without a doubt he was the first person she'd trusted—loved—in years. That was the worst part: ruining the chance she might ever open herself up to anyone again. He could take the loss of his own happiness, but destroying hers was unbearable.

He shouldn't have let her go. All the courage she possessed couldn't make up for how small and fragile she was. Letting her go was a sign he either didn't love her enough or that he'd never be able to deny her anything.

Four a.m.

She understood him better than anyone, so maybe that was in his favor. He'd told her his deepest fear—that he was a monster—and she'd refused to even consider it. Of course, that had been before he'd shown her the nonkilling side of that, his willingness to lie when necessary. To lie to her.

Sometimes people get hurt.

Ash had said it so casually, he hadn't understood then to take it seriously. But it was worse than physical blows, worse than stab wounds and scars. He'd give anything to go back to that first night and start over. To see her smile wistfully and say, *Alex is a nice name.*

That's what he was with her: Alex. Hearing her say his name tonight had uncovered what he hadn't realized had been so deeply buried. Of all his friends, only Cass ever called him Alex anymore, and then only in private when he wanted to make a point. Even to Charlie he was the captain now. But with Sage he didn't have to be always right or always in control. Or rather, he wouldn't have to be. The few minutes he'd allowed himself to be totally unrestrained had been the best of his life, though he thanked the Spirit she'd called him Ash. Had that not brought him to his senses, the night would have ended differently, and she would never, ever have forgiven him. At least now he had a chance, slim as it was.

Five a.m.

In less than sixteen hours it would all be over. If Sage had gotten out, then it didn't matter if he failed—if he died. The right people would know in time to have a chance of stopping the duke, and she would live. Sending her out had been the right thing to do. She was fierce and she was smart. And now she was safe.

He looked up as Casseck came into the room, rubbing his face. It didn't look like he'd slept much. A look passed between them and Alex nodded. Cass smiled in relief. A minute later Charlie appeared, looking pale but almost fully recovered. This time yesterday he'd been in agony, and Alex had cleaned out every bucket Charlie filled as penance. Tonight would be the perfect time to strike.

The page went to fetch water so they could shave. Breakfast was cold stew and stale bread from last night—they'd cooked the rabbits the dogs had brought back. It was almost time for the morning muster with the duke's captain, Geddes. Wouldn't he be pissed to know who had slipped past his net? Alex smiled to himself as he changed into a clean shirt and combed his hair.

There was a heavy drizzle outside, meaning the pass would be cleared in time for the reinforcements to march through. All his soldiers had to do was damage D'Amiran enough that he couldn't effectively close up the pass by the time they arrived. Thanks to Sage's brilliant idea on taking out the barracks, he was more optimistic than ever.

The men filed into their ranks, and Geddes approached, sneering as he always did. Alex couldn't help his own smirk on his own face as he nodded his greeting—he would never salute that ratty-eared bastard. "All my men are present or accounted for."

The captain barely looked at the columns before him. "So I see." He tugged his ear as he looked Alex over. "Long night? You look tired."

"The roof of our quarters leaks like a sieve. It was hard to sleep with all the rain pouring in."

"My profound apologies." Geddes didn't sound sorry at all. "It was a torturous night for me, too."

Alex didn't really care. Now that Sage was safe, he had work to do, staging everything for this evening. "If that's all you have, then we'll see you in a few hours for your next check."

Geddes nodded and turned to go. Alex looked to Casseck and the lieutenant called the ranks to attention for dismissal. They hadn't made any announcements this morning. Every man knew his part and where to go.

"Oh, Captain." Geddes turned back. "I almost forgot. I found something you lost." He dug around in his jacket, muttering, "It's in here somewhere."

Alex gritted his teeth while Geddes searched. The captain had waited for precisely that moment to inconvenience as many people as possible. The rain was soaking into Alex's jacket, and he knew every man standing there had water dripping down his neck.

"Ah, here it is."

There was no way Geddes could have lost an object that big in his jacket for a full minute—

No.

Sweet Spirit, NO.

Geddes held up a black-handled dagger for all to see. The gold initials in the hilt were covered in grime.

Alex's knees began to buckle, but Cass was already grabbing his elbow and propping him up. "Steady," his friend whispered.

He locked his legs in place as Geddes took a step toward him, offering the knife to him with a smile. Rain ran in dark trails down the blade as the grime washed away.

Rivulets of red.

Blood.

71

ALEX BARELY MADE it to his room before vomiting into the bucket Charlie had used yesterday.

How many hours had he sat outside, smug and content? How many hours had she been dead while he thought she was safe? While he smiled and shaved and ate like nothing was wrong?

Another wave hit him and he sobbed through it, not caring if Casseck and Gramwell and Charlie saw how weak he was, because nothing mattered now except that Sage was dead. She was dead, and it was his fault, and he wanted to die, too.

Eventually the heaving stopped, though it went long past the point his stomach emptied. A damp cloth appeared in front of his face, and when he made no effort to take it, Casseck wiped the snot and spit and vomit away for him. Alex was sitting on the floor between his cot and Charlie's, and he leaned back against his.

"I killed her," he whispered.

"No," said Cass firmly. "This isn't your fault."

Alex shook his head and reached for his face before realizing he still held the dagger in his hand. He eased his fingers open—the muscles were cramped from gripping it so hard, and the design of the hilt had pressed into his flesh deep enough to bruise. Reddish-brown blood had collected in the lines of his palm.

Her blood on his hands.

He lunged for the bucket again and heaved nothing for another five minutes.

Alex wiped his own face this time, and Cass offered him a cup of water. Charlie hovered in the background with a worried expression. "Are you getting sick, too?" the boy asked.

"No, I'm just . . ." Alex trailed off as a new emotion began to unfurl.

He would kill them all.

It wasn't until Casseck said "What?" that he realized he'd said it aloud.

"I'm going to kill them," he said. "The duke, Geddes, and every man who stands between me and them."

Cass shook his head. "If he surrenders, you can't."

The rage inside was building, and he warmed his soul on the fire. "Watch me."

"He has rights and privileges by law. It could ruin your career, land you in prison."

"I don't care." Alex pushed to his feet.

There was a knock on the outer door and Sergeant Porter stuck his head in the meeting room. "Beggin' your pardon, sirs, but Mistress Rodelle is here asking for you."

Alex pulled the door closed on the room and the foul-smelling bucket and gestured for Porter to let her in. Casseck whispered some task for Charlie, and the boy slipped out as the matchmaker entered. Her blue eyes blazed in anger as she shook out her wet skirt.

"Where is she?"

"Mistress Rodelle—"

"I'm not a fool. She spent the night here. I've allowed you to use my apprentice for your spying, but I'll not let you make a—"

"She's dead."

The matchmaker froze midsentence, every bit of color draining from her face. "She's what?"

"Dead." Every time Alex said the word he felt calmer. "She was caught making an escape that would have brought reinforcements here several days sooner."

"But . . . are you sure?"

"Yes." Alex gripped the dagger in his hand. "I'm sure."

"You saw her?" the woman pressed.

For the first time, Alex faltered. "No."

"Is it possible she's alive somewhere?"

But Geddes would have taunted him differently if they had her. He would have said—

It was a torturous night for me, too.

Alex swayed and grabbed the edge of the table to steady himself. The knife clattered onto the table, and he sank into the chair he'd sat in all night, waiting while she'd been . . . "I don't know."

"Alive or dead, she's in the keep," said Casseck. "The dungeons or the infirmary or D'Amiran's private chambers."

"Or a void," said Gramwell, speaking for the first time. "There were areas within the keep we couldn't account for. They could be support columns or secret rooms or passages."

"We're accelerating everything," said Alex. "I'm not waiting for nightfall." Darkness was to be their ally, but time was the enemy. "Can we be ready by the noon meal? Everyone will be headed to the Great Hall anyway, so half the work of herding them there will be done."

Cass nodded. The matchmaker gaped at them. "I thought we were just going to leave as though nothing was wrong. You sound as if you've planned to take over."

Alex looked up to her. "We have. It turns out your ladies are what the duke was after in the first place."

Realization dawned on her lined face, and she sat down hard in a chair of her own. "Spirit above, all those marriages of the past two years . . . he was binding half of Crescera to him."

"And now he'll take the rest," Alex finished. "Sage figured it out."

Mistress Rodelle smiled weakly. "Of course she did."

"Which is all the more reason we're going to find her." Every instinct Alex had screamed to charge in now, to tear down the keep brick by brick. But no, he had to wait until the time was right, until everything was in place. He clenched his fists to keep his arms from shaking.

Patience.

"We have a few hours before we can act," Alex said. "In that time I want to find out where she is and if she's alive."

Casseck nodded to the dagger on the table. "That was about making you want to find out. He'll be expecting it. Anyone who snoops will be caught."

"I have an idea who to send," said Gramwell.

72

D'AMIRAN WATCHED THE activity below from his window. The escort soldiers milled about the inner and outer wards, collecting supplies for continuing their journey, but it was only a cover. They were looking for her.

He smiled to himself. They'd never find her.

And as the day wore on, Quinn would get more and more frantic. Geddes had seen the look on his face when he handed him the knife—the boy had almost lost control right there. D'Amiran would enjoy executing him in front of everyone. The escort soldiers would dissolve into chaos, and he'd have them easily.

And then tonight everything would come together.

The last of his nobles were expected to arrive this evening. Scribes were finishing the wedding announcements and dowry demands at that very moment, and the messengers could go out at first light as soon as the bedsheets were collected to prove the permanence of the unions. D'Amiran would head to his army in the morning, and they would march. It might ruin the element of surprise to send young Quinn's head to his father beforehand, but the poetry of it was irresistible.

"Your Grace," came a voice from behind him. D'Amiran turned away from the window to acknowledge his bowing steward. "The morning meal is ready, if you wish to break your fast." The man indicated the table laid out.

"Actually, I believe I'll go to the Great Hall," D'Amiran said. The steward tried to hide his frustration. It was no easy task to bring every-thing up here, but the duke didn't care. He wanted to see Quinn's face for himself, wanted to relish it.

He shrugged out of his robe, and the steward rushed to bring his doublet, hissing to the waiting page that he must delay the meal below until the duke arrived. Once the close-fitting jacket was buttoned and his sleeves straightened, D'Amiran went downstairs, a bounce in his step. He entered the Great Hall from the back, smiling as everyone rose from their seats. With one hand, he gestured for all to sit, eyes sweeping over the table where the escort officers sat. All three of them.

Lady Clare left her seat and came to meet him, sinking into a deep curtsy. "Your Grace honors us," she said.

This one he'd picked for himself. Even if her family was already bound to him through her sister's marriage to his brother, they were still the richest in Crescera. And she was lovely. Castella Carey had been lovely. It almost made up for that disappointment.

One of the officer's heads went up, watching, and D'Amiran realized why Clare had come forward. Oh, he would enjoy this.

"My dear, I could never pass up an opportunity to spend more time in your presence," he said as he raised Clare's hand and put it on his arm. He spoke loud enough for all to hear, and the officer watching stiffened as D'Amiran led her back to the table. When they reached the head, the duke indicated she should sit at his right hand, forcing some shuffling of seats.

The platters came out and the duke waited for his plate to be filled before turning to Lady Clare. "And how are you this morning, my lady? I hope the weather hasn't dampened your spirits."

"Oh, no," she said lightly—too lightly. "I'm worried a bit for my friend. Lady Sagerra fell ill last night. I haven't seen her all morning."

The girl wasn't very good at hiding her intentions. Her eyes kept darting to the officers' table. All three watched silently, their food untouched.

The plan had been to have Geddes drop a particularly vile hint about where the Fowler girl was during the afternoon muster. One that would have Quinn raging to rescue his beloved little commoner. One that would lead him straight into a trap in his private chambers. But this was too good to pass up.

D'Amiran looked back to Clare with a sympathetic smile. "Indeed, she's in my infirmary. I spoke to her only an hour ago."

Clare's back went rigid. "May I see her, Your Grace?"

"Oh, no, my lady," he said. "I'm afraid I can't allow that. I'd never forgive myself if you became ill, too." He glanced over at the officers' table with a smirk. "And she's in no condition to see anyone right now."

73

SAGE WOKE TO the steady drip of water. Her face hurt in more places than she would've imagined possible, and she could barely see out of one eye. She turned her head away from the light and discovered a new pain in the back of her skull. For the next twenty seconds, she battled dizziness and nausea, conquering both only to remember the previous night. The nausea surged, and she rolled to her side and retched the meager contents of her stomach onto the stone floor.

Large hands reached down to pull her hair back from her face as she vomited, though most of it was completely matted to her scalp by dried blood. The muscles that went rigid with her heaving identified even more bruises and scrapes, and she sagged and groaned.

"You'll be all right," soothed a deep voice. Sage's hands were over her stomach. The sash of red blaze was missing. She clutched around for it frantically. It was all that mattered. "We've got it," the man said. "Relax."

He tried to help her sit, but she struggled against him until dizziness overtook her. The man held her upright until the world stopped spinning. Sage blinked at the dark, bearded face that swam into focus. She recognized him now, though it had been dark when they found each other in the woods last night. When he seemed sure she could hold herself up, he tipped a canteen over a scrap of cloth and began wiping her face. Sage flinched away from the wet rag and the pain it brought, but he continued his gentle cleaning. "We didn't realize you were a girl till the sun came up and we could see you better. Sorry if we roughed you up."

"Forget it." She'd been near collapse when she found Alex's scouts, so she hadn't resisted when they pinned her to the ground and searched her for weapons. "The castle guard who found me before you did was far rougher." He chuckled, and she took in her surroundings. They sat sheltered in an overhang of rock on the side of a steep slope. "Where are the others?"

He poured more water over the cloth. "Dell's checking the snares, and Stephen's patrolling. Rob and Jack are probably right at the pass by now. If they push hard, they can light the signal fire tomorrow morning, and we'll have reinforcements in less than a week, thanks to you. Can you drink anything?"

She nodded and discovered it was not a movement she wanted to repeat anytime soon. "Yes," she rasped.

"Here." He held the canteen to her lips. "Just sip for now, even though you want more." She obeyed, swallowing tentatively. Even her throat muscles hurt. The short man eyed her. "The first is always the hardest. Better him than you, though."

Sage recalled waking up with the weight of a dead man on top of her. It was a miracle she hadn't suffocated. After shoving him off of her, she'd vomited all over his body. Belatedly, she remembered leaving the knife behind as she stumbled away, drenched in his blood. "Did you throw up after your first kill?" she gasped between sips.

"I don't know anyone who didn't."

That made her feel better. "Even Captain Quinn?"

"Alex? For days." He sat back on his heels. "You were so worn out last night, we weren't properly introduced." He offered his hand. "I'm Sergeant Ash Carter."

Sage sighed. "Of course you are."

74

SAGE OUTLINED ALEX'S plan to Ash as he prepared a meal over a small fire. The smell of the blood in her clothes and hair killed her appetite, but she forced herself to eat. She had to put food in her mouth carefully, as her lips were split in two places. Chewing was also difficult, with her left cheek so bruised and scraped. At least her teeth and jaw felt intact.

Ash watched her eat a piece of camp bread—basically fried porridge—with her dirty fingers. "Are you a maid, then?"

She resisted the urge to shake her head. "No, I work for the matchmaker. I've been blending in with the ladies and helping Captain Quinn gather information. It's a long story."

"I look forward to hearing it." He offered her a piece of squirrel meat. The way he looked at her made her slightly uncomfortable.

She cleared her throat as she took the piece from his hand. "When I first met Alex, he told me his name was Ash Carter. Are you the *real* Ash Carter, or is that just a name spies prefer?"

He smiled ironically. "I'm the real Ash. Normally it's my job to gather information, but he wanted to give it a try and have me do some scouting. My story was already known and in place, so I suggested he use it rather than make up a whole new person."

Sage considered the idea as she chewed. "You have to create an entire identity to be effective." Ash nodded. "So you know Alex well? You were raised together?" Again he affirmed. "Are you really Prince Robert's half brother?" He nodded. "Are you a sergeant rather than an officer so you won't ever outrank him?"

He winced. "It seems you already know a lot about me."

"Just those details. It might take a while to sort some things out in my head; your history is mixed up with his personality."

Ash snickered. "Yeah, it's kind of hard to keep that under wraps." He studied her for several seconds. "Does he return your affections?"

Sage's head jerked up. *My what?*

Ash looked surprised by her reaction. "Your affections," he repeated slowly. "You care for him a great deal."

"I don't—"

"Oh, you don't? My mistake, then. . . ." Ash popped a piece of meat into his mouth. "But it's nothing to be ashamed of *if* you were—half the ladies I know would choose him over Robert. You should see the fuss whenever he shows up at court."

Sage made a study of brushing crumbs from her jacket. It was still damp and most of them just smeared. "Which explains his expertise in the deception of women."

"Not at all." Ash sat back. "Alex is a bit . . . private with his inner thoughts, but those of us who know him well can usually tell what he's got brewing in there." He tapped his temple. "Once he's decided on something, though, it usually comes out."

"Yes," Sage agreed. "And what 'usually comes out' is a lie. For starters, he said he was you."

Ash smiled without humor. "I bet that hurt."

Sage flinched. "I'm not some silly, sentimental schoolgirl—"

"I meant it hurt him," Ash said calmly. "Did you ever imagine it from his perspective?" He picked up the spit stick and bowed it back and forth between his brown hands. "I tried to warn him. Playing spy is fun until you realize people don't like *you*—they like what you're pretending to be. And if they ever find out . . ." Ash shrugged and tossed the stick into the flames. "Well, then they hate you."

I hate you. They had been nearly the first words out of her mouth. And his response had been—

I love you, Sage Fowler. Of everything I've said and done, that is truth.

Sage had been staring into space, but she brought her eyes back to focus on Ash, who wore an encouraging smile. "If he told you he cares for you, I suggest you believe it. *Your* feelings were obvious the first time you said his name."

Sage squeezed her eyes shut against the threat of tears. It had all hurt so badly because she thought he had lied, but she understood now he hadn't—not in any way that mattered. He had shown her the *real* Alex, the man beneath the rank. The Alex buried so deep even he had begun to forget existed. And then that Alex had laid his heart at her feet, knowing full well how she would react. An ache pulled at her chest from the inside as she remembered their parting and how she'd refused to even let him speak, and how he'd accepted her hate as something he deserved.

But she didn't hate him; anger was a cloak she wore out of habit, even though it never brought lasting warmth. In truth, what she hated was how he'd drawn her out and made her care after years spent wrapped up in herself. She hated that he'd crippled her pride and exposed her flaws and loved her in spite, if not because, of them. She hated that she couldn't bear the thought of a world without him.

She loved him.

She loved him, and she had to tell him before it was too late.

She opened her eyes to find Ash was grinning openly. "My only regret now is not taking that spy job as we'd originally planned—I would've met you first." He shrugged in resignation. "Don't worry, though, I know better than to get in his way."

Stephen and Dell arrived back in the cave just then. Ash had Dell collect a bucket of rainwater, and with it he set about cleaning the rest of her cuts and scrapes. She hadn't even noticed half of them, including a long gash on her forehead at her hairline. The remainder of the water she used to rinse her hair out, but she didn't bother with her clothes. Sage wrung cold water from her hair as the three soldiers readied their weapons and developed a plan to take out the fortress's patrols.

"How many will there be?" she asked.

"We've seen as many as twenty walking sentries," Ash said. "But in the last couple days it's been more like eight or ten."

She nodded. "The sickness."

"Remind me to tell Alex that was brilliant. His father will be proud."

Sage concentrated on braiding her hair, unwilling to brag about her part in it. "So how can I help now?"

"Would you consider staying here? It's safer." At that she looked up, and he snorted in laughter.

She narrowed her eyes. "What's so funny?"

Stephen and Dell exchanged an amused glance. Ash shook his head. "Nothing. I just—I can see why he likes you. You're stubborn as hell."

"So is he." Sage had to smile. "That aside, I'm coming along."

"Can you handle a crossbow?" he asked.

"I doubt it."

"Spear or sword?"

She swallowed. "No."

"Knife?"

"Only a little. And I lost mine." Her confidence faded.

Ash sighed. "Mistress Sage, I hate to say it, but unless you come up with something, I'll have to insist you stay here, and I'm sure the captain would agree with me."

Sage looked down, cheeks burning. She didn't want to be a burden, but she couldn't stay away. There had to be something. The drawstring of Dell's travel bag caught her eye, and she smiled.

While the soldiers sorted through what they would take and what they'd leave behind, Sage got to work, borrowing Ash's knife and cannibalizing a torn satchel for her purpose. When she showed Ash what she'd made, he frowned.

"How good are you?"

"Good enough to hunt with," she replied.

Ash's frown remained, but he agreed to let her come when she promised to obey orders and stay out of the way. Stephen and Dell didn't seem to mind her presence, especially when she proved she could keep up with their pace down the mountainside. When they reached the river, already swelling with the rain and melted snow, Ash halted and gestured for her to go ahead.

Sage picked through the stones along the riverbed, searching for the ones with the best balance and smoothness. Ash watched with crossed arms. He still didn't like the idea, and frankly she didn't blame him. Her own courage faltered when she thought how long it had been since she'd used a sling, and she hadn't yet tried out the one she'd cobbled together with the drawstring and a scrap of leather.

She stuffed several round stones in her pockets. There wasn't time to be picky. Hopefully she wouldn't even need them. "I've got enough," she called as she waded out of the frigid stream.

Ash didn't move. "If you wouldn't mind a quick demonstration."

Sages swallowed nervously. "You'll have to give me the first one. I've never used this sling."

"I'll give you three tries."

She nodded and wove the knotted ends through her fingers. A perfect stone presented itself at her feet, and she swooped down to grab it. It was almost too good to waste on her first attempt, but she settled it in the leather pouch and pulled it taut. When she gave the weapon an experimental swing, she almost laughed. It felt like she'd never put a sling aside.

"Try to hit that greenish knot on the fallen tree over there." Ash pointed at a target twenty-five yards away.

Sage spun the sling faster and focused on the spot he indicated. *Don't think. Just throw.* The leather cup swished past her face right where she wanted, and she snapped her arm to release the stone. It sailed out and hit the log with a *thunk,* embedding itself in the soggy wood just below the target. She'd missed the knot by mere inches. When she recovered from her own shock, she put on a smug smile and turned to face him.

"Will that do?"

75

ALEX DIDN'T KNOW whether to believe what D'Amiran had told Clare or not, but the duke obviously wanted him to think Sage was alive. He wanted Alex to come after her, which meant D'Amiran was ready.

So was Alex.

I'm coming, Sage.

He knocked on the door, and the matchmaker opened it and let him into her suite.

"Everyone's here," she said before he could ask. A glance around told him the count was low, and she gestured to the bedroom. "Some are changing. Their idea of dressing plainly isn't the same as mine."

Alex nodded once and strode through the back door without knocking, eliciting several shrieks. None of the women were truly uncovered, though, and he was not in the mood for propriety. He pointed his finger at one girl and swept it around to the others. "All of you will follow me, be silent, and attract no attention. If you refuse to cooperate or allow yourselves to be left behind, you forfeit my protection."

A tall blonde stepped forward, chest heaving in what she must have believed was an attractive way, and put her hand on him. "What is the danger, sir?" she begged.

He shifted his gaze to the painted nails clutching his arm. *Jacqueline.* He recalled the name and the venom stretching back to the first night.

Sage had risked her life for this wretched woman. Suffered for her. He peeled her fingers off coldly.

"Death."

The women were silent after that.

After a quick nod from the soldier posted in the passage told him all was clear, Alex led them out. Each bride carried a bundled shawl as they walked down the steps to the laundry, three levels below the guest wing. With the shortened staff brought on by the sickness, along with the approaching midday meal, the area was deserted. His soldier brought up the rear and stood outside the door as Alex bent over and pulled the sewer drain open, trying not to think about the last time he'd done so. He looked up at over a dozen shocked faces.

"In there?" cried one of the ladies.

"Yes, and quickly." He held out his arms. "Who's first?"

Lady Clare stepped forward without hesitation, pinning her skirts between her legs to make them smaller. He grasped her arms and lowered her down. "Move along the tunnel to make room." He turned back to the group and held up his arms. "Next." No one moved, so Mistress Rodelle shoved the nearest girl at him. As he lowered her, her dress caught on the opening, and she went down with it flipped over her head. The rest tucked their skirts as Clare had.

Jacqueline arranged herself last, and Alex eyed her voluminous skirt while she simpered at him. "I don't think you can fit through." He pulled out a knife and jabbed it into the fabric and ripped off the excess as she protested. "Quiet," he snapped. Once she disappeared into the darkness, he kicked the remainder of her dress down after her. Now he faced the matchmaker alone.

"I'm going to get her back," he said.

Mistress Rodelle smiled a little. "I know."

She held out her arms, and Alex lowered her below, then tossed a burlap sack down, explaining it contained some food, water, and several daggers. As he sealed the stone grate over them, pressing dirt into the cracks, he overheard the matchmaker warn she'd cut out the tongue of

292

any lady who complained. Alex smiled grimly. He had little doubt she'd be willing to carry out her threat.

⚬❖⚬

Alex and Charlie crept up the stairs of the keep. The duke and his guests had all gone to the Great Hall for the noon meal, so each level was empty or nearly so. The duke's quarters were silent as they passed and continued higher.

Alex headed for the very top of the tower and the watch standers. As always, it pained him to use Charlie, but he couldn't waste a fighter, and hopefully the boy would be safer doing this job. Since Sage hadn't made it to the pickets, he'd decided to call them in, and the signal would also be used to begin their attack. Luck was with them, and just as they approached the trapdoor, it opened and one of the guards came down the steep wooden steps, grumbling to his companion that he couldn't wait any longer to use the privy. When he reached the bottom, his attention was caught by Charlie juggling two small casks. They danced around each other in the dark space as the boy stammered apologies. When the soldier's back was to the shadows, Alex stepped out and clamped a hand over the man's mouth as he buried a long dagger in his back, angling up to pierce the kidney. The intense pain caused the man to jerk once and drop straight down. Alex caught him and dragged him backward down the stone steps and finished the job out of Charlie's sight.

Alex wiped his bloody knife on the man's shirt and ascended again, signaling Charlie to go ahead. The boy nodded and ambled up the steps to the platform. He had the last two packets of red blaze with him, and they expected the guards had a steady fire in the bowl to keep warm. Alex pulled the hinge pins of the stairs and listened as his brother conversed with the remaining guard; then Charlie came bounding down the wet wooden steps as the guard yelled, "What the hell?"

The instant the guard's foot hit the top step in pursuit, Alex released his support and the stairs collapsed, dumping the man in a crash under the trapdoor and smacking his head on the way down. Alex drew his sword and rammed it through the guard's heart before he could untangle himself. He pulled the blade out and looked over at Charlie, who stared at the shuddering body with wide eyes.

Alex stepped over the corpse. "Hey," he said, grabbing the boy's chin and turning his frightened brown eyes up to his own face. "You have a job to do, soldier. Focus." Charlie swallowed and nodded. "Let's go." Alex boosted his brother up through the opening and leaned down to drag the dead guard off the steps. He tossed the staircase up onto the wooden platform. "Use that to help hold the door down."

"His crossbow is still up here," Charlie called as he lugged the trap-door shut.

"Be ready to use it if you have to."

"Yes, sir." Charlie peeked down at him one last time, red smoke billowing behind him. "Alex," he called, and their eyes met. "Good luck."

"Be safe, kid." The door slammed down, and he heard the bar slide across it. Sword in hand, Alex bounded down the stone staircase.

He had a man to kill.

76

D'AMIRAN PACED IN front of the fireplace of the Great Hall as his guests straggled in for the midday meal. The escort's muster would be assembling now, and Geddes would drop his hint that the girl had been in the duke's private chambers all along. Quinn could fill in the blanks. The boy would charge into the trap without thinking, and D'Amiran would have his execution, right in time for everyone to see it.

The ladies would be kept inside the hall, of course, but everyone else could step out to the ward. They'd hang him. Let him dangle and twitch and shit himself while his men watched, surrounded and helpless. The duke could hardly wait.

D'Amiran stopped pacing and looked up. The ladies hadn't arrived yet. Perhaps they were coming to the back of the hall, through the keep, to avoid the rain. Still, they should've been here by now. None were ill as of that morning, which was more than he could say for his own people.

Shouts from the far end of the hall pulled the duke from his thoughts. People rushed in the doors, yelling about a fire in the courtyard. The stained-glass windows scattered drops of color across the room with the flames behind them—flames that raged high and bright despite the hours of rain. Soldiers ushered more people inside, calling for them to run for their lives.

Soldiers in black. Quinn's riders.

Within the space of a few breaths, nearly all D'Amiran's allies were in the Great Hall. The crowd parted as Captain Quinn pushed his way through, his sword drawn and bloody.

It wasn't supposed to happen this way.

D'Amiran took several stumbling steps backward as Quinn grabbed a servant and shoved him against the wall with a sword at his stomach. After a brief exchange, the Demoran captain dropped the man and swept dark, wrathful eyes across every face in the room, searching for the ones he wanted. When those eyes focused on him, D'Amiran saw his own death waiting.

He turned and fled.

77

ALEX SHOVED THROUGH the crowd in the Great Hall. The panicked face of D'Amiran's manservant caught his eye, and he grabbed him by the throat and slammed him against the wall. With the point of his bloody sword against the man's belly, Alex demanded what he needed to know. "Where's the girl?"

"What girl?" the man gasped.

Alex pushed the blade through the first layer of the servant's jacket. "The guards brought a girl in last night. Where did they put her?"

White showed all around the man's irises. "I never saw a girl!"

"Would they have put her in the dungeon?" He pressed harder

The man screamed as the sword pierced flesh. "I don't know! I don't know!"

Alex dropped him in disgust, and the man fell to his knees, clutching his stomach. People scattered out of his way as he continued his search until he found himself facing D'Amiran from across the room. The duke's eyes widened when he saw him, and he turned and ran for the back door, which hadn't been sealed off yet.

Alex sprinted after him, instincts screaming that the duke was going to wherever Sage was being held, and he would kill her. Several yards out of the hall, Alex had to make a choice: up toward the duke's rooms, straight into the keep, or down toward the dungeons and storerooms. He paused and listened for indications of which way he should go. Then he chose down.

78

AS SOON AS the red smoke appeared, the guards on the outer walls began falling, crossbow bolts buried deep in their chests and backs. Once satisfied, Lieutenant Casseck leaned out of the inner gatehouse and gave a shrill whistle. The Stiller brothers and two companions ducked out of the already smoking armory, carrying casks of alcohol and bellows stolen from the smithy. They reached the barracks and split up, one pair leaving a leaking barrel by the door as they passed.

Casseck watched them pry open their casks and pour alcohol into the bellows, praying no one in the barracks had lit a candle or the whole thing would go up before the teams could get away. Both pairs began pumping the flammable mist through open windows on either end, and he held up a hand to signal to Archer down the wall several yards, who lit the pitch on his arrow.

Not yet.

He thought he heard shouting coming from inside the barracks, but the large tent set up in the inner ward had just caught fire, so it was hard to tell with all the noise echoing off the stone walls. Tim Stiller stood up to heave the bellows through the window and his partner tossed in the half-empty cask.

Casseck raised his arm higher and Archer drew back his bowstring, aiming for the open window.

Both pairs raced away from the barracks, diving under the first solid shelter they could find. The door to the barracks burst open, and guards stumbled out, rubbing their eyes and coughing. One tripped over the leaking barrel, and it spilled open.

Casseck dropped his arm.

Archer loosed the arrow, and the barracks exploded before either could duck behind the wall.

79

SAGE, DELL, STEPHEN, and Ash were within a mile of Tegann Fortress when red smoke began billowing from the top of the keep. A few minutes later, one of the flags was pulled down, and the smoke began rising in a pattern of puffs. They couldn't see the person responsible.

Ash grinned. "Looks like the party started early." He pointed to Sage. "You, find somewhere to lie low. We'll take out the sentries as they come back."

Sage looked around. "How about a tree? I can get a better look at what's going on inside as well." She gestured to a large evergreen. Most of the other trees hadn't fully grown back their leaves.

"Good idea. We'll come back and find you when we're done. Need a boost?" he offered.

The walk had loosened her sore muscles and adrenaline flowed through her veins. Sage jumped up to catch the limb she wanted and hooked her legs over the next one. Then she pulled herself up and disappeared in a shower of pine needles.

"I guess that's a no." Ash signaled to his companions and they moved out, weapons ready.

❧

From her vantage in the tree, Sage saw movement on the inner and outer walls of the fortress. With the rain it was difficult to distinguish the colors of the livery. Black smoke poured from the inner ward. Must be the tents. Soon after, flames licked up the walls of the eastern armory. The rain would put out the fires eventually, but they'd been started with oil that was staged in slowly leaking barrels to soak into their surroundings.

The plan was to create panic that made everyone easy to herd into one place, take out as many of the posted guards as possible within the first few minutes, and secure the inner walls. Gaining the entire fortress was ideal, but the soldiers were prepared to fall back to the inner bailey or the keep itself if necessary.

Before making the decision, however, they'd wreck the outer ward as much as possible. The soldier on the top of the keep was barely visible as he swung a sodden flag. Sage caught a glimpse of him through the smoke and realized he wasn't crouched over—the soldier was only as tall as the fire bowl itself. *Charlie.* Her gut twisted, but Alex must've had no choice. The boy was probably safer up there anyway.

As Sage squinted to see if the plan for the barracks had worked, it abruptly went up in one large, expanding flash, though the sound didn't reach her for several seconds. The success gave her morbid satisfaction, and she wondered how many she'd just killed with her idea. A man on the outer bailey was blown off his feet and over the side of the stone wall. His arms flailed uselessly as he fell to his death, and she turned away, feeling sick.

Movement nearby caught her eye. Several birds had lifted from their perches when the explosion echoed through the valley, a large hawk settling back down on a tree a few dozen yards away. With a chill she recognized it as a tame bird. Maybe even the one she'd seen several days ago, though there was no way to be sure. Perhaps the Kimisar weren't gone after all.

Sage pulled herself to a higher branch, wincing as the needles scraped her tender face. From her new position she had a clear view of the hawk, but saw no sign of anyone in the trees or on the ground below. Possibly the bird carried a message from someone far away and belonged to them, but she wasn't searching. She was waiting. Her master was near.

If the hawk was a messenger for their enemies, killing her could be critical. Sage reached a shaking hand into her pocket for her sling and a stone.

She was so nervous her first throw went wide by several feet. The hawk's head swiveled around to follow the stone's path, but she remained on her perch. Definitely trained. Sage pushed herself to a precarious stand on a limb and leaned out to give her arm more room. Anyone on the ground would be able to see her.

She snapped her wrist and let the stone fly. The bird turned back and started to lift off too late. The missile hit the hawk in the shoulder and she screeched and tumbled backward. Sage yanked herself back into the tree and hugged the trunk, listening for indications of the hawk's owner.

She heard nothing, but she felt his eyes.

After several minutes of barely breathing, Sage turned her head to look out into the forest and saw him almost instantly. He stood motionless in an open area on a nearby slope, a dark cloak hanging around him almost to the ground and a hood shadowing his face. One step backward into the foliage, and he would be invisible. His elaborately tattooed arms were crossed as he watched her. Like he was waiting for her to see him.

He carried a crossbow, and she was well in range.

Almost lazily, he swung the weapon from his back but made no effort to aim it. Was he taunting her or debating whether to shoot her? Sage trembled all over. She should move lower, to where the branches and the trunk were thicker, but fear paralyzed her.

"Fowler!" called a voice in the distance. The scouts were coming back for her. She turned her head toward the sound and tried to answer, but her voice came out as a weak croak on the first two tries. When she looked back to the man on the hillside, he was gone.

She scrambled down the tree, breaking half the branches she touched and falling several feet twice. She hit the ground running and never looked back.

80

THE LOWER STOREHOUSE was deserted, except for a few scurrying rats. In the dungeon, one more level down, Alex killed three guards, two of whom were too sick to put up much of a fight. The last managed to open a cut on the side of Alex's leg before falling to his sword. A glance told him the wound was nothing of immediate concern, and he stepped over the guard's body to the foul-smelling cells beyond.

He found one of his father's couriers, broken and unconscious, but the man could be better tended once they were in full control of the fortress, so Alex left him. The other cells were empty.

She wasn't there. He'd chosen wrong.

Alex ran back up to the junction and the infirmary in the first level of the keep, dispatching several sick and weak guards without hesitation, but found no trace of Sage. Though he feared what he might find, he checked the cold room, where he came across the body of a castle guard, dead almost a day from what looked like blood loss. Other than a broken left arm, the only wound the man had was under the right shoulder, where he'd bled out. One of the pickets must've done it.

Relieved, he returned to the sickroom and three stunned healers staring at the bodies around them. "You won't be harmed if you go to the Great Hall now," he told them. "Otherwise you'll end up like them." He pointed with his sword to his earlier victims. At that moment the barracks in the outer ward exploded, and a dozen screams followed.

"Or them," he added before turning and running from the room.

It felt like he had a chapel bell clanging in his skull. Casseck rubbed his left ear as he clambered down the steps to the ground level of the inner gate, his hand coming away bloody. Every noise on that side sounded like it was underwater. Sergeant Porter came up to report the outer gate was secure, and Casseck left him in charge of the area and joined Gramwell outside the Great Hall.

"Have we found her yet?" asked Gramwell.

Casseck shook his head. "I don't think so." Alex was searching the keep from bottom to top.

Gramwell looked up at the keep. "The longer it takes, the more I worry something will go wrong."

Casseck shared his friend's concern. Every minute was a minute D'Amiran had to slit Sage's throat. He peered into the Great Hall. Nearly half the nobles inside had their hands bound behind them. The other half looked dazed and resigned while Corporal Mason kept watch with a crossbow as two soldiers tied up the rest.

Regardless of where Sage was, they still had to capture the duke. "Take two men," he told Gramwell. "Go find the captain and assist him as needed. I'll take charge here."

The red fire burned lower and what little smoke it produced was dissipated by the rain. Charlie gave up trying to direct it with the flag and looked down over the side of the keep. Black smoke obscured almost his whole view of the scene below. Cries of agony floated up from the area of the explosion. He had the last packet of red blaze with him, but Alex had told him to save it for the pickets if they came so they could take it back across the pass. His job now was to stay put until Alex or one of the soldiers fetched him.

Charlie tucked himself under the small shelter the fire bowl offered and warmed his chilled fingers on its underside.

The wooden floor beneath him thumped with the impact of some-one trying to break through the trapdoor.

81

CHARLIE WEDGED THE remaining flagpoles across the trapdoor, but it was only a matter of time before the guards below bashed it open. Too late, he realized the crossbow wasn't loaded. He didn't have the strength to pull the string back without using a crank, and there was none. Charlie cast his eyes to the rope looped around a crenellation. The Kimisar body hanging from it was too heavy for him to lift, which left climbing down. If he cut the body loose, maybe he could swing to a window, but he doubted it. Even if his frozen hands could manage to hold on to the slippery rope, he probably wouldn't have time to cut it before the guards below broke through and pulled him up.

Or until they cut the rope from above.

He leaned over the edge to look down and shivered. Backing away, he tripped over one of the two miniature barrels he'd brought up. Normally they would've contained ale, but Alex had filled them with a purer spirit, one that would burn. Charlie threw himself to his knees and began prying them open with his dagger.

Just as he got the second open by its end, the trapdoor lifted, revealing a straining face beneath. Charlie hastily dumped the contents down the hole and all over the man standing on a box of kindling. The soldier cursed and sputtered as the door dropped shut. Charlie stood and wrapped the wet flag around his hand, reached under the metal rain guard over the fire bowl, and grabbed a burning chunk of wood.

Once again the door creaked and lifted, and this time when Charlie poured the alcohol, he touched the flame to the liquid, creating a waterfall of fire, then kicked the burning wood and flaming barrel at the man's face. The trapdoor slammed back down, and Charlie heard him and another man screaming. He rolled away, slapping at his trousers to extinguish the flames, which had caught him, too.

Charlie cowered against the wall as the wooden floor steamed from the inferno raging below, consuming the men and stored firewood. But no matter how tightly he clutched his ears, he could not block out their screams.

❖

Alex returned to the junction and took the other fork, up toward the quarters of the household. It was foolish to be doing this alone, but the thought of Sage ending up like the Kimisar soldier hanging from the keep drove him forward.

The next level was a large gathering room that served as the Great Hall in the early days of the fortress. At the moment, it was used for storage and housing some of the guests. It appeared deserted, but he couldn't risk anyone coming up behind him. He paced around the room, kicking chairs noisily aside. He saw no one.

Before reentering the passage, he paused inside the door to listen and caught the sound of a guard coming down and around the corner. From somewhere there also came the scent of burning wood, which differed from the oil used to light up the tents and armory. Alex pulled out a knife and stepped back several feet from the opening, making himself visible as the guard crossed in front of the door. The man barely had time to pause when the dagger came flying at him and buried itself in his neck.

Alex retrieved his knife and continued up the stairs.

❖

Charlie crouched on the stone wall between the higher crenellations as the wooden floor smoked and smoldered. One side collapsed as the support beneath burned away. The stack of firewood must have contained several fast-burning items for sending signals, much like red blaze, because green flames licked up through the hole. Though he was more frightened than ever, Charlie was grateful the screaming had finally stopped.

He needed to escape, but the only way down was through the fire. Catching sight of the wet flag, he hopped down and pulled it off the steaming deck. Much of the moisture had baked away, and it was hot to the touch, but it would have to do. He wrapped it around his body as heat seeped through the soles of his boots, and he remembered something his father had told him weeks ago. *When you've chosen your course of action, seize it with all your might.*

Charlie pulled the corner of the flag over his head and launched himself into the breech, pushing and rolling away from any surface he touched. Smoke and cinders blinded and choked him as he bounced his way to the stone floor until he came face-to-face with the burning skull of a man. The body tipped back as he bumped against it, making the jaw open farther, shrieking silently at him. With a terrified sob, Charlie crawled away on his belly, using the direction the smoke was being drawn upward and out as an opposite compass.

Once he was safely away from the furnace above, he rested against the wall and tried to decide if he should stay there. Then the remainder of the ceiling collapsed with a thunderous roar, and he ran down, stumbling over the body of the first guard Alex had killed.

82

THE NEXT LEVEL up, Alex found a family room with several offshoots to bedrooms. Like the rooms below, they were all deserted. The smell of smoke was stronger and included burning flesh, and the building shook with a tremendous crash from above. Understanding came to him: the top of the keep was on fire. A new fear realized, Alex dashed out of the room and up as he heard a high-pitched yell he recognized instantly.

Charlie.

He flew around the corner and around another bend to the duke's level. At the top of the steps stood Captain Geddes, holding Charlie against his body. The boy was singed and covered with soot but otherwise looked unharmed. Alex would've sobbed in relief if the feeling wasn't so immediately displaced by rage.

With his head twisted to the side and pinned against the guard's stomach, Charlie could meet Alex's eyes with only one of his own. Alex tried to give his brother a reassuring smile before shifting his gaze to the leering face of the man above him.

"You have quite a habit of losing things, Captain," the guard said, sliding a large, menacing knife from his belt. He gestured with it. "Drop your sword."

Alex lowered his blade but did not release it from his grip. "Let the boy go."

"Out of curiosity, Captain, if you had to pick one to save, which would you choose?" He cocked his head to the side. "This one, I guess."

He sneered. "But now we have someone who actually matters to you. So drop it."

"I'll drop my weapon when *you drop* yours," Alex replied calmly.

Charlie took the hint and let his knees buckle, forcing Geddes to suddenly support all his weight with the arm slung across his small body. For a moment, the man struggled to keep from losing his balance on the edge of the landing. In the long-practiced move, Alex released his sword and drew his own dagger, flinging it up and into the guard's face in a single motion. The dead man froze for a second before crumpling over the boy now crouched at his feet.

Alex crawled up the steps to pull the body down, allowing Charlie to slither out from under it. He was about to ask if his brother had seen the duke when D'Amiran himself stepped out of the doorway, seized Charlie by his dark hair, and heaved him back up to the landing.

Alex lunged for Charlie's feet, but D'Amiran dragged the boy backward and into his room. By the time Alex reached the door, it was barred shut. He kicked and pounded on it, trying not to scream in panic.

A noise on the stairs made Alex turn away from the duke's chambers and reach for his sword, which he belatedly realized was still on the steps where he'd dropped it. He had only one dagger left, and he clutched the hilt as Gramwell came flying around the corner.

The lieutenant stopped when he saw Alex and glanced around. "What—"

"Charlie," Alex gasped, pointing to the door. "He's got Charlie in there, but I think it's just him left, no guards."

And Sage. She was probably in there, too. It was the only place left.

Gramwell nodded and scooped up Alex's sword and ran up the last few steps to hand it to him. Corporal Denny and Private Skinner came around the corner behind him, wheezing from their sprint up the keep. Alex gestured to the door. "Get it open."

Alex sheathed his sword and pulled Gramwell aside as the men hacked at the door with battle-axes, barely denting the solid oak. "We need to get in another way. We can't wait."

"There are two windows on the east side," Gramwell said. "We can climb down from the top of the keep. I'll go find some rope." He turned to run back down.

Alex grabbed his arm and pointed up the stairs. "There's already some up there."

Together they ran to the next level, Alex praying the fire hadn't burned away the rope the Kimisar hung from.

The stone floor was warm under their boots, but the fire had nearly succumbed to the rain that poured in once the ceiling collapsed. Alex picked up a sodden flag at the top of the stairs and began swinging it at the remaining flames to clear a path. He could see the rope around a crenellation above and thanked the Spirit it was only singed. As he tried to climb up to it, the half-burned wood beneath him gave way, and he fell back down to the floor.

Gramwell grabbed his arm and pulled him to his feet, slapping the cinders that threatened to burn through Alex's clothes, but he barely felt their heat. "I need a boost," Alex said.

His friend dropped to his knee and laced his fingers together. Alex stepped into the joined hands, and Gramwell heaved him up. He reached the wall and pulled himself higher until he could throw a leg over the edge.

"You good?" Gramwell called. Alex nodded and leaned over to pull up the body hanging from the rope. Gram picked up the wet flag and kicked the blackened remains of the ceiling aside. He wrapped the cloth around his hands and grasped a burning chunk. "I'm going to take some of this fire down to the door."

Alex nodded again and pulled out his knife. His stomach clenched as his fingers wrapped around the blood-crusted black hilt with its gold letters, and he began sawing the Kimisar soldier free from his noose. A minute later the body tumbled down the side of the keep, and Alex lifted the loop from around the stone block in front of him. He stood and climbed atop the wide crenellation. With the rope over his shoulder he ran around the wall, bounding from rise to rise, until he got to the opposite side.

There were two windows below: one into the bedchamber and one into the sitting room. Which one? The bedchamber could undoubtedly be barred from the inside. From the sitting room, he could again be on the wrong side of a locked door. But he could let Gramwell in, and the bedchamber door probably wasn't as strong as the outer one.

Sage was likely in the bedchamber, the implications of which made him sick. But if he entered through that window, the duke might panic and kill her if he felt he had nowhere left to hide. As long as she and Charlie were alive, D'Amiran had bargaining chips. Geddes's words came back to him: *Which would you choose?*

D'Amiran would make him choose.

Alex could have help if he got in the sitting room. He'd be on his own in the bedchamber.

He settled the rope so it would hang next to the sitting room window, and began climbing down, bracing his feet against the wall.

83

ALEX KICKED AWAY from the wall to swing in with more force. As he crashed through the window, the duke leapt up from where he straddled over Charlie. Alex scrambled to his feet and drew his sword as D'Amiran yanked Charlie up and held the boy tight with an arm hooked around his neck. Charlie had been gagged and his hands tied together, but his feet were free. He kicked wildly until the duke jabbed a knife in his back. "Enough."

Charlie gave a muffled cry and let his legs dangle. Alex watched in torment as tears streaked down Charlie's dirty cheeks, his brother silently begging forgiveness for being caught like this. Smoke drifted in from the crack under the door. Gram's fire was taking. From the smell, he'd added alcohol to help.

Alex took a deep breath and lowered his sword as he raised his left hand. "It's over, Your Grace. Let him go and give me the girl, and I'll stand for clemency at your trial."

D'Amiran's mouth twisted into a leer. "The girl? So you haven't found her yet?"

She wasn't here.

Alex tried not to panic at the possibilities multiplying in his head. "Tell me where she is, and I'll prevent your execution."

The duke shook his head. "You'd kill me yourself. I can see it in your eyes."

There was no denying he was right. Alex weighed his next words carefully. The pounding on the outer door resumed and smoke clouded the room. The bottom half of the door suddenly buckled, and the duke jerked toward the bedchamber, swinging his knife hand around to Charlie's front. Alex resisted the urge to lunge at him. "Don't make it worse," he said. "There's already been enough suffering and death."

Ice-blue eyes turned back to Alex and the arm around Charlie slackened, lowering the boy back to the floor.

D'Amiran suddenly smiled. "I disagree."

He pulled his arms back, dragging the knife across Charlie's throat before shoving him away.

84

THE BEDCHAMBER DOOR slammed shut as Alex dove to catch his brother before he hit the floor. Charlie's brown eyes frantically sought his as Alex yanked the gag down and pressed it against the gaping wound. Alex held him tightly, begging the Spirit not to take him, promising anything, but he heard the sickening gurgle and knew he could do nothing. His brother's mouth moved, trying to form words Alex couldn't hear. The light began to fade from his eyes, and he looked almost confused. Alex had only seconds. Alex searched for something to say that would give Charlie peace, something to tell him how much he loved him, how proud he was to be his older brother. His eyes flooded as he pulled Charlie close and pressed his lips to the dirty forehead.

"I have never known a braver soldier," he whispered.

Charlie's back arched with one last choking, wet gasp, spraying blood and spit across Alex's own throat. The bound hands clutching his jacket slackened as Charlie's head rolled back, followed by a silence louder than anything Alex had ever heard.

He was gone.

With a sob Alex laid his brother down and pushed himself to his feet, fumbling for his sword. His fingers found and grasped the hilt, and he shook the tears from his eyes and bared his teeth, growling like a wild animal.

Gramwell nearly had the door open, so Alex hurdled over Charlie's body and slammed against the bedchamber door. It gave a little, but he heard furniture being pushed across the floor against it.

Was Sage in there? He doubted it now, but the only man who knew was. And now Alex wanted blood. Needed it.

He sheathed his sword and backed away as the door behind him burst apart, scattering burning wood across the stone floor. Gramwell and the others stumbled inside, weapons drawn. The lieutenant froze at the sight of Charlie lying in a pool of blood.

Alex was already climbing out the window.

85

CASSECK WATCHED ALEX run around the top of the keep and drop a rope down the side, where it dangled next to the duke's sitting room window. D'Amiran must be barricaded in his suite. Maybe he should send more help.

Down in the ward, things were going as planned. The sickening smell of burning flesh and hair mingled with the moans of dying men as the Stiller brothers led the effort to finish off the survivors of the barracks explosion. Tim was bleeding from an arm that dangled uselessly as he hacked and jabbed with the other. There were several bodies around Casseck, but only one was dressed in black. It was the only casualty he knew of so far, but with their few numbers, each loss was costly.

His head jerked up at the sound of four horn blasts. "Did you hear that?" he called to Porter.

The sergeant grinned back. "Sounds like the pickets are coming in."

Casseck gestured for the soldier to take his place at the hall door as he ran toward him. "Inner gate is secure enough. You watch the hall while I let them in."

He tore through the outer ward to the main gate, swinging his sword to slice off an arm clutching at him from the ground. Through the portcullis he saw four men running at the fortress, though not as if they were being pursued—Ash Carter leading the way. Casseck whistled to the gatehouse above, and his man began raising the heavy wood-and-metal barrier.

The four pounded across the drawbridge without waiting for the gate to be fully lifted, ducking underneath and crawling or rolling inside. Casseck signaled for the lifting to stop and pulled his friend up into an embrace. "Damn, it's good to see you."

Ash grinned and thumped Casseck's back. "Looks like you're doing just fine without us." He turned around and pulled the smallest of his companions forward, a battered and bloody man Casseck assumed was the general's courier. "We found someone you'll be missing."

Casseck's jaw dropped. It was Sage.

She grinned up at him. "How are things going, Lieutenant? Can we help?"

"You made it," he said, stunned.

"Did you doubt me?"

"We thought—"

She interrupted him. "Where's Charlie? I saw him on top of the keep, but it looks like it caught fire."

They looked back to the stone tower just in time to see Alex reach out the window and grab the rope hanging next to it. He pulled the line taut and leaned outward to run across the wall and into the other window.

Without waiting for anyone, Sage sprinted for the inner gate.

86

ALEX KICKED HIS way into the window, thankful the shutter panes were pulled open. His feet caught on the tapestries around the frame, and he tumbled head over heels into the room. He struggled to untangle his legs as the duke loomed over him. Alex rolled away, looking up just in time to raise an arm in defense. White-hot pain lanced through his left forearm as a dagger stabbed completely through it. He wrenched away, tearing the knife out of D'Amiran's hand.

His sword came free from its scabbard and Alex swung it wildly. D'Amiran jumped back, stumbling against the heavy wardrobe he'd pushed in front of the door. A wooden trapdoor lay exposed under where the cabinet must have stood. The duke had been only seconds from escaping. He'd killed Charlie to gain time, but it hadn't been enough.

Alex lurched to his feet as D'Amiran yanked a sword down from the wall. Alex parried the thrust like it was nothing and pushed up against the duke, bashing his face with their locked hilts before heaving him backward over the foot of the wide bed.

He stepped back as the duke rolled and tried to recover, using the furniture between them to block his advance. Without taking his eyes off his enemy, Alex reached over to his left forearm and slowly pulled the knife free, barely feeling it slide out of his flesh. Scarlet blood dripped from the blade and his leather armband as he tossed the dagger aside. There was room in his mind for only one thought.

D'Amiran stood panting in the center of the room, leaning heavily on the weapon in his hand.

"Where is she?" Alex asked with deadly calm.

The duke smiled, his teeth bloody. "Still looking, are you? Going to kill me, boy? If you do, I won't be able to tell you about last night." D'Amiran made an attempt to rally as he spoke, but Alex knocked the sword from his hand with his own before it could finish the weak slashing arc. The duke staggered back into a chair by the bed. Alex brought his blade to D'Amiran's throat and held it there.

"Where is she?"

"Rather spirited, your little fowler. I had to tie her down."

Sweet Spirit, no. Alex's sword began to shake with rage and fear.

"Shall I tell you, boy, how she cried? How she called for you in the hopes you would hear, but by the time I was done with her she was cursing your name?" He leaned forward, coughing blood on his linen shirt. "Shall I?"

Alex forced himself not to imagine it. What mattered was where she was now.

D'Amiran laughed a little, though it took all the breath he had. "How does it feel to have the only thing you truly wanted taken from you, as your mother was taken from me?"

"What is that supposed to mean?"

"Castella Carey was *mine*. Promised to *me*. Your father took her. Rather fitting that I should take your little fowler, don't you think?"

"I'm willing to bet either of them wouldn't hesitate to cut your balls off." Alex pressed the point of his sword against the duke's throat and thrust him against the back of the seat. "And I may just let Sage do it. Now, *where is she?*"

D'Amiran smiled and lifted his hand to point at the open window. "I would've stopped her if I could, but she still had one burst of spirit left in her."

The vision stunned Alex beyond his ability to function. His sword dropped from his hand, clattering on the stone floor.

"How does it feel, Captain?" D'Amiran gasped triumphantly. "How does it feel to lose?"

The knife slammed into him, piercing his heart.

"I don't know, Your Grace," Alex whispered in his ear. "You tell me." He stepped back, and D'Amiran looked down at the dagger buried in his chest, focusing on the gold initials in the hilt.

"Rather . . . poetic." His eyelids fluttered, and his head rolled to the side.

Alex stared at the crimson stain spreading across the dead man's shirt. Then he turned and stumbled toward the window, a trail of blood leaking from his arm.

87

SAGE AND CASSECK raced upward through the keep, climbing over two bodies on the stairs. The door to the duke's chamber was charred and bashed open. Inside, Gramwell and two other soldiers were kicking against the inner door. Sage stumbled into the room and tripped across something soft.

Charlie.

She threw herself down and lifted his small face in her hands. "Oh, no! No! No! *No!*" Sage wailed as she clutched him against her bloody shirt.

The door to the bedchamber gave, whatever blocked it groaning in protest, but she ignored it and continued to hold Charlie to her breast, rocking and crying until she felt Casseck grasp her shoulders from behind. "Sage." She shook her head. "Sage," he said again. "He's gone. There's nothing you can do."

Finally, Sage nodded through her tears and kissed the bloody forehead before laying the boy gently back down. She raised her hand for Casseck's help back to her feet, and he dragged her into the bedchamber.

There was blood all over the floor, some dripping from the duke, sitting lifelessly in a chair, a dagger buried in his chest. Most came from Alex, who was on his knees, bleeding from his left forearm. He stared out of the window several feet away, fighting to remain conscious.

"We have to stop the bleeding. He's going into shock," said Gramwell from his side. He yanked the vambrace off Alex's lower arm and pressed his hands against two gaping wounds on either side.

Sage darted around behind them, jerking the knife out of the body on the chair, grabbing sheets from the bed, cutting and tearing them into usable pieces. She knelt in front of Alex and wrapped the cloth around his arm. The fabric quickly soaked through.

"Alex!" Gramwell released the bloody arm to Sage's attention and shouted in the captain's ear. He slapped Alex's face and turned it toward him. His friend looked back with eyes that struggled to focus. "It's over! Where are the girls? Where did you hide them?" Gramwell continued to smack his cheeks to keep him from passing out.

"Last place," Alex mumbled, his voice slurred. ". . . I saw her."

Gramwell looked down at Sage. "What does that mean?" He turned to Alex again. "*Where*, Alex? Where did you put the girls?"

"In the last place . . ." He blinked. "I saw her alive." Gramwell sighed in frustration, releasing his face. Alex returned to gazing out of the window.

Sage looked up with sudden understanding. "The laundry sewer–go! Go!" Gramwell dashed out. She turned pleading eyes to Casseck. "Will he be all right?"

Casseck nodded reassuringly. "I've seen men survive much worse." She sobbed in relief, and he reached down to take Alex's arm so she could let go.

Sage stood on her knees in front of him and grabbed his face in her bloody hands. "Alex, I'm right here! Stay with me! I'm here!"

For a moment he focused on her; then he whispered her name and collapsed unconscious into her arms.

88

ALEX WOKE WITH the feeling of a hard cot beneath him. He shifted painfully and forced his eyes open. As he separated light from dark, he saw Casseck walking toward him to stand over his bed.

"I'm not dead?" he croaked. His mouth was completely parched.

Casseck chuckled. "No, but you gave it your best." He pushed Alex back as he tried to rise. "Stay down. You've lost a lot of blood, but you'll be fine in a couple weeks."

Alex fell back against the pillow and closed his eyes to make the room stop spinning. "How long have I been out?"

"About twelve hours."

Alex nodded, setting off a pounding headache. He massaged his temples between the fingers of his right hand. The left felt numb, but the arm above it ached fiercely. His right thigh also burned, though he couldn't remember why. "Report."

He could almost hear Casseck smile. "Everything's under control, Captain. We have the whole fortress, though we'll probably be able to hold only the inner walls if we're attacked. Duke D'Amiran is dead, which you already know, as are most of his guards. His nobles are sitting pretty in the Great Hall—it's easier to just keep them there, though we put a couple down in the dungeon. The ladies are a little traumatized, but unharmed. Our casualties are manageable: a few minor wounds, one broken arm and some broken ribs, several burns, and lots of splinters from the explosion. Tim Stiller may lose his hand. A few cases of the sickness—I suppose it was inevitable. We lost Corporal Smith and Sergeant Grassley . . . and . . ."

Alex winced with the memory. "Charlie."

"Yes. Charlie."

Alex was amazed by the flood that rushed to his closed eyes despite his dehydration. Charlie, who'd looked up to him in everything, who'd wanted to be a soldier like him. Charlie, who would never grow up.

Charlie he had failed to protect.

And he wasn't the only one Alex had failed. Had they found her body yet? "And Sage," he choked.

Soft fingers brushed his cheek. "No, Alex," he heard her voice say. "I'm right here." His eyes snapped open, and he turned his head toward the sound. She sat only two feet away, smiling anxiously.

A large purple bruise spread across her left cheek and a shallow cut ran along her hairline. Her lower lip was swollen and split on one side, and she had several other scrapes, but the injuries were already a day into healing.

Sweet Spirit, she was beautiful.

"Sage," he gasped. "I'm sorry. I'm so sorry." His words came in a desperate rush. "He hurt you, and I didn't know until it was too late. . . ."

She came off the stool to her knees beside him, wiping his tears away. "Shhh. It's all right. I think I hurt him worse. I broke his arm and stabbed him in the armpit, just like you taught me. Between all the blood and the throwing up after, though, I left your knife in him." She smiled crookedly. "I saw you got it back, though."

He struggled to understand her words. "What?"

Casseck cleared his throat. "She escaped, Alex. D'Amiran never had her."

Alex sobbed and rolled toward her, reaching out with his good arm. Sage shushed and soothed him, combing her fingers through his hair, planting gentle kisses on his face. Cass excused himself and left them alone.

"Sage," he whispered, "I—" but she put a finger to his lips.

"My turn." Her gray eyes glistened with tears. "I'm sorry I was so hateful. I know you never meant to hurt me. I love you." She smiled weakly. "That is truth."

He didn't know how long he kissed her, but it wasn't enough, it would never be enough. Sage eventually pulled away so she could wash his face with a warm, wet cloth and make him drink some water. The effort of sitting up to swallow made him sleepy, but he couldn't bear to close his eyes while she was there.

Finally, he began to fade back into unconsciousness. "Will you still be alive when I wake up?" he mumbled.

Sage leaned in to kiss his dry and cracked lips. "I'm not going anywhere."

89

THE SMELL WAS horrific, like something out of nightmares, but the land was too rocky and the bodies too numerous to bury them all. Continuous light rain meant they had to use oil and alcohol to get the fire burning, but fortunately there were also plenty of wood scraps from the guardhouse and the armory. The putrid smoke rose from the cleared area outside the main gate. Sage turned away from the pyre and saw Alex weaving toward her.

"What are you doing?" she scolded as she tucked herself under his right arm and propped him up. "For Spirit's sake, you need rest."

"I need *you*," he said as she led him to a place to sit. Alex tugged the handkerchief that covered her nose and mouth down and kissed her. "I woke, and you were gone."

She set him down and checked his injuries. "I'm sorry. There's just so much to do and so few to work."

"You shouldn't be out here. This isn't something I want you seeing."

"I think it's too late for that." His wounds seemed fine, and she smiled in relief. "Besides, I put the women to work in the kitchen and laundry. If I wasn't here, I'd have to put up with them."

Alex relaxed against the stone column at the end of the drawbridge, and she thought he'd passed out again when his eyes snapped open. "Did you hear that?"

"Hear what?"

As if in response, horns all around the walls sounded. "It's too early for help," Alex said, struggling to his feet. "Get everyone inside!"

Casseck was already calling for that, and they'd just secured the portcullis and drawbridge when a dozen riders approached and halted outside, staring at the smoldering pile of bodies and the Demoran flags flying from the gate and the keep. Corporal Mason came running to report. "Hundreds, sir. Approaching from the south and west on foot."

"Don't you dare," Casseck told Alex as he made for the steps to the top of the outer wall. "I'll handle it." Alex leaned on Sage, nodding gratefully. "I think I can convince them to stand down," Casseck said. "But we should prepare to fall back."

"Who's their leader now?" asked Sage.

"The count may be with them," said Alex. "But this must be the army they gathered."

"Tell them D'Amiran's dead," she said.

"I'll tell the riders," Cass said with a shrug, "but I'm not sure whether it will get the troops to turn back. The closer they get, the less likely it is they'll leave."

"Hang D'Amiran's body from the keep," said Alex. "That was his preferred method of dealing with former allies. I'm sure they'll get the message."

∞❖∞

Alex was walking in the garden on the fifth day and trying to convince Sage he was well enough to go on a patrol when the sentries sounded the approach of riders.

"Do you think they've come back?" she worried as they made their way to the inner gate. The troops had melted away after two days of surrounding the fortress, but everyone was on edge, waiting for them to reorganize and return.

The signal for all clear sounded. "I'll be damned," Alex said twenty minutes later as his father rode in at the head of a rider company. Sage followed but stood back several paces as he saluted the general and formally presented command of the fortress.

General Quinn looked around the wrecked ward in amazement. "I feel quite a report is coming."

Alex nodded. "Yes, sir. But first I ask that you accompany me to the chapel."

"The chapel?" his father said sharply. "Why there?"

Alex couldn't bring himself to say the words, but his father read it in his face.

"Charlie?" he whispered.

Alex nodded.

"Take me to him."

The general walked beside him silently until they reached the chapel, and Alex stopped and let his father take the last few steps alone to stand before the smallest of the three coffins laid out. Alex had no more tears left. On the third night, he'd managed to describe his brother's last minutes to Sage alone, and she held him as he was sick several times and cried for hours. She'd taken care of Charlie's body, cleaning and dressing him and clipping a lock of his hair for their mother.

Now Sage stepped forward. "I can open the casket for you, sir," she offered.

The general focused on her for the first time. She wore a plain wool dress, and her sandy hair was plaited in a single braid down her back. Most of the swelling in her face had gone down, but he blinked at the colorful bruises across her cheek and forehead before turning back and placing his hand on the coffin. "No, thank you, my lady," he said. "I prefer to remember him alive."

Sage nodded and backed away, but Alex reached for her hand and drew her forward again. "Father, this is Sage Fowler." She bit her lip and looked down as she blushed.

The general's eyes dropped to their linked fingers. "I'll take that report now, Captain."

Alex led his father to the keep and the chamber they'd taken for a strategy room—the old Great Hall. The ladies were now housed in the rooms above, and most of the soldiers slept in the infirmary below. His father paced the room while Alex rested in a chair, flexing his left hand and admitting to himself he still had a long recovery ahead of him. It took over an hour to describe all that had happened, but he laid the credit for their success at Sage's feet.

When Alex finished, his father filled him in on what had happened in the south. "The Tasmet brides' escort vanished a week after you left," he said. "I knew something was wrong, but I thought it had more to do with the pass in the south. We took a full regiment to Jovan, and the count disappeared right about when we stopped hearing from you. I feared the worst."

"Is that why you were already halfway here when the river flooded?" Alex asked.

His father snorted. "Patience isn't always a virtue." He paused in his pacing. "I'm proud of you, son."

"It wasn't just me."

"You said that. But I also know you." He leaned his fists on the table. "You made some hard decisions."

Alex swallowed. His father had no idea, and he never would. And D'Amiran's taunts had no place in the official record. In the end, they'd been meaningless, empty. But Alex did have one thing he wanted to ask. "The duke said a few interesting things before he died. About you and Mother."

"Really?" His father looked surprised. "Like what?"

"He said you stole Mother from him."

The general sat down across from him, but said nothing.

"Is there a story behind that?"

His father looked at his hands. "Did your mother ever tell you she was picked for the Concordium?"

"Not that I can recall. I never considered it, seeing as I was born a year before one rather than a year after."

"Well, she was, so I can assure you she wasn't promised to anyone." The general paused. "We met at the celebration of her sister's engagement to the king. Everyone was making a fuss about her, too. Because of her family and her new connection to the royals, she was expected to be the most desirable match at the next Concordium."

That surprised Alex. "I didn't realize you knew her beforehand. I thought it was purely political, even though it was an off year."

His father shrugged. "Most people did. That suited us just fine."

"But it wasn't."

"No, it wasn't." He smiled a little. "I was smitten."

"So you bribed a matchmaker to put you together?" said Alex.

His father looked down at his hands again. "We may have done a few things that made matching us necessary to prevent scandal."

The union of two powerful families was so rarely about love that Alex had always taken his parents' marriage for granted. Ironically, it was the affection they had for each other that had made him fear matching—he could never be as lucky as they'd been. That they were as much a love match as Sage's parents stunned him.

His father cleared his throat. "This Fowler girl . . ."

"Her name is Sage."

The general looked up. "This Sage. What are your intentions?"

"I intend to marry her."

"Is there a *reason* you must marry her?"

"Because I love her, and I will have no other."

"I meant—"

"I know what you meant, Father." Alex looked at him squarely. "The answer is no. But if you try to stop me, I'll make sure there is." He raised an eyebrow. "And now I know there's precedence for it."

"Relax, son, I like her. I just needed to know what to tell your mother."

90

SUPPORT POURED THROUGH the Tegann Pass two days later, and the bridal group prepared to continue on to Tennegol. Alex was tied up in meetings, though he often slipped away in quieter moments to the tiny chapel near the burned-out armory. Clare was surprised by Sage's sudden inclination to go there to pray, sometimes several times a day, but when she discovered why, she and Lieutenant Gramwell developed a new sense of piety as well.

Once they left the fortress, however, Sage rarely saw Alex. Had it not been for his injuries and Charlie, she suspected he would've been sent after the count or the Kimisar soldiers now raiding Tasmet, so she forced herself to remain satisfied with occasional glimpses of him as they traveled. At one point, she started to worry Alex might forget her, but the next night she found a note tucked into her trunk. The contents made it clear he hadn't forgotten any promises whispered in stolen moments.

Their arrival in Tennegol created quite a commotion, as news had traveled well ahead of them. The escort received a hero's welcome as they paraded through the city and up to the palace gates, though none of them were in the mood for celebration. Alex and his father stayed only one night, spent mostly in conference with the king and his council, and early the next morning they left for Cambria to take Charlie home. Alex did find time to write Sage another letter and departed with her reply tucked in his jacket.

Sage and Darnessa had only one week left before the solstice, when the Concordium weddings traditionally took place, so they got straight to work. Though the dominant concern was keeping the country stable, especially now, heavy weight was given to what was best for each individual girl. Every morning and afternoon, all three apprentices present were kept busy recording diagrams of compatibility and the political advantages of each possible pair.

Despite the reduced time, the process went smoothly. As the ladies' guardians had relinquished their consent to the matchmakers, most outsiders assumed the brides had to accept whomever was chosen for them. In truth, the women were allowed to turn down their match, ironically giving them more power than they would have had outside the Concordium, but such refusals were rare.

Sage listened in amazement as the matchmakers predicted (with accuracy, she had no doubt) which noble families would be granted the forfeited properties and titles in Tasmet and matched women to them accordingly. The women in that room played the nation's strings of power like a quartet of musicians, creating a balance of power that had served Demora well for over two hundred years.

In the evenings over tea, the regional matchmakers traded information for the future in a more casual setting. The most talked about men were the now famous escort officers, and the women pushed Darnessa to approach Captain Quinn for his thoughts on committing to a long engagement. She deferred their requests as Sage flushed over her ledger, saying with the recent death of his brother, it would be inappropriate to address just now.

Despite the reduced time, the deals went smoothly, due in part to the lack of representation from Tasmet, and several additional pairings were lined up for the near future. Even Gabriella Quinn was matched in her absence, as she'd returned home with her father and brother, though her wedding was postponed until at least winter.

Three days before the grand ball and ceremony, Sage received a visit from Prince Robert, who asked if Darnessa could spare her for an hour or two. Feeling flustered, she took his arm and let him lead her around the palace. She suspected he took her through the garden past nearly all the brides lounging about, just to make them stare. They chatted casually, and Sage found him a merry fellow with a streak of recklessness. He looked distractingly like Alex, except in the eyes.

After a few minutes he shared some news. Lieutenant Gramwell had heard from his mother that morning, and she'd agreed to accept Lady Clare into her house. "Mistress Rodelle will be working out the details." He smiled. "I think Luke is telling Clare now, but then he'll have to break the news he's leaving in four days."

"Have you heard from Alex?" she asked.

"He'll be back soon," Robert replied, looking slightly guilty. "But in the meantime, there's someone who wants to meet you." They'd stopped in an unfamiliar section of the palace. He knocked and then opened the door to a small library. A balding, fortyish man with Robert's cheerful hazel eyes stood from his seat by the fire. "Father," said Robert, "may I present Mistress Sage Fowler of Garland Hill?"

The king smiled, and she curtsied and kissed the offered hand, blushing scarlet.

"Mistress Sage," he said kindly, gesturing for her to sit across from him. "I've heard so much about you."

Sage took the indicated seat and shot a dirty look at the prince as he plopped down in a third chair. He winked back, seeming to enjoy her discomfort. Alex should have warned her about the prince's love of surprising people. Maybe he had, but she'd forgotten in favor of remembering more pleasant moments.

The king, fortunately, was determined to put her at ease. "Both my sons and my nephew told me about your role in thwarting the D'Amirans' plot. They spoke very highly of you."

Sage's annoyance with Robert kept her embarrassment at bay. "I'm not sure how well His Highness got to know me. I never really spoke to him until today."

King Raymond chuckled. "Well, most of my direct information came from Captain Quinn, though some also from Ash."

Sage nodded, flushing at both the thought of Alex and of how she thought she'd been in love with Ash. She hoped the king didn't know anything about *that*. "Your Majesty, I was only acting as any true Demoran would in defense of her country."

"You may believe that," the king said. "It may even be true. But the fact is, I owe you a debt that can never be repaid."

"Nor would I expect such a reward," Sage said quickly.

King Raymond smiled. "Perhaps not. Yet I believe there is something you wish that coincides with a need of mine."

Sage had no idea what that could be. "I will serve Your Majesty in any way I can."

"I've heard you speak Kimisar," he said.

She answered him in that language. "I am better in reading than in conversation, but yes, Your Majesty."

He nodded. "Reyan?"

Clare was much better, but Sage had been practicing with her since she'd found out. "Moderately well, My King," she replied in Reyan.

"As your father was a fowler, I imagine you know a great deal about natural sciences."

Sage looked back in puzzlement. "I'm not sure what you mean by natural sciences, sire."

"You know and understand animals and their behavior, how plants grow and which are useful, weather patterns and land erosion, that sort of thing."

"Oh, yes!" Sage replied, then blushed at her eagerness. "I just never thought of it as science."

"Just about everything is science, once you break it down to its process." He paused. "Geography?"

"My experience is limited, but I have studied many maps." Sage's suspicion as to what this was about began to grow. Alex—acting as Ash—had offered to introduce her to the king and find her a job teaching in the capital. But why the king should take the time to question her before recommending her for a position was unnerving.

"And how is your history?" he asked.

Sage glanced at Robert, who wore a secret-keeping smile. "History is like a story, Your Majesty. Easy to learn if it is made interesting."

The king nodded. "What about mathematics? Can you do more than sums?"

She winced. "I can multiply and divide and my geometry is good. Algebra is my weakness." Father had been teaching her algebra just before he died, and trying anything beyond the simplest equations had made her heartsick.

The direction of this conversation was now so obvious she could no longer hold back. "May I beg to know why you ask these questions?"

The king smiled almost exactly as his son did. "After you answer one more of mine, Mistress Fowler. I'm told you enjoy teaching. What is it you love most?"

Sage blinked. She'd never really thought about it, but her love of teaching was something Alex, Darnessa, Clare, and her aunt and uncle had all seen clearly. "My father found joy in learning and in teaching me. I suppose it reminds me of him. But what I enjoy most is how I bring something useful into the life of another. I give my student the tools to build a life that suits them." Sage looked down, embarrassed.

"And what life suits you, Mistress Sage?" the king asked, his voice gentle.

What if Alex wanted to marry her? He talked like he did, but it would be years before he could. A lot could happen in that time. She took a deep breath. "I should like to teach and also to learn more where I can. That is what brings me fulfillment."

She heard a smile in the king's voice. "I have two young ladies in need of a tutor. Would you like to meet them?"

Sage's head snapped up. Surely he didn't mean . . . ?

King Raymond turned to Robert. "Go fetch Rose and Cara, please."

The door closed behind the prince before Sage found her voice. "Your Majesty, you cannot be serious! I'm not qualified to educate royalty!"

"We would proceed only if you wish, but the queen has expressed concern that the princesses aren't enjoying their studies. She also desires them to have a proper female companion closer to their age. This would all be subject to a trial period, of course, but I'm very optimistic."

Sage twisted her hands. How had she found herself in this position? "And if it doesn't work out?"

"We will find you proper employment elsewhere. The kingdom owes you a great deal; I find it only fitting to reward you." He paused and tilted his head to the side. "Unless you wish to continue apprenticing with the matchmaker. Mistress Rodelle and Lady Clare seemed to think you would rather not."

He'd already talked to Darnessa and Clare about her. Sage might have been angered that everyone—including Alex—had gone behind her back in arranging this, but they had all done it for her. And if so many people thought she deserved this honor, this happiness, perhaps they weren't wrong.

Sage wiped her sweaty palms on her skirt and raised her chin. "Your Majesty, I accept your generous offer. I shall endeavor to be worthy of your trust in me."

"I do have one condition, Mistress Sage," said the king, hazel eyes twinkling. "You must be honest with me about the girls' progress and also about your own happiness in this job."

"Sire, you may count on the first part. As for the second . . . ," Sage hesitated. "When I'm unhappy, I think everyone knows it."

The king was still chuckling when the princesses arrived, eager to meet their new tutor.

91

BETWEEN WEDDING PREPARATIONS and Sage's dizzying orientation to her new position, she and Darnessa barely crossed paths over the next two days. The matchmaker released her from her apprenticeship when Sage related the king's offer, but said little about it. Sage felt too awkward to attempt a discussion.

To her great embarrassment, Sage also discovered she was somewhat of a celebrity, especially now that she was connected to the princesses. The final banquet and ball before the traditional mass wedding at midnight were exhausting, and she was introduced to face after face until they all blurred together. As the dancing began, Clare slipped up to her and pressed a note into her hand. Sage's heart skipped a beat when she recognized the script. She looked up with a start, scanning the room for the dark face she craved, and spotted him near the door, watching her with a hungry expression.

She tore open the note and devoured the words inside.

> *After living the longest and worst days of my life, I cannot*
> *wait any longer to hold you again.*
> *Make your excuses. I'll be in the garden.*
> *–Alex*

Sage looked up again, but he was gone. With shaking fingers, she refolded the paper and planned her escape. She thought she was finally finished with acknowledging everyone she felt necessary when Darnessa approached. "There you are. I haven't seen you in days."

Sage grimaced. "Sorry. It seemed like you had everything in hand, and there were so many people and things to attend to. I've barely had time to breathe."

The matchmaker waved her hand dismissively. "Don't worry about it. You look lovely, by the way."

Sage brushed her hands over her simple but pretty blue skirt, a gift from the queen, who'd taken her under her wing. She couldn't wait to show Alex. "Thank you. So when do you head home?"

"In two days. Tomorrow will be mostly packing. They're sending a squad to escort me back, but it'll be just me. All the maids are staying with various ladies, even Poppy. Is there anything you'd like me to take back to your aunt and uncle?"

Sage laughed at the thought of her family reacting to all the news. Stunned as he would be, Sage looked forward to putting her uncle's mind at ease that she was well taken care of, though both her aunt and uncle might be disappointed it didn't include a match. Yet. "I think I'll spend most of tomorrow writing a very long letter."

"Good idea." Darnessa smiled at her fondly. "I'll miss you, Sage, but I'm happy for you. You deserve this opportunity, this life."

Sage hugged the taller woman. "I'll miss you, too, though maybe not the job so much. I don't think I'm cut out for being a matchmaker."

"Wild Sage, I never thought you were." Darnessa squeezed her tight and blinked back the moisture in her eyes. "But I did want to help you."

Sage pulled back but kept her arms clasped on Darnessa's. "Are all your matches made, then? Is there anything else you need help with before you go?"

"I just have one more deal to close up, and actually I do need your help."

Sage raised her eyebrows. "We'd better hurry, then. What do you want me to do?"

Darnessa tilted her head in the direction of the door and said, "Go down there to the gardens and talk to that soldier who's waiting for you." Sage put her hands on her hips and scowled at the matchmaker, who only winked back. "Don't worry about my fee on this one, either." She patted her cheek. "Now go."

⚜

Sage found Alex sitting on a bench by the giant willow tree at the southeast corner, his dark uniform contrasting with the silver fountain of branches flowing down behind him. He jumped up when she came along the path and folded her in his warm arms.

"Did anyone tell you how beautiful you are tonight?" he whispered. Before she could answer, he pulled her up the sloping grass into the shelter of the drooping tree branches, hiding them from any passersby. He turned her face to his and brushed her lips with the gentlest of kisses.

"You know," she said, slipping her arms around his neck. "You've told me that several times, but I've never gotten a chance to tell you how good-looking you are."

He shrugged. "I'm all right."

She laughed and threaded her fingers in his dark hair. "You were a major topic of conversation among the matchmakers. They'll be coming after you in droves."

"Tough for them. I'm taken." He pressed his forehead to hers and pulled her lower body closer. A familiar heat spread through her. If he pressured her for more than kisses, Sage didn't think she'd be able to say no. He did not, however, though from the way he was breathing she knew he felt the same things she did. He didn't even try to kiss her again, as if it would tip the balance of his self-control.

"Marry me, Sage," he whispered.

It was too much. She didn't doubt his sincerity, but the proposal took her completely by surprise. "But it's late; I don't have time to find a proper wedding dress before midnight."

"Dammit, Sage, you know what I mean. I want you to promise me now." He released her from his hold, angry beyond what her nervous joke merited.

She understood him too well to be hurt. "What's wrong, Alex?"

He closed his eyes and ran his fingers through his hair, scratching the back of his head. "I'm leaving tomorrow." Her heart squeezed painfully in her chest as he continued, "D'Amiran's conspirators and the Kimisar are stirring up trouble, and we still haven't found the count. I've been ordered to go after them. After what they've started—what they've taken from my family—I have to go."

She nodded. "Yes, you do."

"The next few months will be rough, but I can get through them if—"

"I promise," Sage interrupted, reaching for his hands. "I'll wait for you."

Alex sighed and laced his fingers with hers, pulling her close again. "Thank you."

Sage lay her head against his collarbone, breathing him in. "How long will you be gone?"

"Till midwinter, I expect. I'll write as often as I can."

"As will I."

"Then if you want, I'll resign and we can marry as soon as I'm free."

Sage leaned away and shook her head. "Don't be ridiculous. You can't do that for me."

"I'll be a farmer."

She laughed. "Be serious."

"I am. As long as you're there, I'll clean the pigsty every day."

She looked down at their interlaced fingers and shook her head again. "No, it's *because* I love you that I could never take you from the army. It's your life."

"I think you underestimate my feelings for you." His tone was light, but there was a trace of hurt.

Sage raised his hands to her lips and kissed his fingers. "What I have now—a home with friends, respect, a useful and important occupation, a chance to learn more . . ." She looked up. "Would you want to take these things from me?"

"Not for the world."

She pulled her right hand free to trace the scar over his eyebrow. He closed his eyes and exhaled heavily. "That is why I can't take you away from the things you have now," she whispered. "They're part of you. They're inseparable. And that's one of the things I love most about you."

Alex caught her up in his arms and kissed her with a passion that made her seriously reconsider her words. "Damn your persuasiveness," he muttered in her ear before trailing his lips down her neck to her shoulder.

"And yours," Sage managed to gasp. He lowered her down to the soft grass at their feet, and there was no more talking. Alex paused to pull his jacket off and put it behind her head as a pillow. Then, starting at her fingers, he teased and explored every inch of her bare skin with his lips, making her dizzy by the time he moved past her wrist up her arm. He never tried for more than what was already exposed, but she almost wished he would, though she doubted she had a clear enough mind to stop him. Then his hands gripped her skirt, like he was trying to prevent them from doing something else, and he moaned in her neck in a way that made her shiver.

For a long time he held still against her, and she instinctively didn't move, knew he was struggling with the same desires that left her breathless. Then he whispered her name and wrapped his arms around her again. She sighed into his chest, trying not to cry at the thought of missing him. Two months ago she hadn't even known he existed, yet now she couldn't live without him.

Alex nuzzled her temple. "You'll want to fix your hair before we go back in," he murmured. "It's a real mess."

Sage laughed into his shirt. "That is truth." She pushed up to look down at him. "Yours isn't much better."

"I guess we'll just have to stay out here all night, then." Alex sighed with mock sadness.

"No argument here. It'll be one hundred and eighty long days and nights before I can muss your hair again."

Alex traced her lips with his thumb. "Who's counting? Not me. Too depressing."

He leaned up to kiss her forehead, and she settled back into his arms before daring to voice her deeper concern. "Alex?"

"Mmmmm?" he breathed into her hair, deliberately tousling it further.

"Three years is a long time." His arms tensed around her. "I just . . . I know things can change, especially with distance." For several heartbeats he remained motionless. Then he relaxed.

"I guess if you forget me, I'll just have to use my persuasive powers. Let me practice them now." He moved to kiss her neck.

She scowled and shoved him away. "I'm serious."

"So am I." Alex leaned in again, and this time his lips hit the mark. "Besides," he whispered, the heat of his breath curling around her ear, "it's not three years, it's two and a half. Nine hundred twenty days, to be exact."

Sage grinned. "Who's counting now?"

ACKNOWLEDGMENTS

First thanks go to you, the reader, who made it this far and for whom Sage's story was written. I hope you enjoyed getting to know her as much as I have. She is way cooler than me.

I could not have brought this book into reality, however, without the tireless support and efforts of others. Most important is God, from whom all things come. Right after are the intercessions of Francis for words and Dymphna for sanity. *Deo gratias.*

In a more corporal sense, I owe so much to my champion and super-agent, Valerie Noble, who picked me out of the slush and dreamed big when I was afraid to. I wouldn't be here without you. To Erin Stein at Imprint, who said "Wow" and not "Whoa." To Rhoda Belleza, editor extraordinaire, and her sidekick Nicole Otto, who rolled up their sleeves and dug in. To Ellen Duda and her design team for making things pretty inside and out, and to Ashley Woodfolk in marketing. To Molly Brouillette and Brittany Pearlman, the publicists with the magic touch, and the Fierce Reads Team, who voted to let me in their clubhouse before I was fully housebroken. And for all: God bless you for your patience with me.

Special thanks to Devon Shanor for her beautiful photography and for meeting me at the dinosaur park in the middle of nowhere. Also for not thinking it was a weird idea.

To Kim, who read Alanna with me in junior high and then twenty-five years later read my roughest of drafts and said *Yes!* All my other readers (alphabetically): Alissa, Amy, Brit, Carol, Carolee, Caroline (who printed the whole dang thing out!), Dan, Kammy, Katie, Kim M., Kim P., Leah, Melissa, Natalie, and Ron . . . at least one scene was made better by each of your comments. To Ryan, for his non-legal advice and foolish optimism (which turned out to be not so foolish). To my critique partners Joan Albright, who gently educated me on what I had screwed up, and Sarah Willis, who polished. I will meet you on the bookshelves someday, if not in person.

To Mom, for showing me that girls loving science and math was normal and for letting me pursue everything I wanted to, even when you didn't understand why; and to Dad, for going fifteen rounds with me on every paper in high school (and not even telling me what was wrong until round ten). And to both of you for unfailing love and support, letting me read whatever I wanted, and for teaching me my limits were only set by myself.

To Krav Maga Nebraska (and also Dad), for teaching me how to kill people (all in the name of self-defense, of course).

To Kisa Whipkey. We didn't end up working together, but getting your e-mail in a time of despair was the lifeline that probably saved this book.

To Andrew Jobling, who lit the fire by showing me what would kindle the flame. (Spoiler: It has little to do with actual writing.)

To Tamora Pierce, who inspired me as a person with books I wanted to read.

To my kids: being your mother has been the greatest privilege of my life. Thank you for coming out so well despite my clumsy efforts. Yes, you can have a snack. After you clean your room. Okay, you can have it now, but then do your chores.

And Michael, because when everyone is thanked, when every word is written, when every day is done, it's always you who are at the end of it.